THE IMPERIAL AGENT

Kim could discern only a dark silhouette, but he knew the man was already struggling to get the revolver out of the bag. Kim lunged at his feet, striking his ankle twice with the lathi. He heard the bone crack. The man howled and hopped back again. Kim followed him up, jumping forward to within striking distance. He knew where to hit to paralyse him. As he lifted the cane the revolver came free and the man fired. In mid-stroke, Kim felt a tremendous blow and a strange sensation of flying as he fell back.

He felt his life escaping from his body, and struggled to hold on to it. With a huge effort, he searched his kurta and drew out the pebble. 'Ram . . . Ram . . .' he whispered to it, and slumped against the wall.

TAJ

'an exotic, passionate novel, sensual and violent by turn, always compelling'
Woman's Own

'tells the passionate love story behind the creation of India's most beautiful building, the Taj Mahal'
Daily Mirror

'one of the greatest love stories that's just been told'
Edinburgh Evening News

'A complex novel which recaptures the colourful sensuality of 17th-century India'
Huddersfield Daily Examiner

'From its wry humour to its warm humanity, with a blend of Eastern mystery, it was like incense to an acrid world'
Sunday Star

About the Author

Born in Madras, T. N. Murari's highly
acclaimed novels include FIELD OF
HONOUR, LOVERS ARE NOT PEOPLE and
THE SHOOTER. His worldwide bestselling
novel, TAJ, received ecstatic reviews. His new
novel, THE LAST VICTORY, the continuing
story of THE IMPERIAL AGENT, is now
available in hardback.

THE IMPERIAL AGENT

T. N. MURARI

NEW ENGLISH LIBRARY
Hodder and Stoughton

For my sister and friend
Nalini

Copyright © 1987 by V.A.S.U.
Limited

First published in Great Britain in
1987 by New English Library

First New English Library
paperback edition 1988

Printed and bound in Great
Britain for Hodder and Stoughton
Paperbacks, a division of Hodder
and Stoughton Limited, Mill
Road, Dunton Green, Sevenoaks,
Kent TN13 2YA (Editorial Office:
47 Bedford Square, London
WC1B 3DP) by Richard Clay
Limited, Bungay, Suffolk.
Photoset by Rowland
Phototypesetting Limited,
Bury St Edmunds, Suffolk.

British Library C.I.P.

Murari, Timeri
 The imperial agent
 I. Title
 823[F]   PR9499.3.M85

 ISBN 0-450-42403-0

That is the land of lost content,
  I see it shining plain,
The happy highways where I went
  And cannot come again.

A. E. Housman
A Shropshire Lad

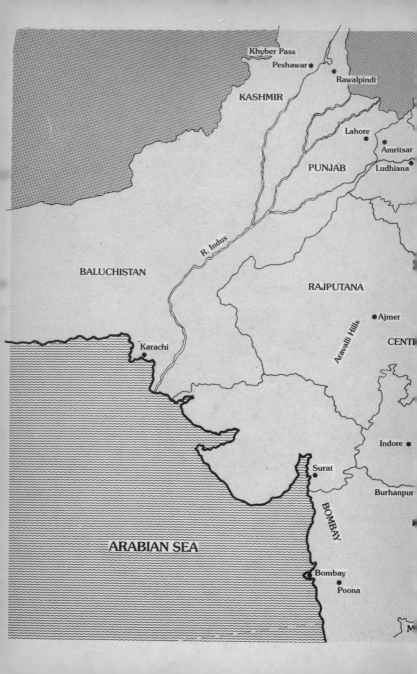

AUTHOR'S NOTE

WHEN AS a child I first read Kipling's novel *Kim*, I thought of it only as an exciting adventure story, and on finishing it I wanted to be Kim. I wanted to be that orphaned boy who could move effortlessly through the cities and bazaars and temples of late nineteenth-century India. I wanted to travel on the Grand Trunk Road in the company of a wise yet innocent old man in search of a mythical river. I wanted to be recruited by the British as a secret agent and help them in the Great Game against expansionist Russia. I wanted to learn the tricks of being a spy, even as Kim learnt them from an array of marvellous teachers. I wanted to be a free spirit, like Kim, and I wanted to be the friend of everyone I met on these great adventures. I wanted . . .

The realisation suddenly dawned on me that I couldn't be Kim. Kim was British. I was Indian. Yet so persuasive was Kim's story, and so Indian his thinking and beliefs, that I overcame this minor obstacle. Kipling might have made Kim physically British, but deep in his soul Kim was truly Indian. As an Indian child I could identify totally with him, just as people everywhere, whatever their age or race, have managed to do since the novel was published in 1901.

Thirty years later I re-read *Kim*. I still saw him as very much an Indian, but what had once been accepted as a sheer adventure story turned out to be something far more profound. In my youth, I'd skipped that part of Kim's travels and conversations with the Buddhist Lama, the teacher he adopts and guides across India. This time

I read about Kim as a mystic in search of truth and the meaning of life. He is divided between the reality of his world and the inner knowledge that life must have far deeper meanings. Also, when reading the novel as a child, I completely missed the sexual undertones of the story. Kim was, in modern parlance, streetwise; he had known all manner of evil, and yet he retained his innocence. It is to Kipling's credit as a storyteller that he could grip the imagination of the adult, as he had the child so many years ago; that is, until one reaches the end of the book. The end still disappointed me, for Kim is left suspended between his mystical yearnings and the reality of his life as a secret agent, between being an Indian and being British.

I had long wanted to write a novel about the British in India, but not a novel about mutinies or the Raj. I wanted to write about Indians in a British-ruled India slowly coming awake. At the start of this century, British rule in India was unshakeable and seemed permanent. It would last for centuries to come. There was no doubt about this in the minds of the British or the Indians as together we entered the twentieth century. There was, however, a small handful of men and women, British and Indian, who thought differently, and were persecuted for their belief that India should be free. India was slowly beginning to change. I thought I would like to write a novel set in the first two decades of the twentieth century that would attempt to capture the complexities of this change.

I needed a major character for this novel, one who was quintessentially British, yet also Indian. He had to be accepted by both without question as one of their own, a person who would reflect the conflict of loyalties. A person who one day would have to choose on which side he wanted to fight. As a Briton would he support the continued rule of his people? As an Indian, would he oppose it? He had to be famous enough for the reader to be familiar with him, to understand his terrible dilemma. And if by chance this character should be an

Imperial Agent, would he one day betray his masters? Or would he betray his friends, the men and women who opposed British rule? At the same time, he had to capture my own interest in the magic and mysticism of India, to undertake a spiritual quest even as I once had done.

I just could not resist taking up the story of my childhood hero, Kim.

1

THE SINISTER whisper 'mar', *kill*, spoken at midnight when the land is at its darkest and the whine of cold wind blowing down from the mountains awakens sleeping spirits, was to alter for ever the lives of men who heard it. The one who spoke of death on this night was an insignificant man. Harmless. He could not summon evil spirits to do his bidding or command armies to march. He would die unknown, ignorant of the effect his whisper would eventually have. It would bring down an empire and change the destiny of the man who heard him with such interest.

This 'mar', like an 'om' reverberating through the universe, echoed in the minds of those who listened. There were about twenty of them, squatting in the shelter of a deodar tree. They shifted away, fearing this fellow coolie who spoke of death.

His whisper was heard by the great mountains, silvery and screne, filling the horizon. They listened to the whispers of every man, they heard too his unspoken thoughts and prayers, for God had his abode in those eternal icy folds. Involuntarily the listeners turned towards those peaks, silently invoking their protection. They were too distant to be seen clearly on this dark night, but the Himalayas had long filled their imagination, filled their myths. They knew the mountains had power to protect, to grant them boons.

'Where did you hear of this "mar"?' asked the young man. His life, from that moment on, would change. He too had begun to look towards the mountains, but then stopped himself.

'In the bazaar,' the coolie replied. Only when he sucked on his beedi did the glow outline a gaunt, unshaven face with dark, dull eyes. A turban masked his forehead.

'And who spoke of killing?'

'Two men.' He peered through the darkness. Drizzle, fine as mist, settled on their shoulders, soaking through threadbare shawls. 'One was your age, the other older. I carried them in my rickshaw from the railway station and dropped them in front of Ramchand the chaiwallah's.'

'Did they go in?'

'No. They went off in different directions, as if they no longer knew each other.'

'And did you find out who they were going to kill?'

The coolie shrugged. 'The Angrezi.'

'All of them?'

The man laughed. 'There are too many. Only a few. Why all this interest?'

'It is better to know such things. Then I can avoid them.'

The exchange had been overheard by others. It would ripple out into the bazaar and beyond. Betrayal had already begun. A secret had been released. India was a country where nothing ever remained a secret. One man could whisper into the ear of another hidden deep in the jungle with only the kite and the langur as witnesses, and within the day it would be heard a thousand miles away. No one had ever understood how such things happened; it was the mystery of the country that words – truthful and dishonest ones, rumour and gossip – moved even more swiftly than the telegraph.

'I am tired,' the coolie said. 'When will this tamasha finish?'

'Only when the sky turns as pink as a memsahib's cheeks,' another replied. 'Then they will order us: jaldhi karo, jaldhi karo, and we shall kill ourselves to rush them home.'

Together they stared at Viceregal Lodge. It was a turreted wooden palace, quite unlike any other building in this land. They did not know that it was a dream place, a symbol of collective memory from a distant island, transposed here to the foothills of the great mountains. The ghostly night air gave it a sense of make-believe, as though it were a palace from a fairy tale that could suddenly vanish. It was now ablaze with lights, bursting with music and swirling with shadows, filling the night air with gaiety.

Two bodyguards in resplendent uniform flanked the gateway. Their lances glittered in the electric light. More guards lined the curving drive, fading into the night. Mist blurred the porch lights and the bearers waiting for the guests, who by now had all arrived. The bearers remained at their posts, as still as the guards. The Lodge, a modest name for such a seat of power, was the summer residence of the Viceroy of India. In winter he ruled from Calcutta, so this visit to Chota Simla in the October of 1905 was a special occasion, a farewell ball for Lord Curzon.

The dining-room was a dark, sombre chamber with mahogany panelled walls. Though lovingly polished, they reflected little light. In the days of lamps and candles, the room was always filled with shadows, and even the electric chandelier above the dining-table could not dispel the gloom that lurked in the distant corners. Its decorations were solemn and formal, a constant reminder to guests that they were dining in the presence of supreme imperial power. On one wall hung a portrait in oils of the King-Emperor Edward VII. It was almost life-size, and none in the room could escape those regal eyes. On the other walls were the martial symbols of the empire: faded pennants of famous regiments, ornate lances plundered from defeated native princes, muskets, jezails, swords and shields. It was a room crowded with memories.

Twenty-four ladies and gentlemen had been dining for the last time with Lord Curzon. He sat at the head of the table, facing the large windows framing shadowy deodars, a slim, aristocratic man.

'Gentlemen!' Curzon called. The guests all stood, facing him as if in homage. They raised their wine glasses. Curzon turned to the portrait of the monarch.

'The King-Emperor.'

They drank the toast, reassured by the familiar ritual, and sat down again.

The Vicereine, Lady Curzon, at the foot of the table, now rose to signal the withdrawal of the ladies. The whole company rose, their chairs pulled back by bearers looking splendid in white uniforms with scarlet sashes, who had stood silently behind them all evening. The Viceroy was the last to stand, and even such a simple movement appeared to cause him discomfort. As she passed her husband, Mary Curzon paused to whisper, 'Thank God all this will be over soon.'

She was as tall as he, and they were handsome, like a prince and princess. Her shining hazel eyes were set in a delicately boned face; auburn hair was piled high on her head. For an American, a Chicago heiress, she had played her role well, but had long grown impatient with the pomp and ceremony of her husband's office. Curzon looked drawn and weary. He kissed his wife chastely.

The Colonel, half-way down the table, noticed the discreet show of affection. It had always been so between them, as if to dispel the rumour that he had married her for her money. It was untrue, for Curzon was a moderately wealthy man, but the Colonel still relished the gossip. As the bearers flung open the door for the Vicereine and the ladies, there was a gale of music and English laughter; dancing figures dressed as pirates, beefeaters, Elizabethan ladies, came into view like spirits from another world. Then the doors closed and they vanished.

Bearers filled brandy glasses and the men selected

4

cigars from carved humidors. Now they raised their glasses in salute to the Viceroy.

'To Your Excellency. May God go with you.'

'Thank you.' He sipped, sitting stiff and imperial. 'No doubt you are all relieved at the news of my resignation.'

They mumbled their protests, but the sentiments lacked passion or belief. Curzon took note of the tone. In private they were celebrating. He too was relieved; Lord Kitchener, the Commander-in-Chief, had made his life here impossible. That man, Curzon reflected, is a monster. I began this task with hope, and now I taste only ashes. I had always dreamed of being Viceroy of India, and it came true, but too soon. Forty was too young and now forty-seven is too old. I failed all that early promise. I live with pain when I should be bathed in the pleasures of power. Success has eluded me. I feel like a draught-animal weary beyond belief. I am ready to drop. What more did they expect me to give to India?

The great dining-room depressed him. Looking around at the dark panelling, the portraits, he thought it all a sham, a brooding womb in which they sat enshrined. Normally on his summer visits it was his custom to pitch a grand, many-roomed tent, as magnificent as any Mughal's, rather than sleep within these walls.

'Oh, God,' he said deliberately. 'How I hate Simla.' His companions flinched as though they had been slapped. He felt a small satisfaction at this repayment for their accumulated ill-will. They too had betrayed him, a dozen Judases. 'We come here every summer, year after year, retreating from India, cutting ourselves off from the people. This town's nothing but a fortress against the Indian.'

'It's the summer heat, Your Excellency.' St John Brodrick spoke patiently as though lecturing a child. He and Curzon had been at Eton and Balliol together, and were friends. Brodrick, unwinking eyes set in a square, stubborn face, was now his friend's inferior. It had turned him venomous. 'No Englishman can be expected to stand it.'

'Sheer self-indulgence is a trait I will never accept,' Curzon said. 'You people are lazy and self-satisfied. We are supposed to set a good example to the native, but when he sees us disporting ourselves in this little England, cutting him off, how can he learn?'

'He is not meant to,' the Colonel responded. 'We are his rulers. We do as we please.'

Curzon felt the Colonel's displeasure. 'For how long?'

'For ever.'

'Such complacency!' Curzon said. 'We can, if we allow them a certain degree of self-rule. We are here by divine right but that right carries with it some degree of compassion.'

'Totally unnecessary,' said Brodrick. 'They'll botch it.'

'I agree there isn't one native with the ability to sit on the legislative council but we must ensure that one day there will be.' Curzon's disparagement of the Indian, the Hindu especially, equalled theirs and he did not wish them to doubt this. 'I am leaving behind a secure empire and I have faith that our rule will continue here for centuries to come. I think we should join the others for my farewell.'

His companions rose. The Colonel remained while the others left the room. Bearers silently poured more brandy.

Curzon, like all who looked at the Colonel, was drawn by his eyes. They were circled by thick brows and deep pouches, like the markings of a predator who watched and waited with immense patience. The observer experienced the uneasy realisation that those eyes knew one's most secret thoughts, and that if he were disturbed, he would reveal one's weaknesses to the world. They were not meant to frighten, but to warn. The remainder of his features were concealed behind the shadows of those eyes, so that later one would not be able to recall them.

Curzon distrusted the Colonel's power as head of the political and secret department of the Indian government. It was a wrong judgement. The Colonel's loyalty lay not with a single man, but with his belief in the empire. It was the rock on which he rested. If a man, even a Viceroy, were to betray this idea, he would be ruthless in his opposition.

'Will the Prince and Princess of Wales be safe during their visit here next month?' Curzon asked at last.

'Assuredly,' the Colonel said after a pause. 'There are bazaar rumours of an assassination plot, but we'll nip it in the bud.'

'Maybe we listen too much to these bazaar rumours,' Curzon suggested.

The Colonel's reply was silence. He did not have to remind this Viceroy of 1857, the Mutiny. The Colonel had been only a baby then, but the memory of his whimpers still echoed in his deepest sleep. And what he could barely remember was reinforced by the telling and re-telling of those terrible days. He had smelt blood, seen it blackening on the bodies of his people, heard the sated buzz of flies. Worse, he remembered fear. It had its own peculiar odour: sweat, urine, smoke. It could not be scrubbed away. It had passed into his very soul. Then he had seen sepoys strapped to zam-zamah, the great cannon that stood opposite the Ajain-Gher in Lahore, and blown to shreds. Seen others hanging from trees like giant flying-foxes. It had been pleasurable, this sense of cruel vengeance. 1857 haunted them all; like a monsoon cloud it threw its shadow across their sunlight. Except, of course, for men like Curzon, who only lived in India as viceroys and listened to London's drum. The Colonel was determined that 1857 would never repeat itself.

'I believe,' he said, watching the Viceroy carefully to assess his reaction, 'that we need more stringent laws to keep control of the situation.'

'Such as?' Curzon gave no hint of his thoughts.

'Detention without trial for a start. Exile.'

'And no doubt a few executions? You want more power, Colonel, and my answer is "no". I will not tolerate such draconian methods.' The Viceroy silenced the Colonel before he could protest. 'I know you would

7

like to keep this country under lock and key, but we are English and we cannot rule as tyrants.'

'I believe it to be only a temporary necessity.' The Colonel decided not to pursue the matter with this man. He would wait for the next Viceroy and then push hard for legislation. Bazaar rumours were now to be believed, pursued, crushed, broken.

'By the way, who's going to do the bud-nipping?' Curzon changed the subject, knowing what the Colonel thought.

'I have an agent – my best man – making enquiries.' He waved the bearers out of the room with an authority equal to that of the Viceroy. The two men sat alone, listening to the strands of music and laughter. It sounded more of a celebration than a farewell.

The Colonel thought Curzon was a weak man. He had seen him weep when Kitchener defied his viceregal authority. India had broken him – no, he'd broken himself, unable to grasp the task of ruling this country. 'He'll hunt out the seditionists and then I shall crush them.'

'You seem to depend a lot on one man. Who is he?'

The Colonel hesitated, displeased at the question. 'He's called Kimball O'Hara.'

'For God's sake! An Irishman! He'll stand out like a sore thumb in the bazaars! He'll make a complete mess of it.'

'You have not met him, sir. He looks like an Indian and behaves like one. He can think like them; he knows the crevices of their devious minds.'

'With a name like O'Hara?'

'His father and mother were Irish, but he was orphaned early and grew up in the bazaars of Lahore. Kim is, I can assure you, one of us. And I would trust him as I would my own son.'

2

KIM LOOKED north, not in worship, but in memory. It was gradually becoming light and it seemed, at first, a trick of the eyes grown used to the Indian night. The mountain peaks were just visible. Soon they would turn pink as the sun brushed the snow.

'Somewhere up there is the home of my old companion, the Lama. Long ago we travelled from Lahore to Benares in search of the sacred river. He found what he was looking for. He was fortunate. God blesses the innocent – and he was a child. I have never known such innocence. What chance had I, with the bazaars of Lahore and the Grand Trunk Road as the gardens of childhood. It is true I have survived and thrived, more fortunate than many of my chokra companions, dead, disabled, begging. My friend found strength in his belief that God guided him. I have no such belief yet. But one man, the Colonel, is the father I have never known. My mother is India herself; the sun, the dust, the waters, the odour of the hot earth. One day I too will have belief, I too will search. From up there in the mountains my friend's spirit will be my guide in life.'

Kim stood up and stretched. He strolled over to a deodar, untied his pi-jama and urinated. The steam and smell imparted an earthiness like the smell of cattle, the sweet smoke of dung fires. It gave him life against this wintry chill. After retying his pi-jama he approached one of the Sikh bodyguards.

'Sardar, when will they finish?'

'When they are good and ready, and not when

chuthias like you want it. Now return to the other coolies.'

'Salah,' Kim swore cheerfully. 'You too would be squatting with me on the road if it wasn't for that fine uniform. Where are you from?'

The bodyguard chuckled. 'Near Ludhiana. And you?'

'Lahore,' Kim replied, conscious that his past was partly fabricated. He could not claim with such certainty a place in India; he had no village, no ancestors. 'Do they pay you well to stand here like a statue?'

'Well enough to feed my wife and children and to buy my own farm one day.'

'Buy? For your bharti the sarkar will give you one free from their Crown lands, reserved specially for loyal sardars like you.' The Crown land, Kim knew, had been confiscated from those who opposed British rule. 'That is, if you don't die in battle first.'

'Sooner or later we all die,' the Sikh said. 'For you it may be all the sooner unless you return to your filthy companions.'

Kim spat to within an inch of the polished boots. The Sikh started, controlling an impulse to strike at Kim.

'If that had touched me,' he hissed, 'you would be dead the next time you looked on my face.'

'Sardar, any woman will tell you that looking on your face shrivels and dries the passage between her legs.'

The exchange would have continued, but a bearer approached to summon the Colonel sahib's rickshaw. Kim fetched the vehicle. It was painted green with brown upholstery and brass lamps. He followed the bearer up the drive, stopped under the porch and squatted between the shafts. Through the open doors he could see the guests, sweeping back and forth in dance. If he crossed that threshold, he thought, he would enter another country, familiar only from the pictures in books he had seen at school. The tableau appeared to be enclosed in glass, filled with fluttering butterflies, strangely exotic.

The Colonel came out, wrapped in an evening cape, and settled into the seat. Kim rose, and felt those eyes strip the flesh and bone from his back as he walked to the gate, passed by the coolies and began to trot.

'There's no sense in overdoing it, Kim,' the Colonel said. 'What have you learned?'

The Mall was deserted. Kim's breath came out in short bursts of steam. The light had turned grey and Simla unfolded on either side of them. Bungalows, small and cosy, reminded him of his picture-book villages, set in small hills. Below the Mall, he saw the early-morning smoke of the bazaar. The morning mist, thin and patchy, hugged the ground, and tendrils clung like lace to leafy branches. Kim ran round a curve into a thick patch, ghostly and foreboding. He ran through it swiftly, expecting it to be brief, but it continued. He imagined shapes and shadows haunting it. He slowed down. The mist chilled him, though its touch was soft on his skin.

'Two men have come here to kill,' Kim said. 'One young, one old.'

'Can you find them?'

'Possibly. They have hidden in the bazaar.'

The Colonel spoke English, Kim Hindustani. He was not as yet comfortable with another tongue. He thought and dreamt in the language of his childhood. The Colonel preferred him to use it; Kim was too valuable to be taught fluent English. It would only distance him from the country and the people. The Colonel had seen this happen with educated natives, who now thought no end of themselves because they spoke English. Such signs, omens, made the Colonel uneasy. He sensed the flick of leaves and dust, quick and darting, warning of the coming monsoon.

'Whom will they kill? Us?'

Kim waited until he was clear of the mist. The sunrise was turning the sky a delicate peach colour. He considered the question, approaching it cautiously.

'Why do you hesitate? If it is an Englishman, I must know.'

'Colonel sahib, all I can tell you is what others have said. It is not always the truth, for they only half hear

11

what men talk about.' He paused, then added: 'Yes, the Angrezi. But that is the word of a coolie.'

'Maybe you're right, Kim. The bazaar is always full of rumours. I wouldn't bother to chase them.'

'But the Viceroy travels tomorrow,' Kim said, surprised at the Colonel's lack of interest.

'Don't worry. I'll put on extra police to patrol the line.'

The handful of Indians violently opposed to British rule were not generally given to such bold strokes. They were cowardly; they murdered a Commissioner here, a Collector there, and then faded into the vast folds of India. They were hunted down, caught, hanged, for the Colonel always took his revenge. The Great Game on the North-West Frontier against the agents of the Russian empire no longer preoccupied him. It was the game unfolding here in India that now tested his skill and patience.

How could he use the Indian National Congress? The political party of rich landlords and lawyers had been founded some twenty-five years ago in Bombay by an Englishman, Allan Octavian Hume. Hume had thought it necessary for the native to have a political forum, an escape valve for nationalist aspirations. The government had reluctantly given permission for the Congress to be formed, and monitored its activities closely. Its demands were modest: a small morsel of power, especially for themselves.

The Colonel thought: we must not concede. Erosion is dangerous; a crumb of power now, a slice later. Congress wasn't violent but humble, and they could be more easily appeased than the extremists. I will use them as our buffer. The Congressmen are corruptible. Position is all they want, plus a little baksheesh. When their usefulness ceases, I will sow the dissent and division. It will be easy. Muslim and Hindu now sit together, but I will have them at their throats when the time comes.

'I'll walk now, Kim,' the Colonel said in a kindly tone.

Kim's kurta was sticking to his back and lines of sweat streaked his face, making his moustache limp. It was

12

black and curled at the ends, resembling a bison's horns. He halted, wiping his face on his shawl. The Colonel dismounted and strolled alongside Kim. The Mall remained deserted. Only the British were permitted on this ridge, which ran from Viceregal Lodge at one end to the Secretariat at the other. It was hallowed earth, lemon coloured, flanked with English stores, English banks, English tea shops. In the centre, like a pivot, stood the Gaiety Theatre.

'You must help me, Kim,' the Colonel said. 'We shall fight together. Everything we stand for in this country is being eroded by fools like Curzon. The mice are allowed to nibble at the foundations. I don't want things to change. Ever. You do understand, Kim?'

'Yes, Colonel sahib.'

They breathed in the cold air and looked over to the Himalayas. The dark slopes soared upwards and the peaks turned white with snow and age. Even on the blackest night, those peaks glowed like beacons, somehow phosphorescent. The eye could not see them all, they faded into the lightness, becoming a part of the distant sky.

'Who is supposed to live up there?' the Colonel mused.

'Parvati, Siva's consort, is called the Daughter of the Mountains.'

'She's not been of much use, has she? Every invader has marched right past her. It's a wonder they still believe.' The Colonel turned to the handsome youth pulling the rickshaw 'We came from the south, from the sea. And now we rule India. Not only a part of it like the Mughals, but all of it. We have a greater divine right to rule than the monster deities who live up in the mountains.'

High above, a lone bird circled. For some strange reason Kim thought of the vulture Jatayu, who had fought the demon king Ravana in the popular Hindu story of the exiled Prince Rana and his wife Sita. In the Ramayana, Jatayu had tried to rescue Sita from the clutches of Ravana, and had died in the battle. His wings and legs were hacked off, but he did not yield until the demon king finally thrust his sword into his chest.

'My father fought and died for the Crown.'

'Yes, he did,' the Colonel agreed. He knew Kim's father had perished in an opium den. 'And we must keep safe the India he gave his life for. We will fight together.'

The Colonel laid his hand on Kim's shoulder, feeling the hard muscles, and squeezed affectionately. He had known Kim since he had been but a boy. Kim had been wandering the roads in the company of a strange fakir, in search of some damned mythical river. He is mine, the Colonel thought. I found him, trained him, honed him. He is my weapon, unseen, unrecognisable, dangerous. He is my eyes, my ears, my nose. I envy him. He does what none of us can do. He can move through this land, mingle with the people, unseen.

'I will start my search for those two men,' Kim said, and before the Colonel could reply, he strode easily down the slope towards the bazaar.

The road wound round the edge of the hill. At a corner, Kim paused. The earth plunged down beyond the stone wall and the view of the distant hills falling away to the south was clear and sharp. Kim looked up and saw that the bird had continued its circling, but with each great circle it was dropping lower and lower.

Suddenly the bird stopped its circling. It hovered a moment high in the sky and then dived down towards Kim. As it drew closer, it became larger. His huge wings tilted, first this way, then that, holding the great body steady, aiming at Kim. He skimmed the tops of the deodars and his giant shadow rippled over the earth, turning day into darkness where he passed. The air was filled with the sound of the wind whistling through his wings, and his eyes had terrible beauty. The talons were as large as sabres, and his speckled chest was as powerful as the prow of a sailing ship.

Then the eagle checked its downward plunge with a beat of its wings, sending the leaves flying as though

14

driven by a storm. Kim felt the draught chill his sweat-soaked body and watched the eagle circle just above his head.

The eagle called down to him. 'Namaskaar . . . namaskaar. I am the same Jatayu, the one who fought Ravana and was dismembered by his sword. For my courage, Brahma granted me the boon of eternity and changed me from a vulture into an eagle.'

'Then why remain a bird?' Kim asked in a voice cracking with nervousness and awe.

'Brahma asked if I wanted to be a man, and I refused. The burden of being a man was too heavy for my atman. I had no higher ambition than to soar in the air and observe the actions of men. But I have a message for you. A man awaits below on the plain. He has only the height of a child, but the mind of a great sage. You must find him. Namaskaar.'

Jatayu's wings beat the air and Kim could barely stand upright against the blast. Deodars swayed and their branches snapped like twigs. Houses shuddered as the eagle rose up into the sky, growing smaller and smaller with each beat until it became a speck against the rising sun.

Now he knew. Once this duty was done, he must search out the man waiting for him down on the plain.

The bazaar lay in the shadow of the Mall. The small wooden rooms on either side pushed against each other and pushed outwards. Kim felt the compression of space and people, as though they all teetered on the edge of the world where the solid earth ended. They cascaded down, fighting gravity, fighting to be nearest the Mall with the sun above their heads.

The night's drizzle had cleansed the air and left a glistening gauze over every shack. Life stirred; children sat in the watery sunlight, pi-dogs curled in tight, thin balls, women swept the ground in front of their stalls and homes. Shutters were being taken down from stalls and the fresh perfume of channa, sweet tea, treacly

15

jelabis frying, chilli, mustard, dhania, slowly stained the smell of rain. Men and women squatted behind rows of fresh tomatoes, potatoes, onions, green chillies, garlic, the dew still spotting them, placed on scraps of gunny, patiently waiting for bearers and cooks to come down from the Mall to make their day's purchases. Bunias sat cross-legged in stalls, presiding over riches of silks, cottons, gold and silver, brass vessels, spices.

Kim felt himself sink back into this familiar life. It was rather like being immersed in the warm waters of the Ganges. He greeted many he knew, and the others he didn't – the new faces of those down from the high foothills arranging shawls and pullovers in orderly piles – he salaam'd. He parked the rickshaw in front of a small shack and went in, stepping lightly over prone sleepers. Then he found the man he wanted.

'Ahre, Suresh.' He shook the curled blanket and a grizzled, thin face appeared over the edge. 'Here is money for the loan of your rickshaw.' Kim handed over a few coins which were gratefully accepted.

The chai-wallah Ramchand stirred a dekshi filled with tea and greeted Kim warmly. He poured sugar and milk into a clay mug, dolloped in the tea and handed him a piece of fresh thick bread. Kim squatted by him to eat and drink.

'I am looking for two men,' he said. 'One young, one old, who got down from a rickshaw in front of this place yesterday. Did you see where they went?'

The tea stall was a small, makeshift room which stood at a cross-lane. Ramchand presided over not only the tea, but also a few dekshis of food cooking on the clay braziers. He wiped his hands on a rag and dropped fresh bhajis into hot oil. He was a thin, stooped man with a squint in his right eye and bony knees.

'One young and one old? Yes. They were visitors, it seemed. The young man carried a case.'

'They parted as strangers.'

'No. They spoke. I overheard the old one say that he would meet his companion at the Prince Hotel down

16

below the Mall. They were staying there. They looked as though they could afford it. I hear it's an expensive place.'

Kim had already noted the distortions in the tale. The rickshaw wallah saw and heard only half of what happened, as all men did. They saw what they wished and made it whole.

He finished the food and lit a beedi. He smoked it through his closed fist, as any Indian would, instead of holding it pinched between two fingers in the European fashion.

'How were they dressed?'

'Like Angrezis. Very "posh".' Ramchand spoke this last word in English and hooted with laughter at his own wit. He waved away Kim's money and was still chuckling as Kim walked to the hotel.

The Prince Hotel was a modest bungalow strategically located between the bazaar and the Mall. It stood on the side of the hill, surrounded by a small lawn. Indians, those who could afford its equally modest prices, stayed here on their visits to Simla. They came in the summer, apeing the habits of their rulers. Though not permitted to stroll on the Mall, they and their families would walk among the stately deodars in the hills. Now, in winter, the Prince had an abandoned air. A uniformed chowkidar dozed at the gates in the gruel of sunlight. Kim nudged him awake.

'Chowkidar sahib, I am owed money by two sahibs who are staying here. One is young, the other old. Is it possible to see them?'

'You cannot go in,' the chowkidar replied. 'If you wait, maybe you'll see them when they come out.' He watched Kim lower himself and squat in the sun. 'You may have to wait a long time.'

'Why?'

'Because they have already gone out.' He pointed up at the hills.

'Did you see where they went?'

'Up there. Where else can they go?' The chowkidar

spat paan into the gutter. He was irritated at being woken by a coolie for no financial reward. As a retired government chowkidar, he had status and didn't waste his time talking to ruffians like this man.

'But they will be returning?'

'Yes. Now go away.'

'Did they carry their tiffin?'

'Tiffin, and a strange-looking instrument. It could have been a jezail.'

Kim thanked the bad-tempered old man politely and hurried to pass on this new piece of information to the Colonel sahib. He hoped the two men meant only to shoot quail, but he couldn't take any chances. It would be best if the police were alerted. At midday, the Viceroy would begin his journey to Delhi.

3

THE MOUNTAINS inspired poetry and the young man looked south, enchanted by the play of light on the slopes of the foothills. They undulated in the haze, quilted by black shadow and delicate, lemon sunlight. He had never seen such beauty: the green of forests, broken by tiny patches of wheat and dotted with the white specks of bungalows. He could scarcely imagine where he sat – on the brow of India looking down at her vast body. Immediately surrounding him were deodars, their heads touching the blue sky. Their trunks had grown twisted and curved, misshapen by the steep slope of the hill. The earth was a carpet of cones and leaves.

His uncle sat some distance away, propped up on his shooting-stick. Both men wore tweed jackets and plus-fours and stout brogue shoes. Anil Ray was bare-headed; his uncle wore a deer-stalker. Except for their dark skins they might have been English.

The shooting-stick was a favourite possession of the older man. He had seen English gentlemen using them at Goodwood, and thought them a wondrous invention. He had purchased his in Bond Street. It was made of steel with a sharp point and a small disc at one end, at the other a curved handle which opened up to form a leather seat. The shaft was bound with leather and engraved in gold with his initials.

'It reminds me of Switzerland,' he said.

'But more beautiful. Vast.' Anil spoke English with a public-school accent. 'I wish I'd seen all this before. I've seen more of England and the continent than my own country.'

'You have plenty of time.'

The tiny regret remained, like the sigh of the breeze in the trees. He did have time. Anil was young, just returned from England. He had been educated at Eton and Oxford, and had then taken three years for his Bar exams. It had been a strange exile. He had been moulded into an English gentleman, and there lay his regret, but he understood the need. He was now familiar with the language and ways of the English, and had begun to practise law in Calcutta. Success came easily to him; the English judges looked kindly on him.

I have become another person without ever really knowing who was the original. It happened too swiftly, but I mustn't regret it. Obviously it's for the best. I am the most fortunate of men. When I return home at the end of this vac, I shall get married. The girl is young and shy, but she is my mother's choice and I shall obey tradition in this matter.

Far below them, Anil saw the glitter of the railway line. It curved around and disappeared into a hill. There were 103 tunnels on the way to Simla and he could not help but admire the spirit and inventiveness of the English.

We would not have cared for such labour, nor have been able to build such a miracle. And only because they wished to reach Simla conveniently, he thought.

He saw several figures moving along the track. Two of them looked up and he caught the glitter of glass as they stared at his stand of trees.

'I feel happy,' Anil said. 'The air makes one drunk; clear and smooth, like good Scotch.'

He opened the basket beside him and spread out a tablecloth. He laid out plates and forks and served cold chicken, potatoes and bread. From a Thermos flask he poured chilled white wine. In his college days he had been on many picnics, both at Oxford and during his travels on the continent.

20

'Cha-cha,' he called, 'lunch is ready, but I'll need your pocket knife to cut the chicken. The bearer didn't pack one.'

His uncle was grateful. He wasn't used to such invigorating exercise and his stomach had been rumbling for an hour. Anil took the knife, opened the five-inch blade and cut the chicken. They sat opposite each other, with the shooting-stick beside them, and ate voraciously.

They did not look much like each other. The uncle was stout, balding, with a stump of a nose. Yet he was not unattractive. He carried himself with grace and was known to be a most courtly man with exquisite manners. He spoke five languages fluently, including French and German, and he was known for a weakness for fine women and bad horses.

Anil had an athlete's physique. He had played cricket for Eton and won his blue at Oxford. Yet he had an air, not of activity, but of quiet languor: of dreaminess.

As they ate, they bickered good-naturedly over the choice of Simla for their holiday. Anil was deeply fond of his uncle and considered him a close friend. They had spent many pleasant days together whenever his uncle visited England.

'What else can one do here except stroll?' his uncle said. 'It's an awful English habit, like their weather.' He always joked about the English with great affection. Like his nephew, he believed that there were no finer people on earth and had fashioned his manners closely on the many friends he had made in England.

'Well, it's healthier than sitting up in a machan waiting for some poor animal to come so you can kill it.'

'Hunting is the sport of princes.'

'But we aren't princes. We don't have to imitate them by killing ten tigers a day to prove our courage. And that with expensive rifles. A week here, cha-cha, and you'll feel as good as new.'

'What a ghastly thought! I enjoy the exhaustion of over-indulgence and even prefer to kill than to walk.'

They were so preoccupied that they did not notice the

cautious approach, slowly encircling them. The men stepped softly on the crisp matting of leaves and moved behind the protection of trees.

The tall, bony man who led the police constables signalled them to move in closer. Richard Goode was young to be a Deputy Inspector of police. He had been in India for only six years, and had earned the reputation of an honest and meticulous man, though on occasion over-zealous. But he had earned his promotions through this last trait.

He halted twenty yards from the two Indians seated on the ground. He noted their dress, and in the cold, thin air, heard the talk of killing. On the ground beside them, hidden in the folds of the tablecloth, lay the rifle. He had been informed about it; now he unholstered his revolver and cautiously flicked off the safety catch. When he saw that his men were all in position, their Enfield rifles at the ready, he leaped out from the cover of the deodar.

'Stand up!' he shouted in Hindustani.

Anil and his uncle started. They saw Goode with the revolver pointing at them and sensed the presence of the other surrounding men.

'I say,' his uncle began. 'What's all this nonsense? We are having a picnic.'

'Stand up. At once,' Goode shouted again. He was nervous, tense. The revolver was clutched tightly so that his knuckles had turned white.

Anil noticed Goode's red moustache. It was a peculiar colour, and balanced like a carrot beneath his nose. In the strangeness of the moment, he focused on that as he began to rise. His uncle, too portly to manage this feat, reached for his shooting-stick and half rose to one knee, holding it. The shot hit him in the chest, throwing him across the remains of the picnic. The sound of the shot seemed to echo long after his death, reverberating around the hills like a drum-roll, fading finally into silence.

Anil stared down at his uncle. There was a small black

hole, little blood. His face was caught in a grimace, the final moment of pain frozen there. He could not believe it; this was a charade, the kind he had played as a small boy. His uncle would roll over, rise and lumber away for a chota peg to revive his energy. Anil shivered. God, he felt cold, he felt dead himself; his body and mind had ceased to function.

Then he was pushed up against a deodar. The bark scraped his face, drawing blood, but the pain served as a momentary relief. It warmed him, and the smell of the wood was sweet after the sour and angry odour of cordite. Two constables held his arms around the tree. He saw only one: a dark, expressionless face, fathomless eyes above a black moustache. No hint of sorrow. Other hands searched his body.

'Oh God, a bloody shooting-stick,' he heard the Englishman mutter.

His arms were released. They fell to his sides. He could not leave the comfort of the tree. He pressed his face cruelly against the wood, tasting bark and tears. He was roughly turned around. The sunlight was a harsh blur, exposing him to the eyes of the Englishman. The revolver remained pointing at him. He found the black muzzle hypnotising:

'What the hell were you doing up here?'

Finally, Anil looked up at Goode's face. The moustache was no longer a point of focus. Now Anil looked at his eyes, which were blue, matching the sky and matching too the emotionless expression in those of the constable. Fathomless.

'You have killed my uncle for no reason,' Anil heard his own whisper from far away.

'Answer my question. What the hell were you doing up here?' The response too sounded distant.

Anil thought: we live in different worlds. I say one thing; he another. I cannot understand his question; he doesn't understand my answer. This is madness. Why can't we both step into the same world? We are both men of the same age. Yet I can hear nothing but silence.

The trees are silent, the sky is silent, all these men are silent, cha-cha is silent. But I cannot be silent.

'You have killed my uncle for no reason.'

Inspector Goode spoke carefully. 'Please answer me. What were you doing up here?'

Anil gestured to the basket, the plates and tablecloth, now a shroud for his uncle. 'Picnicking.'

'You were waiting for the accident, weren't you? You came up here to gloat.'

'Accident? Gloat?' He knew the meaning of the words, even their linguistic roots. His mind went to the bleak classroom in Eton and the blackboard on the wall.

'The railway line has been tampered with. The Viceroy's train would have toppled down the hillside. Killing everyone on board.' Goode made this last statement sound like a newspaper headline, dark and bold.

Anil looked down. The rails glinted like silver bangles encircling the hill below. The sun shone, the sky was blue and the hills still green, and yet they had darkened before his vision, fading into a terrible gloom. He did not look at Goode, but heard himself speaking.

'I would never harm the Viceroy.'

'You're an anarchist. You'd have bloody well killed him.'

Again, there were the two worlds. Suddenly Anil could not bear the one Goode inhabited, aloof, angry, murderous. He could not understand it. His life had been spent with pleasant companions from that world; their skin was the same colour as Goode's. They had laughed and drunk together. He thought of the pretty English girls who had flirted gaily. He had wanted to step back into that world, it had been his comfort; but he could not desert his uncle.

His uncle! How quickly the flies took note of death. They buzzed greedily around the dark little hole, feeding on the escaping spirit. He knelt and waved his hand. They buzzed wildly, unafraid.

'You must pay for . . . this.' Was that all his uncle had

been reduced to? A 'this'. A repayment, like a financial transaction?

'I shot him in the line of duty. He was a suspected criminal.'

'We are not criminals. We were just taking a picnic when you murdered my uncle.'

'The railway line has been sabotaged, and you are the only natives to be found near the scene of the sabotage.'

'Do we look like criminals?'

'I don't care what you look like. What is your name?'

'Anil Ray.'

Goode pounced, delight and relief in his exclamation. 'A Bengali!'

He had good reason for pleasure. Some Bengalis were violently opposed to British rule. They had formed secret sects and had marked officials down for assassination. Since Lord Curzon had partitioned Bengal into Muslim and Hindu, east and west, their murderous activities had increased. They believed they could drive the British out by using murder and violence, and they were actively encouraged by seditionists in other parts of India – like Lokamanya Tilak, the Maharati political leader who had his base in Poona. Admittedly, Tilak had no proven connections, but it was only a matter of time. He provided the rhetoric, the Bengalis the violence.

Goode had no doubt he had caught the right villains. This English-speaking native claimed innocence, but Goode had been thoroughly inculcated into believing that every native was a liar.

Anil failed to notice Goode's reaction. He held his uncle's hand. It was warm but lifeless; it didn't return his tight grip. If he held on, he might waken his uncle, pull him back into this world. The shock was wearing off; disbelief was turning to rage. He wanted to scream, but, inarticulate, he only sobbed. Under his uncle's hand he saw the gleam of the pocket knife, greasy with chicken. Goode's polished black shoes were a few feet away, turning now as he issued orders to the constables.

'One of you stay with the body. I'll send porters to

bring it down. You others take this man to the lock-up.'

Anil gripped the knife, stood and lunged at Goode. The knife was sharp, and the force of his rage drove it into Goode's side. They both fell and rolled down the slope. Anil tried to withdraw the blade, to plunge it into Goode's heart. He could not make room. Goode gripped him tightly, beating at his back and head. Neither had any real hold, rolling like children down the hill. Instead of laughter, one grunted in effort, the other screamed out commands.

They hit a deodar and the wind was driven from both. Anil left the knife in Goode's side and took a grip on his throat and squeezed. He used all his strength, concentrating fiercely until the rifle butt cracked down on his head.

4

KIM SAT stiffly in the Colonel's office. It was a small room in the Colonel's bungalow with a view of the Simla Secretariat building. The furnishings were spartan: a desk, three chairs, an almirah. A large map of India hung on the wall. Files, bound with red tape, lay in a tray. A peon was meticulously packing others into a trunk. One door led to the garden; the other into the bungalow.

There were several photographs. They were yellow and dark, stained by the damp air. The Colonel featured in all of them: with be-jewelled princes outside ornate palaces; at a clubhouse in the company of cricketers and admiring ladies. In others he stood, rifle in arm, behind the body of a tiger, or of a panther; even an elephant. In each portrait the Colonel's pose remained the same, as if the pictures had been taken all at the same time, though with different beasts.

In a large photograph in the middle of the display, he stood with his hands resting on the shoulders of a boy and a girl in front of this very bungalow. Two golden Labradors panted at their feet. The Colonel was younger then, and full of hope, but with eyes which had already begun to sink beneath the shroud of his eyebrows. The children looked happy, but aware that his presence marked a special occasion. They were too neatly dressed. The photographs suggested a fairy-tale sort of life; except for the one with the children. There Kim saw a sadness in the Colonel's eyes.

'We caught two of them.' The Colonel addressed Kim,

then emerged holding a file. He smiled and clapped Kim on the shoulder. 'Excellent work, Kim. Without your help, there might have been a frightful disaster.'

'Who were they?'

'Bengali trouble-makers, again. How stupid can you get? They were sitting, plain as day, above the track, waiting to see the train go by. I would have been miles away.' He bent over his file. 'One of them was killed, resisting arrest. Goode, the DI, was wounded in the struggle. Not seriously. A minor knife-wound. He'll be up and about in no time. Lord Curzon sent his personal congratulations. The damn train will be delayed for an hour until they mend the line.' He initialled the report and dropped it in the tray. 'Doubtless these two were the source of the bazaar rumour of "mar". Now I have to ensure that nothing will spoil Their Highnesses' arrival next month. I'd like you to go to Bombay . . . just to keep an eye open.' The Colonel opened a drawer and took out a bag of rupees. He counted some out and passed them to Kim, who put them, without counting, into the side pocket of his kurta. The Colonel wrote on a slip of paper and held it out for Kim to read and memorise. 'Here is the name and address of your contact in Bombay.' When Kim leant back again the Colonel tore up the slip.

'What happened to the other man?'

'He was injured resisting arrest. He'll get a stiff sentence for attempting to kill the DI.'

'How much?'

'That depends on the judge. Fifteen years, possibly more. He will make a good example to others. If Goode had died, though, naturally the man would have been hanged.'

Kim noted the regret, but was distracted by a flash of colour. A woman strolled through the garden. She was wearing a blue frock and a white topi. A dog lolloped behind. Under the hat, Kim glimpsed fair hair, and the sun silhouetted a young, slim body. She waved to someone beyond his vision, then turned and came up the path to the office.

Her face, with the sun behind her, was at first indistinct, but when she entered and stooped to kiss the Colonel, he saw she was very pretty. The wide topi shaded the upper half of her face, but her mouth resembled the Colonel's – sensual, yet hinting of no sexuality. The scent of lavender filled the small room with a gentle fragrance.

She paid no attention to Kim, though she noted that he showed no deference to the Colonel. Any other Indian would have sat there fawning. Most Indians were servile; she accepted their servility as a part of her life. It was his distinctive self-assurance that made her remember him later.

Kim noticed the Colonel's hand hover, wanting to hold her. Then it fell emptily back on the desk.

'Did you enjoy the dance, darling?'

'Oh yes, Father. So many people knew me, but I honestly couldn't remember them all.'

'You've been away for a long time. I suppose they were as surprised as me. A gawky little girl left to go to school, and a pretty young lady has returned.'

'Thank you, kind sir.' She had a merry laugh, and Kim wished she would notice him. But they both behaved as though he wasn't in the room. 'It's not quite the same as the balls in London. I wish—'

'You'll get used to India again. It takes time. By the way, I told Cook to make sandwiches. The train's been delayed.'

'Oh, then I'll have time to see Sally. She's announcing her engagement at Christmas and I promised to come up for the party. You won't say "no", will you?'

'But Richard might get leave for Christmas. You'd miss him.'

The news delighted her and she laughed. 'In which case Sally will have to celebrate alone. Oh, how I envy him. Dashing down some dark defile. Men have such grand adventures.'

She brushed past Kim's chair and went into the bungalow, humming. The light and scent went with her.

The Colonel's face had softened and Kim saw then his vulnerability. He loved his daughter deeply, and yet even as Kim watched, a shadow, some deeper, darker thought, arose unchecked, in which Kim saw something akin to dislike. He looked at the photograph on the wall and saw again the Colonel's closeness to his children.

I feel sad that I have no such reminder of my own past, Kim thought. The memory of my father is dim. I believe he was a handsome, jolly man, full of charm and wit. But of that I cannot be certain. The mind plays tricks, and of course I want to believe in this image.

'Richard's up in Rawalpindi. No dark defiles for him at the moment. Just parade and drill, spit and polish. Since we withdrew from Afghanistan it's been a quiet posting. Thank God.'

When Kim remained silent, the Colonel continued. 'Well, I'll see you in Bombay, Kim. If you haven't eaten, Cook will give you tiffin. By the way,' he added as Kim paused at the door leading into the garden, 'I think we should avoid being seen with each other from now on. It could be dangerous for you.'

Kim squatted in the shade of an apple tree in the back compound. He had eaten chapatis and subji, and now lit a beedi. Out of curiosity, he had remained, and now waited patiently for the right moment. He had seen the miss sahib step out on the back verandah and call for the bearer. She appeared to notice his presence, but made no sign. Her ayah also emerged from the bungalow, having completed her mistress's packing. She sat down near Kim and a mali who was also seated there.

'Hurry-burry, hurry-burry,' she complained. 'I was up all night waiting for miss sahib to come home from the tamasha. I thought she would return when her father did, but she has a mind of her own, that girl. She only came back as the sun rose. I put her to bed, but still she got up to say goodbye. I spend all morning packing, now the train is delayed. If only I had known earlier.' She leant over and spoke conspiratorially. 'They caught those Bengali terrorists. Useless people. Why do they cause such trouble for us? Don't they have better things to do?'

The mali ignored her, while Kim clucked sympathetically. Mary ayah was of indeterminate age with hair black as a crow's wing, a fine-boned face and broad nostrils, which flared in indignation. Her body appeared supple beneath the folds of her sari, and she knew that men watched her with fixed intent. She knew their thoughts – a waste of a lusty woman – but she spared none her glance. They were not for her, servants like herself. Kim, however, was different. He was sturdy and strong, with humour hidden in his eyes, and a certain difference she could not define.

'You are employed by Colonel sahib?'

'Yes, in a way. I do this and that. You have worked for him long?'

'Since I was but a child. I was six when Richard sahib was born, eight when Elizabeth baba came. I have looked after them both, Richard is now sub-al-tern in the army, but Elizabeth baba is like my own daughter.' Her eyes became moist at the thought. 'Then their father sent them to school in England and when Elizabeth miss sahib was due to come home again, the Colonel sahib asked me to be her ayah. I was so happy to be remembered.'

'She is indeed a fine woman. But what happened to her mother?'

'Dead.' Mary ayah's mouth snapped with the finality of death. She looked suspicious. 'You ask too many questions.'

'I only ask because I notice no burra memsahib,' Kim said. Her answer had been harsh, too brutal for death.

'Dead, dead.' She made it a chant; a mantra to ward off evil spirits. In spite of her Christianity, her mind was still filled deeply with Hindu superstitions.

She would have to be Catholic, not Anglican. The splendour of that ritual, with its divine images, was akin to the Hindu. Kim guessed too the reason for her

31

conversion: to escape the purgatory of her Hindu caste. It was better to be Christian or Muslim or Buddhist than to be a sweeper or one even lower, the dread of those born to the religion yet denied the embrace of God. He had been educated at St Xavier's by the Fathers, but had only once entered a cathedral, the great one near Lucknow Station. It had been cavernous and silent, flooded with brilliant light which burnished the ivory image on the altar. It was formal and reverent. He preferred the temple or the mosque, with the crush of people, the chanting of priests, the smell of jasmine and luddos, the presence of sadhus and pirs, intense in worship.

'Such a fine miss sahib should be married by now. Have they not found her a husband?'

'The sahib-log are not like us, you know that. My miss sahib will find her own husband.' She sighed in admiration. 'She told me: so many men came to see her in England, but she was not interested in any of them. She will choose the right one when the time comes.'

'And the Colonel sahib does not wish to marry again?'

'That,' she said haughtily, 'is not our business. But,' and she became conspiratorial again, 'the memsahibs look at him with interest. They come in big boats from their country to find husbands here, and a few have come to see him.' She rose. 'I am wasting time talking to the likes of you. I have work to do.'

Kim strolled back to Ramchand's. There was a small space in the rear and he curled up and slept. It was a restless sleep, haunted by silence and emptiness. He dreamed that he was in a large garden, not planted with flowers and shady trees, but barren and dusty. He stood alone and smoke coiled around his body. Like broken twigs, bodies lay scattered around him. The dead faces were all familiar and he wept for his lost companions.

He woke at dusk, chilled. The lamps were being lit. Ramchand's wife, a small, plump woman, prayed briefly to the light, smiled shyly at Kim and went out. Kim joined the chai-wallah to drink tea and gossip with customers. It was only by chance that Kim noticed the rickshaw-wallah again, the man who had whispered 'mar'.

'Huzzor,' Kim called, 'come and join us and rest for a while.'

The man gratefully lowered the shafts of the rickshaw and squatted down by Kim. He took the tea and a beedi, closing his eyes in exhaustion. He looked even thinner now, and more tired.

'You have had a profitable day?'

'A few annas,' he said with no expectation in his voice. 'Enough only for food for tonight.'

Kim was sympathetic. 'That is all we can expect nowadays. Do you recall that last night you told me of those two men? One young, one old, who got off your rickshaw just here?'

'Yes. I heard they have been caught.' The bazaar usually learnt of every police activity as soon as it occurred.

'Were they dressed like Angrezis?'

The man laughed. 'No. They were dressed like us. Kurta and pi-jama.'

At that, Ramchand protested. 'I saw two Angrezi-dressed sahibs get down.'

'Was I not the rickshaw-wallah? I would notice something like that. No, they were just ordinary men like us.'

'Have you seen them since?'

'No.'

'Then the men the police caught are the wrong ones.'

'This man's a fool,' Ramchand said. He was determined to prove himself and called over the cloth merchant from the next stall. 'You remember yesterday two sahibs dressed like Angrezi got down from this man's rickshaw?'

The cloth merchant squinted in thought. 'Yes, I saw them, I think. One was budda, so.' His hands outlined a fat man. 'The younger man looked around him in wonder, as if he were truly an Angrezi and not one of us.'

'I am telling you,' the rickshaw-wallah insisted, 'the men were dressed like us. The older man was tall and thin.' Across the lane squatted a barber, shaving a customer. The rickshaw-wallah called out. 'You see everything, Hari. Those two men who got out of my rickshaw yesterday: how were they dressed?'

The razor hovered in the air, coated with soap. His customer, half-shaved, turned to take part in the gossip as well. 'Like kissans.' The young man had been shaved badly and his moustache was crooked. It rose too high on one side.

The customer said, 'I heard that three men have been shot by the police.'

'Only one,' Kim murmured, but his comment went unheard as several others joined in the debate. A small crowd collected. The lamplight only half illumined them, inquisitive, kindly strangers greedy for diversion. The rickshaw-wallah rose to take his leave. Kim asked: 'Is there anything else you can remember about these two men?'

'The older one had a thadi. It was grey and reached his chest.'

'Nothing else?'

The man scratched his gaunt face. He looked too weary even to remember that he lived. Unlike Kim, who had been taught to observe and memorise every minute detail, the man's memory was blurred. Kim took out a rupee and pressed it into his palm.

'Did they speak of anything else apart from "mar"?'

It took another minute of scratching before he finally said, 'I heard the older man say he would be going to Bombay immediately. Someone . . . someone . . .' He gave up. 'To see someone.'

Kim slipped away, uneasy now. One man was dead, another was being held in prison. He was now certain that they were not the saboteurs. These two others, through a quirk of fate, had crossed their paths and had escaped. And if they were travelling to Bombay, the only 'someone' they could mean were the Prince and Princess

of Wales. Karma, he thought, had set its trap. He had
to undo the work. The Colonel had left on the Viceroy's
train. He had no one to turn to.

Between the bazaar and the Mall was the police
station. It was a neat bungalow, painted red, set in a
carefully tended garden. This was meant to lessen its
menace, but somehow only heightened it. A constable
stood on guard, at ease with a rifle. Kim approached the
head constable, a burly, middle-aged Panjabi.

'Thanedar sahib.' Kim elevated the man flatteringly to
a sub-inspector. 'Is it possible to see the DI Goode?'

'He is sick. Badly hurt. He will not be on duty for
many days.' The head constable examined Kim. 'Why
would he want to see a coolie?'

'Because I work with the Colonel sahib of the political
and secret department,' Kim said softly. 'It is important
that I see the man you have arrested.'

'I cannot do this without permission. He is a dangerous prisoner. He was the one who stabbed the DI sahib.'
He clung to the ledger in front of him, the only symbol
of authority.

'Thanedar sahib, if I disturb the DI with my request,
which I know he will grant, he will only get angry with
you. This is your authority.' Kim pressed his thumb and
fingers together, a mere morsel of time. 'Half a minute.'

The head constable stroked his moustache. Kim was
too confident to be a coolie. He had a superior air of
power beyond the head constable's vision. He decided
and beckoned a constable. 'Go with him and stay by
him. Half a minute only.'

It was cold in the cell. The air wasn't chilly, but the
spirit shrank within the bars and granite walls. A figure
was huddled under a threadbare blanket in the grim
shadow. Kim took a lamp and knelt down. He noticed
one foot shod in a brogue shoe, the other was bare.
He lifted the edge of the blanket, raised the lamp and
grimaced. The police had taken their revenge. The man's
face was swollen and discoloured. A bandage, dark and
stiff with blood, was wound around his forehead. The

man did not move for a moment, and then fluttered one bruised eye.

'Water,' he said in English.

Kim went and drew water from an earthenware chati. He held the man's head up and poured it gently past puffed lips and broken teeth. He saw the Angrezi clothes, torn, muddied and blood-stained.

'Salahs,' Kim swore.

'Thank you.' The eye opened wide enough to glimpse Kim's face in the flickering light. The eye was red and dull at first, and then Kim saw the leap of rage, the body coiling.

'Lie still, my friend. You will only suffer more. I will try to help you. Did you sabotage the railway? Think carefully and speak the truth, for I shall discover it eventually.'

'No. I am innocent of that. Who are you?'

'It is unimportant.'

'My uncle . . .'

'I cannot raise the dead.'

Gently Kim lowered the man back to the floor and went out. The cold air partially cleansed his sense of dismay and disgust. The only all-night post office was on the Mall. Kim hurried to it and composed a short message which he could send in code: COTTONSEED CALCUTTA STOP WRONG MAN ARRESTED STOP SUSPECTS PROCEEDING BOMBAY STOP

The Colonel would right the wrong.

Kim left the train at Kalki, at the base of the foothills. From here the plain of India stretched a full thousand miles south to the Deccan. Once out of the small town, he looked up at the sky. Jatayu circled interminably, moving to the south and west. Kim followed the eagle. Occasionally, as he strode along the Grand Trunk Road, he would ask travellers if they knew of a man the height of a child. No one knew. The Grand Trunk was an ancient silk route, used by countless conquerors who had invaded India. Like a river, it rose in the mountains, beyond Kabul, and ran through Delhi to Agra.

On the third day, Kim stopped to address three sadhus travelling north. They wore saffron robes, had long grey beards and equally long grey hair, knotted on top. Two carried tridents, the third a begging bowl. They had fierce, dark eyes that fixed with unpleasant intent on Kim's face while he questioned them. They reminded him of three cobras circling a mongoose.

'Why do you want to find this man?' asked the sadhu with the begging bowl. He was smeared with ash and dust. 'If you seek a guru, follow us. If he can do miracles, so can we. Give me money and I will show you.'

'I have none. Use your own to perform this miracle.'

'A rupee, then.'

Kim gave him an anna. The sadhu took the coin and, staring fiercely into Kim's eyes, began to squeeze the coin. From the bottom of his fist fell a steady drip of water. Then the sadhu opened his fist and in his palm lay a crushed rose-bud.

'Can your guru perform such a miracle?'

'He does not need tricks.'

Kim gripped the hand that held the rose. The sadhu tried to wrench it free, but Kim kept hold and with a fingernail drew a sharp line across the open palm. The skin split easily: the palm had been covered with a flesh-coloured pad which when squeezed dripped water. The coin, doubtless, had already disappeared into the folds of his robes.

'We curse you!' the sadhus shouted as Kim continued on his way.

'Be careful,' Kim called back. 'I have stronger mantras than you lot possess. I could turn you all into bandicoots. Then Jatayu up there will swoop and eat you all up.'

'Ahre,' he muttered to himself. 'There are more charlatans claiming to be the representatives of God than pebbles in a river bed. They will perform "miracles", recite the vedas, walk on coals, hypnotise you. Only fools believe in them, hoping for salvation. All they end up with are empty purses.'

When he woke on the morning of the fourth day, Kim saw Jatayu much lower in the sky. The eagle circled over one place. Kim looked ahead, but in the shimmer of the heat he could see nothing. He walked on, looking up, but the eagle remained in the same circling position. At midday, he came to a white temple by the river. It was on the outskirts of a small village and was shaded by a huge peepul tree. When he looked up, Jatayu was not to be seen.

Kim passed through the gateway, giving a coin to a beggar, and stepped into the courtyard. In the centre stood a small, simple shrine to Vishnu. Apart from a few monkeys in the tree, the temple was deserted. He sat in the shade beneath the tree to wait. Sequins of sunlight fell around him on the ground, and wavered with the moving leaves. In the branches, monkeys chased one another and nibbled on the fruit. A baby one ventured closer to examine Kim. He smiled at the wizened, child-like face, but made no move to frighten it. The mother, fierce and matted, watched from a distance.

He must have dozed, for when he opened his eyes a child stood directly in front of him. Except that this child had a beard, hair piled on its head in a knot, and a string of rudhrakas around its neck. The dwarf beamed at Kim and he felt himself suffused by the warmth of the smile. The smile felt like a physical touch, as though he had been blessed. The dwarf, standing, was the same height as Kim sitting, so he immediately started to rise.

'No, no, sit. If you stand I shall get a crick in the neck staring up at you. It is a nuisance being so small, but if I were to reveal my other self, you would get the crick.' The dwarf came and peered at Kim. 'Yes, you *are* the one. Sometimes Jatayu brings the wrong person, and that causes endless trouble.'

Kim stared at the dwarf uncertainly, wishing to believe, but wavering. He studied the dwarf from head to toe and found him perfectly formed, with wheat-coloured skin and a small pot-belly. Kim knew his mythology. Vamana was the dwarf reincarnation of Vishnu. And

Trivakrama, the giant reincarnation of the god who with three strides had defined the boundaries of the universe. He wanted to believe, but wavered still, uncertain.

'Didn't you believe Jatayu? I know men are full of deceptions, like those three badmashes you met on the road. But if you can believe in a bird, why not in me?'

'I think I believe.'

'But you need proof. Always man wants proof. Miracles, turning rocks into bread, changing shape, raising the dead, as though this last is much of a miracle. Death is mere illusion. You were the chela of the Lama, were you not? And you believed in him.'

'Yes.'

'He asked me to see you.'

'But he was Buddhist.'

'Buddhist, Hindu, Muslim, Christian. Those are men defining themselves,' the dwarf said crossly. 'I don't define myself. Now, will you listen or do I have to give you a lecture? If men ceased to talk for a minute or two, they would hear more clearly.'

'I am listening,' Kim said meekly.

'The end of your journey is in the garden of smoke, the dream you dream often, I know. It is a dangerous path, but you have a duty to perform which you cannot escape. You will be tested, but you must remember Krishna's advice to Arjuna in the Gita:

> *To action alone hast thou a right*
> *and never at all to its fruits,*
> *Let not the fruits of action be thy motive;*
> *Neither let there be in thee any attachment*
> *to inaction.'*

He then chanted the lines in Sanskrit, and music seemed to hang in the still air.

'I wish to attain moksha. Will this duty eventually lead to that?'

'In time. You must perform your duties as a man to men before you can escape this life. I know it is difficult being a man, but I will guide you from time to time. However, don't call on me day and night. It becomes very tedious.' He rose and walked about, searching the ground. He pounced on something and brought it back. For a moment he held it and then gave it to Kim. It was a river pebble the size of a chicken's egg and as brown. 'I could have materialised this, but that is a magician's trick. Keep this by you. It is my ears, and when you call, I will hear you. But, as I said, not every five minutes, please.'

The pebble was hot, and even as Kim watched, it changed colour. It turned to an old yellow, touched with streaks of red.

When Kim looked up the dwarf was already half-way to the gate. Kim was surprised at the speed at which those short legs carried him. He rose immediately and ran after him. The dwarf reached the gate without looking back and turned east.

Kim reached the lane, expecting to see him just ahead. But he saw only villagers, carts, vendors; no sign of the dwarf. He had vanished. Beyond the walls of the temple were fields of shimmering wheat, the sun bending the backs of men, women and bullocks. Kim turned this way, then that, not believing that the dwarf could disappear so swiftly.

'A dwarf came out of the temple,' Kim asked the beggar at the gate. 'Did you see which way he went?'

'Only you have gone in and out today.'

Kim set his face south. If he was to perform his duty, it must be to serve the Colonel. Within a week, Delhi was visible on the horizon. Between him and the city lay scrub jungle and the ruins of the city of the Lodhi kings. The walls of the eight-hundred-year-old fort ran along the low hill like the broken crown of a monarch.

He spent one night in a village three miles outside Delhi, nestled in a ruined fort. Where kings had once slept, villagers now made their home, knowing nothing of the builders of the great granite walls and ramparts.

But Kim felt at ease here. To travel by night, even so near to this old city, invited dacoits to cut one's throat.

He left the village before sunrise and reached Delhi an hour past dawn. The Lal Qila and the Jama Masjid drew his eye. They dominated the city, towering over the sprawl of low buildings crowded together around them. Delhi lay upon Delhi in layers. There were thirteen Delhis beneath his feet, each one built by a different dynasty, and these two great buildings were relics of the latest one, the Mughals. He threaded his way through narrow streets. Dust had long soaked up the blood of many defeats. Nadir Shah, the Persian, had massacred the inhabitants on the fall of the Mughal empire, and in 1857 this earth had also witnessed the last bloody battle between the British and the sepoys. The sepoys had rallied here, in the Lal Qila, around the ageing Mughal, Bahadur Shah. But his empire was now only a faint memory. The Red Fort had fallen, the sepoys had been executed, and Bahadur Shah exiled to Burma. The last Mughal had died in an alien land, sent away like an errant child.

The British flag drooped in the hard sunlight above the Amar Singh gate. British soldiers stood guard under the great archway. On a previous visit to Delhi, Kim had gone inside. Except for the Diwan-i-am and Shah Jahan's palace, the original interior had been razed by the British after the mutiny. It was a sort of punishment against the people, this destruction of the last Mughal glory. He did not know why they had spared the palace. The fort, a massive pile of red sandstone, a military symbol from another age, still served its original military purpose. It now contained the barracks for British troops and was the army HQ for Delhi district.

Kim moved unerringly through Chandini Chowk to the railway station. The dust of Delhi settled on his shoulders. He passed men squatting in the sunlight with the tools of their trade wrapped in bits of gunny: carpenters, bricklayers, iron workers, carvers. They waited to be hired, patiently, quietly. Each skill had its own lane in the chowk. And what could one not purchase from this ancient market? Anything and everything was to be had, a catalogue of which would fill tomes. The city was full of vitality and fluid movement. Camel caravans came and went, following the old silk routes which neither time nor the changing of empires could erase. They existed not on maps but in the memories of these traders.

Delhi was now only a backwater, but Kim had heard rumours that the sarkar intended to move the capital from Calcutta to Delhi. Lord Curzon had already approved plans for the building of a new Delhi some distance from this old one. Kim was certain that this new city would outshine the glory of the previous empire and last for a thousand years of British rule. It was to be a milestone in the continuity of Delhi. But he also remembered the legend of Delhi – or was it a curse? – every 'new' Delhi marked the end of a dynasty. He wondered whether an Indian curse would work with the Angrezi.

The entrance to the railway station was crowded with rickshaws and tongas. The building was also of red sandstone, with a great clock tower in the centre. Kim pushed his way through the crowds and queued up at the third-class ticket window. The waiting hall was cavernous and cool. High on one wall a blackboard showed the train schedules. The Frontier Mail was due to arrive from 'Pindi on its way to Bombay at eight o'clock.

He bought a modest meal from one of the station vendors, and wandered curiously about the platforms. Blue-shirted coolies with red turbans carried trunks, holdalls, baskets of fruit. Monkeys scavenged the platforms, pi-dogs the tracks. Kim enjoyed the expectancy and chaos of the station and squatted against a wall to wait. The whole country was distilled here, so unlike Simla railway station. Pathans, Sikhs, Jats, British soldiers, Indian jawans, Tamils, Europeans, Gujeratis, all swirled together like dyes in a cauldron. He heard strange tongues and gazed at outlandish costumes, but saw them all as one people. They had an indefinable harmony, a strange composition beneath which ran a familiar chord. If a mirror had been shattered, each fragment was separate, yet it still belonged to the whole.

Suddenly, through the ebb and flow of people, he caught a glimpse of furtive movement. A youth moved, crouching behind a mail trolley to hide beneath the stairs. He wore baggy pi-jamas and a kurta, and his turban was badly tied. It looked too large for his head.

Kim stood up, and a moment later the head poked out to search the platform hastily before ducking back down. Kim too now gazed over the platform, looking for anyone else doing the same. The youth's furtiveness had not been criminal. Kim sensed the fear, he'd seen it in the jungle as a sambar picked its way through the undergrowth, all eyes, ears and nose. Kim saw no searchers in the cheerful chaos.

A few minutes after eight o'clock a ripple ran over the platform and the Frontier Mail, a drab red train pulled by a gleaming black engine, came round the curve. The great engine bathed people in steam as it passed and exhaustedly came to a halt, belching and wheezing. Coolies leapt into the carriages, soliciting the travellers, and before anyone could even disembark the waiting passengers were pushing themselves in. Kim was convinced that Indians were the most impatient travellers in the world. They seemed to think the train would fly away without them. Many doors were jammed with this impatience except, of course, for the first class, which was reserved for Europeans. They were orderly in their coming and going, aloof from the frenzy.

Kim strolled by the stairwell and peeped in. There was no sign of the youth now. In the distraction he had probably slipped into a carriage. Kim pushed his way into a third-class compartment and found a window seat. A fat Marwari and his thin writer squeezed in beside him. Their girths reflected their positions.

The Marwari opened *The Statesman*, spreading right

across Kim's face. It was a sign of importance to read in English, and the Marwari wanted his fellow-passengers to know that he was no ordinary man.

'Disgraceful,' he said in English, and then continued in Hindustani, 'the British murdered Subash Ray in Simla. A fine man, a gentleman. Very learned and an excellent cricketer. They have imprisoned his nephew, Anil Ray. A terrorist, they say.' In English he added, 'Nonsense.'

The writer, crushed against his employer, crushed too with worry, murmured assent. He would have agreed if the Marwari had said the opposite. His sole intent was to echo his employer. The Marwari looked at Kim for agreement as well.

'Sahib, they could have been. The Bengalis are a very excitable people.'

'Some, but not Subash. I saw him playing once in Calcutta. An excellent batsman. Beautiful strokes. A man like that would not turn to violence.'

'Then the British have made a terrible mistake.'

Kim looked closely at the Marwari. His cheeks wore the sheen of rich food and shone with a fresh shave. His moustache was oiled and curled. He smelled of talcum powder.

'Yes, they have gone too far. This DI Goode will no doubt be promoted. He should be tried for murder, but because he's British he will get away scot-free. We should demand an enquiry.'

'I believe you should, sahib. You must call for one immediately, start a petition.'

'I was speaking figuratively. I'm a businessman and cannot be involved in politics. If they had passed the Ilbert Bill, why, this Goode would have been tried by one of us.'

The Ilbert Bill had been an attempt by a past Viceroy, Lord Ripon, to allow Indian judges to try Europeans. The bill had caused such an uproar in the European community that it had been abandoned. Europeans could still only be tried by Europeans, whatever the offence.

The train's whistle interrupted the discourse. Kim looked out and saw the youth dart through the crowd as the train began to move. Far behind he saw his pursuers. The two in front looked like chaprassis, dressed in grubby clothing and brandishing lathis. The third man moved sedately, confident that his men would catch the youth. He seemed to be their employer, for he was dressed in an elegant cream suit and carried a malacca cane.

The train gathered speed and the youth ran faster, stumbling with panic. Kim had never before seen such fear in so young a face. Behind, the two men were gaining on him. Kim pushed his way quickly to the open carriage door.

'Hai ladkha, give me your hand. Quickly.'

The youth stretched out his hand and Kim caught hold of it grimly, swung the youth off his feet and into the carriage. He wrenched himself free of Kim's grip, scurried into the latrine, and locked himself in. Kim looked back at the receding platform and saw the three men, together now, staring intently at him. He was glad of the distance, for they couldn't distinguish his features.

5

'I PRAY to you to help me, Colonel sahib.'

The man's face was damp with tears and sweat. His palms were pressed together, trembling with intensity. If this force of strength alone could bring salvation, he deserved it. He perched on the edge of the chair, suspended between sitting and kneeling, willing to sink to the floor and place his forehead on the Colonel's foot. Humility gave his face a strange complexion; it drained his flesh and left it the colour of dried river mud. It had reshaped his frame too, bowed broad shoulders and imprinted a curve on his neck. His silken clothes appeared grubby. The gold thread in his turban looked dull as brass and the stiff, starched cloth had wilted.

'I cannot,' the Colonel said.

He had seen such submissiveness before, it disgusted him. What if a thousand years of civilisation once lay on the man? It had been shed as swiftly as a snake shed its skin, and had been as deep as that skin. His own people would have remained unyielding, not grovelling for clemency. Men like himself accepted karma stoically, they did not twist and thrash and weep.

'If you use your influence . . .'

'I will not interfere with the judiciary of this country,' the Colonel said. 'Are you offering me baksheesh?'

'No, no, Colonel sahib. I would not offer such an insult. But, if you should speak to the judge, ask him to be lenient. He is only a boy and innocent of the charges.'

'For God's sake, man, how on earth can he be innocent? Your son stabbed Deputy Inspector Goode.'

'In blindness, Colonel sahib. In rage. He lost his head. His uncle, my brother, had just been mur . . . killed in front of his very eyes. You must understand how this upset him.' He paused, eyes brimming with tears. 'He went to Eton and Oxford. He would not have done such a thing unless he was provoked.'

'Englishmen would not do such things, whatever the provocation.'

'He has also been accused of tampering with the railway line. I assure you, Colonel sahib, my Anil would not behave as a miscreant.'

'That will all come out in court.' The Colonel pulled out his gold hunter and stood up. 'I have an appointment.'

The man remained seated, as if cast adrift in a boat. He could not rise, and the eyes in his shrunken face looked around, searching for land. His thoughts were revealed to the Colonel: What else can I do? What else can I say? What else can I pray? I will do anything to save Anil. I cannot leave without further effort.

'Colonel sahib . . .'

The Colonel waited, knowing that the man was drained. Mr Ray scrabbled through the dust of mourning, only to find nothing. The man rose wearily, palms still together, and turned away to the door. He paused half-way.

'He is a brilliant lawyer.' It was a thought spoken to himself, all that was now left of the promise of a son in whom he'd invested affection and wealth. The peon opened the door and ushered Mr Ray out.

The file on Anil Ray contained only a single sheet. It stated his birthplace, family background – wealthy landlords – education and reason for arrest. It was a spare sketch of a life now in ruins.

The Colonel was pleased. He knew Anil Ray was innocent of the rail sabotage, but his attack on Goode was most convenient. It gave him proof that the government and the police needed more powers. The new Viceroy would be persuaded easily.

Kim's telegram lay on his desk. He hoped Kim

wouldn't interfere further in this matter. A judge would find Ray guilty of the stabbing. Ray had proved to the Colonel the waste of educating a native. The Indian was generally a good and kind man, though weak and incapable of his own betterment. Eton and Oxford! Discipline had not been instilled into Anil; he had sipped at it only, the veneer worn as lightly as a suit from Savile Row. Beneath remained the loin-cloth. Thank God he hadn't controlled the murderous impulse.

Beside Kim's telegram lay another, also in code. It irritated him. An agent moving without an order or a reason given. It was to Cottonseed: BOMBAY GOING STOP DADDAJI STOP. It was as if, on the Prince of Wales's visit, the whole of India was seeping towards that city. Daddaji had no right to proceed to Bombay. He had been placed in Delhi for a purpose, and now the Colonel could not countermand the move. Nor could he meet or acknowledge the man if he saw him in Bombay. Daddaji was special, and no suspicion that he was the Colonel's agent could fall on him.

The Colonel's office in Calcutta was a handsome room, with high ceilings and huge windows looking out on the city. It was cooled by a punkah and by a breeze off the Hoogli river. One window framed a glimpse of the Hoogli to the east, another the straight avenue leading to Government House. The Calcutta air was not as clear as Simla's, instead it was murky with heat, foetid with too much life. It broiled too with intrigue and seismic shifts of power.

The Colonel summoned his carriage; the day was to be interrupted by a farewell luncheon for Lord Curzon. He had accepted only because Elizabeth was one of the hostesses of The Calcutta Ladies Association. He normally took a light tiffin in the office or at home. Most men lunched at the Gymkhana Club or the United Services. The Colonel hated club life; it bred boredom, gossip, adultery. He saw the same faces, heard the same talk, and saw men lust after the same women. The sameness of life, the consuming of their own entrails

48

impelled the Colonel to avoid contact with them as much as possible. By keeping himself aloof, he had their respect, if not their liking. He was different from them. India was his life, not a brief posting or a commercial venture. He loved this country, its people, the heat and the dusty air. It was a paternal love; he kept faith with a giant child, protecting it from its own self-destructive impulses. If he had been told that he was in fact an enemy of the land, an occupier, he would have stared in disbelief.

He strolled through the Writers' Building. It was a vast brick hill, honeycombed with offices, corridors, titles. It smelt of imprisoned men, ink, glue and dusty paper. Peons leapt from stools to salaam, clerks pressed against the wall to give him passage. All India was ruled from here, its blood and brains were the papers that moved sluggishly down corridors, held together with familiar red tape. The system of administration had not changed since the Mughals. The Viceroy was the new Mughal and he governed through four departments: the army, justice, commerce and agriculture. These offices were duplicated all the way down from the nine provinces to the smallest district. India never changed.

The Viceroy's residence was at the end of the maidan. It was a splendid copy of Kedleston Hall, Derbyshire, completed in 1802. Six acres of beautifully tended gardens surrounded the mansion. A bearer offered the Colonel a cool drink, but the Colonel waved it away and moved through the ornate reception room, looking for Elizabeth. There must have been a couple of hundred people there, most of whom he knew. He smiled at them in turn, but kept on moving. He had to stop for Lady Shearer, the wife of the Lieutenant-Governor of Bengal and a woman aware of her importance as the second lady in the city. Her husband sat with Lord and Lady Curzon, and they acknowledged his presence, Lord Curzon somewhat curtly. A shamyana had been set up on the lawn, with a buffet laid out, mostly cold meats and salads.

A smaller table was set with vegetarian Indian food for the few Indian ladies present, who clung together, looking like a knot of brilliant silks. They glittered with gold, wearing diamond nose-rings, necklaces, bangles and ear-rings. The Colonel estimated that even one woman's display probably surpassed his year's salary. They were the wives of landowners, princes, lawyers.

He felt sorry for them. Like chital, they appeared ready to bolt. One or two European ladies, including Lady Shearer, would try to engage them in conversation, but would then drift away. He was about to turn when he caught one woman's eye. She allowed a small smile to move over her face, so subtle that he wondered if he had imagined it. She wore a gold-bordered blue silk sari and choli.

'Father!' Elizabeth kissed him. 'Are you enjoying yourself, dear?'

'Haven't had time to yet. Just popped in to show my face, really.'

The Colonel was seldom at ease in the company of women. He conducted himself stiffly, mechanically formal. He had little small-talk and the art of flirtation was unknown to him. With Elizabeth, whose bloom into womanhood still caught him by surprise, he made a real effort to relax, but each time he looked at her he found himself in the presence of this new, daunting woman. Part of him wished she would become again the darling child he had sent away. Nevertheless, he strolled round with her, murmuring to her friends, and when finally Elizabeth left him to attend to the other guests, he found himself alone. He glanced at his watch. Duty done, he could now slip away.

He hesitated a moment too long. A woman thrust a plate and napkin at him. The Colonel helped himself daintily and retreated to a corner table. The Indian ladies sat at the next one, silently picking at the food. Knives and forks were held awkwardly; very little food made the perilous journey to their mouths. They giggled and whispered to each other. He saw that secret smile again, veiled by shadow. It was not sly nor shy, but boldly done.

'Sitting alone, Father?' Elizabeth picked up his plate and moved to the next table.

'Begum sahib,' she addressed an elderly, grey-haired lady with a beak of a nose and button-bright brown eyes, 'this is my father. I hope you won't mind if he joins you?'

'Not at all,' the Begum said. 'Won't you, too?' she added diplomatically, and Elizabeth wedged herself next to her.

Silence fell, but Elizabeth filled it readily enough. She spoke of the weather, the departing Curzons, the food. The women listened with politely strained, frozen smiles. The Colonel glanced around. The blue-saried woman's smile was now pleasant, quite natural and open.

'Miss Creighton,' she said, 'you really are trying a little too hard to entertain us.' She spoke English with a poetic lilt. 'The weather never changes in Calcutta, whereas in England it is never the same. Which part of England are you from, Colonel?'

'My great-grandfather came from Bristol. I was born in India . . .'

'. . . And you serve her faithfully. I never managed to visit Bristol. It seemed so far from London. You know, there is a gulf of difference between you people here and the English in their homeland.'

'In what way?' the Colonel asked, uneasy at her tone. He was not used to talking to Indian women as equals. This was a bold girl.

'I would say the English here are so snobbish, quite unfriendly towards us. The English in England are kind and friendly people. They show a greater curiosity about us than you do sitting here.'

'I believe I know as much about India as you do.'

'Then can you tell me if I am married or not?' Her smile was open, yet he sensed a sly humour. The Colonel looked at the other ladies. They said nothing, speechless with embarrassment.

'I believe you are.' She had the markings: the tilak, the thali (it hung between her breasts, though he could not be certain of the symbolic pendant), but he could not peep down at her feet for toe-rings.

'Wrong,' she said. 'See!'

'That was an unfair question.'

'Oh, I know that. But nothing in India is ever fair, is it?'

The Colonel looked down at his watch again. 'Duty calls. I must return to the office. Elizabeth, ladies,' he rose, bowing curtly.

The woman laughed. 'The British concept of duty. Is it the same as ours, Colonel?'

'In any language, it remains the same. Mine to my office, yours to . . .'

'. . . Being a dutiful wife, though duties do change over time.' She held out her hand and, in some surprise at her boldness, he took it. It was soft, subtle, like a fluttering bird. He noted the saffron colour on her palm, turning her skin even more golden. 'I am having a dinner party tomorrow, Colonel. I hope you and your daughter might attend?'

Automatically, the Colonel made to refuse. Instead, he said, 'It will be a pleasure, Miss . . .'

'Mrs Basu. You will be able to resolve the mystery tomorrow, Colonel. India is full of romantic enigmas, isn't it? I will tell Miss Creighton how to get to our place.'

'She was a strange woman,' Elizabeth said.

'Who?' asked the Colonel.

They sat together on the verandah, gazing out at the darkened garden. Behind them the bungalow glowed erratically as the lights pulsed to an uneven breath. The air was moist and warm on their skins and filled with the hum of crickets and cicadas and the chic-chic of lizards on the walls. An occasional bat wove fleeting patterns between the stars. The canna bed rustled with sly movement, setting Elizabeth's teeth on edge. The lawn and bungalow were ringed with saw-toothed tin to keep out snakes, yet still they wound their way into her imagination and involuntarily she drew her legs up under her.

'That Mrs Basu who invited us for dinner. I didn't like her much. She didn't seem to know her place. Why did you say we'd go? Usually you refuse.'

'Just to be friendly,' the Colonel replied, knowing it to be untrue. He sipped his whisky and soda, uncertain of the real reason. She had needled him with that remark about the difference between the English in England, and here. He should have responded by saying: 'We rule, they do not. And that makes us different, but not disparate.' Yet . . . he wanted to be accepted by Mrs Basu.

'You didn't need to be. I couldn't refuse after that.' Elizabeth sounded petulant. 'We had to invite them to the luncheon, but that doesn't mean we need to go to one of their dinners.'

'It might be interesting.'

'Boring, rather. I just can't talk to them. They smile and simper. We have nothing in common.'

'India.'

'No. Theirs is a different India. We don't belong. We are not welcome, either.'

'We do belong,' the Colonel said firmly.

'To each other, in a kind of prison. We are not invisible here. Even in Calcutta, they stare at us in astonishment. And in the countryside they stare in . . . I don't know what. That horrid silence of the villager. It broods like those ghastly gods looking down at us from their temples.' She stopped for reassurance. The crickets too had waited and now their chorus grew louder. 'What do they think? I don't know what they think.'

'Of what?'

'Anything. Us.'

He noted the despair in her voice. It teetered on the edge of hysteria, and he took her hand. At night, as a child, when the darkness turned ominous and she would cry, he would cradle and comfort her. Richard showed no such fears; in Elizabeth they ran deep.

'She was rather beautiful,' Elizabeth said abruptly.

'Was she?' He remembered the smile and the curve of her breasts, hidden in the soft folds of her silk sari. He pushed back the memory of warmth and softness.

'You never liked England, did you, Father?'

'Not much. I always felt the cold, and there was too much green. I missed India.'

'I loved that cold. It made me so . . . brisk, I suppose. It's this heat I can't stand . . .'

'As a child, you loved it.'

'Tastes change, Father. I'm no longer that child.'

He had long stifled all memory of England. Only the chill remained, buried in his bones. He had made the immense journey as a boy, in the company of other children. They were sent to different schools, spartan and harsh. And in the summer he spent his days alone in a house in Bath with cousins who did not like him or understand him. He had felt a stranger there. Yes, imprisoned by the memories of an Indian childhood, suffocated by that dainty landscape and incapable of forgetting the mountains, plains, jungles; interminable and vast. He longed for sights of people, things, that he could not explain to the others. They would not understand the fantastic kaleidoscope of India because it did not exist in England. He had then gone to Sandhurst and, with his knowledge of India, joined a regiment being posted there. The moment he landed, he had felt himself immersed.

'Dinner, sahib,' the bearer interrupted his thoughts.

They went in to join Mrs Parkhurst at the table. She was always there first. 'Aunt' Emma, who wasn't a real aunt but a distant relation of the Colonel's, had not changed a bit over the years that Elizabeth had been away. She was a tall, thin, straight-backed woman with bright blue eyes and a discreet manner. She had no family of her own either in India or England, and Elizabeth suspected her father paid her a small stipend to run the household. It was hard to believe Aunt Emma had once been married but she did collect a small army pension. All her money was spent on bridge at the club. Elizabeth had heard she was a reckless card-player.

Her menus, however, were still unimaginative: tomato soup, boiled ham, boiled potatoes, boiled carrots, cabbage and tapioca pudding. Elizabeth had hated the pudding as a child. Not everything had changed.

Mrs Basu's home, on Mir Jaffar Lane, was a good mile and a half from the European quarter. The broad avenues narrowed and lost their straightness, houses and people crowded in. The very air became strangely darker, coloured by the smoke of cooking fires, certainly, and yet it was more than that. Elizabeth held her father's arm and the Colonel wished now he had refused. He felt a foreboding – not fear, nothing frightened him in India; it was home and he could walk through the darkest bazaar with confidence.

The carriage halted at a heavy wooden door, intricately carved and set in a high blank wall. The syce knocked and the door swung open immediately as if people within watched for them. Bearers flanked their passage as they passed under an archway and entered a beautiful garden. Built in the Indian style, the house surrounded the garden and trellised windows looked down on rose and canna beds, bougainvillea, and an immaculate lawn. They followed a bearer across to an exquisite room, all of marble, its floor covered with Kashmiri carpets. An elaborately carved wooden swing hung from the ceiling, white divans were the only furniture, apart from two silver tables and an ancient ivory chest. They were left there.

Elizabeth gazed around. On the walls she saw paintings, frescoes painted directly onto the walls; scenes of princes hunting, of battles between Indians and British soldiers, of a beautiful, sad woman. In the soft light they pulsed with brilliant colours. Elizabeth settled on the swing; the Colonel lowered himself to a divan. A bearer returned with a gold and crystal ewer of water and a whisky bottle. He placed these beside the Colonel and waited as the Colonel mixed his drink.

'There don't seem to be any other guests,' whispered Elizabeth.

'I think you're right. She made it up.'

He drank. It was an expensive malt whisky. Three men approached across the garden. They were of descending ages, but alike in their dress: silk kurtas and pi-jamas. The father was slim and stood very straight, with a thin, aristocratic face. A pair of gold wire spectacles perched on his nose, making him look immensely learned. He bowed formally to the Colonel.

'Colonel sahib, I am Sudhir Jyoti,' he said in English. 'It is a great honour for us to have you enter this humble house.'

'The honour is all mine. I admit that I expected a dinner party. Mrs Basu . . .'

'My daughter. But we certainly do have a dinner party, one especially for you and Miss Creighton. These are my sons, Satyajit and Chandra.'

Shyly the two salaamed. Neither acknowledged Elizabeth's presence and she felt herself to be swinging in an empty room and hearing disembodied voices.

'Will your daughter be joining us?' Elizabeth asked, her voice now too loud against the soft tones of the men, and they looked startled.

Mr Jyoti turned and whispered to the youngest boy, who then ran across the garden to another room. They waited in silence, the Colonel seated a little awkwardly, the two men standing.

'My son spent a few years in your country, Colonel sahib. He was very impressed with it.'

'Where were you?'

'Cambridge,' the son replied. 'I read politics and philosophy. I wish now that I had learned to play cricket before going up. I missed that side of the social life.'

'It's a fine game,' the Colonel said. He saw the evening

stretching ahead, filled with such small-talk, littered with politeness and no exchange. He sensed a movement, and then Mrs Basu strolled unhurriedly across the garden. She smiled in the same way, soft as a breeze trembling on water.

'I'm so delighted that you and Miss Creighton could come.' She joined Elizabeth on the swing and finally the men sat down on the divans. 'My father was very shocked that I was so bold as to invite you for dinner. It is not the done thing, you know. He nearly locked me up in my room!'

'It is certainly not usually done. Why did you?'

'We must change, Colonel. Our ideas are old, yours are new. I find the new exciting.'

'The old's good enough for me,' her father grumbled, but he spoke with affection, in admiration of the daughter who had been brave enough to ask a European to eat with them.

Though Mrs Basu spent the evening modestly talking to Elizabeth, the Colonel could sense her interest in him. Whenever he glanced at her face, the soft smile returned, and he had an uneasy feeling that she was flirting with him. Her father was a charming man, a tea merchant who owned his own estates. He had read Dickens and Walter Scott and spoke with enthusiasm of English writers. He also extolled the greatness of one of their own, Rabindranath Tagore. The Colonel regretted he had not read the man's work, though he had heard of him. It seemed, however, that the topics had been chosen beforehand, like a menu, and were to be followed strictly. The Colonel knew it was all an attempt to make him feel at ease. The son talked of England as if it were his home, not the Colonel's.

At last after four drinks they had their meal. The round marble dining-table was set out in the garden. The light from the lanterns glittered on silver plates and tumblers, and on the two sets of metal spoons and forks. The bearers served biryani, chicken korma, fish curry, vegetables, parathas. There was enough food for an army.

'My wife is too shy to join us,' Mr Jyoti said suddenly, half-way through the meal.

'She will never change,' Mrs Basu said. Then she turned to the Colonel. 'You have yet to solve the mystery of my marital status. Married or not?'

'Are you perhaps a widow?'

'I should be wearing white then, Colonel, and my hair would have been shorn. I am married, but separated. My husband prefers his estates and his cronies to my company.'

'Sushila, you go too far,' her father said.

'Well, he does. I came back to my family and travelled abroad with my father. Where is your wife, Colonel?'

'My mother died when I was a baby,' Elizabeth answered abruptly, hoping to stifle this Indian curiosity about one's personal life.

'Oh, how sad.' The chorus echoed around the table.

'How did she die?' asked Mrs Basu.

'Of cholera.'

'And where did this tragic incident occur?'

'Here in India.'

'Of course,' Mrs Basu persisted. 'Everyone dies in India. Don't we all see those sweet little cemeteries littered around our country? Babes and women. What a price for the empire! But where?'

'In the south,' the Colonel said, rising. He liked this curiosity even less. 'Elizabeth?'

Dinner was over. They all rose and walked to the gate in silence. The lane was deserted and they had to nudge the syce awake. The moon was a slender curve of lemon and the sky so clear that every star was visible. Mr Jyoti opened the carriage door and helped Elizabeth in. His sons stood at a respectful distance.

Mrs Basu had been studying the sky. She recited softly in Urdu:

> *'The old Enchanter, in his patchwork cloak,*
> *Sits weaving spells to bind us to his throne,*
> *While, seeing nothing in the turquoise vault,*

> *We dwell in fear, uncertain and alone –*
> *Forgetting that one night he made the moon*
> *(By magic from a fish with silver scales),*
> *Which in his blue glass bottle, flecked with stars,*
> *Unerring on her course serenely sails;*
> *He closed the stopper with a thousand seals*
> *Of wax the candle of the moon supplied . . .'*

She stopped and smiled at the Colonel: 'I'm sure you can finish the poem, Colonel sahib.' He heard the challenge in her voice.

The Colonel recited:

> *'Since when no mortal has evaded Fate,*
> *However long, however hard, he tried.'*

The silence was soft and enchanting, and the Colonel had never felt a greater longing than at that moment to belong to the land and the magical dome of the sky. He smelt the sweetness of Queen o' the Night nearby, and the settling dust.

'That's very good, Colonel sahib.'

'I didn't realise you understood Urdu.'

'That shouldn't be a surprise,' she laughed, 'even for a Bengali. But that I should know you do.' She turned from him, then, 'Goodbye, Miss Creighton, and thank you for coming.' With that formality, she stepped back into the shadow of the gateway. The Colonel caught a last glimpse of her gold sari and heard her lilting chuckle.

He shook hands with the three men and joined Elizabeth in the carriage. She yawned and leant against him.

'What was she saying?'

'It's an Urdu poem, by Nishani, court poet to the Emperor Akbar. It was written originally in Persian.'

'What is it about?'

'Fate,' the Colonel replied.

All the way home, the Colonel puzzled how Mrs Basu knew that he translated Urdu poetry as a hobby. It gave him a sense of tranquillity and accomplishment, making him feel a part of this country, but also imparted a sense of infinite sadness. The poems spoke of lost love and death, as though they were inseparable.

The chowkidar was still alert and opened the gate. He would fall asleep the instant the Colonel did. He was supposed to be a Gurkha, but was only a Nepali posing as one for employment. The two Labradors (descendants of those in the old photograph) barked and trotted behind the carriage. The bearers, asleep on the verandah, came awake slowly when they heard the dogs. They turned up the lights and awaited orders. The Colonel dismissed the carriage and followed Elizabeth indoors.

'Nightcap?'

'No, thank you, Father.' Elizabeth's lips brushed his cheek. 'Good night.'

'By the way, what was Mrs Basu talking to you about?'

'England,' Elizabeth said. 'Speaking as if it was her home, and how it felt to stroll up Piccadilly.'

'We were invited for a reason.'

'What?'

'I don't know. I'll find out eventually. A favour, probably.'

The Colonel sat alone with his brandy. All the furniture in the room, the sideboards, sofas and tables, was equally dark and sombre. It was made of oak, lovingly polished, and precious, for they had been shipped all the way from England. On the walls were landscapes of the Cornish coast, with blustery grey skies and the bite of winter in the pink cheeks of fishermen. Pride of place was given to a few watercolours of Englishmen and women on picnics and at the races, painted by Elizabeth. They were well executed, but the poses were stiff as photographs.

Against a wall stood an oak bookcase, filled with a set of encyclopaedias, and other books of a factual nature on India. There were studies of customs, birds, beasts, the flora of the land, most published by A. H. Wheeler. In a rosewood cabinet opposite was a small collection of

Dresden china, old pistols and family photographs. The room itself was large with a very high ceiling that dwarfed the furniture.

We reflect what is within us, the Colonel thought. The reflection is of the interior world we long to inhabit, by which I am ruled. Very little of our exterior, India, intrudes here. We shut it out, as does every European. And by keeping them separate, we pass from one soil to another with just a few steps. This stone floor, these pieces and paintings, are a bit of home. Then we can imagine the soft rains and the gentle sun. An Indian's home is empty, except for those who have Europeanised themselves and imitated us, and reflects the emptiness of India. They put little value on possessions, only the gold jewellery they wear. Even in the design of their homes, I can see so many differences. We sit square in a garden looking outwards; they look inwards. For centuries they have looked within, and that is why they are weak and intellectually bankrupt.

Mary ayah had waited up for Elizabeth, though the woman no longer needed her as much as the child had. Her love had not faded over the absent years, and she was happy to serve her 'daughter' again. While Elizabeth was in the bathroom, Mary ayah turned down the bed-cover. By the bedside was a photograph of Elizabeth and Richard with their mother. Elizabeth was only a tiny bundle. She was held snuggled in her mother's arms, draped in a lace christening gown. Richard, not much bigger, sat on a high stool. Mary ayah always tried to avoid looking at that photograph; it brought tears to her eyes. Mrs Creighton was tall and pretty, an older Elizabeth, with her rich hair piled high, and her dress was delicately embroidered. She stared boldly out of the photograph, not at the camera but at something in the distance. Something in her face looked wistful and longing.

Elizabeth, now changed and wearing a severe nightdress, climbed into bed. Mary ayah tucked her in and withdrew to the dressing-room where she slept.

By the bedside was a library novel. Elizabeth returned to the story.

> *The dashing young captain, whom Marion had seen in the bazaar the previous evening, now rode up beside her. The caravan had come to a halt, and the natives looked around them hopelessly. They were unable to organise themselves since the attack by dacoits, and now looked to the captain to take charge of them. The afternoon sun lit up a handsome, devil-may-care face, and when he reined in and swept off his helmet, Marion saw that he had burnished blond hair and sparkling blue eyes.*
>
> *'Ma'am, your humble servant, Captain Johnson of the Khyber Rifles, at your service.'*
>
> *Marion could not help but blush at his bold stare.*
>
> *'Captain Johnson,' she managed to whisper. 'Thank God you came to our rescue. I was going to join my father in 'Pindi when the caravan was attacked and the officer was killed. The natives seem incapable of going on.'*
>
> *Captain Johnson had acted so swiftly; she could not but help admiring his strength and courage. He whipped the natives back into the caravan and shouted his orders out in a loud clear voice . . .*

Elizabeth marked the page and slid deeper into bed. She looked around at the shadows. She was glad they no longer moved, leaping and cavorting to the flicker of the old oil lamps. At times she felt she was afloat in a tiny craft on a dark, endless sea. The library novels regaled her with adventures of dashing, romantic Englishmen, and even if that world didn't truly exist, she knew it to be the one she wanted to believe in. They reassured her of her place in the scheme of things, and of her feelings for England and India. Before shutting her eyes, she fondly kissed the photograph of her mother, as she had every night of her life.

6

KIM WAITED for an hour for the youth to emerge from
the latrine. He passed the time sitting on the steps of
the open carriage door, watching the land gently drift by
the train, and gossiping with his immediate neighbours.
There was a small, slim Tamil Brahmin, returning to his
home in Madurai after years of service with the sarkar
in Simla; a group of Rajput women, brightly plumaged
in their brilliant reds and blues, making a pilgrimage to
Mathura; a Jat sepoy on his way to join his regiment in
Agra. It was only when the Marwari pounded on the
latrine door demanding entry that the youth poked his
head out and emerged cautiously to face the curious
stares of his fellow travellers. They had all been witness
to the rescue, and now wanted to know what wrong he
had done to be thus pursued.

The youth's nose wrinkled in thought, and now that
the fear had left his face, Kim noted that he had large,
amber eyes. Because of the delicacy of his features it
wasn't possible to judge his age, but the swift calculation
in his gaze made him seem older.

'Don't you even have the gratitude to thank your
saviour?' one Rajput woman said indignantly before the
youth could speak.

'If you had waited a moment longer, you would have
heard my thanks. Why are people always so impatient?'
The boy turned to Kim. 'Sahib, if your feet were not
hanging outside I would place my head on them to
show my gratitude for saving me from those terrible
miscreants.'

'No doubt you had stolen something from them,' Kim said dryly.

'A thief? Me? Is that all you can think of? Am I carrying a wallet or a sack of gold? See, I am empty-handed. If you believe me to be a thief, you may hand me over to the police, or beat me.'

'Before we do that,' the Tamil Brahmin said, 'and before you bore us to death, tell us: why were you being chased?'

Instead of addressing the others, the youth spoke only to Kim. 'You are the only one who deserves an explanation, sahib. I am not a thief. My father died but two days ago, leaving me the sole possessor of his estates. We grew tea, indigo, cotton, wheat . . .'

'All in one place?' Kim asked.

'Of course not. They were scattered all over India. But his wicked brother, who has always hated me and wanted to kill me to gain the inheritance, immediately set about trying to assassinate me. I had to flee for my life. I was most fortunate that my uncle's wife was my lover and she aided me in my escape.' He sat back breathless and awaited Kim's judgement.

'Why did you not go to the police?' the Jat sepoy enquired.

'Just because you wear a uniform, you think all men in uniform are honest. The local police are in my uncle's pay, and even now they may be searching for me.' He turned back to Kim and shaded his face and winked. 'You believe me, sahib?'

'It is possible,' Kim said, amused by the bald lie. He doubted the truth of the whole story, but was now convinced that the youth was innocent of theft.

'Good. Because of your kindness, I will sit with you.'

The boy stepped over the others squatting in the corridor and slid down to sit beside Kim. The travellers turned their interest to other matters and the boy, having escaped their inquisitiveness, now fell silent. Though there was barely enough space for two, he managed to make no contact with Kim, and instead sat pressed against the door. One hand tightly gripped the handle, and Kim noted the exquisite shape of his hands.

'Is it possible,' Kim whispered, 'that you were being pursued by a lover? Many men like boys and you are indeed a pretty one.'

'You have a most evil mind.'

'I have seen many kinds of evil in my life. I only want you to understand that I do not condemn such strange things.'

'I read that the Mughal emperor Babur loved a boy.' The youth shuddered dramatically. 'It seems a vile practice for kings. As a prince . . .'

'Oh, so you're a prince now?'

'I must be modest. A minor one. Our kingdom is north of Lucknow. I didn't wish it to be known to the others. Who knows? One of them might betray me.'

'To whom?'

Kim received a suspicious stare and the grip on the handle tightened. Beneath the gaiety, Kim noted, the fear remained just out of sight.

'Who are you?' the youth asked.

'I am Kim.'

'That's a strange name. You look Kashmiri, because you are so fair.'

'I'm from Lahore,' he said, and made no effort to explain further. 'What is your name?'

The youth's nose twitched, the signal for his imaginative mind to spin another invention. 'Prithivi. I live in Delhi.'

'Where in Delhi?'

'Why do you want to know?'

'I am familiar with Delhi, so I may know your princely family.'

'I never said they came from Delhi. I said I lived there.'

'You are the most suspicious person I've ever met. I have a good mind to throw you off the train.'

'Kim sahib, please be kind. I am all alone in the world, and if I lie, it is for my own protection. I have committed no crime.'

'Then why can't you speak the truth?'

'Because . . .'

Kim felt a hard nudge against his behind. He looked up to see the peaked hat of the ticket collector, with his punch machine and clipboard. His white uniform was stiff with starch and faintly blue from the dhobi's cheap soap. The man was as fair as a European, with hard blue eyes, but his official position revealed his pedigree. He was Eurasian, as were nearly all the railway staff. The railways were their special preserve, a vital machine which the British entrusted only to those who were totally loyal. The Eurasian was the bridge between the ruler and the ruled. Both their bloods ran in his veins but, in the manner of those who are below the seat of actual power, he preferred to believe himself akin to the ruler, and not to the ruled.

The man's shoe deliberately nudged again.

'Ticket, munktha.' He spoke bad Hindi.

Kim stood up. 'Sahib, if you had asked me first, I would have given the ticket. Do not let your foot touch my body again.'

He was a full head taller than the ticket collector, who was a sturdy man in his twenties whose face was florid and now suffused with bureaucratic superiority. The collector's name was engraved on a small brass badge: M. S. Richardson.

'I will do as I bloody well please,' he said in English, not caring if Kim or the rest of the carriage understood. 'And I will kick you bloody well off if you don't have a ticket.' But even so he took a step backwards, bumping into his native assistant; he swore at him in English.

Kim ignored the remark and took out his ticket and money. 'This is to buy my companion a ticket to Nagpur. He did not have time to make the purchase.'

The collector snapped his punch at the ticket and wrote out another.

'Name . . . nahm?' he asked.

'Pritiviraj Chand,' Kim replied, and the name was entered on the ticket and handed to Kim.

'But I want to go to Bombay,' the boy whispered.

'He will be asked if he saw you. And he will truthfully reply that you are going to Nagpur.'

'Why are they always so rude?'

'Because they do not know who they are. They are neither Angrezis nor one of us. They are the buffer between the two.'

Once, the Eurasian was as respected as the Englishman and the Indian. There were many, in that long-ago time when Englishmen who made their name and fortune in India took Indian wives and mistresses. General Skinner, whose lancers were considered the finest soldiers, was known as Sikander-sahib (for Alexander the Great was still remembered). But the Eurasian multiplied too swiftly and the English turned against him. With the coldness of supreme rulers, they pushed him down from grace. And then, when English ladies began to arrive in numbers in search of husbands, his fate was sealed. The memsahib brought middle-class social customs with her and forbade any sexual liaisons between an Englishman and an Indian woman. As for the Eurasians, trapped now by their past, they were venomously called chi-chi or blackie-white. Their loyalty was never questioned, only their blood. The Eurasians found themselves trapped between two races, for the Indian had his own derogatory term: kutcha-butcha, half-baked bread.

'I'm hungry,' Prithivi announced.

'Ahre. Not only have I saved your worthless life and bought your train ticket, but I am expected to feed you as well.'

'I have no money of my own, but when we reach Bombay, I will tell my aunt to repay you in silver rupees. Consider all your expenses a loan only.'

'I have heard more fluent liars than you. But I will feed you a little. When you tell me the truth you will get a full meal.'

He purchased a couple of samosas and an orange from a vendor. Prithivi wolfed down the food and licked his fingers clean. The slow, majestic passage of the train through the noon heat silenced the chatter of the carriage, and Kim returned to his rightful seat. He pushed and heaved enough space between the window and the Marwari for them both. Prithivi promptly fell asleep and Kim began to doze, but not for long. Prithivi stirred and cried out in fright, startling Kim and the other travellers, who protested sleepily at this disturbance. Kim nudged Prithivi, but to no avail. He nudged again and his hand accidentally touched the firm, rounded shape of a breast beneath the loose kurta. 'Prithivi' struck his hand away without awakening, turned 'his' back but now slept quietly.

Aha, thought Kim. I admit I was taken in at first by this youth's tale, but I always thought him too pretty to be a boy. Now that I know this 'Prithivi' is a woman, I can see that the prettiness is really beauty.

It was dusk when 'Prithivi' woke suddenly in fright and turned to Kim for reassurance.

'You had a bad dream?' Kim asked.

'My dreams are not bad. It is life that is bad. Where are we?'

'A few miles from Mathura still. Is this person who pursues you . . . your uncle . . . a powerful man?'

'Very.'

'In which case you should get off the train. He could have the police waiting for you in Agra, or further along the line.'

'Will you get off too?' 'Prithivi' looked out. It had grown dark swiftly. The familiar landscape of hills and plains was now invisible and menacing. 'It's dangerous for a . . . young man.'

'Very,' Kim said.

'I could be killed.'

'That is possible. Most probably your throat will get cut.'

'Prithivi's' eyes grew moist and she turned away to hide her sadness. Kim saw that he had succeeded only too well in frightening her, and now felt sorry.

'I will come with you and get you back on the train later.'

'Oh, thank you, Kim sahib.' She turned back to him and he found himself lost for a moment in the gaze of those amber eyes.

His reason for accompanying 'Prithivi' was partly chivalrous, but Kim also possessed an insatiable curiosity about his fellow human beings. He was determined to discover his lovely companion's secret, even if he had to walk all the way to Bombay.

Night came swiftly now, and the air turned cooler. The travellers, all of whom except for Kim and 'Prithivi' had brought their own tiffin, wrapped themselves in blankets and shawls and fell asleep. Kim was lulled by the rhythm of the wheels, and he also fell asleep.

By early dawn the train had reached the outskirts of Agra. Kim woke 'Prithivi' as the train wound slowly along the Jumna river, and they caught the first glimpse of delicate lemon light slowly settling on the dome of the Taj Mahal. The whole carriage came awake and clapped in delight at such a wondrous sight. In the pale, clear air, the great tomb appeared to be afloat, serene and aloof from the cares of the everyday world. It looked scrubbed too, the white marble glistening like a tear. For over two centuries, since the death of Aurangzeb, it had stood neglected and forgotten, like the skeletal remains of other empires. And then Lord Curzon had thrown his great energy into restoring India's past. He had founded an archaeological department, and one of their first tasks – his personal quest – was to restore the Taj Mahal and save it from neglect.

'Oh, it's so beautiful. It makes me want to cry,' 'Prithivi' said, and tears slipped down her cheeks.

'You have seen it before?'

'What am I? A jungley? Of course I have. Years ago I came here with my parents. We sat out in the bagh and waited for the full moon to come out.' She shuddered. 'Pah, it's only then that you realise it's a tomb. It looks cold and sad. It's lonely too, you know. Who can be its companion? If Shah Jahan had built his black tomb, it would have had a friend. Now I only see it as a lonely creature, waiting for its own death.'

Kim stood up and stretched casually. Taking 'Prithivi's' hand, he went to stand by the open carriage door. He waited for the train to slow and jumped down. She faltered.

'Jump,' he shouted. 'I will catch you.'

She jumped down. Though he stumbled he held her tightly. Their faces were an inch apart and he saw from her eyes, widening first in surprise and then in panic, that she knew he was aware that she was no boy. She struggled to escape and began to cry when Kim kept a firm hold on her.

'You will take me back, now.'

'No. I mean you no harm. But I am very curious to know why you disguised yourself.'

'How else can a woman travel alone to Bombay?'

'But not every woman is pursued by men brandishing lathis. Come. Tell me while we walk.'

She followed meekly, one step behind, as they walked along the railway line.

'I am waiting,' Kim said after a while. On looking back, he saw her nose twitching. 'Why don't we start with your name?'

'My name is Parvati. How did you find out?'

'By accident. While you slept.'

'You . . . you . . . touched a defenceless woman?'

'I didn't know you were a woman, remember? Now, continue your story. Remember also that you will be fed only if I believe you.'

'It is a simple and sad story,' and her voice quavered as her imagination began once more to spin her tale. 'I am an orphan. My mother and father died when I was a small child . . .'

'No brothers or sisters.'

'They all died, and you mustn't interrupt. I was adopted by a wicked aunt and uncle who, because of my beauty, planned to marry me off to the terrible man who chased me in Delhi station. The marriage was arranged for tomorrow . . . today . . . and I ran away. He is already married to three other women.'

'You do not look like a Muslim.'

'How can I be with a name like . . . Parvati.'

Her hesitation confirmed his suspicion that she was still not telling the truth.

'My parents too are dead, so we are both alone in the world,' Kim said. 'My father was a great prince. We ruled a large state on the border of Kashmir. My evil elder brother plotted against me and I have been escaping his searchers ever since.'

'I admit that you look like a prince, but you don't behave like one. You're too kind to people. Princes are not kind. They're cruel.' Suddenly she stopped and Kim went on for a few yards before turning back. 'Now will you feed me?'

'You truly are an ill-tempered little bird.'

They found a dubba a few kos further along the Grand Trunk Road. The food in these establishments was always good, for they catered to the caravans that plied the route, and the competition for customers was fierce. For a slim woman, Parvati ate like a wrestler. Kim watched her consume large quantities of meat, chicken and parathas, washed down with lassi, until at last she gave a contented burp. A few yards away was a splendid tamarind tree, and Kim made himself comfortable under it. It was time to rest, like all wise men and beasts. Out of the corner of his eye, he saw Parvati settle her back against the tree and gaze out at the shimmering distance. In repose, her beauty was shadowed by a deep sadness as her thoughts turned inward. When he awoke, she hadn't moved.

'Who were those men?' he asked again.

She rested her chin in her cupped hand. In profile, she resembled a temple carving of an aspara, those beautiful nymphs who were the seducers of gods and men. She had a gracious nose, and distinctive, high cheek-bones. Her skin was as brown as a walnut, its smoothness like the caress of warm marble.

'Goondas, I told you. They wanted to kill me.'

'Why would they do that?'

'Because . . .' She stared out into the distance, now not caring whether Kim believed her. She was fabricating a life, and Kim knew it was a deliberate ploy.

'But then, what would a girl know of anything? Especially one who has never worked in her life, but has always lived in luxury.'

'I have not lived in luxury.'

'Your hands are like a begum's.' He took the free one. The palm was soft and pink and the life-line long and strong. The bend in her line of thought was slightly exaggerated, attesting to a fertile imagination. She snatched her hand away.

'What do you see?'

'A liar.'

'Oh, I'm that. Let's see now. They were going to catch me and sell me into prostitution. I would have been forced to dance in front of men and drink wine.'

'Is that all you would be made to do?'

'What else do nautch girls do, then? I would live like a maharani . . .'

'And grow fat and coarse on jelabis, doudh pheda and rassagoulas,' Kim teased her. 'You would make a good nautch girl. Your stories are quite unbelievable.'

'I think they're good. One day I shall write stories. I have written poetry.'

'About love?'

'What is that?' she asked with a sudden bitterness. 'Poems of love are stupid lies.'

'About sadness, then?'

'Yes. Many poems. I left them all behind, but I could write them again. They are kept in my head and heart.'

'Would you recite one for me?'

'No. They are my special secret. Do you intend to spend the rest of the day idling under this tree? My . . .

betrothed might send his men back to look for me.'

Kim sighed and got up. True to her inborn tradition, the woman who now called herself Parvati remained one step behind.

'Now will you tell me where you live in Delhi? After all, you are trusting me with your life now.'

'My life is worthless, but I will tell you. We live about four kos from the Lal Qila.' She went on to tell him the size of the house, how many servants worked there, and other details.

He only partly believed her, but listened with attention. Even her vivid imagination could not invent every detail, and he knew when she spoke of landmarks that they were real. The miles passed in spirited conversation, each teasing the other from time to time, and growing increasingly comfortable in one another's company.

Kim was experienced with women, and his tongue could be silver in praise of them. He spoke of her eyes and her mouth and her undoubted beauty, and though she protested, she smiled with delight. He did not flatter, but remarked only on her good points. Her bad points, like her inability to tell the truth, he avoided. But when she fell silent, he saw the veil of melancholy cloud her face. Then he wanted only for her to laugh and look on him with those grave, amber eyes.

It grew darker as they walked for a while in silence. Then, just before it became impossible to see the road, Kim saw the flicker of firelight and the shapes of three men sitting by it. He thought he could also see the dark forms of sleeping animals, but was not sure. They could smell the evening meal being cooked.

'Hazoor,' Kim called. 'We are travellers. May we spend the night in your company?'

One man rose and beckoned. The other got to his feet and nudged the third awake. Kim saw it was a bear. When he was fully in the fire's light, the two men peered at him and Parvati, and then warily out beyond them into the night, for they could easily be dacoits.

73

'We mean you no harm. We are brothers, travelling to Bombay.'

'That is a long way from here. I am Nadir Shah, and this is my son, Salim.' Kim saw a large, handsome man with a great moustache that curved up his face and into his turban. His son was half his height with a round, mischievous face; he could not have been more than ten years old. His turban was the same colour as his father's. The bear was on the end of a chain and came and sniffed at Kim and Parvati, who immediately hid behind Kim. There were also two monkeys, and they scolded Kim angrily for having disturbed them. 'The bear is Babur. One monkey is Daniel, the other Aziz. We are magicians and entertainers. Come, sit, you must eat with us.'

'I will only have half a chapati. My brother is not hungry, but tired.'

Out of politeness, Kim ate half a chapati. Their meal was simple and poor, chapatis, a watery dhal and raw onions with coarse salt. While they ate, Nadir Shah told him of their travels. He and Salim journeyed all over India, moving from village to village, entertaining the local people with their performing animals and their magic.

'My great-great-great grandfather performed in front of the Emperor Jahangir with the ancestors of these same animals. So impressed was the Emperor, that he gave him a bag of gold, and wrote of his magic in his book, the Jahangir-nama. My ancestor could cut off his arms and legs and then make himself whole again. Sadly, we lost that great trick.' He took a beedi from Kim. 'And we lost the bag of gold.'

Kim gave a beedi to Salim as well, who smoked it with great satisfaction. Parvati nudged him for one, too. He lit hers and watched calmly as she choked and spluttered. Nadir Shah settled back against his sleeping bear.

His home, Nadir Shah went on, was in Delhi, as it had been for centuries. He had two younger sons who now lived with their mother, but when they were old enough, they would accompany him and Salim. He and

Salim would travel for nine months of the year, not only performing their tricks, but also carrying gossip and news from village to village, which is traditionally how India learns of things that happen a thousand miles away. He was eager to know about Kim, who told him about Lahore and Simla and the adventures of his youth.

By the time the fire had died down, Parvati had long since fallen asleep. Kim went to lie close to her for warmth, but without even awakening, as though the feeling of dread was deep-seated, she pushed him away fiercely and turned her back to him. It was the action of a woman who had slept beside a man she did not love.

But in the morning, with the dew sparkling on the cool earth and the air cold and fresh, he found Parvati pressed up against him. She had woken, realised he was not the man she had repulsed in her subconscious, and had huddled next to him. He looked down on her for a long time. She slept like a lovely child, mouth half open, all sadness erased. Her turban had come undone and the morning sunlight glistened on long, perfumed black hair. His stare finally woke her. Her eyes snapped open, startled and afraid, but she saw Kim and smiled. Then she sat up, groaning.

'I have never spent a more miserable night in all my life. I am stiff from sleeping on the ground, and the bear rumbled all night long.'

'You will get used to it. I cannot afford a serai.'

Their progress was leisurely. Each time they met a group of travellers or a caravan, Nadir Shah and Salim would perform all their tricks. The bear would dance, the monkeys would play their instruments and then came the highlight: Nadir Shah would cover Salim with a sheet, talking all the while to his audience, mesmerising them with his voice and gestures, and Salim would rise from the ground until the sheet hung free. Then Salim would float around before gently settling back on the ground. Kim could not understand how it was done. Each time he saw the trick he would circle Salim, shut his ears and eyes to Nadir Shah. But each time he opened his eyes, there was Salim, afloat.

'How is it done?' Parvati asked the first time.

'It is our family secret. If I told you, how would we earn our living?' Their living wasn't grand. They only gathered an anna here and there.

Kim then asked Salim, who looked at him with the wise eyes of a child who had seen all manner of things, and trusted no one except his father. 'I fall asleep,' he said simply.

He had as much luck getting Parvati to tell him more of herself. Quite deliberately, wanting him to know she was making up the story, she would say she was born in Lucknow. Or Jaipur. She was a rani one day, a servant the next. He had never come across such a vivid imagination.

'I am one of six children,' she might say. 'I have three brothers, all older, and two sisters. I am the youngest. My father was a doctor and practised in the old city. If you know Lucknow, our home was near a Nawab's palace. He was the Nawab's personal doctor and I grew up playing in the palace. Ah, it was a place of great luxury. We had everything we could wish for as children, and the Nawab was a very kindly man. But then, when I was twelve years old, my father died during the epidemic. He was trying to save the lives of too many people and lost his own. My mother was heartbroken, of course. In order to survive, we moved in with her brother in Delhi, which is where I spent my life until this moment.'

But she took a great interest in his life as he talked, marvelling at his travels and envious that he was a man and could wander so freely. Women, she would say angrily, were trapped by the traditions and customs imposed on them by men. She wanted to know too whether he was married or betrothed and he truthfully replied that he was not.

Her identity, naturally, did not go unrecognised by Nadir and Salim. When they bathed in a river, they saw how Kim's 'brother' would seek a private place, far away from their gaze. And they couldn't help but notice when the 'brother' returned damp from the water, the outline of firm high breasts.

'We are,' Kim confided to Nadir Shah, 'lovers running away. Neither of our families wishes us to marry.'

'I understand,' Nadir Shah said kindly. 'We will not betray you.'

Kim found himself wanting her. The thought and the dream became an ache inside him, but he knew he needed to be patient. She had been wounded by a man and still cringed from physical contact. He deliberately kept his distance at first, but as the days passed, and they walked on and on along the dusty roads, they would fall further behind Nadir Shah and his son. They moved at Babur the bear's shambling pace, prizing their secrecy. When Kim reached out to hold her hand, at first he found her palm rigid, but slowly, like clay, it began to mould itself to fit into his own.

'I have never been with a woman who has made me feel not alone,' Kim said. 'Do you understand that? The world is solitude, it is loneliness. With you, I feel that loneliness melt away. There is a feeling of comfort inside me, so that I can wake each day and see you, and when I sleep at night, I am calmed by you sleeping beside me.'

'I understand. If you hadn't found me, I should be desolate and alone in a world where I had no reason to live. My life has not been happy. It has been filled with despair. I cannot yet tell you all the reasons for this state, but one day I will and I pray that you will understand. Until then, I want to make up stories about myself which I believe should be true. Is that so wrong?'

Kim kissed her hand, first the wrist and then the soft, scented palm. She closed her hand around his face, caressing his cheek and lips.

'No. What a man or woman says is less important than how they feel and act.'

Parvati giggled. 'You know, I've never before caressed a man's face and felt such an ache of tenderness. I don't

77

. . . don't . . . want to think of anyone else but you. If I could wake and sleep and serve, my life would be fulfilled.'

They saw, as lovers will in their heightened state of ecstasy, a similarity in the world around them. They were in harmony with their surroundings, being a part of the roadside flowers, a part of the parrots swooping in the sky, a part of a mother with her child, a dog with its pup, even the entwining of a creeper with a tree. Pain and death and destitution and suffering vanished from this special world which they had created for themselves. The sun became gentle, the nights cooler, and after their evening meals with Nadir Shah and Salim, they would withdraw some distance to make their beds on the hard earth. Gradually, even in sleep, where her mind had once erected defences, Parvati allowed Kim to move closer to her. They would wake in the early morning when the sun was just tipping over the horizon to find themselves in each other's arms. When they regularly ended their sleep in such a way they soon began it, too, and Kim would gently caress and kiss her, soothing her fears, his love driving away the darkness in her heart. It could not happen on the first or the second night, but by the third their desire for each other had left them drained all day. They could think of nothing else, or breathe or talk but of making love. Parvati stifled her fears, her deep dislike of the touch of a man. Kim was so different, so gentle, that she, in spite of herself, was weak with longing. When they withdrew for the night and he kissed her face and mouth she took his hand and placed it beneath her shirt against her breast. Another man's touch would have seared, this soothed and then filled her with longing for him. Shyly at first, then urgently, she caressed him, and when they could wait no longer, they made love to each other with insatiable greediness.

'I love you,' Kim said when they lay exhausted. 'I don't know what the future holds for us, and I only wish these days and nights would never end.'

'I cannot *say* I love you, although I do. To say such things would be to tempt God to cast me back into the evil past. Here, feel my heart – let it speak my love silently, only for your ears.'

When they continued on their journey the next day Nadir Shah took note of the dream-like manner in which they moved and the soft glow that shone from their faces.

At the end of two weeks, they reached Gwalior. The town nestled at the foot of a cliff. High above, suspended in the clear blue air, was the Scindia fort and palace. In the Mughal days, princes and nawabs were imprisoned in the fort. But the Scindia had taken possession once again. He was now a dear friend of the departing Viceroy, Lord Curzon.

'May Allah guide you,' Nadir Shah said, embracing Kim and salaaming Parvati outside the railway station. 'If you should ever need our help, tell any traveller to pass word to Nadir Shah and Salim. We will come to your aid.'

Kim and Parvati watched them disappear into the crowded streets and both felt sad at parting from such good companions. They did not have long to wait for a passenger train to take them to Jhansi. And at Jhansi, they caught the mail train for Bombay.

By now Kim knew he loved Parvati. He had never felt such passion for a woman, and it was not mere lust. He wanted to remain with her, to have her as the companion with whom he could spend his life. Her sadness had receded in his company, and the past she had escaped was for the moment banished. She laughed more easily now, and grew increasingly trustful of him. He felt that perhaps she returned his love, and yet . . . but yet . . . Something inside her remained withdrawn and secretive. There were times when an iron veil would descend which he could not penetrate. She would withdraw deep into herself. But then later he would catch her looking at him with the same longing, and when he reached out to touch her, she would allow him a brief moment of this pleasure before pulling away. She could not yet give herself to him completely.

As they drew closer to Bombay, they both grew quieter. Kim sensed that it was the end of a dream-time, soon would come the awakening. He would ask her about her aunt. Where did she live? How would Parvati find her? But Parvati, like a distrustful child, would stubbornly shake her head. She would take him with her, but she could not tell him about this aunt.

'When you meet her, you will understand. You will come with me, won't you? Promise.'

'I promise. And then you will tell me everything?'

'Yes. You will know my life and the feelings of my heart, dear Kim. But,' tears welled up in her eyes, 'once you know, you will shun me.'

'I swear I never will,' he said, but he saw the disbelief in her eyes.

The train arrived in Bombay four hours late. It was midday. They clung together, pushed and jostled by the huge crowds in Victoria Terminus. Kim should have been more alert, but he had been lulled by love and the warm feel of Parvati's hand in his. They were now indeed lovers running away, but from whom he had yet to discover.

They had just passed through the ticket barrier when he was suddenly grabbed and knocked to the ground. He lost his grip on Parvati's hand, and even as he tried to rise he was struck hard in the middle of his back. He rolled over and away from his assailants and caught a glimpse of Parvati being dragged by a man through the crowd.

'Kim! Help me!' She struggled with the man, but he had a tight grip on her arm.

Kim couldn't escape his two attackers. They were not trying to kill him, only to distract him long enough for their companion to carry Parvati out of sight. Kim managed to strike out at one of the men and then grappled with the other. Someone came to his aid, pulling away the man and beating him with an umbrella. Then in a flash his two attackers slipped away from him and scuttled through the crowds.

He didn't give chase but ran in the direction he had seen Parvati taken. The crowd blocked his way and he weaved and dodged through them until he found himself outside the Terminus. He felt helpless. The crowds of Bombay pressed in all around him and, though he sprinted back and forth he could see no sign of Parvati and her kidnapper.

HE HAD lost his Parvati, but he would not give up. Systematically, Kim went down every street and lane around the station, gradually widening his search. He asked beggars and chokras and tonga-wallahs and rickshaw-wallahs, but nobody could help him. No one had seen a boy being dragged away by a man. However, they had seen one man stab another, if he was interested. Was he with a boy? A slim, pretty-looking boy? No, there was no boy.

At last he rested on a step and drew out the pebble. Its heat warmed his palm and he studied it for a long time. If he asked for help, would he be answered? A god might not consider this matter one of life and death, but Kim, whose heart wept, would gladly have given up his life to find Parvati.

'Help me,' he whispered to the stone, not knowing what to expect. Nothing happened. 'Help me to find Parvati.' The pebble remained inert in his hand; no dwarf materialised. In rage and frustration he nearly hurled it away. Instead, he slipped it back in his pocket and continued his search.

At the end of the second day, he knew it was hopeless. She had vanished as suddenly as she had appeared in his life, and left him with a wounded heart. He had already squandered two days of precious time. Their Highnesses were due to arrive in Bombay – at Apollo Bunder where they were building the special pandal for such illustrious visitors – and he had yet to find out whether the two assassins were here. This was his duty and reluctantly he obeyed it. He had also to find the man the Colonel had told him to contact.

He threaded his way through the narrow lanes of the bazaar, crowded in by gaudily painted buildings. Here, like grain crushed into a vat, were thousands upon thousands. He saw every kind of person, Maharati, Gujerati, Bengali, Nepali, Portuguese, English, Arab. It seemed every corner of India and the world gathered here to roam these alleys. The busyness of everyone, from merchant to urchin, was a constant amazement. But then, it was the wealthiest city in India.

The address he had memorised turned out to be a two-storey building; like all others, made of wood, carved elaborately and painted in reds and blues and greens. It was in a lane of jewellers. A bunia sitting on the divan was absorbed in selling a gold and emerald necklace to two elderly Maharati women.

To one side of the shop was a narrow, dark passage. Kim passed a room in which men sat cross-legged, bent over handfuls of precious stones – diamonds, emeralds, rubies. They were the setters. In another room, the gold was being melted and poured into delicate moulds. Threads of the fluid, priceless metal gleamed dully in the firelight. The men, bare to the waist, glistened with sweat and looked like gnomes imprisoned in a dungeon. The passage ended in a small enclosed courtyard. Kim crossed it and climbed a staircase. At the top he knocked on a green wooden door and waited, watching the activity below. Women washed clothes and dekshis, children played in the confined sunshine, men hurried to and from their tasks. He heard the door open cautiously and a head, small as that of a bird with round spectacles perched on its nose, poked out and examined him from head to toe.

'Isaac Newton?'

'Kim?'

'Yes, sahib.'

The door opened wider and Kim stepped into a large, cool room. The man was tall and thin and bird-like in his body, too. He resembled a crane, his shoulders were stooped and his head stuck out. He had bright, inquisitive eyes behind the wire glasses that studied Kim with the interest of a crow. He sat down cross-legged at a low desk, pulled out a gold snuff box, inserted a pinch into each nostril, inhaled and sneezed. The sneeze scattered a fortune in diamonds over the desk. One diamond fell on the floor, but he ignored it. He examined another with a jeweller's glass.

'I have been expecting you,' he said quietly, then continued with his work. Occasionally he would jot a word or number in a cheap notebook beside him. 'You had a pleasant journey?'

'Yes. I heard in Simla that two men who sabotaged the Viceroy's train are in Bombay. I suspect they will make an attempt on the lives of the Prince and Princess of Wales.'

'These two men. What description do you have?'

'Little.' Kim squatted down. 'One is old, the other young. The younger one was clean-shaven in Simla, the elder had a beard. Beyond that, nothing. They came and went like ghosts.'

'And what of this Anil Ray?'

'Innocent. It was his bad luck that the descriptions happened to fit him and his uncle. He had nothing to do with the sabotage attempt. Poor man.'

As Kim's eyes became accustomed to the gloom, he saw that the room was filled with all manner of things. There were strange and wonderful instruments made of brass and wood. He went around exploring. He saw two objects which looked like cameras but which were not, a large metal machine the size of a table with small squares on which were impressed the English alphabet, a two-wheeled machine with a heavy cylinder attached to it. Other objects were heaped one on another, broken and exotic. It would take at least a day to examine everything.

'All mine,' Isaac Newton said in a conversational tone. 'These are all my inventions. Science is my obsession. It will save us from drudgery, starvation, backwardness. We still live in the tenth century, while the British live in the twentieth. I marvel at their genius constantly.' He sighed. 'Sadly, none of my inventions work. I cannot make the leap between my mind and that damn stupid metal.'

'And those?' Kim gestured to the wealth that lay scattered carelessly around Newton.

'My living. I am the greatest diamond cutter in the world. With one glance I can tell a stone's worth and precisely how it should be cut. But my true passion is these objects that surround us.' He stopped his work to gaze first fondly, then angrily, at the wreckage cowering in the dark corners. 'Stupid things. They should work, but they refuse point-blank. Point-blank.'

'You are an Indian Christian, then?' Kim wished to pinpoint the man to his native place. With a name like Newton, he could come from somewhere along the west coast. Trivandrum or Cochin.

'No, no, no, I'm not. Why do people think along such ancient ruts of thought? I am Hindu. My name was Gopal Krishnan, but I changed it to honour that great English scientist, Sir Isaac Newton.' He brooded for a moment, forgetting about the stone in his thin hand. 'I thought I should call myself "sir" but that would be too presumptuous of me. You have heard of Isaac Newton?'

'Yes.' Kim dimly recalled his schooldays in Lucknow. The name was in a book, but he could not remember why.

'He discovered the laws of gravity. What luck, I tell you!' Another pinch of snuff was pushed up a nostril. 'The man is sitting under a tree when an apple falls on his head. I have sat under trees, but only crows aim their droppings on my head. Are there any crows in England? I have long wondered about that.' Snuff entered the second nostril and he sneezed and wiped his nose with the sleeve of his jiba. 'But you are here on a mission and I am talking about science, wasting your precious time. Indians have no concept of time. The English always

85

carry watches. We imitate them, but we cannot read those hands. They have no meaning, absolutely no meaning, I tell you, to us. What do they point to, I ask?'

'I ask what you have to tell me,' Kim murmured.

'And I ask,' Newton said triumphantly, 'who was that girl?'

Kim started. Newton smiled sweetly. 'Do you think I just sit here all day and invent and do this jewellery nonsense? I listen, too. If you put your ear to the earth you can hear every secret in India. We talk non-stop, I tell you. And we are like crows, cockeyeing every damn thing. Nothing is missed. Yes, yes, the girl who travelled with you from Delhi and was kidnapped or woman-napped in Victoria Terminus.' He was blinking with the curiosity of a parrot. 'You had designs on her, did you not? She was pretty, I'm told, beneath a turban which no Panjabi would ever have worn. Maybe a sardar, for they are quite mad.'

'I don't know who she was,' Kim said shortly. 'And I don't care, either.'

'Ahre, baba. He doesn't care! For two days my men have followed you hither and thither through Bombay until they have grown sick and tired and ask for more baksheesh because their feet hurt.'

'Did you have her followed?' Kim asked eagerly.

'No. They lost her. One of my men attacked her 'napper and stabbed him, but then she ran away.'

'She is safe, then,' Kim laughed, then fell silent. 'But where?'

'God alone knows. And he doesn't tell us these things.'

'How did you know about her? She was dressed as a boy and was with me only a brief moment in Victoria Terminus.'

'I was told about her. A message came: "Kim with girl".'

'Who sent it? From where?'

'That I cannot tell you.'

Kim sat back on his haunches, uneasily reflecting on

the past journey. Who had seen them? Countless people on the train, but few had guessed her secret. Or did they just pretend ignorance? The Marwari who listened, feigning sleep, but had those sharp eyes that could tally a column of figures in a moment? The writer, crushed beneath the weight of his poverty? The ticket collector? The man who had pursued Parvati? He wished now that he had discovered her real name. Nadir Shah?

If Newton knew, the Colonel knew. They were connected; intelligence, gossip, whispers passed from one to the other. The Colonel knew who watched him. Another agent had been on the train. The thought intensified Kim's unease. The watched and the watchers, a serpent coiling endlessly in and around itself so that eventually one could not tell where was its head and where its tail; its evil beauty hypnotising the eye.

'You like her?' Newton broke the silence.

'I love her.'

'I will find her for you.' He waggled a finger, thin as a claw. 'But women are big troubles, big troubles. They expect you to feed them and clothe them and take them out to tamashas. What other creature, I ask you, does that? Does the tiger? No. He says to his woman: you look after yourself damn quick. But he is a courageous fellow and I am not. This woman will cause you trouble. Big troubles because I suspect she is up to some mischief.'

'What mischief?'

'That I don't know. But why does she run away? Why does she dress like a man? Why was she womannapped? Too many whys. Like a scientist I will ponder these things. But you should be on your way. We must find those two men before they do any mischief to Their Highnesses. Mischief, mischief. Why can we not sit quietly and accept the bounty of the British? Anyone who produced Isaac Newton must be very good.' He raised his voice suddenly and screamed, 'Oh, Narain! Narain!' They waited. 'You will have some khanna, my friend Kim? Some rest, and then the search will begin.'

A small, wiry young man with curly hair and a grinning smile slid softly into the room. His face looked creased with sleep and his dhoti was half falling off. He blinked through spectacles at Isaac Newton. He seemed to know Kim, for he didn't need to look at him once.

'This scoundrel is Narain. He is an absolute loafer. A BA (Hon) loafer. He will loaf here, there, everywhere. It is his profession. He loafs in toddy shops, coffee shops, race tracks, opium dens, prostitute dens, goonda dens, smugglers' dens and any other den. After food and rest he will help you find the two men. If Narain cannot find them, they are not in Bombay.' Newton sighed this time over a bad invention. A mourning sound. 'He is my sister's son. Why my sister should have such a son is beyond even my great mind. And why she should burden me with him even my small mind can discover: to get rid of the scoundrel and hold me responsible. What are you supposed to be studying, Narain? Tell Kim.'

'To be a lawyer,' Narain said softly.

'And will you ever become one?'

'No. Because I want to be an inventor, like you.'

'See! The scoundrel! He flatters me. Now, get Kim food, give him your bed, and then go with him. If one hair on his head is harmed, I will thrash you and feed you to one of my machines.' He turned to Kim. 'Yes, one of them can eat people, but what happens to them I do not know. They do not come out of the other side. The stupid machine will not defecate. I shall have to solve that problem.'

Kim wasn't sure whether to believe him or not. Narain, however, glanced around nervously. He did not doubt his uncle's genius to invent contraptions that worked in peculiar ways. Kim followed him out, along a narrow balcony to a small, stuffy room. The only furniture was a charpoi and an elegant antique English chair, gloriously out of place and piled high with newspapers. A rope had been strung from one window to a nail in the wall and served as a clothes rack. Before he could rest or eat, Kim needed to wash off the accumulated grime of the journey and Bombay's dust. Narain lent him a clean dhoti and jiba, gave him a towel and soap, and led him down. In one corner of the courtyard was a tub of cold water and Kim stripped to his loincloth and bathed under Narain's unblinking gaze.

'You are so fair, like the Angrezi,' Narain remarked in envy. He himself was quite dark.

Kim's face and arms were brown, but from chest to knee he was pale. He was used to such comments; most people had a cobra's eye for the most delicate shadings of a man's skin. 'This comes from being washed in buffalo milk as a baby,' Kim said and from the shape of Narain's mouth, he knew he was believed. Narain accepted Kim's explanation as he did his uncle's inventions. These things worked for some, not for others. He had been washed with mere water and that, everyone knew, had no effect on anything except the earth.

She cried softly at having lost Kim, knowing she would never see him again. He had saved her in Delhi, and the journey had become wonderful in his company; the hours and days had passed swiftly. He had made her laugh and she had been at ease in his company. Mohini, who had been Parvati, also felt love for him. It was the cruelty of her life that, having found a man to love and trust, he should be snatched away by the evil of her past. It was her dharma.

She had managed to twist herself free of the man who held her, and had run away. He had given chase and had just caught her kurta when suddenly she heard him fall. She had caught a quick glimpse of another man, this one dark and thin with spectacles, plunging a knife into her attacker's side. But she did not stop. She did not know who her saviour was, for when he had looked up at her, he still held the bloody knife, and fear gave her speed, and sent her twisting and dodging through busy lanes until she no longer had the strength.

Where could she find Kim? She didn't dare return to Victoria Terminus. Was he still alive? She had seen two men attacking him, had seen him fall. Maybe he too had been knifed and now lay wounded, or worse, dead. She wept again, for herself and for Kim and for their love that was irrevocably lost.

Now she had to hide. Others might still be looking for her. Obviously they had been waiting for her in the station. They must have watched every train for days. Such patience and tenacity frightened her.

It was dusk before she ventured out from hiding in a doorway and hurried to a rickshaw stand. Carefully she chose the oldest, most emaciated man she could find. It was not out of compassion. She thought she would be agile and strong enough to escape his intentions, should she be discovered to be female.

'Malabar Hill,' she told him hoarsely, coughing to feign consumption. He paid no attention, but wearily rose and stepped between the shafts. 'How much?'

'Eight annas.'

'Eight! You are a thief. Four annas.'

He sat down again and made no effort to move. She was reminded of a weary bullock, sitting dumbly and being beaten by the carter for cheating him with its impending death.

'Eight, then. Quickly.'

It was an old, decrepit rickshaw and she made him put up the hood. Though it was not raining and the sunlight was fading, he did this mutely. She shrank back into the shadows and anxiously watched their route. She didn't have a single pice on her, so she prayed her 'aunt' would be at home to pay for the rickshaw. She prayed too that she would be accepted into her 'aunt's' home. If she were turned away, where could she hide, where could she find shelter? If Kim had been there, such things would not have worried her. He would have cared for her and seen that no harm came to her.

To distract her mind from these worries, she thought

about Kim. He had not really told her what he did, and she dreamed that he was a prince in exile, a Rama, and that one day he would find her and rescue her from the demon who relentlessly pursued her.

8

IT DIDN'T remain dark for long. A full moon rose and bathed the land with bright, ghostly light, turning the black sea to silver. At any other time a sight as strange as the sea would have delighted Mohini. She had never seen such an interminable expanse of water. Now she cringed, drawing the edge of the turban across her face and sinking deeper under the canopy.

The rickshaw had left the comfort of the city and moved at a snail's pace along the shore. The road was deserted and filled with black shadows. She did not know where Malabar Hill was, and prayed the old rickshaw-wallah was not planning a ghastly murder. Vividly she pictured her throat cut, and found some solace in the thought. Death would at least solve her problems.

'Jaldi . . . jaldi.' His pace didn't quicken, he hadn't even heard. She peered back, imagining pursuit and seeing new threats in the strange shapes the moonlight cast. The air was still, as though the night too held its breath. They passed the occasional bungalow, set back deep in a garden. Lamplight glowed balefully yellow through a few windows.

Slowly, the terrain changed. The rickshaw inched forward as the man strained to pull it up the gradient of the hill. Finally, just as she had dreaded, the hill began to defeat him and the rickshaw stopped.

'You will have to walk to the top.'

Mohini climbed down, not daring to look around. The old man was company, wheezing and weak as he was.

They walked, the wheels squeaking, to the top, and then she climbed back in.

'Is it still a long way?'

'Not far.'

There were more houses here, grander ones than those they had already passed. From the brow of the hill she could look back on the glow of Bombay and the curve of the great necklace of white sand. The rickshaw turned off the main road into a lane, plunging into the darkness of large trees. She longed for the pleasing sight of another being, a chowkidar, a chai-wallah, Kim. She longed for Kim to be by her side, to protect her from the menace of her own imagination. She had travelled those nights on foot through even greater darkness in the company of strange men and beasts and hadn't felt a moment of fright. Now fear accompanied her and, if she should be turned away, this deserted hill would give her no shelter.

The rickshaw stopped at a wooden gate at the bottom of the lane. Beyond was a small bungalow, deep in shadow. One window glowed with light, but nothing moved. There wasn't even a chowkidar.

'Wait,' she whispered, and opened the gate. It squealed, silencing the cicadas for a moment and she felt their tiny eyes watch her creep up the gravel path to the steps. Her knock on the door was a whisper too. No one called out, no one moved. The lamplight was a beacon still beyond her reach. She knocked again, louder, and with relief heard the scrape of a chair.

'Kaun hai?' a woman called.

'Mohini, Aunt Alice.'

The light moved, passing down a hall and approaching the door. An Englishwoman in a dressing-gown held a lamp high and peered out at Mohini. There was alarm at the sight of a man, so Mohini snatched off her turban, allowing her hair to cascade down her back. It reached her waist and reassured the woman.

'Mohini?' There was no recognition. 'It is very late. What do you want?'

'Aunt Alice, you must help me.' She knew she should have explained who she was, but in her panic at being turned away her thoughts were in chaos. 'I shall be killed. I need shelter. I don't have any money to pay for the rickshaw. He wants eight annas and I don't know whether he is cheating me.'

She began to cry, not knowing what else to do, and the woman's face softened. She stepped aside and Mohini ducked under the lamp into the refuge of a small drawing-room.

'I'd better pay the man his eight annas and then find out your story.' She left Mohini in the darkness while she went into her bedroom to get her purse. Mohini heard her footsteps crunch down the drive and then return. She crouched in a far corner of the room, so that the lamplight revealed her pressed against a bookcase.

'Now, who are you?'

'Mohini. I . . . I . . . you gave my brothers lessons in Delhi. You taught me English. You were not supposed to. I was a little girl, and you would spend time with me in the garden. I have sent you poetry I wrote and . . .'

'Of *course*! My dear.' Alice Soames clapped her hands in delight and took the frightened girl into her arms. 'It's just that it's so late, and I haven't seen you for so long. You've grown into such a lovely woman. Just imagine. That little girl in plaits! And you're a good poet. Come and sit down.'

Alice Soames watched Mohini slowly lower herself to perch on the end of a rattan chair. There was some resemblance to the child of ten years ago. A shy, curious child, dressed in bright silks, who had looked at her with such awe and had held a book as though it were sacred. In the whole of India, only a handful of Indian women could read or write in their own language. Even the rich didn't believe in the education of their wives or daughters. When she had seen the struggling curiosity of this girl, Alice had spent an hour or so each day teaching her at the bottom of their garden beneath a mango tree. In the three years Alice had spent tutoring

94

her brothers, Mohini had mastered English well enough to write and to devour books.

For the men to learn English was of great importance. The best jobs in the government as well as in law depended on a command of the language. Any fool who knew the language could earn good money in a 'situation' with a wealthy Indian family who wanted to better themselves. Alice had replied to an advertisement in the *Pioneer* and Mohini's father, a doctor, had, after some hesitation, given her the position of tutor to his sons.

It had been a comfortable job. They were a kindly family, until Mohini's parents and both her brothers had died in the cholera outbreak. An uncle and aunt had come to care for the little girl, and Alice had been dismissed. Over the intervening years she had received a few poems in the post from Mohini. The early ones were childish but gradually, as she matured, they had become better. They were moving and melancholic. She had written letters trying to encourage Mohini, but the only replies were the poems, scribbled on scraps of paper like notes in a bottle from a castaway. They were more informative than any letter, and recorded the disintegration of the young woman's life.

Alice saw the panic in Mohini's face fade gradually. The girl seemed on the edge of breaking down, so Alice moved to embrace her. For Mohini the gesture was everything. She buried her face in Alice's shoulder, and felt a tremendous release from fear.

'First, you must have some food. Then you're to go to bed. In the morning we'll talk and find out what this ghur-bhur is all about.'

While Mohini ate, Alice made up a camp cot in the study where she worked. Then she led Mohini by the hand and tucked her into bed, kissing her forehead. Mohini was recollecting that first meal she had eaten in the dubba in Agra with Kim watching, and she fell asleep even before Alice had closed the door.

Alice's own bedroom was spartan, furnished with only the bare necessities of comfort and a bedside table piled high with books. The whole bungalow reflected the life of a single woman, and one who was not tidy. Clothes lay piled on a stool, and shoes had not been put away. The room also reflected a busy life, for papers and notebooks were strewn on the bed.

Alice slipped off her dressing-gown and returned to bed. She picked up a note pad, but Mohini's unexpected arrival preoccupied her, a frown only strengthening an already strong face. Her eyes were a clear, pale blue, almost chilly, but when she smiled her warmth and sense of fun dispelled the sternness. She looked like a woman with an appetite not only for pleasure, but also for hardship. Both would be met and either enjoyed or overcome with equal enthusiasm. And even now, with a sense that she was wasting time brooding, she pushed the thought away almost physically and returned to writing her article for the *Manchester Guardian* on the preparations for the visit of the Prince and Princess of Wales.

Though Isaac Newton scientifically classified Narain's many haunts into different kinds of dens, they were indistinguishable from one another. All were small, stuffy rooms, some of brick, others of mud, frequented by men. Their professions, in the gloom of lantern light, smoke, and the sour odour of toddy and arrack, were never apparent. They were united only in their suspicion of the stranger.

However, there was no doubt that Newton's definition of his nephew was accurate. He was an expert loafer and this quality was recognised by all. He was greeted warmly in most of these warrens, hidden from the eyes of the law. He and Kim slipped furtively in and out, and Kim felt adrift in this netherworld of Bombay life. They would float from one den to another and spend two, three, even four hours sitting on benches, gossiping with strange companions. Kim was introduced as Narain's cousin-brother, though they were completely unalike. If the answer needed expansion, Narain would inform them that Kim's brother's daughter was married to his uncle's wife's brother. Such convoluted relationships were accepted, though if expanded indefinitely, as Isaac Newton postulated, every bloody Indian was related to another through some rigmarole nonsense or the other.

They sat now on a wooden bench, clay cups of toddy in hand. Kim pretended to drink. He did not like the taste. The men who were sitting around squandering time were smugglers. They plied the Arabian Sea between the Gulf and Bombay, running contraband. The goods varied according to what was in demand. Gold, silk, English cotton goods, French brandy, guns. Narain said the famous gun-smuggler, Ahmed Sait, a man with a formidable reputation, occasionally frequented this den when not on the high seas in his dhow. He would take women out to the Gulf for the brothels, and return with guns. Guns fetched a high price because Indians were not allowed to own them; the English could. Ahmed Sait might be persuaded to inform if two men – one young, the other old – had purchased guns from him.

'Does the Colonel sahib know about Ahmed Sait?' Kim spoke very softly.

'Of course not. Who would dare to inform on him? He has enough goondas to cut my throat in a dozen reincarnations.' Narain peered at Kim over the rim of his cup, brows furrowed in worry. 'Please, you must not think such thoughts. If Ahmed Sait discovers that you are an Imperial Agent, he will chop you into pieces and sell your remains in the meat market – as goat.' In consolation he added: 'But the local police know who ho is, of course. They become blind when he passes by.'

'Then if we ask him about these two men, won't he be suspicious?'

'We shall lie to him. Tell him these two fellows ran off with your brother's daughter and despoiled her. He understands vengeance. We shall purchase a gun as well, then he will gladly help us to get our revenge.'

They had to wait a further two nights for Ahmed Sait.

Narain had discreetly enquired as to his whereabouts, and a man whispered that Ahmed Sait would be there 'soon'. The time was intentionally vague; it kept them pinned down.

The two men Kim was searching for formed part of a large and curious crowd watching Lord Curzon. The younger of the two, dressed in a conflict of colours – a red turban, blue shirt and white pi-jamas, his lips matching the shade of his turban from the paan in his mouth – stood at the rear. His eyes flickered constantly back and forth over the scene in front of him. He looked watchful, coiled as a serpent waiting to strike. The people near him felt the tension in the hard, muscled body and edged away from his touch. His companion, many years older, was a contrast. He stood right in front, directly behind a police constable, ignoring his companion completely. They had arrived separately. The older man talked to the men and women around him, cracked jokes and related salacious gossip. He looked like a harmless shopkeeper. His clothing was simple, white and fairly clean. He carried a small gunny bag with what looked like the day's shopping: a few tomatoes, two onions and a banana protruded from the top.

Lord Curzon sat resplendent in an open landau, shaded by a huge, ornate umbrella held by two bearers. Two footmen stood behind the landau, and two syces held the horses' heads. The men all stood still as statues. Beside the open carriage door stood Curzon's retinue, a handful of British officials wearing linen suits and topis. Still further away were their assistants, all young Englishmen, carrying files which detailed the order of the procession. And beyond them, furthest from this seat of power, were the Indian officials and their clerks. The chain of commands flowed out to the most junior who relayed instructions to the participants, harrying them like hunting dogs, nipping at a heel here and there to hurry them up.

Curzon, ever the perfectionist, turned away to look

beyond the dust haze of activity. He wanted to remember things now, for soon he would leave. The hard blue sea off Apollo Bunder was flat and smooth as a pond. It murmured along the stretch of glaring white sand, and he thought of it as a huge beast, too lazy in this afternoon heat to stir itself beyond the flick of a small wave. Its roar was muted to a soothing whisper, calling to him to stroke it. Some distance away, he saw fishermen's huts and small black dots, men mending nets. He turned away and looked in the opposite direction: the sea was filled with a line of great white ships, metal veins feeding England, waiting to enter the clutter of docks that stretched further than the eye could see.

The sea's continual murmur took on a sad note to his ear: 'Empire, Empire, Empire'. His rule was ending, the empire would pass to another man. A stranger would suddenly be initiated into this power and pageantry, the magnificence of which still took his breath away. 'Viceroy of India,' he whispered to himself. The sound was sweet, it left an echo that reverberated through the land.

This afternoon, Curzon, watching this modest affair of welcome, could not help remembering the durbar he had organised two years earlier, to celebrate the coronation of Prince George's father, Edward VII. King Edward himself did not attend, but sent his brother, the Duke of Connaught, to represent him. This had pleased Curzon, for it kept him paramount in India. Only the King-Emperor in person was superior to him.

The coronation durbar in Delhi had marked the very apex of British rule in India. He had planned it as a monument; only a Great Mughal could have matched its splendour. Every nawab, maharajah, rajah and rana had been summoned, along with their entire entourage of elephants, retainers, soldiers and dancing girls, to pay homage to Edward VII. Ambassadors and Arab sheikhs, governors and lieutenant-governors of provinces as large as England, had marched in the procession.

In true Mughal tradition, a great tented city had been

erected outside Delhi, and a special railway line had been laid through the encampment to ferry guests from their residences to the central amphitheatre built on the maidan outside the Lal Qila. The durbar started on December 29th, 1902 and had lasted ten full days.

If the pageantry was mediaeval, Curzon had deliberately planned it so. The British were the Mughals now, and Curzon had wanted every Indian, from prince to kissan, to grasp the fact. The people could compare the past with the present, for even as Shah Jahan had once sat on his throne in the Red Fort, so Lord Curzon mounted his own throne to review the new India that passed in front of him in homage. Sixty-seven squadrons of cavalry and thirty-five battalions of infantry and artillery had marched past the dais, followed by all the princes of India and their retinues. Each horse and elephant was so bejewelled that even the trappings of one animal would have fed whole provinces. Curzon's heart, as he listened to the fifty-one-gun salute, beat like that of a true Mughal Emperor. The pomp and ceremony of power were sweet and heady as wine, laced with the opium of homage.

Now, even as he watched these rehearsals, a mere shadow of that other durbar, Curzon remembered his own words. They came floating back to him now, on the eve of his departure, with peculiar clarity as though just spoken. From his throne, Curzon had addressed the princes, the governors, the masses of India. He had begun his speech by expressing his hope that India would enjoy an improving future, with the people sharing more wealth and comfort.

Then he had added: 'Under no other condition can this future be realised than by the unchallenged supremacy of the paramount power. Under no other controlling authority is this capable of being maintained than that of the British Crown.'

The words now gave him some sense of achievement. He would be leaving behind him this philosophy of permanence, and he felt a deep satisfaction. The courtiers surrounding his carriage were good, if stolid men; they would continue to give India the security and the justice of British rule. Curzon had envisaged a future for India and looking around him he could not imagine change.

Yet ironically, Curzon, who so loved the empire, was already an unknowing witness to great change. Had he looked beyond his aides and his entourage, he would have seen a slow stirring in the blurred faces of the crowds. His legacy, in spite of the stirring words, was not permanence, but change, change, change. In his zeal for an enduring reign, for Indians to turn into subordinate Englishmen, he had built schools and universities for them. Their minds, long dormant, long suppressed, had now begun to waken.

For the arrival of Prince George and Princess Mary, the first visit by the son of a ruling emperor to his dominion, Bombay was being thoroughly prepared. Roads were being resurfaced, buildings painted afresh, banners stretched over streets – 'Tata & Sons Welcomes Their Beautiful Highnesses the Prince and Princess of Wales', 'Ibrahim & Sons Welcome Their Most Illustrious and Glorious Highnesses to Bombay'. Every building sported a banner. A hundred-yard-wide arch of bamboo and matting had been erected, and the Union Jack was stretched across from one side to another. Flanking the flag were huge paintings of the royal couple. They did bear some resemblance to them, but the colouring was an exuberant pink and red.

Some distance from the Viceroy's carriage, an immense pandal that covered one hundred square yards was nearly complete. Kashmiri carpets were laid on the ground and a line of chairs, the central one throne-like for Lord Curzon, were lined up on a dais. On either side and lower, were chairs for Prince George and Lord Minto. Facing them were row upon row of chairs. A barricade of bamboo poles had also been erected to keep back the enormous crowds that would gather to glimpse Their Highnesses.

The rehearsal went smoothly. A Sikh cavalry regiment, bright as hibiscus in their uniforms, mounted on coal-black horses, trotted past the pandal. Elephants and the retinue of princes ambled behind them. The dust eddied in the air, and the watching men held handkerchiefs to their noses. Following the elephants came a camel corps of Rajput soldiers, and then came the spectacle of a different, less martial India. Folk dancers from various tribes and a long procession of schoolchildren, mostly English, though here and there was an Indian child. On the day they would carry small British flags, but today they trudged in the dust.

'I scrape a living by writing,' Alice said, and then chuckled. Mohini couldn't help smiling. She remembered that chuckle from her childhood, and it was comforting to find that Alice hadn't changed much. She looked older, but Mohini found it impossible to judge a European's age. They all looked older than anyone she knew. It came with their authority and confidence.

They sat on the porch of the Regent Hotel watching the tamasha. The table between them was laid for tea, and Alice's notebook was on one side. Frequently she would jot down a thought or an observation.

Kim would not have recognised Mohini if he had passed by at that moment. She was wearing a blue cotton sari, a pink choli; her hair was tied in a neat bun. She looked elegant, though she wore no silk or jewellery except for a few cheap glass bangles. The return to her true identity had imparted to her a heightened sexuality.

'But wouldn't you prefer to be . . . looked after?'

'Good God, no. I had that once. It didn't work. Now I can travel, I can be inquisitive and, best of all, critical. Look at that pompous ass, Curzon. Sitting in that carriage like a nawab. He's leaving behind the biggest mess ever with his partition of Bengal – which no doubt Minto will botch.'

Mohini was shocked at Alice's remarks. She knew that if she had spoken these same words, calling the Viceroy

an . . . an ass, she would be taken away to a lock-up.
Yet she also felt excited. This woman had a swagger that
she envied. No, she could never be quite like her. It was
too dangerous, but even partly to emulate Alice would
satisfy Mohini. 'But if you don't get enough money, how
do you live?'

'Oh, I don't have to pay rent, food is cheap. Drink,
admittedly, does cost a lot, but then I have . . . a friend,
shall we say . . . who makes a contribution. It's the best
of both worlds, my dear. Kept and not kept. Women
must walk the tightrope. Ah, His Imperialship is leaving
at last. No doubt this will be yet another grand and
expensive gesture. We suck your blood, my dear, and
shall continue to do so until we are thrown out on our
necks. Who knows? One day it might happen.' Then,
sourly, she added, 'Though not in our lifetime.'

'But what a tamasha it will be,' Mohini said. 'Have
you ever met Their Highnesses? What are they like? Are
they like our Maharajahs?'

'My dear, I'm just a little scribe, and not one who is
all that popular with our lords and masters. I've never
met them and I doubt that I ever shall.'

'Who are all those men with the Viceroy?'

'The lords and masters, our true rulers. Viceroys come
and viceroys go, but the government of India trudges
on for ever, guided by their firm and fair hands. Or so
they would have us all believe.'

'You don't like your own people.'

'I don't like these particular people. The English are
not all alike, thank God. Well, the work has been done
so I can reward myself with a drink, and you with a cup
of tea. Then we'll find out what to do with you. Come
on.'

They had to pass quite near the Viceroy's carriage and
Mohini stared fixedly at Curzon. He had bent down to
converse with one of his subordinates. She saw only the
lower half of their faces for the shade of their topis hid
their eyes and noses. As they approached, Mohini heard
Alice draw a sharp breath and avert her face. None of

the men paid any attention to them, but were turning instead to listen to further instructions from the Viceroy.

'Did any one notice us?'

'No.'

Alice looked back briefly. Her face tightened, became clouded with pain.

'Who was that?' asked Mohini.

'You always were a most inquisitive child, Mohini, with eyes as sharp as a mongoose.' She hailed a gharri and they climbed in. This time it was Alice who sank back into the shadows and fell silent, her eyes distant. 'I just saw someone I knew in a previous incarnation. When one so desires, one can force oneself to forget people, places.'

'Was it the Viceroy?'

'I have never met the Viceroy. Asking all these questions will not get you the answer. I need that drink more than ever. Jaldi!' she called to the driver who whipped the bony horse to a trot which lasted but a minute.

They rode in silence along the wide, tree-lined avenues, now cooled by the evening breeze. The traffic and swirling dust of people, rickshaws and gharris decreased as they left the city. The journey was beautiful and pleasing. Alice stared moodily out to sea and Mohini, not wanting to impose, looked down at her twisting fingers.

When they reached the bungalow, Alice strode ahead, and when Mohini reached the drawing-room she found Alice already nursing a tall glass in her hand.

'I told the boy to prepare tea for you. I don't like to be haunted by memories. In some ways we are rather alike, my dear. Running away from things. Why do I say, "things"? Men. Men. I love them, but sometimes I wish they had never been invented.' She reached out to pat Mohini's hand. 'Don't fret about me. I'll recover. Nothing fatal.'

The boy, an elderly man who acted as both bearer and cook, brought out a tray of tea and biscuits. It was the time of the day that Alice took the greatest pleasure in:

dusk slowly creeping across the land, the smell of the sea. When she was alone, she would collect her thoughts before beginning her work, or reading. She wasn't afraid of her solitude, but rather she treasured it. Mohini had now taken up most of these times, but she did not begrudge it.

They sipped and nibbled in silence, listening to the crows and the screech of a nearby parrot. The shadows of the trees crept along the ground and came into the room, turning it dark.

'I had a husband once,' Alice began. 'And a family. He and I ended up hating each other and, like you, I had to run away.'

'Was he cruel?'

'I couldn't, even in my foulest moods, call him cruel. Stern, yes, and very formal. A rigid man who lived by codes that only other men could understand. I was supposed to obey them, but I found it impossible.'

'At least you had a husband who wasn't cruel,' Mohini cried. 'Mine was. I am supposed to revere him, worship him. I am supposed to place my forehead on his feet. I would do this gladly for a good husband, but he is a man I can only hate. I hate him and I am frightened of him. He will kill me if he finds me.' She burst into tears.

Alice put her arms around Mohini and let her weep, rocking her and stroking her hair as she had done for the child so many years before, when her parents and brothers had died. She knew from those haunting poems that Mohini had been married off to a man much older than herself when she was only thirteen. Alice could not stifle her abhorrence of a religion that permitted the evil practice of child marriage. Hinduism, she thought, was barbaric, but she did not mention this to the young woman crying in her arms.

9

'DID YOU find the woman?' asked the Colonel.

'Colonel sahib, I cannot find her,' Isaac Newton reported. 'I have made my men look high and low and high, but she has truly disappeared from the world.'

The Colonel sat on the verandah of Government House. It was a large building in the centre of a spacious garden. He looked out at the sea, watching the phosphorescence shimmering along the beach. The night was still and calm.

Isaac Newton stood stiffly. He felt ill at ease in his cotton suit which seemed at odds with his shape. It was tight under the arms and one sleeve was longer than the other. The buttons did not align with their holes and the trousers folded down around his ankles. He had paid a damn tailor a lot for this sartorial elegance and he was proud of it. But his brown shoes were dusty and his tie badly knotted. His tailor, Aziz Khan, had handed it to him pre-knotted, and neither of them was aware it was an MCC tie. Newton believed it was the British equivalent of the subtle knot tied by thugs for strangling their victims. He had forced himself into these clothes for his audience with the Colonel, and the effort had made him perspire. He did not dab at his face, but instead allowed the sweat to run down into the collar of his shirt. The starch cut into his thin neck. He had studied a book on etiquette for Indians meeting Europeans and, failing to comprehend the complicated instructions, logically concluded it best to remain absolutely still.

In the Colonel's presence Isaac Newton was subdued.

He felt shrunken in these clothes; he could not speak his mind with the ease and humour that Kim had enjoyed. He gripped a cheap leather briefcase, quite empty, but he hoped it would give him an air of importance in front of his superior.

The Colonel knew little of the different personality standing before him. For years, ever since he had recruited Newton, the skinny man had behaved with pleasant humility. Isaac Newton was a reliable if eccentric person who spoke only when spoken to and accorded him deference. He had a network of informers and could, given time, discover most of Bombay's secrets. The Colonel did not claim to understand the workings of his subordinate's mind, nor was he interested. The man was loyal to the Crown and, for the Colonel, that was enough.

'I want you to keep up your efforts to find her. When you have found out, only tell me. No one else.'

'Not even Kim?'

'No. Was Kim . . . affected by her?'

'Colonel sahib,' Newton said, understanding the Colonel's thoughts and wishing both to please him and to protect Kim, 'I cannot tell the heart of another man. But,' he lied, 'I think not.'

'How is Kim getting on with his work?'

'Greatly well,' Newton said enthusiastically. 'He is a very keen observer of many things and he is a true gentleman in his behaviour to one and all. For Kim, all men are equal. He and my agent, Narain,' (Newton had no wish to let the Colonel know that Narain was his nephew. The British frowned on nepotism, but it one didn't employ one's nephew, who else in this damn world would employ such a loafer?) 'are even now discovering the whereabouts of the two men from Simla.'

'I didn't send him here to look for those two men,' said the Colonel, irritated.

'He believes that those men can clear the good name of Mr Anil Ray.' The Colonel's indifference to the two men Kim was hunting surprised Newton.

'Anil Ray stabbed a policeman. I want Kim to concentrate on finding the other seditionists, not waste time on a wild-goose chase. Have you discovered any others?'

'No, Colonel sahib.'

Newton flinched before the intense stare. It seemed to pin his chest to his spine. Sweat beaded on his forehead. He was glad all the seditionists, violent and otherwise, were confined to Bengal. He prayed that none would suddenly materialise in his own Bombay.

'Bombay only wishes to give Their Highnesses a truly rousing welcome. Hip, hip, hooray.'

His exuberance faded under the Colonel's acid stare. He could not read those predatory eyes. He sensed deception, a kind he would never be able to fathom, for he was only a small man. The deception in those eyes functioned on a higher plane.

'Have you put a man on watching Tilak?'

'Oh, yes, Colonel sahib.' Newton was relieved. 'I have my best man, who has become an ardent follower of Mr Tilak.'

'Tilak is not a mister,' the Colonel said.

'Of course, Colonel sahib. A scoundrel man if ever there was one.'

Lokamanya Tilak was watched not only by Newton's man, but by others in the Colonel's employ as well. Tilak, a Maharati Brahmin, was openly antagonistic to British rule in India, and had begun to advocate driving them into the sea. He was popular in this part of India, for he conjured up the return of the great Maharati warrior, Shivaji. Shivaji was the chieftain who had brought down the Mughal empire, and Tilak was now being regarded as another Shivaji, if not in action so far, then in rhetoric. He attacked the Indian government, and his paper, the *Kesari*, propagated a call for swaraj. It was the most widely read of the Indian vernacular newspapers, and it set every government official's teeth on edge.

However, there was another side to Tilak's coin. Gopal Krishna Gokhale was at this time a friend of Tilak's, but he was a man far more moderate, both in his manner and in his demands. He was a friend of the Viceroy and his main plank was the reform of Indian society before independence. He believed this independence could only be achieved by patient negotiation with the British ruler. He did not believe in force.

'It's only a matter of time before I have Tilak arrested,' the Colonel said, almost to himself. He was thinking of Agent Daddaji, who was now in Bombay. Daddaji would influence the event, carefully spinning a noose around Tilak's neck.

Newton was ignorant of Agent Daddaji, but vigorously nodded in agreement. He would have nodded to any pronouncement, for he wished the Colonel only to be pleased.

'One day he will resort to violence, and I hope it will be very soon, so that we can rid ourselves of him. Damn seditionist.'

Newton was dismissed. The moment he was out of sight, he stripped off his jacket and tie; his shoes too, they pinched his feet badly. He carried them in his hand, pleased with his report to the Colonel. However, his mind now turned to the vexing problem of his new invention. It was only a draft on paper so far, a machine that would carry real words along an electric line, not mere little click-clicks like the telegraph. He was determined to perfect this invention soon, and his mind soared into a daydream of his machine. Newton did not dream along financial lines, but along those of fame. He only wanted to live up to his name.

The Colonel remained on the verandah. Bombay glittered behind him, a city far busier and livelier than Calcutta. It was good to be here, distant from the box-wallahs in Calcutta. In Bombay there were freebooters and the hum of unfettered commerce. But his mind then reluctantly turned inward. The lines along his mouth deepened, his mood darkened. He was not sure what he'd seen, and suspected that his sight had played a trick on him. That very afternoon, while talking to the

Viceroy, he had glanced straight up into the sun and seen two women, one European, the other Indian. He had had a fright, seen a nightmare shimmering in the glare. It must be a touch of sunstroke, which made men see terrible visions swimming at them through the haze.

Elizabeth hardly knew Bombay. She had only visited the city twice, once on leaving India for school in England, and once on her return. Each time she'd spent exactly two days there. Now she sensed an air of excitement. The city had a vigour about it that Calcutta lacked. Bombay promised adventure, and so far it had not failed her in this promise. She was new to Bombay society but not entirely friendless. Her dearest friend, Sarah Rushton, lived here. Sarah and she had led very similar lives. Both were the children of Anglo-Indian parents, who had been sent to school in England, 'come out' in London, and then returned to India. She'd written to Sarah and had promptly been invited to a dinner party and to stay the night. The invitation had included the promise of an interesting young man as a dinner companion. In reply, Elizabeth had written:

. . . There is no lack of young men in Calcutta, but *interesting* ones are thin on the ground. Most of the eligibles lead horribly staid lives in the government, or else are box-wallahs, and one certainly wouldn't want to mix with *them*.

Bombay sounds so different from Calcutta. Here, I am stifled by the stiff formality of behaviour. I *can* do this and *can't* do that. If I stray even an inch, it's noticed at once. So, Sarah, I look forward so much to the dinner and the 'interesting young man', but seeing you again will be enough to give me great pleasure. With my best regards.

Elizabeth had specially prepared for this evening's party. She had found an excellent dressmaker in Calcutta, a Goan woman, Mrs Pereira, and had got her to make a perfect copy of a gown she had seen in a fashion plate in the *Illustrated London News*. It was by now a trifle behind the very latest fashions, but it was the best she could do for this exciting occasion. Elizabeth had also brought a trunk of clothes so as to be prepared for any event, including the possible invitation to a ball for Their Highnesses. She took her bath, then opened her almirah and looked through the carefully hung clothes. They had all been freshly ironed. Elizabeth searched through the wardrobe, her anger slowly rising. She stepped back to allow the light to fall into the almirah.

'The wretched woman!' Elizabeth spat. 'Mary ayah!'

Mary came through from the bathroom. She saw her mistress's face and shrank back into the doorway.

'Come here!' When Mary ayah remained unmoving, holding the door handle, Elizabeth strode over, grasped her hand cruelly and dragged her to the almirah. Neither noticed Mary's glass bangles break and scatter. 'Just look in there. Stick your stupid head in and see if you can find the new silk dress. Look, you fool.'

Elizabeth pushed Mary right into the almirah. She stumbled and slid to the floor, and wept. Elizabeth hauled her to her feet. 'Well, where is it?'

'Elizabeth baba, don't be angry. I must leave it behind. Hurry burry . . .'

She didn't finish. Elizabeth slapped her hard and a moment later regretted it. Disappointment, on top of the expectation and excitement of the past weeks, had been too much.

'I'm so sorry I hit you, Mary ayah, but you really are a stupid woman. A simple thing like a new dress, and you left it behind. You're useless. I don't see why I put up with you.' She ignored Mary ayah's tears, and the pricks of blood on her wrists where the bangles had cut into the skin. 'Now, what shall I wear? You tell me.' Deliberately she waited, the silence unbearable.

'The . . . pink . . . silk, Elizabeth baba? You look . . .'

'Pink . . . silk?' Elizabeth mocked Mary ayah's sobs. 'But I don't *want* to wear the pink silk, you stupid woman. Pick another.' Elizabeth pulled the pink dress out of the almirah, crushed it in her hands and threw it on the floor. Mary ayah picked it up, but it was snatched from her and thrown down.

'The . . . flowered muslin frock . . . Elizabeth baba. It makes you . . . beautiful, like . . . the Virgin Mary.'

Elizabeth dragged out the frock, crumpled it and threw it on top of the pink silk. This time Mary ayah allowed it to remain, and chose another, mutely, taking it lovingly off the hanger. It was a satin ball gown, with lace along the shoulders and sleeves. Again Elizabeth balled it up and threw it down on the floor. In silence, they went through the whole almirah until it was empty and the floor awash with silks, muslins, printed flowers and swirling colours.

'Iron them all, you fool.' Elizabeth fell on the bed, close to tears. Her pretty new frock stuck in Calcutta, while she was here with nothing at all to wear. 'Get out. Hurry. Jaldi, jaldi, you idiot. I have to go in half an hour.' Elizabeth shut her eyes tightly. She could kill her.

Mary ayah gathered up all the clothes in her arms, as carefully as a child, and left the bedroom. Her cheeks stung and she ignored her bleeding wrists. Elizabeth baba was not to blame; it was herself. Her baby had every right to be angry. Mary ayah could not remember where she'd put the new dress. She was sure it had been packed, but in the confusion of leaving, no doubt it was still at home. She went down to the servants' quarters at the rear of the Government guest house. The Colonel's valet, Balram, was ironing the Colonel's trousers. He saw Mary ayah with the dresses and silently stepped aside. The iron was a heavy metal box, filled with hot coals, and Mary ayah, who had spent the whole afternoon ironing the frocks, now began once more.

Elizabeth wore the pink silk. It felt soiled against her skin, shabby. She tried to stifle her shame. The dress was barely in fashion. But she absolutely could not wear muslin to a dinner party, and was still angry with Mary ayah, who stood silently watching her mistress powder her face. Elizabeth looked very pretty, her cheeks flushed with anger. Her shoulders were straight and stiff. Ready at last, Elizabeth grabbed her evening purse and stalked out without another word.

The Colonel had changed for dinner and had taken his whisky out onto the verandah. Elizabeth bent and brushed her lips against his forehead.

'Has the gharri come for me yet?'

'Abdul,' the Colonel called his bearer. 'Go and see if a gharri awaits miss sahib.' The bearer padded out into the darkness and returned with the gharri. The lanterns on either side barely threw enough light. The Colonel followed Elizabeth, helped her in. 'Don't wait up for me, Father. Remember, I'm spending the night at the Rushtons'. Sarah and I have such a lot to catch up on.' She closed the door. 'Are you going out, too?'

'I may go down to the Club later. Enjoy yourself.'

The gharri drifted up the long gravel drive into the night that was still and waiting. He knew it waited for him, and heard the silence. All at once he was overcome by such a sense of loneliness that he felt an enormous pain in his chest, like a blow that winded him and stopped his breath. It was a loneliness visited upon him like an attack of fever. He had not thought of Elizabeth's mother for years now. He could not bring himself to allow the venom of her name to soil his lips; his mind could not utter it, even in silence. But there were times when a shadow fell across Elizabeth's face; then another face rose mistily from the grave of his mind. That face remained a mask, mocking his youthful passion. Too many years had passed for him to recall the woman physically, but there still remained an emptiness in his life, like all those poignant ruins in India, filled with nothing.

'Damn sun,' he whispered, and sent Abdul to fetch a gharri. He would dine at the club. Ever since that fleeting recognition this afternoon, a feeling of unease had haunted him, as if evil spirits filled the air.

113

Generally the Colonel disliked club life, but tonight, on entering, he felt saved from the dark. The rooms were ablaze with lights, English voices and laughter. He showed his Calcutta club card and signed the register. The main room was spacious, with polished teak floors. The walls were hung with heads of wild buffalo and tigers, lances and muskets, insignia of bravery. The whist tables were filled with lively players, and on the lawn, in the lamp-light, he glimpsed groups of Europeans. The club provided a haven for the British, as did Simla. They could gather here, remote from the eyes of the natives. The hum and chatter in English cadences comforted them all. The Colonel looked into the billiard room, and found a vacant table in the bar. He ordered a whisky and soda and studied the dinner menu.

'Colonel!' An officer in mess kit stood beside his chair. He was a square-faced man with pale blue eyes. A cigarette hung from his mouth and he held a cigarette case and matches in one hand, a whisky glass in the other. 'We met in Lahore a few years ago. Reggie Dyer. Your boy is in my regiment.'

'Of course.' They shook hands and Dyer pulled up a chair. 'How is Richard?' the Colonel enquired.

'An excellent man, excellent. A bit of a madcap, but that's to be expected, what?' The major stubbed out the cigarette and immediately lit another. 'I'm down here for the tamasha with some of the regiment. I'm afraid Richard had to be on duty.'

'How are things up there?'

'Simmering,' Major Dyer said. He ordered another burra peg. The Colonel sensed a tightness in his manner. His cigarette jerked in his mouth like a nervous tic. 'The Russians are causing endless problems as usual, stirring up the tribes. We have our hands full. I think we should have more men there, teach the damn tribals a lesson. Hang a few, they'll quieten down. But now that we've pulled back, they're up to their old tricks again. Hang a few, is what I say.'

Yes, the Colonel thought, hang a few. But is the Great

Game now to be played with the Russians or here, within the empire? He had enjoyed playing the Game against those Russian agents constantly filtering down through the mountains, probing the borders of the British empire. But they had been outwitted by an empire greater than the Czars, and could not extend down to the warm waters of the Arabian Gulf through Afghanistan.

'I'm sure you chaps are doing a fine job,' the Colonel said. 'You just keep on holding the frontier against those Russians. Kill a few of them whenever you can.'

Like the Colonel, Dyer was an Anglo-Indian. He had been born in India of Irish parents and came from a wealthy family. Brewery people. He had been sent to school in Ireland then to Sandhurst. He was a good man, but not imaginative. The army discouraged such traits.

'I say, did you read *The Times* this morning? That bastard Tilak is suggesting a bandh against Their Highnesses. I would have him flogged. Yes, a good thrashing would teach him his place.' He drank greedily. 'What are you people doing about him?'

'Just keeping an eye on his activities.'

'Well, I'd flog him and throw him in jail for a few years.'

'We might yet do that. Are you dining?'

Over dinner, the Colonel managed to steer Dyer to talk about Richard. He was eager to have a first-hand account of his son's progress. He missed Richard, although they'd never been particularly close. The years in England had made Richard almost a stranger to his father. He hoped they could get leave at the same time, and shikar in Kumaon. Richard was popular and liked by his men and fellow-officers. Once he settled down, he would go far in the army. Throughout dinner Dyer drank whisky. He ate sparingly, and by the end of the meal he was unsteady on his feet. The Colonel guided him to an armchair, then wished him good night.

Dreams do shape desire. Those wispy events imagined in sleep and even when awake begin to take shape as the will hardens and forces them into reality. If God is the dream, then God becomes real; if wealth is the dream, then wealth becomes real; if love is the dream, then love becomes real. Elizabeth cared neither for God nor wealth. Her daydreams, and those that flitted through her mind at night, were of romance.

She felt this evening held significance. All day she had felt herself a-tingle, as did the heroines in her novels when they realised they would meet the man they would love for ever. Elizabeth had always known that such a thing would happen to her. At eighteen, she desperately willed it for herself.

The Rushtons were neither military nor ICS, but well established in Bombay, as Mr Rushton was the managing director of a business. They lived not in a bungalow, but in a sizeable house set with its face to the sea. A long gravel drive led up to the brilliantly lit porch, and Elizabeth saw that the other guests had already arrived. Mary ayah had delayed her too long.

Sarah Rushton ran forward to embrace and kiss Elizabeth. She was no beauty, being plump with a mane of curly brown hair which tended to stand on end in the heat. They hugged and Sarah dragged her away to a corner, giggling with joy at seeing her friend again. Sarah always bubbled. She was a veritable fount of words, even at school, and constant fun.

'Oh Elizabeth, I'm so happy to see you. You *are* staying the night, aren't you?'

'I brought my things. I wouldn't have missed the chance to spend the night talking like we used to at school.'

'Getting ticked off by Miss Bannister!'

Elizabeth gave Sarah another peck on the cheek. 'I *have* missed you so. Bombay sounds so exciting from your letters.'

'And Calcutta so dull from yours. But still, it's not London. I do enjoy being a memsahib, don't you?'

'Not much. It's boring, to be honest. Now, who's this "interesting young man" you've stuck me with?'

116

'I wouldn't stick you with just *any* young man. He's the one I wrote to you about. He's a bit mysterious – the kind you like, though they always make me feel a bit silly, which I know I am. But then, you always could cope with a man far better than I could.'

'Where is he?' Elizabeth felt excited, looking around at the men and women crowding the room.

'You'll meet him soon enough. He'll be taking you into dinner. Now, come and meet the others.'

'I hope he'll like me.'

'Of course he will, silly. He'll fall in love with you!' Sarah always wished she could look like Elizabeth. Elizabeth had the height and the shape, and all that soft blonde hair. She looked as though butter wouldn't melt in her mouth, but Sarah suspected otherwise.

'Who's on my other side?'

'Oh, an old bore, I'm afraid. Mr Jenkins. He's retired ICS. Came down from Mount Abu for this tamasha.'

At dinner, Elizabeth scarcely noticed Mr Jenkins. Peter Bayley was a head taller than she, with broad shoulders and a tapered waist. He had an aristocratic face, finely chiselled, with dark hair, tightly curled. At first she could not help feeling gauche in the presence of such sophisticated appearance, exquisite manners and languid, even arrogant behaviour. She listened, wide-eyed like a schoolgirl, to his account of a life spent exploring Africa, Russia, and now India. He appeared to have no profession except adventure.

Even as she listened Elizabeth thought: Dear God, this is the man I have dreamt about all my life. I want him and I don't care how I get him. I want to stroke his face, kiss his mouth, feel his body against mine. He will banish all the dullness of my life.

Peter Bayley was aware of his effect on Elizabeth. She looked unaffected, wearing a frock that went out of fashion two years ago but at least did not conceal the luscious shape of her body, the candid desire in her eyes. Each time she leant towards him, he saw the hollow between her firm breasts and smelled the delicate

117

lavender scent. She was the only coolly sexual woman he had met in Bombay during the past month.

'I haven't seen you before in Bombay, Miss Creighton.' His hand very lightly brushed her thigh, and she didn't flinch.

'We're from Cal . . . cutta. I came here to see the celebrations for the Prince and Princess.'

'HRH will be tickled pink by all this.' Peter made it sound as if he were speaking familiarly of an old schoolfriend. 'It will be a bit of a bore for him, missing the pheasant season. But then, duty takes precedence.'

'Do you know the prince?'

'We've met,' he said casually. 'Mostly on shoots up in Scotland. But that's enough about him. Tell me about yourself.'

How swiftly the evening passed. She would have clung to him after dinner too, but once in the drawing-room, he remained with the men. Though when it came to saying good night he held her hand a moment longer than was strictly necessary and squeezed it.

'When do you return to Calcutta?'

'The day after tomorrow, I'm afraid. But won't you come there? You must!' She couldn't hide her desperation at this parting.

'With you there, I'll be over like a shot. I might even catch the same train.'

Elizabeth hummed and sang as she undressed. She felt afloat. She bounced into bed like a schoolgirl, and Sarah felt as happy as Elizabeth. She'd been certain they'd like each other.

'Now, tell me all. And I mean *all*.'

'Oh Sarah, I'm so happy,' Elizabeth began, knowing they wouldn't get much sleep that night, as there was so much to tell.

10

KIM AND Narain were eating a huge meal in the same
den as Ahmed Sait. The rows of tables and benches were
crowded with men. At last the smuggler belched, rose,
and washed his hands in a corner. He found a toothpick
and, watched by Kim, walked to the doorway. One of
his chamchas came and whispered to him. The message
was received with a curt nod.

'Come,' he called back. Kim and Narain finished their
meal, washed their hands and joined him on the charpoi
outside. The air was scented with food and wood smoke.
A hookah was lit by a chokra and passed to Ahmed Sait.
The water bubbled angrily and he passed it to Kim. 'So,
you wish to purchase guns?'

'One gun, Sait sahib. I am not rich enough to buy
more,' Kim said.

Ahmed's beard was red with henna. He was proud to
have made the haj to Mecca. Not once, but thrice. His
one ambition, apart from becoming rich, was to die in
Mecca. When it was time, he would make the final
pilgrimage and, God willing, would remain there for
ever. His profession did not interfere with his belief.
Other men tilled the land or owned shops; Ahmed Sait
owned dhows and smuggled. His family had done this
for centuries. Sometimes men died on these ventures,
but that was their kismet. He was stocky and square,
with strong arms and sharp eyes that missed nothing.
He knew Narain and did not believe Kim to be his
cousin-brother, but the lie did not worry him. If Kim
had the money, he could purchase a revolver.

'Even one is very costly,' Ahmed said. 'I go to great trouble to get them. They are like gold. If you should be found carrying a revolver by the British, you will end up in jail. Or hanged. Maybe you would mention whom you bought it from?'

'No, no,' said Narain. 'He is not like that, Sait sahib. He is my cousin-brother; he would not betray a man like you. I told him you'd cut his throat if he did. I will do it personally for you if he should betray you.' He sucked nervously on the hookah and held Ahmed's steady stare. 'You know me well, Sait sahib. I have a good reputation. I keep my mouth shut.' He added in English, 'Damned tight.'

'Sait sahib,' Kim said, 'I will tell you why I want this revolver. My uncle gave his daughter in marriage to this thakur. She was a pretty girl, and because of this my uncle did not have to pay a dowry to the thakur. However, what happened then was that the thakur tired of her and sent her back to my uncle. Now what kind of life does she have? Since no dowry was paid, my uncle cannot blame the thakur. But he wants his revenge, and I must fulfil it for him, as he is an old man. I have heard the thakur is now in Bombay, with one of his men.' Kim paused dramatically. 'They know I am in pursuit, and may even have purchased a revolver from you.'

Ahmed Sait beckoned the paan-wallah, bought a metai paan and stuffed it into his mouth. Kim and Narain took theirs. This paan-wallah was the best in Bombay. They chewed for a while in satisfied silence.

'It is possible.' Ahmed Sait believed in revenge. It kept people in check. India was full of revenge, blood-feuds, murders. Business for guns was always good. And if one Hindu killed another, that was no loss. 'What do they look like?'

'The thakur is an old man. He had a grey thadi that comes down to his chest. His chamcha is my age, and only wears a moustache.'

'It may be possible.' Ahmed Sait gave away nothing. 'How pretty?'

'Beautiful,' Kim said. 'She has skin the colour of wheat, it feels like silk. Her face is round and her lips are the colour of pomegranates. She has breasts that an acharya would carve, firm and high and round.'

'You have noted her well.'

'Only as a brother,' Kim said. 'She was married at twelve, and now at eighteen, with her life still ahead of her, she is an outcast. I must avenge her.'

'If I tell you where to find the thakur, it will make the revolver more expensive,' Ahmed Sait said. He plucked a number from the air. 'Two hundred rupees. Have you got it?'

'I can get it,' Kim said. 'I would not carry such a large sum on my person. We all know a man can get his throat cut for half that price.'

Ahmed Sait laughed. 'I like you.' He said this to every customer until he disliked the person. 'Obviously you are a man who appreciates women. Your descriptions of your cousin, and I mean no insult, have whetted my appetite. I have my fill going to the west with my cargo, but on the return journey I carry only guns and they cannot satisfy my lusts.'

He led them towards the Fort, stamping bow-legged through the small, narrow streets where the prostitutes were to be found. Kim accompanied Ahmed Sait out of politeness, but Narain was eager for a woman. As a single man he had no other means to sate his lust. Ahmed Sait's two chamchas followed, watching their master's back. Ahmed spoke of the problems of his profession and poured his complaints into Kim's ears. The navy harassed his dhows; other smugglers attacked his cargo on land; he had to bribe the police, and finding suitable buyers was always difficult and dangerous. All the world conspired against him.

In a lane crowded with patrolling men, they stopped at a smallish, narrow building. Within, women of all shapes and ages beckoned. Some were not women at all, but men dressed in saris with exaggerated breasts and painted faces. Ahmed led the way up a flight of narrow stairs, barely a shoulder's width, into a large, luxurious room. A plump old woman with drowsy eyes, gaudy in silk and jewellery, sat on a divan eating paan. A boy knelt behind her, preparing the leaf. She would reach back without looking, and he filled her palm. There was a group of musicians. One played a sitar, another a sarod, a third, tablas. Music filled the room, and the old woman was adrift on the sound. Sitting together near the musicians, just as rapt, were six young women. They were swathed in flowing, brightly coloured cotton saris, their hair decorated with flowers. They wore silver anklets and delicate glass bangles from wrist to elbow; their eyes were dark with kohl and their mouths touchingly red. They looked young and innocent and when they glanced up, they giggled. To Kim, they appeared to have come from various corners of India. Panjabis, a tribal girl, two or three from the south, a dark one from Cochin. They might have been kidnapped as children and sold to the old woman; a few would have been religiously initiated into their profession. A family would give their daughter in marriage to the goddess Yellama, and from that temple she would be sent to Bombay to sell her body for men's gratification. After a few years she would return to her family and village with her savings, and she would be accepted. By sanctifying prostitution, Hinduism saved the girl from the damnation of family and society. It understood the needs of men and the barter of women. But those poor girls who were kidnapped and not religiously trans-muted could never return to their homes.

The old woman beamed and her eyes sharpened. 'Bhito, Sait sahib, bhito,' and she patted the divan beside her.

Ahmed, Kim and Narain lowered themselves and leaned back against the bolsters. The boy handed them paan, but it was not of high quality. Ahmed, a valued customer, was also given a hookah and, like a prince, he stretched out, closed his eyes and sank into the evening raga played by the musicians.

'Which one?' Narain asked. 'I will take that fair one who keeps looking at you.'

'I don't have the need,' Kim said. Narain's eyebrows rose. 'I am betrothed.'

Almost against his will, he thought of Parvati, as he had done so often since he lost her. Her memory was like a veil at the back of his heart. He had merely to open it to see her in those shabby clothes. The thought of her alert, lovely face made his heart ache.

A few other men shuffled into the room and took their places, remaining separate. The girls paid no attention. That would come later, and anyway they had little choice in the matter.

Kim saw the girl Narain had pointed out glance frequently at him. Solemn eyes would flicker in his direction, linger a moment, then return to the musicians. He was not sure whether it was a professional ruse or genuine interest. She had an oval face with an upturned nose, rather similar in feature to his mythical cousin's.

The evening's entertainment continued with a woman who joined the musicians to sing gazuls. They were love songs, sung in Urdu, from the Mughal court. The woman had a clear, strong voice. The setting for this musical event did not surprise Kim. In Lucknow, he had attended performances by nautch girls in the old quarters, and had enjoyed the company of one on many a night.

When there was a lull in the proceedings, Ahmed Sait leant over to Kim. 'Which one will you choose?'

'Sait sahib, I am honoured that you allow me first choice, but I feel a man like you has the greater need. Those many days on the kala pani must have whetted your appetite.'

'No, no. The choice is yours,' Ahmed said. 'But don't take too long.'

'That one, then,' Kim pointed to the girl who had been watching him, and glanced apologetically at Narain who accepted it with grace. One body was like another.

Ahmed chose the youngest. He was an elderly man and needed rejuvenation. She was slim with a child's

123

face, and when the old woman signalled, the three women rose gracefully and came over smiling.

The room Kim entered with the girl was small, with curtains dividing it off from the passageway. There was a small divan on the floor, a low table and a lamp. The girl silently turned down the wick, lit incense and sat cross-legged on the divan. The incense mingled with her own perfume. She removed that part of her sari thrown over her shoulder to reveal large round breasts squeezed into a small choli.

'That isn't necessary,' Kim said. He sat beside her, waiting for the others to finish. He still had work to do. 'Where are you from?'

The girl accepted the rejection with a shrug. 'Near Benares.' She touched his arm gently, then his face. 'You look kind and you are very handsome. Mostly only ugly men come here and they always choose me because I have a fair complexion. Do you like it?'

'Yes.' Her colour was important to her. It made her popular. 'Do you miss your family?'

'Very much,' she said. 'I had brothers and sisters once. I was stolen and I can't run away. Some girls do try, but they are caught and beaten and sold to Ahmed Sait. God knows what happens to them. We never hear from them again.' Suddenly she looked frightened. 'I did not mean that. Sait sahib is a very kind man.'

'I am no friend of his,' Kim said.

She sighed. 'I must learn to guard my tongue. I get carried away too easily. What is your name?'

'Kim.'

'Keem,' she repeated. 'I am Lakshmi. My father was a wheel-maker. I suppose he is still alive. I miss them all so much. The village was small, near the Ganges . . .'

As he listened, Kim saw the lost child rise to the surface of the woman. Life had become a nightmare; she would remain here until death, never to awaken. He thought too of villages and rivers and another woman who lived in fear. Was she another Lakshmi escaping her master?

He touched her arm. 'I could help you return to your village, if you wish.'

She laughed and gently pinched his cheeks. 'You are young and brave, and there is nothing I would like more. But it is too dangerous for you, wasting your life on one such as I.' Shyly, she leant across and placed her lips delicately on Kim's cheek. 'I dream, sometimes, not often, that I shall have a husband one day. Someone like you. He appears in my dreams and we return to my village. But then, those are just dreams.'

'I will help you as soon as I have finished my work here,' Kim said, and got up. He still had to find Parvati before he could rescue this girl.

'What do you know of Ahmed Sait?'

'Very little. He does business with Durga amah.' She sat and watched him for a whole minute. 'Do you really mean it?'

'Yes. Now I must go, but in a few days I will return and we can talk further. Find out how you are guarded, who the men are and so on. I will bring money, too.' He stopped before stepping out of the cell. 'But I am not the husband you look for.'

'I understand. But why are you helping me? I am only a prostitute.'

'You are alone and afraid. And I wish to help.'

Having spent an appropriate time in privacy, they emerged. The musicians softly plied a night raga which filled the listeners with melancholy. Narain sat contentedly by the old woman and they waited a while for Ahmed Sait to emerge before they could leave the establishment. It was nearly dawn and the streets were deserted as they made their way back towards his den.

'Bring the money tomorrow,' Sait said, 'and you will get the revolver, three bullets and the information you need on the thakur. I know where he is staying.'

When Kim awoke near midday, damp with heat, Narain was still asleep. Isaac Newton was sitting in the same pose Kim had seen him in on the first day. Instead of diamonds there were scraps of papers and crazed drawings. His brow was furrowed in contemplation. Kim sat by in silence.

'This invention is the most problematical,' Newton sighed finally. 'If a wire can carry click-clicks, it should be able to carry a voice. The only solution is that, instead of speaking in Hindi, we should learn to speak in click-clicks. But that isn't my intention. Now. What is it you want, Kim?'

'Paisa. Two hundred rupees. It will pay for information about the men I am seeking.'

'But the Colonel sahib wants you to give up this search and look for other mischief-makers.'

'They will lead me to others,' Kim said. How strange, he thought. Once more the Colonel wants me to forget about these men. It is true that Anil Ray stabbed a policeman. Of that crime he is guilty. But these two men haunt me.

Newton was in a quandary. He had relayed the command, but Kim persisted. He hated damn quandaries, but he hadn't the authority to command Kim.

'Ah, you will have to sign a chitty for the money. The Colonel sahib always makes me give him chits in duplicate before he repays my expenses. It takes so long too, and I'm but a poor man, and the sarkar doesn't understand these things.' He took a cheap notebook from the table and wrote carefully in pencil. 'Received for expenses pertaining to the purchase of information as to the whereabouts of two mischief making individuals, the sum of Rs200 (two hundred only) from Mr Isaac Newton.' He read it and copied it twice over. 'Sign all three.'

Kim signed and Newton counted out the money twice before handing it over. Kim too counted it, for it was a large sum to be carrying on his person. He hid the coins inside his kurta and left Newton grappling with his invention. He found his way easily back to Ahmed Sait's haunt, but he had to wait an hour before Ahmed came for his afternoon breakfast. He was in a jovial mood and insisted Kim join him for the meal.

'You have the money?'

'Yes. You have the revolver?'

'It will be brought.' He signalled to his chamcha, who immediately slid out of the room. 'The thakur you look for is staying in a lodging house by the grain merchant Amar Singh, outside Crawford Market. The house is run by a Tamil family called Gopalan. They are dark people; you can easily recognise them. The thakur has a room at the back. You are pleased?'

'We shall see,' Kim said, and by the time they had finished the meal, the chamcha had returned with a small bag of rice.

Ahmed took the sack, hefted it and passed it to Kim. He thrust his hand through the rice and felt for the revolver.

'I want to examine it before I hand over the money.'

'There is a small room at the back.'

'No. I don't want to have an accident. Here.'

'You are wise not to trust me,' Ahmed said with a brief laugh. 'I most probably would have been tempted to cut your throat. But I'm also a man of my word. It is safe for you to take it out here. These are all my people.'

Kim drew out the black revolver. It was a British army Webley; well-oiled and cared for. There were three rounds in the chambers. He spun the chamber and pulled the trigger. The gun worked. Kim handed the money to Ahmed. He passed it to his chamcha who counted the money thrice before agreeing that it was indeed two hundred rupees.

'If you need any more weapons, remember Ahmed Sait. Salaam.'

Kim did not want to carry the revolver on his person, so he returned to Isaac Newton's and left it under his pillow. Narain still slept, exhausted.

Crawford Market was Bombay's belly. It hummed with noise and movement. Here, in a huge hall with an iron roof, and a central fountain designed by Lockwood Kipling, Bombay fed itself. The interior was cool and moist, and the fresh fruits and vegetables laid out in

127

such abundance made the air sing with their sweet odours. Mangoes, plantains, apples, watermelons, nungus, coconut, jack fruit, red chillies, green chillies, tomatoes, beans. The abundance of the land overflowed here. Their smell mingled with fresh fish. The ground was littered with discarded fruit and vegetables, while above sparrows and crows hungrily eyed the feast. Kim threaded his way through the countless stalls, pushing past housewives and servants bargaining vociferously with the stall-holders.

By the east entrance to the market was the grain merchant Amar Singh, and behind him a small, modest building. A board proclaimed in English: The Excellent Madurai Hotel. In front, cows and pi-dogs scavenged the plantain leaves for left-over food. Ahmed Sait's information was correct, so far.

Kim sat on the bottom step of a dye merchant's shop opposite. The air within vibrated with colour. The powdered dye dazzled and mesmerised the eye with open sacks of reds, greens, indigoes, blues, pinks, yellows, oranges. A round woman in a purple sari, with eyes black as grapes, presided over this sumptuous palette. She wore heavy gold studs in her nose and gold cubes that enlarged the lobes of her ears.

'Ahre, coolie. What do you think this is? The station waiting-room? How will my customers enter if you sit your fat self on my step? Chulo, chulo.'

'Maharani,' Kim said, 'a woman of such beauty should be gracious towards a tired stranger like me. I travelled to Bombay only because I heard tell of the glorious beauty of its women. Truly you are a Padmini and I can see now why men talk of Bombay women's beauty. If I should be fortunate to sit at your feet for a while, that alone will have made my journey worthwhile. If I could but touch your hand and kiss those red lips, my heart would sing out for joy.'

'You are a badmash indeed,' the woman laughed. 'Sit, sit. But at least make space for my customers. Where are you from?'

'The city of Lahore, Maharani. A truly wondrous place, but the women are as cold as the winter winds that come down from the mountains.'

'Did you come here only to gaze on the women?'

'Only? To gaze on a woman's beauty is like looking at the sunrise above Badrinath. It is to watch the seas caress the sands and turn them into the colours you see at Kanyakumari. But I also came to see the Kaiser-i-Hind's son.'

'He will arrive tomorrow. Tilak sahib has called for a bandh, but I cannot afford to close my shop, even for one day. We are small people, poor. We have to pay for our goods, pay taxes, rent, buy clothes and feed ourselves. Grand men like him say bandh kharo. Bandh.' She looked neither poor nor underfed; she was like a rani in her comfort.

'Tilak sahib wishes to rid us of the Angrezi. A bandh would register our protest at the Kaiser-i-Hind's son's visit.'

'The Angrezi at least bring us peace. They let us get on with our business. What shall we do with this swaraj Tilak offers us? Eat it?'

A customer interrupted and Kim moved to the top step, where it was cooler. The air tickled his nose. Later they continued their conversation, and the topics ranged from the price of dyes to local gossip. She was Maharati and disapproved of the Madrasi across the lane who owned the hotel.

'He has become very rich,' she said, taking a pinch of snuff. She offered some to Kim from a small gold box, but he refused. 'And even richer now, because people have come to see the tamasha tomorrow.'

'Why begrudge him his success?' asked Kim. As he himself placed little value on either money or possessions, he could not understand envy.

'He should stay where he was born. Open his hotel there, not here in my town.'

Kim sighed. Tilak's call for swaraj really was too optimistic. Freedom would require a concerted effort, and if they could not live together in harmony even on a Bombay lane, what chance had Tilak of uniting all India against the Angrezi? It was a dream that would never happen. Ever.

'Where can I purchase a lathi?' he asked.

She directed him to a lumber merchant on the corner. The freshly cut wood still held the sweet smell of sap. Kim chose a sturdy cashew cane about his own height, paid for it and returned to his seat. The woman watched him twirl it like a baton.

'Who are you looking for? And don't talk to me of my beauty again, young man. You are watching that hotel.'

'Two men,' Kim admitted, flexing his fingers around the cane, causing it to twirl over itself. Gradually it became a dazzling blur at the end of his arm, then suddenly stopped.

'Where did you learn kalaripayyatu?'

'From a guru called Kutty. I met him in Lucknow and offered him prayers, and he taught me his art.' He twirled the weapon again. It was called a kethi kayeri. He could rain blows down on an opponent at the rate of three a second, and knew the sixty-four points of the human body called kulumarmams. If he should hit any of these vulnerable parts, he could maim or even kill a man.

Kim saw her look at him now with new respect. His skill in the martial arts made him dangerous.

Kim had come across Kutty one summer holiday. Kutty had been a small, muscular man, supple and as graceful as a dancer, but who moved with the rolling arrogance of a prince. He had been summoned from Malabar by the Nawab of Oudh to teach his children the martial skills of fighting with swords, bare-handed, and with the kethi kayeri and the cheruvedi (a much shorter and more lethal stick). As Kim watched, he knew he had to learn these skills. Kutty accepted him as a chela, and Kim undertook the harsh regimen of disciplining his body, his mind and his soul. Each morning they performed puja to the fierce mother goddess Bhadrakali, then meditated. Only when the mind was purified did Kutty teach the acrobatic art of combat. He could leap and twirl and hurtle through the air like a magician. Swords and sticks thrusting and cutting the air around him missed by inches. Gradually Kim perfected the art, and at the end of the year received from his guru the special therapeutic massage that made his body more supple and powerful.

'You too could learn these skills,' Kim said. 'Did not one queen, having mastered these arts, fight alongside her husband in battle?'

'I am too lazy,' she said. 'But . . . to be supple again would be most sensual.' She fluttered her eyes at Kim, and he smiled back with a look full of promises. She would indeed be a woman to give him pleasure. He would take it later.

At dusk, she rose and lit the lamps. Above her cushion was a statue of Lord Ganesh. She performed her evening prayers before settling down again. Kim watched the shadows gather in the street. He could not see the faces. The lamps were lit in the Excellent Madurai Hotel, but the guests' rooms remained dark.

'I shall spend the night in the hotel,' Kim said, and the woman's eyes flashed disappointment. She had aroused herself for the conquest, and now had to be content to see Kim slip across the street into the hotel. She sighed; it had been some time now. Her husband, a weak, scrawny man, was incapable of satisfying her sexual appetites.

'But I will return soon,' he added, and saw her look of satisfaction.

Gopalan was a bare-chested Brahmin who wore his thread like a shield. His forehead was smeared with the three horizontal lines of a Shivite. He looked haughtily down a thin, pinched nose at Kim. He did have a room free, though it would cost him eight annas. Kim tried to bargain him down, but Gopalan was a mean and impatient man.

'Take it or get out,' he ordered.

131

Kim paid for the room at the rear, and handed over another anna for an evening meal. The two men had yet to make an appearance, so he asked the chokra serving the food whether they would return.

'Sometimes they don't come in until midnight,' he said, 'and I have to wake up and let them in. Even then they do not even give me baksheesh. They talk very little.'

The hotel was similar to Newton's house. Kim's room was above the central courtyard and adjacent to the locked room of the two men. Kim settled himself to wait at the window in the dark. He looked up at the clear sky. Every star was visible, the universe unending. The lights of the city blurred the edges of the great cosmic dome. Below, in the courtyard, he watched the chokra hurry about his tasks, constantly lashed by Gopalan's scalding tongue. The man loved his voice, it went on and on. The chokra now scrubbed the utensils with coconut husk and sand, often pausing to wipe his face, as though he wept.

Kim felt compassion for him. The boy had survived yet another day of petty cruelty. Cruelties abounded for him, for the prostitute, for Parvati wherever she slept this night, for Anil Ray, for countless others. All those small, unnecessary cruelties that could make life unbearable. It was not the cruelty of gunshot and sword, but these tiny cuts inflicted on the souls of children, men, women, beasts. There was no cure, no balm for them. They learnt to live with them. If not, they would die.

Kim dozed. He dreamt again. Of friends and companions, the smoky clearing, their disappearance. He now saw a well not far from where he stood and heard cries and moans, hollow and vibrating, coming from within. Slowly he moved towards it, forcing himself to place one exhausted foot in front of the other. He didn't want to see what called him from the depths, but he knew he could not escape it. A bloodied hand rose up, its fingers like talons, stripped of flesh, to hold the edge of the stone. Kim wanted to run away, but his body was pinned down and he felt a force from behind, pushing. He looked around but he was alone. Another hand, a woman's now, equally bloodied, stretched up to grasp at the air . . .

He started awake and wiped the sweat from his face. He shook as if with fever, then gradually calmed. He didn't want to remember, didn't want to sleep again and look on such spectres. He looked out and saw the soft glow of light thin as twine falling from the next room.

Cautiously he opened his door and crept along the balcony until he was beneath their window. He listened and heard the rustle of movement, the click of metal on metal, but no voices. He removed his turban and raised his head until his eye aligned with the thin crack of light that escaped beneath the shutter. At first he saw only the back of one man, broad and bent. The man moved and Kim saw his companion, a man with a hard, handsome face. He was concentrating on dismantling a revolver and cleaning it. His movements were practised and expert. The older man settled back on his bedding with a sigh. He had a pleasant, fatherly face, but hard watchful eyes, which began to close as he spoke. 'Aim carefully tomorrow, Madan, . . . Your bullet is worth a fortune to us if it hits the mark.'

The younger man grunted, reassembled the revolver and loaded every chamber. He tucked the gun under his pillow and blew out the lamp.

11

SHE BARELY saw the spectacle unfolding before her, except as another dream. The real became fantasy; the hard blue sea a glaring mirror. Figures moved, slowly, hurriedly, manipulated by the Viceroy who sat a few feet away. She looked towards the city and at the huge crowds awaiting the arrival of Their Highnesses. The press of bodies was stifling; bearers waving fans of peacock feathers only stirred the heat. The grey destroyer, diminishing the sea with its proximity, hurt the eye, but she stared out at it. The Viceroy's barge began its slow return to the shore and the massed regimental bands struck up a rousing march. Princes, glittering in silks and jewels, sat in rows beside provincial governors bedecked with orders and medals. At the last moment Lord Curzon wasn't present, to everyone's surprise. He had decided to receive Their Highnesses and the new Viceroy, Lord Minto, in the Governor's residence. The gesture of a true Viceroy.

Elizabeth sat with the ladies, pressed against Sarah Rushton. The air was heady with lavender water and talcum powder. Elizabeth searched the faces of the spectators, longing to see Peter Bayley. The men were sitting some distance away and she could not pick out the handsome face, the gleaming hair. Those distinctive features dissolved into the blur of pink and red, dissolved too in her dreams of him.

He was fresh as an English peach, perspiration lay like dew on his skin. Elizabeth decided he was unsullied, though she knew it could not last. There was corruption

134

in the air, a voracious need to spoil. A lump of sugar left out for a minute would be consumed by ants, a dress by moths, a piece of furniture by white ants, men and women by the heat and the boredom. Peter still had about him the bloom of something freshly grown.

Even over the past few weeks, she felt that India had begun to change her. She had returned eager and unspoilt, but now felt that innocence seeping out of her. India aroused mysterious passions in her, long unrecognised in an English climate, an English civilisation. The veneer was paper-thin, tearing already. The passions weren't sexual, although she was aware of such a force as she searched for Peter Bayley's face, but more far-reaching. She felt their simmering violence within her: anger, love, disillusionment, hate. She loved the India of childhood memory, and it was that innocence which was escaping now.

Here we sit, she thought, blindly staring out to sea, atop a grand howdah, while below us is the beast we do not want to see. That's why we remain distant, not wanting to be corrupted by the evil of the poor, the deformity of the beggars, the beauty of the people and the land. Our deliberate blindness is our corruption. I just don't know how I can survive this existence again. The child I was, was ignorant, oblivious. I am not.

'Can you see him?' Sarah asked.

'Who?'

'Mr Bayley. He might be in the welcome party.'

'Oh, is he here?'

Elizabeth turned away in feigned uninterest from the row of faces and gazed out at the approaching barge. Normally, passengers disembarked down the gangplank at one of the quays, but Lord Curzon, with his sense of history, wanted the Prince of Wales to arrive in the splendour of a barge, setting foot on Indian soil in the traditional manner, before the ports existed.

Kim saw none of the tamasha. He had slept briefly and woke before dawn to trot through the deserted streets to Isaac Newton's house. It took some time to rouse the household. When Newton came down, Kim told him of the two men and asked him to send a message to the Colonel immediately. He would wait for the police in the Excellent Madurai Hotel.

'I will go myself,' Newton said, and hurried off to don his suit.

By the time Kim returned to the hotel, dawn was streaking the sky with pale pink sunlight and people were stirring. Bullock carts and hand carts lined the narrow lanes, filled with produce for Crawford Market. The hotel chokra was awake, lighting the hamam for guests' baths. He sniffled drowsily. Kim stayed outside, waiting for the police to arrive. Gradually the street filled and the shops began to open. Here and there, one or two remained shut, obeying Tilak's call for a bandh. The dye woman, however, greeting him cheerily, took down her shutters and settled herself for the day. Soon the heat began to beat down and Kim drew back into the shade, fretting for the Colonel's police.

The two men had emerged from the hotel, the elder carrying a bag of vegetables, and then Kim had to follow them. They walked at a leisurely pace, not talking to one another. Kim kept close to them as the crowds began to build up. The British firms and stores and banks were closed for the public holiday, so by now it was impossible to tell whether the Indian shops had obeyed the bandh or the holiday. People were dressed in their finest, as if they had received a personal invitation to meet Their Highnesses. Fathers and mothers carried children, and the children, scrubbed and clean, eyes round with excitement, carried small flags. They began waving them and the air fluttered with reds, whites and blues. Police constables lined the route for the procession and a Eurasian superintendent was stationed every fifty yards. Occasionally a mounted English police officer patrolled the street.

The two men continued their stroll, stopping to buy paan, stopping to buy cigarettes, stopping for tea. They knew they had plenty of time and had already chosen their position. Kim kept them in sight, bobbing along with the flow of people, patiently waiting for his quarry to settle. Instead of heading towards Apollo Bunder, they turned off into Church Gate Street. Here the crowd was settling down to see the Viceroy and Their Highnesses drive past in an open carriage. People crowded balconies, boys climbed trees. The men stopped at a corner leading off into a narrow gully and squatted with their backs to the wall. Kim moved some distance away and settled on his haunches. The two men looked unconcerned, the older one striking up a conversation with his neighbour, the younger remaining aloof and impassive, with the bag of wilting vegetables by his side. One hand rested on it constantly. Kim noticed his sweating face. He was already visualising his act of violence, watching the bullet find its target. An hour passed. Kim could not be sure whether this was their appointed position for the assassination, or whether they would suddenly move on.

'Kim sahib!'

Standing a few feet away, watching him with a cheerful smile, was the Marwari from the train. His writer was with him, still thin, still worried. The Marwari wore a loose pink shirt and European-style trousers. He ambled over to Kim as though he were a long-lost acquaintance.

'What are you doing here?' Kim asked.

'All business is bandh kharo. I have come to watch the procession. And how is your business getting on?' His dark eyes were expressionless, though his face was still wreathed in smiles.

'It is good.' Kim remained squatting in the shade, looking up at the Marwari. It was possible that his presence was a coincidence. But was it? Kim looked over at the two men. They hadn't moved. The younger one looked half asleep. The Marwari's presence unsettled Kim, for the man did not seem surprised to run into him. Was it he who had informed Newton about Parvati?

'Why are you standing here?'

'My business, cloth merchants as I told you, is just beyond that archway.' He dusted off a step with his handkerchief, spread it out, and slowly lowered his bulk. 'Will you have some tea with me?' Before Kim could refuse, the Marwari took out a couple of coins, handed them to his writer, and sent him scurrying off to find a vendor.

In the distance they heard the soft murmur of the crowd. The news that the Kaiser-i-Hind's son had set foot on Indian soil fanned through the people. They stirred, stood up, rippling like blown wheat. With all the speeches and ceremonies, it would be some time before the procession began the drive to the Governor's residence. The tea came and Kim noticed the writer had not brought one for himself. He insisted that the man drink his.

'No, no,' the Marwari said. 'He will buy his own. Go.' The poor man turned back to the vendor, digging into his own depleted pocket.

'It's a nuisance, I say, this Prince of Wales's visit. Causes disruption to everything. And look at us fools. We crowd the streets to stare at the son of a foreign emperor. If we went about our own business, the British would know we no longer want them to rule us. We can rule ourselves, I say.'

'And what government would we have?'

'We would muddle through,' the Marwari said vaguely. 'Democracy as the British practise it. Elections, prime ministers, etcetera. We are treated like butchas now. Do this, do that, don't do this.'

'Then you should demonstrate in front of the Prince,' Kim said.

A British police inspector reined in his grey mare on the other side of the road. He sat regally straight, staring down at the quiet crowd. A topi shaded his eyes and he looked like a proud young warrior. One hand rested on his thigh. The brown leather of his gunbelt was lovingly polished and his boots gleamed.

'What, and get arrested and beaten up and God-knows-what-else? I am a coward. I cannot help my nature.' The fat Marwari chuckled good-naturedly, then continued, 'I am allowed to think and voice my opinions, am I not? So that is what I do. I hear that in London men stand on boxes in one Hyde Park and call their government all sorts of names. But if we were to do that, we would be called seditionists. Why are they not seditionists? That is a puzzle, is it not?'

'Yes. I agree we should be permitted to speak out. To keep thoughts suppressed is to destroy the true self. Words become like steam in a closed dekshi. Eventually it will explode. But they do not believe we can look after ourselves, and of course it is to their advantage for them to remain here. For ever.'

'In India there is no for ever. We are not a "for ever" people.' He rose and patted Kim's shoulder. 'I must return to my shop.'

'But it is closed.'

'One doesn't know what mischief can happen when there is a bandh. I will take my leave then, Kim sahib. Perhaps we shall meet again one day.'

He tossed away the clay cup and beckoned the writer to follow. Kim watched them melt into the crowds. He turned to look for the two men. They had gone.

The brief escape from her thoughts, the relief from pain, was but an illusion for Mohini. She knew the spectacle was a mere distraction. She clapped and laughed with a child's delight at the sight of Prince George, though he was too distant to be seen clearly, or to be heard. It was the sense of occasion, the pomp of bands, soldiers, elephants and camels, that gave an illusion of normality. Alice was pleased to see the change in Mohini. She too ached for the girl's dilemma, the tragedy of a young life broken by an ancient tradition that could not change. Love did not exist, not in the conventional sense that she understood, between husband and wife, parent and child, man and god. Duty, an alien idea of discipline over emotion, suffocated everyone. The duty of the wife to the husband, the duty of the parent to the child. Like railway lines, duty guided the passage of people's lives. There could be no diversion except at tremendous emotional cost.

It was best that Mohini never saw Kim again. She could not destroy him with her wretched life, and escape was once more the only solution she could think of. But all escapes ended eventually; they had to. Roads, lives, all ended in cul-de-sacs. Death was the wall at the end which none could escape.

The Prince and Princess climbed into a carriage and the procession moved off. Mohini envied them their ordered lives, that they could be regal and be above such awful pain.

'Well, we'll have to sit and bake for a while longer before they open the pen,' said Alice. She put away her notebook and pencil and examined the dignitaries, praying she would not see a familiar face. She only saw a blur: princes, burra sahibs, memsahibs with parasols, here and there a suited Indian, a member of the legislative assembly or a businessman. Their dark faces stood out against the others.

But then Mohini saw a familiar face and nearly cried out in fright. She wanted to run, but didn't dare to move. A slim, elegantly dressed Indian wearing a silk suit was conversing with a companion. Their heads were bent close together. Mohini had recognised her husband, from the way he toyed with his gold-topped cane and the incline of his shoulders. There was coldness in the way he held himself, a man superior to the world, full of his own importance and intellect.

If he should but lift and turn his head, she would be discovered. He had legal rights to her, all rights. Her body, her mind, her life itself. She was his possession, as real as the cane he held in his hand. She dragged the end of her sari over her head and across her face, now feeling she was the only one he would look at.

'I must leave,' she whispered to Alice in blind panic.

'Is it your husband? Where is he?'

140

'Over there.' She didn't point. To her, his presence was everywhere.

'Get behind me and wait. The crowd will start moving soon and we'll get away by sticking with them.'

Eventually the police allowed the crowd to seep away. Alice caught hold of Mohini's hand and quickly they edged into the heart of the moving body of people. Mohini glanced back. Her husband was now looking around him with his accustomed regal air of ownership. They stayed deep within the crowd, drifting with them, using them to shield her from her husband. She saw him stroll with the others towards their own carriages. He climbed in and the gharri inched its way through the people and slowly moved out of sight.

'He's going.' Mohini felt her heart start to beat again.

They drooped with relief. Suddenly, a whisper swept like a fire through tinder wood.

'A shooting, a shooting. Mar, mar, mar.'

The crowd rustled, heads turning like a huge beast towards the rumour. They were not sure of the direction, but saw the sudden urgency of the British police officers. They ran here and there, issuing instructions. The people were driven back with lathis, as though they were to blame. Mohini and Alice were pushed and elbowed as those in front tried to escape the anger of the police.

Just as Kim crept up the stone steps, he heard the shot. It came from one floor above. From the street he heard the sudden silence of the crowd. He could not tell who had been shot. In the distance he could see the Viceroy's carriage. It had stopped and now was turning. He followed the averted faces of the crowd and looked directly down at the street. For a brief moment, all was chaos. Then he saw the grey mare and the empty saddle. Two police constables leant over the fallen British officer and Kim saw black blood spreading over his starched khaki shirt. He felt himself to blame for the young man's death, and yet, even as he looked on the face, he could not understand why they had killed him.

The Prince, the Viceroy, they were more important, their lives worth more than that of a police officer. Yet the men had been paid for killing him. Kim knew it was not a mistake. The two men had deliberately selected their place, and the target, both decisions made by their paymaster. It had taken him some time to find them. He'd asked a dozen people before one of the children pointed back down the gully to a door. It was unlocked and Kim had just begun his cautious search when the shot was fired.

'Jaldi, jaldi,' he heard the whisper and the clatter of chapals as the two men ran down the stairs. He drew back into a doorway, holding his cane ready. The older man came first, half stumbling. Behind, in less haste, came his young companion. He was pushing the revolver back into the vegetable bag.

Kim lunged at the older man, striking him in the belly. The surprise and shock, the pain of the blow too, stopped the man. He staggered and fell, choking for breath. Kim knew he had made a mistake. The younger one stopped and stepped back. The light was behind him and Kim could discern only a dark silhouette, but he knew the man was already struggling to get the revolver out of the bag. Kim lunged at his feet, striking his ankle twice with the lathi. He heard the bone crack. The man howled and hopped back again. Kim followed him up, jumping forward to within striking distance. He knew where to hit to paralyse him. As he lifted the cane the revolver came free and the man fired. In mid-stroke, Kim felt a tremendous blow and a strange sensation of flying as he fell back.

He felt his life escaping from his body, and struggled to hold on to it. With a huge effort, he searched his kurta and drew out the pebble. 'Ram . . . Ram . . .' he whispered to it, and then slumped against the wall.

The man whimpered. His ankle was shattered. He wanted to punish Kim further for causing such excruciating pain. He lifted the gun to fire again.

'Go. Hurry. The police.'

The older man struggled to his feet, gasping for breath and, as he stepped over Kim, he kicked him. The man with the shattered ankle tucked the revolver into the waistband of his pi-jama and hobbled awkwardly down the stairs after his companion.

12

It was night and an eerie silence hung over Church Gate Street. The unease could be felt all over Bombay, especially here in the city centre, where most of the Europeans lived. The police had immediately imposed a curfew and the streets were deserted. A lone gharri stood at the corner, hidden in the shadows. The only sound was the jingle of the horse's bit and the click of hooves as it shifted its position.

The Colonel had been waiting half an hour. Normally, he would have become extremely impatient. He valued punctuality, though he never expected it from an Indian. This night, he remained sunk in thought, unaware of time passing. Indeed, he wished it would turn back. The last hours had scarred him; the lines around his mouth had deepened.

Dear God, how does one live with the death of an innocent man? It was not meant to be; I calculated every detail with care, even allowing for bungling. But then, events can take on a life of their own, slipping out of control. In their own strange way, they fulfil the final purpose, but at a cost far higher than I had calculated for. But to keep control I have to bear the burden and live with death. Forgive me, forgive me.

The gharri door suddenly opened, framing a man's head and shoulders. He had come so quietly that even though the Colonel was expecting him he had heard no sound. No doubt his damned driver was asleep. The man salaam'd.

'You bloody fool,' the Colonel whispered. 'You killed

a British policeman and one of my own men will be dead by morning. Your orders were to wound, not to murder.'

'Colonel sahib,' the elderly man spoke calmly; the Colonel's anger failed to move him, 'we fired, but it was a bad gun. If you had given us one of yours, we would have been more accurate.'

'I couldn't risk having you picked up with an Army-issue weapon. Have you thrown it away?'

'Yes. As for your man, how were we to know that he was employed by you, as we are? He attacked us. He would have killed us both. I was struck in the belly and Madan's ankle was broken. He will never walk normally again. He had to shoot.'

'Can Madan travel?'

'He will have to.'

'Go then. Hurry, but be careful. The police are searching for you. Wait until you hear from me again.'

The man faded away swiftly, making no sound. The Colonel had little fear that he would be caught. Even if he were captured, he would not utter a word. He was completely loyal to the Colonel.

The next morning, the Colonel accompanied the Commissioner of Bombay Police to a special audience with the new Viceroy, Lord Minto. Both men were ushered into Minto's temporary office in the Governor's residence.

Lord Minto was a complete contrast to Curzon. He was a much older man, of less elegant build. He had little ambition other than to enjoy the office of Viceroy at a princely salary. Again, unlike Curzon, he had no private wealth. He had come directly from serving as Governor-General of Canada; his had been an undistinguished term. Minto, ignorant of the complexities of India, intended to depend entirely on his staff to guide him. As long as India remained peaceful during his term of office, he would be content.

The Colonel bowed and shook hands with Lord Minto, assessing him as a bluff and genial man. The Police Commissioner, a grave man a few years younger than the Colonel, gave a report on the murder of the police officer. They were scouring the city, had clamped down on everything, but they had yet to trace the assassins.

'Colonel, you're experienced in these matters.' Lord Minto turned to him when the Police Commissioner fell silent, embarrassed at his failure. 'What do you suggest?'

The Colonel spent a little time considering the implications of the question. The Viceroy didn't expect him to reply immediately, and waited patiently.

'I don't believe in panic measures, Your Excellency, but there are several men such as Tilak inciting people to violence. Some have already turned to such tactics to redress their imagined grievance over the Bengal partition. These two assassins could well have been Bengalis or seditionists, given to extremes. For all we know, that bullet might have been meant for you. I feel that we should be granted additional powers in order to nip the situation in the bud before it gets out of hand, as it did back in 'fifty-seven.'

'Of course. I shall take your advice in this matter. What er . . . powers did you have in mind?'

'For certain elements, arrest without warrant, imprisonment without trial. If necessary, hanging. This would make our task much easier, and once we get rid of these trouble-makers we can rescind those laws. Eventually. But we must show them that *we* rule India, and that murders such as this will never be tolerated by us.'

13

'YOU ARE two peoples. One I have known well and amongst them I have spent many happy years of my life. I shall always remember them as friendly, decent, compassionate, open to intellectual debate, believing deeply in the freedom of the individual. Those people believe that men and women have an inalienable right to freedom of thought and expression, as well as the right to express these thoughts. They are vigorous in the protection of these freedoms, and the greatness of those people has been based on such simple and universal ideas. Those people have produced some of the greatest thinkers and philosophers, not merely of our age, but of mankind. To read Shakespeare, Macaulay, Dickens, Scott, Swift, is to understand a race who stride this world as colossi. You cannot open a page and not be stirred by the ideas these men have propounded. Their words and ideas are immortal and they have opened the windows of the minds of human beings everywhere . . .'

'Mr Ray, we are not in the Houses of Parliament,' the judge interrupted in a bored tone. 'I must remind you that this is a court of law. You are on trial for attempting to murder a police officer.'

'I am well aware of where I am, but not with whom I am dealing,' Anil Ray said.

He stood manacled below the judge, John Spencer. He had changed a great deal since that fateful afternoon in the mountains where he had been picnicking with his uncle. Months had passed, and waiting in various mean cells for trial had profoundly altered him. Prison turns

147

ordinary men into philosophers or criminals; it can shape them in ways they do not understand. Another man might have become a philosopher, accepting the cruelty of fate and musing on its perversity.

But Anil Ray raged. He had paced and cursed and fought, and was beaten. Prisons confer power on one group of men over another group of men, and in an Indian prison, low caste over high, the poor over a scattering of the rich. It is a place where centuries of revenge can be brooded upon. Anil Ray had wounded an Englishman with intent to murder, and was punished accordingly. He was now heavily bearded and wore a grubby kurta and pi-jama. There was a badly-healed break in his nose, making him look fierce. The glitter in his eyes chilled Spencer, and he wanted to draw back from such a display of hatred. It was as visible as a placard around the man's neck. And yet, when he closed his eyes and listened to the voice, it evoked green hills and cloudy skies, with cool drizzle against the cheeks and softly flowing rivers. He could hear the muted chink of china cups in drawing-rooms. It reminded him of languid summer afternoons, standing at long-leg boundary near a small pavilion set under ancient elms.

A breeze riffled the papers on the judge's desk as though in search of a particular piece of evidence. The clerk, sitting one step below and dressed in a suit and turban, yawned and sat contemplative, waiting for the trial to continue. He did not care to listen to Anil Ray, for in his words were the seeds of destruction. He could not look on Anil Ray either.

John Spencer too wanted the whole business to come swiftly to an end. He had planned to get home quickly for tiffin, then a short nap, and then he could spend the late afternoon and evening playing cricket. He looked out through the huge windows; the sky was clear and the mountains faded into the blue air. Sparrows flew in to sit on the beams and peep down, chirruping. Police constables leaned against the wall, waiting to finish with one prisoner and bring in the next. Every now and then a peon would stroll in with an armful of files, confer with the clerks and then leave. There was a casual air to the proceedings, boredom. Spencer had no jury; he alone passed judgment and sentence. His career had been made in the judiciary and, with care, he could become a High Court judge in Bombay or Calcutta. At one time, administration and justice had been dispensed by the same man, but in the last decade these things had changed and a young man coming out from England had to choose one or the other.

Behind the railings, some distance from the bench, sat Anil Ray's father. He had come alone to witness his brilliant son defend himself. He kept his gaze fixed on the floor, his shoulders now had a permanent slump. He could not understand what his son was talking about. He knew it sounded dangerous, but it was too late to heed that now. Too many police witnesses had seen Anil stab Inspector Goode; it was only a matter of passing sentence.

Deputy Inspector Goode had already been called to give his account of the incident. There had been shown just cause; all charges against him had been dismissed. Mr Ray could not understand the words 'just cause' either. How could a shooting-stick be mistaken for a rifle? There was a great difference between them. But, to the English mind, the mistake was understandable. A witness, not brought to court, had reported that one of the men had indeed carried a rifle.

'Sir, I believe I do have the right to summation.'

'This is not exactly an English court of law, Mr Ray,' John Spencer said. He was a few years older than Anil Ray, and his gown was a size too large. He could have been an amusing figure, wrapped in the black cloak, except for the authority vested in his small frame. Wearily he waved Anil Ray to continue, and sat back, daydreaming of playing cricket, not in Simla, but at Lord's.

'Sir, have you ever read the novel, *Dr Jekyll and Mr Hyde*?'

149

'Mr Ray, I presume this reference has a direct bearing on your case?'

'Yes.'

'In which case, I have.'

'Then you will understand my analogy all the better. In the novel we have a good, kind man, incapable of doing wrong. I believe he could be called an English gentleman, though once I felt the word "English" was quite superfluous. A gentleman was axiomatically English.' He noted Spencer's thin, satisfied smile. 'But there is a darker side to this man's nature, a black, frightening side. We see it not only in his change of character, but in the very house he inhabits. Mr Hyde slips furtively in and out of the rear of the house, which is shabby and run-down, compared to the front, which looks out on a charming London street. For me, the Englishman can be personified by these twin characters existing within the physical and mental frame of one individual. The dark side, the one which lacks humanity, lacks compassion and understanding of another race, the one who treats the other race as his inferiors, who shuns its company and who forgets the laws of justice and democracy which he practises at home, is the Englishman who rules this land. Fools like me believed that certain ideas could cross oceans. I was mistaken. They undergo a change in their passage, and what arrives on these shores are thousands of Mr Hydes, tyrants who exile us from our own land on mere whim, imprison us because we want freedom from tyranny, execute us for our rage, suppress our thoughts with impunity. We must, and by this I mean as a people, rise up, holding swords, jezails, cudgels, and drive you from the land. We must call upon God for slaughter of a kind that has never been seen before . . .'

'Mr Ray, your tongue will put the rope around your neck,' Spencer spoke incisively, losing his daydream in the face of such hatred. 'The court no longer has time to listen to your ravings. I shall pass sentence.' He peered down at the clerk, who waited with his pen poised. 'There are certain extenuating circumstances in the case.

You were provoked. However, this does not excuse the act of violence you committed against an English police officer in the execution of his duty.'

'He murdered my uncle. Do you call that duty?' Anil Ray shouted.

'I can pass sentence without you standing in front of me. The next time you interrupt me, you will be escorted back to the cells. Where was I?'

'. . . an English police officer in the execution of his duty,' the clerk read back the line.

'Yes. However, your closing . . . should I call it, summation, or tirade . . . I found disturbing. Your call for violence is certainly an act of sedition against the Crown, the King, and his people. Under the circumstances, I have no alternative but to sentence you to twenty years in prison for your attempted murder of Deputy Inspector Goode. And a further four years for sedition.'

'An act of violence equals an act of words. Even though the words were spoken in a court of law.'

'The place has no bearing. Only the person to whom you spoke them, and I am a representative of the government, Mr Ray. I have been lenient, having taken account of your background and education. Others would have received a harsher punishment.'

'Why should you be lenient with me, then? Because I speak English with an accent soothing to your Angrezi ears? I am *Indian*. I am *manacled*. I insist that you treat me as you would another of my people.'

'I have passed sentence.' Spencer rose. 'Court is adjourned.'

'Do you believe you will be superior to us for ever?' Anil shouted at the departing Spencer. 'We will rise up and defeat you, even as the Japanese nation defeated the Russian empire.'

'But you are not Japanese, Mr Ray.'

Anil Ray was led out of the small courtroom, his arms held by a constable on either side. He saw his father, so small and frail now, alone and bereft as if his son had already passed away and now only looked back at him from another world. Anil took a step towards him, but the constables jerked him back.

'I want to receive my father's darshan before I go to prison.'

They understood and allowed him to step one pace away from them. He prostrated himself on the cold floor and placed his head on his father's feet, feeling his father's touch on his head and then his hands lifting him up. He stood a head and shoulders above the older man and was momentarily shocked at the difference in their height. He had always thought himself smaller than his father. Most of his life he had looked up at him, and had forgotten the changes that occur.

'How is Amah?'

'Crying. She cannot stop. But that must not be your burden. I am very proud of what you have done, and what you said to the Englishman. We do not speak of these things, but hold them inside and suffer.'

'I only increased my punishment,' Anil said bitterly. 'But I could not control myself. Twenty-four years!' It was not the passage of time, but the passing of people. He would suffer the loss of his grieving mother, the further disintegration in his father. He embraced his father and smelt the familiar odours that remain in the memory; he placed his lips against his father's forehead.

'It will pass swiftly. I will visit regularly.'

'Two exiles, one after the other. One to their land, the other to their prison. What chance have I of ever leading a normal life now? I cannot control the passion and they will watch and wait for me. I feel like Bolingbroke saying goodbye to his father when Richard sent him into exile. Except that I shall not be wandering in a foreign clime, but pacing an island of earth, as small as a grave.'

'I do not know this Bolingbroke of whom you speak,' his father said. 'But, if he was sent away, then I know how his father felt. Pain and an overwhelming sadness. I hate them now for what they have done to our family.'

Anil felt an impatient tug from the constable and released his father from his embrace. His father wept,

152

but Anil had no tears; his eyes were dry as pebbles on a long-dried river bed. He did not look back as he walked to the waiting bullock cart. A bamboo cage, the height of a man, had been constructed on the platform. Within were other prisoners, thieves and murderers. Anil was pushed in. The door was locked and, escorted by policemen, the cart slowly made its way out of the compound.

He did not look at his fellow travellers, all wretched and silent, but out at the streets, the sun, the clouds, the mountains fading into the distance. He had journeyed far over the past months, yet he had remained in the same town. People stared back at him, small boys followed the cart, wide-eyed with awe. One or two poked sticks through the openings.

The man next to Anil growled. It was only a rumble in his chest, but the boys heard it and hesitated. The mere sound threatened, but when Anil turned to him, he could see the glint of humour in the man's eyes. His turban was Rajput, wildly coloured in reds and golds, perched on his head like a nest of serpents, and his moustache curled up his cheeks. His dress was shabby but none could mistake the pride in his face. He turned and spat out paan at one boy, striking him on the front of his shirt. That sent him roaring with laughter as the boy, crying, scampered away.

'That will teach the little chuthia to poke a stick at Man Singh. You have heard of me? No. But I have heard of Anil Ray, the man who opened his mouth too wide in front of the Angrezi magistrate and got another four years. Stupid man, I say to myself. Why doesn't he keep his mouth shut? See, when I am in front of the magistrate I always keep my mouth gup chup. "Yes sahib, no sahib." And they think I'm a jolly good fellow.' He chuckled.

'Who is this jolly good fellow then?' Anil asked.

'Man Singh is Man Singh.' He smiled to reveal broken teeth with many gaps. His face was thin, sharply chiselled, and his right eye was afflicted by a squint. He addressed the man next to him. 'Tell him who Man Singh is, fool.'

'Man Singh,' his companion respectfully addressed Anil, 'is the most terrible dacoit in all of India. He has killed countless numbers . . .'

'Countless!' Man Singh interrupted. 'What does that mean, fool? It can mean big numbers, or it can mean nothing. Tell him how many. No, I will. Over one hundred have I killed.' Then he whispered, his breath sour with paan and spittle. 'But they can prove nothing. People disappear from this earth, never to be found. So how did they catch me this time? All because of this woman I took away. A nice partridge, plump and pretty. But I made a mistake. Her husband is a landlord, a small one. He gets very angry and reports to the police. The thanedar sahib usually leaves me alone, but this time an Angrezi says all this nonsense must stop. The woman remembers where I took her and she leads them to my hideout. Never trust women, my friend. I gave her a good time, but because I sent her home she gets very angry with me. But how could I have kept her?'

'That would be difficult,' Anil agreed. 'How many years did they give you?'

'All my life. Man Singh is to die in jail, so they think. But one day Man Singh will vanish back into the hills!'

'But for the kidnap of one woman, a life sentence is extreme.'

'Obviously you are a big fool. Or rich. Do you expect justice in this world? People like us expect none.' He shrugged. 'Ah, but there are those other things. I am a terrible miscreant, they tell me. But, ahre, what else can one do?'

They fell silent then. The cart was not taking them to the lock-up, but to the railway station. It stopped in the shade. Constables with rifles now joined their colleagues and two of them carried a long chain. They opened the door and the first man to climb out was locked to one end of the chain. It was run through all their handcuffed hands and locked to the last man. Anil found his companion was Man Singh. They were made to squat by the roadside and wait to board the train. When people passed them, Anil noticed how they drew away, as if an invisible barrier had been erected between them.

'Where are they taking us?' Anil asked.

'Tihar Gaol.'

Anil was not yet so hardened that he didn't feel despair at the mention of the name. Naïvely, he'd believed he would remain in the lock-up, for he still did not consider himself a common criminal, but rather one who'd fallen from grace by chance. Somehow, he would be rescued, and all his privileges would be restored. Eton and Oxford were now only a dream, and he wondered whether he had ever really been there. Was this just a nightmare, from which he would waken, sitting in front of a fire, sherry in hand, surrounded by good companions?

Lost in thought, weeping inside for his carefree youth when the only concern was to lead a life of comfort, Anil did not notice the approach of two police officers. They moved purposefully towards the convicts – Anil had yet to understand this transformation, for he still considered himself a prisoner, prisoner of circumstance, of karma, that had taken charge of his life and would not let him escape. The officers stopped in the shade and the constables saluted them. Anil only noted their presence when he saw the polished black shoes and the creased khaki trousers blocking his vision.

'Stand up, stand up,' a constable ordered, prodding the convicts with his lathi as though they were cattle dozing in the shade.

The convicts stood and Anil saw Deputy Inspector Goode. He had seen him once in court, giving evidence, and didn't need to study him any further. Eyes shut, he could recall the trim of the red moustache, the hollow of the eyes, the jut of the ears. Goode had glanced at him only once. He had spoken firmly, quietly, and had sealed Anil's fate.

Even as Goode closed the door of imprisonment on Anil, he opened another for him. A sense of purpose in a life which had lost its purpose. Although he could not yet admit it to himself, Anil knew that one day he would kill Deputy Inspector Goode. He accepted the thought as easily as he had once accepted his good fortune. Goode's voice intruded on his reverie.

'I heard about your speech. That was foolish of you, provoking the magistrate.' There might have been a note of sympathy in Goode's voice. Anil remained silent and watchful. 'Well, I haven't come to say I'm sorry but it was an honest mistake. I do regret it. But you should have controlled yourself, man. What did they teach you at Eton and Oxford? Didn't they teach you a little good, old-fashioned English discipline?' He turned to his companion, a young Englishman, ruddy from the sun. 'It was an honest mistake,' he explained, immediately receiving a sympathetic murmur.

Anil fixed him with a baleful glare. 'What do you expect from me, Mr Goode? Absolution? I am a prisoner, not a priest. You murdered my uncle. You must, if we are going to be biblical, expect retribution.'

'Don't make idle threats, Mr Ray. You will only regret them later. Again, I will say I am sorry for what has occurred, but I was only carrying out my duty.'

The sincerity of Goode's tone did not move Anil Ray. He was impervious to compassion now, though he did slightly change his opinion of the policeman before him. He had thought him to be a sinister man, but now, looking at the round face creased in concern, he saw only a simple and stolid one. This same idiot call of duty would no doubt see the murder of other men.

Goode had meant every word he spoke. He had carried out his duty and was now appalled at the consequences of what he still considered to be the right action. He had been engaged in protecting the life of the Viceroy of India when he'd shot Anil Ray's uncle, and had nearly been murdered by Ray as a result. Still, like most other Europeans in India, Goode did not believe in the English education of the native. He was aware that, in fact, he and Ray had led similar lives, a thought which made him uneasy. He too had been sent to school in England (a minor public school, though, certainly not Eton) and had returned to serve India in the police service, as his father had. Goode's only ambition was to follow in his father's footsteps, to retire as a Deputy Inspector General of Police, and he hoped this unfortunate accident wouldn't put a blot on his career.

'I will, with your permission, visit you in Tihar Gaol, Mr Ray. It won't be a pleasant experience, but I hope my continued interest will make it easier.'

'Would it make a difference if I refused?'

'Not much.'

Goode spun on his heel and both Englishmen strolled back up the slope.

'What were you talking about?' Man Singh asked, when they settled back in the shade. He looked at Anil with fresh interest. 'You said something that made him angry, and you speak English like he does.'

'I told him he was a chuthia,' said Anil.

'And did you tell him you will kill him one day?'

'How did you know that?'

'It showed in your eyes. I am a dacoit. If I didn't understand the signs men give, I would not have stayed alive this long.' He hunched closer to Anil. 'When I escape from Tihar, I will take you with me. I like you.'

14

EVEN AS Kim lay dying in the gloomy stairwell, his blood spreading in a pool which had already begun to drip down the stairs, his last whisper was heard. It carried through the air more swiftly than a flash of lightning to the ears of the dwarf, and before the words had even faded from Kim's lips, he sensed the presence at his side. The loneliness at the moment of death faded, and the agonising sensation around his heart melted away.

'Why is it that when I grant boons to men, they always have to make use of them? It is fortunate for you that it isn't your dharma to die just yet, so I came when you called. Ahre, men are ingenious in inventing so many new ways of killing each other. Even we cannot keep pace with them all.'

Kim felt him place his child-sized hand on the wound. There was a brief flash of pain as the bullet was drawn out, and then he experienced a deep sense of exhaustion.

'You didn't come when I called before.'

'I have the power to perform miracles, and you ask me to mend a lover's heart? You should not waste the boon. Broken hearts abound in this world. If I was summoned for each heart-ache I'd never have a moment's peace.'

'Is she still alive?' The dwarf had begun to fade, transparency was spreading over the small body, so that Kim could see only dimly the large glowing eyes and grey beard.

'Yes.'

'Where can I find her?'

If the dwarf had answered, Kim did not hear him. Exhaustion crept over him. He had seen such magic before, in the bazaar, and wondered where the dwarf had gone. After all, he was only the size of a child. He fell asleep then, and the slumber lasted for many, many days.

When Kim woke the first face he saw was the Colonel's. He felt comforted by the sight, and when he tried to move his hand, he found that the Colonel was holding it tightly. A look of sheer relief came over the Colonel's face, and for the first time that Kim could remember, the smile was warm.

'I prayed you would live, Kim. Dr Malcolm keeps mumbling about a miracle. I'm sure it is. You must rest now. You lost a great deal of blood.' And then, very softly, as Kim began to fall back into that deep sleep, he heard the Colonel whisper, 'I am sorry.'

He did not know why the Colonel had apologised to him. It seemed he was sorry that Kim had been wounded, sorry to see him in a hospital bed. Yet it had been said in a deeply personal way, as though the blame lay with him.

The Colonel was back at his bedside two days later, looking down at Kim cheerfully.

'I think it would be best if I have you transferred to Calcutta for a while. I can keep an eye on you better there. You should work at a desk in the department until you are fully recovered.'

Kim had lost a great deal of weight during his fever, and his skin was an unhealthy chalky hue. It would take at least two months for him to regain his strength and his old spirit. He wanted to protest, but he still felt too tired and listless. The Colonel's determination was a force he couldn't fight yet.

'All right. But, tell me, sir, why weren't the police sent? I asked Newton to carry the message.'

'They were, but in all that crowd they were delayed. I sent a sergeant and five constables, but they couldn't find you when they reached that hotel. It was too late.'

The Colonel spoke the truth. He had wanted to prevent Kim following his men, but there again lay a miscalculation. To round up the sergeant and constables had wasted precious time. He placed his hand affectionately on Kim's shoulder. 'I'm sorry about all this.'

Again Kim wondered at the personal tone, but gave it no further thought.

'I don't understand why they killed the police officer. What was his name?'

'Fraser. A young Scot. He was single, thank God for small mercies.'

'But why? If they had waited, they could have killed the Prince.'

'Who knows? Panic, probably, lost their nerve at the enormity of the plan. But the end result is that we have been given greater powers to control the situation. Lord Minto has recommended arrests without warrant and imprisonment without trial for seditionists and anarchists. He realises the importance of such legislation at the moment. There are a few rotten apples in the barrel who would like us to leave India. We shall never leave, but we must pick them out. The majority of Indians, ninety-nine per cent, want us here.' The Colonel reached into his waistcoat pocket and drew out Kim's pebble. 'They found this clutched in your fist. It was nearly impossible to open your hand.'

Kim took it. Its colour had changed from old gold to a dull, greenish brass. He slipped it into his pi-jama pocket.

'A miracle, a bloody miracle. When I tell people you are my walking miracle, no one believes me. Damn fools. They should know better.' Dr Edward Malcolm was a small, thin man with a cigarette permanently stuck in the corner of his mouth. Nicotine had stained the edges of his peppery moustache dark yellow, and two fingers of his right hand a deep brown. Each time one cigarette was finished, he would toss it over his shoulder like a fire cracker and light another. Kim had seen these cigarettes fall on people, dogs, Persian carpets. This time they were falling on polished teak floors. 'Here you are, alive and well, sitting in this bloody gymkhana club eating lunch, when by rights you should be dead. You were shot at point-blank range, I tell them. The scar from the bullet is still on your chest, but I was damned if I could find the bloody bullet. It went in just above your heart; I know it did. I've seen men with far less serious wounds than you succumb to their injuries. Good God, I've operated on soldiers in the Khyber. I've known many men die from the slug from an old jezail. Yet here you are. A miracle. Magic, in fact. You still won't tell me how it happened, I suppose?'

Kim shook his head and continued to pick at his mutton cutlet, boiled potatoes and peas. He had heard his companion re-telling the story of his recovery countless times. He liked the doctor for his irreverent, unconforming attitude even though the man had been mentioned in dispatches for his service on the Frontier. Dr Malcolm was Kim's only real friend in the Calcutta European community. The doctor reminded Kim of a busy gnome because the end of his nose turned up sharply, giving him a mischievous look. He also had an unusual knowledge of an India beyond the high walls of this club and European life. He was researching for, and intending to write, a book on sexual practices in India, and constantly regaled Kim with his stories.

'It's all delightfully lewd and absolutely filthy,' he told Kim the first time, though he would go on to repeat himself often on the subject. 'The native takes his sex with curry, y'know. Up in the Khyber they've perfected the art of pederasty to an exquisite level. They shove cucumbers up the you-know-where to ease the passage of the you-know-what. We have so much to *learn* on that special subject. Good God, there can't be an educated Englishman who hasn't bent over in love for one of his heroes, but they don't get much fun out of it. Then, down in the south, they use a cucumber – or is it a

161

watermelon, it's in my notes somewhere – to push up between a nubile young thing's legs. Ah, I wish I were that cucumber at times. I suppose they must enlarge the hole enough to drive a bloody train through. Must be a frightful loose fit.' The doctor was convinced that his was a book which would do well.

Every Tuesday, the doctor took Kim to the club for lunch. Malcolm, who had recently been transferred from Bombay, had been delighted to encounter his young patient once more. They would sit in the high-ceilinged dining-room with huge french windows opening out on the well-watered bowling green. Beyond were the rattan walls of the tennis courts. The atmosphere in the dining-room was imposing. Men and women sat at distantly separated tables, gleaming with white linen and silver, speaking to each other in hushed tones. Lone Englishmen sat with *The Times*, lowering it only when a bearer served them. All the bearers were very ancient and moved at the speed of snails.

Kim wore a European suit now. Though it was made of cotton, it felt heavy and constricting, and the collar and tie choked him. He found the tie the most uncomfortable part and had never understood its purpose. He thought the whole costume totally inappropriate for the weather, but the Colonel said that it was expected of him if he was to work in the office. Even the Indian clerks wore western dress and Kim, superior to them, couldn't let the side down. Kim felt he had gone back in time to that dreadful school in Lucknow. The doctor's voice broke into his train of thought.

'Well, must be off. I now have the delightful pleasure of examining young Mrs Martin's heat rash! What a body that woman has. Her breasts would make a bloody goddess look flat-chested. But when she opens her mouth she's such a damned bore. Gives herself the most frightful airs and graces. A barmaid, I'd say, who's done well for herself. My finger applied up the right place should keep her calm. Might even cure her rash.'

162

He tossed a cigarette over his shoulder as they left the dining-room; it fell into a retired brigadier's soup. But he was reading *The Tatler*, and failed to notice.

'Same time next week?'

'Certainly,' Kim replied dutifully.

Kim's office was in the Writers' Building. He had a cubbyhole where he was expected to read and analyse reports sent in from every district and province in the country. Reports were filed on all natives involved in one political movement or another. Kim was surprised at the thoroughness with which people were investigated, their words carefully recorded and filed away. Though many of the reports were written by district collectors, deputy magistrates and lower-echelon policemen, the Colonel also had a network of informers scattered all over the country. Kim had long since memorised every agent's name, code and location.

He owed his present position as a junior officer in the political and secret department to the Colonel. He received a salary of three hundred and fifteen rupees a month, and could, by the time of his retirement, expect to be earning seven hundred rupees. However, he would not be able to rise to the level of a private secretary because he did not have the precious initials ICS after his name. Only an Englishman could claim the privilege of being an Indian Civil Servant. The exams were held annually in London and, though they were open to Indian candidates, the cost of travelling was prohibitive. The Congress Party wanted the examination venue and requirements changed so that all eligible Indians could sit it. The most important government jobs were reserved for ICS men. The Colonel wasn't ICS, but the Army were considered the aristocrats of the European community.

Today, the file lying open on Kim's desk reported on the recent split in the Congress Party. The Congress Party only met once a year, to elect a president. For the rest of the time, the members went their separate ways. This year the meeting had been in Surat. Kim had once

163

passed through this small town on the west coast about two hundred miles north of Bombay. It stood squeezed between a long high wall and the broad expanse of the Tapti river. There was one main road, which led from the railway station through the town to the castle built by Khudawand Khan in the sixteenth century. The rest of the town was a warren of narrow, twisting lanes and small houses.

Once it had been a city contested by the greatest powers on earth. Huge armies had fought desperately to gain possession of Surat, a prime toe-hold on India, but now all that had been forgotten; the city lay dreaming in the heat of its once great glory. Surat was a beautiful woman, long forgotten by her suitors, who had found other attractions. First the Portuguese had fought to win her, then the Mughals under Akbar's land army won her back; his descendants lost her again to the Portuguese, who lost her in turn to the Dutch. And the Dutch to the British. The cost of these wars was chiselled in marble headstones in the cemeteries. Even in death, the nations lay within their boundaries – Portuguese, Mughal, Dutch, British. Their names and deeds had faded, brushed smooth by India's eternity.

Kim thought Surat a strange venue for the annual meeting of the Congress Party. Rooms had been scarce, as the Congressmen flowed in from all parts of the country. Many sheltered in small tent cities outside the fort walls. A huge pandal had been erected nearby, and the agenda was busy with daily meetings and speeches.

Kim skimmed through the file until he came to a personal report on the proceedings.

Surat, December 1907. On the first day, I was astounded at the reception given to Gokhale. The narrow streets were packed with Congress supporters and the road was covered in rose petals and discarded garlands. It took him two hours to pass from the railway station to the pandal, and the air rang with cries of 'Bande

Mataram' (Hail to the Mother India). This show of unity is totally false, for otherwise, most of the Congressmen remain strictly in the company of their own kind. Madrasis stick with Madrasis, Bengalis with Bengalis, Maharattas with Maharattas, and so forth. They seldom mingle; they seldom even converse with each other. Naturally one could put this down to the difficulties of language, but most of these men are highly educated. They all speak English and have gained degrees from one university or another; some even abroad, Oxford or Cambridge. Yet they remain narrow in their attitudes and habits. Each group has brought their own cooks so that they will not have to taste the delicacies of another province, nor have to sit with those of a different caste. The Madras Brahmins are the worst; arrogant, priggish and very superior.

Of course this makes my task much easier. As per instructions, my followers and I will create a major disturbance when it comes to voting for the president. I have seen your policemen stationed about the ground, ready to come to my aid at the signal.

We spend our days listening to interminable speeches. How they love to listen to themselves talk and talk and talk. One of them can speak for four hours, even five, and end up saying very little. They speak the language of Gladstone and Macaulay more elegantly than either ever could, and they take pride in flourishes of the English language. All, that is, except Tilak, a short, round, cocky man His speech was full of fire and brimstone against the British I could not help but feel the unease among all the listeners. Congressmen, after all, only wish to win themselves comfortable jobs in city legislatures. They have no higher ambitions. Not one of them is able to represent the people of this country as one, villager with landlord, Madrasi with Kashmiri. Congress is a party for the élite, not the masses. India is too vast, too diverse. And if someone did rise up to make India one nation, it would always be a fragile unity.

On the final day of the meeting, the party planned to vote for their new president, one Reshbehari Ghose. My own nomination for this post was Somnath Joshi, a Maharatta Brahmin and supposedly a Tilak supporter. I had around fifty men in my camp, all of whom I had brought with me at great cost [this was underlined]. When the voting began, my candidate's name was accepted, but then, as we had planned, he stepped down in favour of Tilak. Naturally, Gokhale's supporters refused to accept this move. My men immediately began to shout and insist on Tilak, which in turn incensed Gokhale's supporters. When my men began to start a fight, our opponents responded. It was at this point that I signalled for the police to calm the situation down and, as you know, a number of arrests were made, including that of Tilak. Soon, when the situation is calmer, I will place myself in a position to take over the leadership of the party. [signed] Daddaji.

Kim had read in that morning's edition of *The Statesman* that Tilak had been found guilty of sedition and had been committed to Mandalay Prison in Burma, where the British had once exiled the last Mughal, Bahadhur Shah, for seven years. An editorial praised the government's action of imprisoning a very dangerous man.

'Why was it necessary to split Congress?' Kim asked the Colonel that evening as they rode along in the Colonel's gharri. The Colonel had found Kim a place to stay quite near him, and it was his habit, if he didn't work too late, to offer Kim a lift. 'It would have happened anyway, sooner or later.'

'Yes, that is so. I'm only surprised that it lasted as long as it did. It could have gone on even longer. We thought the time was ripe to help along its demise. Besides, we needed to arrest Tilak, and his speech was certainly extremely seditious. Don't you agree?'

'He's been saying much the same thing for some years. You could have had him arrested long ago.'

'It wasn't the right time then. Now that he's locked up, I'm pretty sure this stupid call for swaraj will die a natural death.'

But even as he spoke, the Colonel could sense Kim's unease. He wanted to reassure him that what he was doing was for the greater good of the country. He did not pursue a personal vendetta against Tilak or any of the others. He only opposed their betrayal of the Crown. He would have explained this, except that for the first time he felt a degree of uncertainty. Every European he knew had expressed delight at Tilak's arrest. In fact, most thought he should have been hanged. But Kim seemed to be mutely sympathetic. Admittedly, he hadn't actually praised Tilak or any of the other seditionists, but neither had he directly condemned them. The Colonel had to remind himself that Kim was not quite what he looked, a handsome young Englishman. Deep down he was an Indian. He was valued by the department for his ability to disappear into India, and India, the Colonel knew, absorbed all those who came too close to her. Every invader had disappeared into that smothering embrace, leaving only a little evidence of their existence, in a palace or a tomb, or a pair of blue eyes set in a dark face. And even the English had nearly succumbed. It was only by distancing themselves that they had managed to keep their identity, to keep power.

So the Colonel decided to say little to Kim now. He would watch and wait for Kim to make his choice. It might take years, it might be sooner, but he had no doubt that Kim was nearing the point when a man had to choose sides.

And when that time came, he wondered what he should do with Kim.

The Colonel stopped the gharri, still some distance from their usual place of parting.

'I have to go on into town. Richard's on leave next

week, we're planning a shikar.' He didn't invite Kim to join them. Despite his deep affection for the man, Kim was still an employee.

Kim took off his tie and stood by the roadside undecided about what to do next. He felt freer; the act of stepping out of the gharri was like stepping out of a glass case, though he knew from the glances of passing Indians that they saw nothing different about this young sahib. He didn't want to return 'home'. 'Home' was a comfortable room in a bungalow owned by an ICS man and his wife. They had no children and certainly didn't need a lodger, but the Colonel was a good friend, so they had opened a back room and furnished it with a bed, an almirah and a huge chest-of-drawers. Since he had few possessions, Kim's clothes virtually disappeared into this ocean of space. He ate his meals with the couple and often joined them for a peg or two out on the lawn. He listened to their chatter but, in spite of their congenial company, he still felt an immense loneliness.

But the loneliness emanated from them. It was infectious. Never before had Kim felt lonely in India. There had always been such a lot to see and do, so many friends, so much gossip to exchange. He belonged to no particular family or caste or sect; his sense of belonging came from something far beyond that. It came from India herself, and was so strong that he never questioned it.

After a while he looked up and saw three paper kites. It was the kite season, an annual event in Calcutta which filled every Indian boy with passion. Once, long ago, Kim too had fought great battles up in the sky, had chased 'cut' kites over roof-tops, across maidans and down gullies. He too had patiently coated the long string with a mix of manja and crushed glass so that it would cut another string like a knife. It took great skill and patience to master a kite fight. You had to know when to pull away, when to dive, when to saw through the opponent's string.

He watched the battle overhead, feeling drawn to the source of it. He wondered whether English boys played with kites as well, or whether they had different toys. It was a fairly long walk; obviously these boys had let out a great length of string. The kites were all of different colours, one green and gold, another red, a third blue and white, all sporting short tails. A long-tailed kite could get itself caught in another's string and be pulled down. He turned off the avenue into the narrow lanes. Life exploded and swirled around him in these dim passageways, crowded in on both sides by mud and brick huts, men, women, children, goats, pi-dogs, cows. He moved easily through the lanes, yet couldn't help being aware of the deference and amazement of the local people at his presence. Old men immediately stood up, women covered their faces, children gazed at him with round eyes, dogs bared their teeth.

He found the kite flyers. They were perched on the frail roofs of the huts a hundred yards apart. Each kite string was surrounded by twenty or so boys, the eldest about twelve years old, the youngest naked and still crawling. Each also had a special assistant who held the large bamboo spool of thread. None of the boys saw Kim. They were concentrating on the sky and the raging battle up there. The onlookers shouted encouragement to each champion, yet poised ready to sprint the moment that a kite was cut, to catch it. Unseen by both Kim and the kite flyers would be yet another hundred boys, watching and waiting. They all wanted the prize, and the moment a kite was cut, they would spurt off like bullets on the chase.

'Sahib hai,' called a youth, suddenly noticing Kim, who was climbing onto one roof. Every boy fell silent. Even the kite flyer lost his concentration. The boys were bare-chested and wore loincloths. Their slim bodies were brown and supple and their hair shone with oil.

'Ahre, kite flyer,' Kim said. 'If you keep on staring at me for long, you will lose your kite. See, he is already diving down on you. You must dive too.'

'Yes, sahib.' He turned his attention back to the kite, but Kim's presence had unsettled him and the others. They backed away to stare at him in wonder.

Kim would have liked to take the string from the boy, and had he asked he would have been given it. Quietly and without protest. Yet, in Kim's own boyhood, if he had been asked, he would have replied, 'Chulo ji, chulo' for what red-blooded boy would give up his kite in mid-fight? Instead, Kim passively watched the fight, still feeling their eyes on him. Suddenly the string of the kite on his roof was cut and the kite rolled and drifted away. The boys hesitated only a second, then ran screaming, 'Cut! Cut!' They scrambled down from the roof and gave chase. The lane erupted with the swift darting of the boys and suddenly Kim found himself alone, except for the crawling baby, on the roof.

Dusk had fallen and lamps had been lit in the shops and homes, when Kim saw Nadir Shah squatting on the ground and Salim floating in the air. He hovered above a bazaar crowd and circled twice, like a silent kite. First he was on his back, then lazily, swimming in the air, he turned to float on his stomach and looked down on the people. They shifted uneasily, for his wide stare was unsettling and they couldn't understand how he managed to remain suspended for so long. As he approached the crowd, Kim heard again the familiar sound of Nadir Shah's rolling voice.

'I will tell you how to do this. It is not a trick, but magic. Any one of you could perform this if . . . and I say *if* . . . you made a journey deep into the Himalayas and performed all the tapas that I have performed for God to grant me this one boon. I spent years in all that ice and snow. Yes, I prayed constantly for fifteen whole years, and when God appeared to me at last I asked him for the power to perform this miracle. He came in the form of a sadhu, a young man full of vigour and strength. He took compassion on me and said, "Nadir Shah, because of your great faith in the power of the spirit, I

170

will grant you this one boon: to make men fly." See? I have but to raise my hand, and the boy rises.' Salim hovered up a foot or so. 'And I have but to lower it,' and Salim fell a foot, continuing to circle. 'As he moves he can look deep into your minds, too, and knows everything that you are thinking about. He knows the future, if you should dare to ask.'

Babur the bear growled and clapped his paws, while the monkeys Daniel and Aziz jumped up and down, chattering. Kim was delighted to see the old travelling companion, for the sight of Nadir Shah brought back strong memories of his beloved Parvati. He pushed his way through the crowd, who fell back to stand around Salim and gaze at him. Nadir Shah was squatting, but when he saw Kim, he immediately stood up.

'See, even the sahib has heard of us, and has travelled many miles to come and watch this miracle. I will stop the boy over the sahib so the sahib can attain his blessing. Salim! When you come over this great sahib, you will stop and bless him.'

Salim circled once and came to a gentle halt above Kim's head.

'Nadir Shah . . .' Kim began.

'See . . . see, the sahib even knows I am the great Nadir Shah. He will tell the other sahibs and they will all come to look upon this miracle. Baksheesh, sahib. Show them you are generous in your rewards and Allah will bless you.'

'It is true. Even I have heard of the great Nadir Shah.'

With a flourish Kim drew some money from his pocket and scattered it on the sheet. A few in the crowd followed suit, and then Nadir Shah brought Salim gently back to earth. The boy lay quite still for a moment or two, then sat up. He looked as mischievous as ever, though he had grown at least a foot taller. The crowd drifted away, though a few remained, as did Kim. They were curious to see what Kim would do next.

'Nadir Shah, don't you remember me?'

Respectfully, Nadir Shah stepped a foot closer to peer at Kim's face in the fading light. Salim too stared for a moment, then bent to scoop up the money.

'Sahib, I have travelled to many places and I meet many people. Forgive my poor memory.'

'I am Kim. Two years ago I travelled with you from Agra to Gwalior. I had a companion whom first I said was my brother, but then revealed to be the woman I love.'

'Ah!' Nadir Shah stared at Kim again, and then pulled Salim to look as well. They scrutinised him carefully. 'Yes, you do look like him, but in these clothes . . . it is difficult to tell, sahib.'

'How have you been?'

'We are well. And where is your woman?'

'I don't know. I lost her. In Bombay.'

Nadir Shah clucked sympathetically, but although he claimed to recognise Kim, Kim could feel his distance. He remained respectful, waiting for Kim to speak first, though Kim was the younger man. Salim too stood away, gathering up the animals and the familiar bundle of belongings.

'Where are you going from here?'

'We are returning to Delhi. It has been nearly nine months. It is time to go home.'

'And your other sons?'

'One died. In two years the other will be old enough to accompany us. We must take our leave now, sahib,' and, bowing respectfully, he and his son and their animals threaded their way down the lanes and were soon lost to sight.

Kim felt abandoned and stood irresolute before turning to make his own way home. He was grateful that his hosts had not waited up for him. Before he turned out the lamp, he took the pebble from his pocket. He had been watching it change colour again over the months, from that greenish brass to what it was now, the colour of mud, long dried. He understood now that it reflected the colours of his own spirit.

He always found it difficult to sleep comfortably on a bed, so he stretched out on the floor. The darkness closed in on him and the ceiling pressed down on his chest, making it impossible to breathe. He was isolated by the four walls and the tiled roof from the starry sky under which he'd spent most of his life.

15

ELIZABETH SAT in the garden with a novel open on her lap and the dogs beside her. Overhead, a blue and white kite drifted past unseen, and the distant excitement of boys running on the road went unheard.

She was staying at home alone out of choice. There was no lack of social life in Calcutta. The gaiety was almost frenetic, desperate. There were fêtes and fancy-dress parties, dinners and picnics, shikars and soirées. Reading societies, dramatic clubs. If she didn't want to attend one function, another always beckoned. This evening she was expected for dinner, but she was dreading it. There would be the same people from the night before, relating the same malicious gossip, all drinking too much warm wine. This life of false and frantic pleasure seemed to drain her like a leech. She yearned to escape back to England where the faces changed, the places changed. The only real excitement in her life would be Richard's leave next week.

The bearer, Abdul, crossed the lawn carrying a silver salver.

'A sahib has called, miss sahib.'

'Tell him the Colonel isn't home yet. Is the burra memsahib in?'

'He wishes to see miss sahib.'

She took the visiting card. Mr Peter Bayley. The curling name with flourishes on the 'y's so angered her that immediately she ripped the card in two.

'Tell him . . .'

What did he expect? That she would run out and

throw her arms around him, as though it had been only yesterday? At first she'd waited impatiently for him to come. The anticipation had kept her on edge for weeks. For days after her return from Bombay she hadn't gone out at all, in case he called; later on she left instructions with all the servants from the mali to Mary ayah to inform Bayley sahib that she was at such-and-such a place, and would he please call again. But the weeks had turned into months, and his promise to come to her had not been kept. Then her heart darkened, turned to despair. Some time ago she had written to Sarah Rushton, confessing her expectations and disappointments. She'd received a sympathetic reply: 'I told you he was a mystery. It seems, as far as I can discover, that he may have gone to Arabia. Father thinks he's a spy!'

And now he had arrived, with no warning, just at the point when she'd nearly forgotten all about him. But she hadn't, not completely. The memory of the dinner, of his sensual charm, had been hidden like a love-note tucked into a corner of her mind, and which now burst out as large as a novel.

'Ask the sahib . . . to wait. And ask him what he would like to drink.'

She dropped her book and raced through the back door of the bungalow. She looked frightful. It took her over half an hour of feverish activity to make herself presentable. She had absolutely nothing to wear, except that eau-de nil chiffon frock. It looked simple but elegant; she'd seen a drawing of Lady Grosvenor wearing one like it for informal entertaining.

'Mr Bayley!' She entered the room casually, and she felt her voice held just the right note of polite surprise and distance. She wished she hadn't torn up the card. It would have been more effective if she had had to read out his name. 'I'm sorry my father and my aunt are not at home.'

He stood, taller than she remembered. Slimmer too, and sunburnt. He had the wicked smile of a buccaneer, cheerful and bold. With the flick of an eye she felt herself undressed and stroked by that amused gaze. It was a pleasurable feeling. She held out her hand. He ignored it and came right up to kiss her on the cheek with all the intimacy of a lover. Not a peck, but a lingering caress. Abruptly, she pulled away.

'Has Abdul brought you a drink?' He held her hand now, and, not letting go, drew her to sit next to him. She had thought to take the most distant chair to emphasise her coolness.

'You're as beautiful as I remember.'

'I'm glad you have such a good memory. It's been some time.'

'Two years and nineteen days precisely.' This accuracy took her breath away. He held her hand intimately, palm to palm. Hers was damp.

'Where have you been all this time? I waited and waited for you. You never even wrote.'

'I'm not very good at composing letters. I had some business that took much longer than I expected, also a trip back to England. Then, an old friend invited me to go on safari in Africa which I just couldn't resist. I'd been there before and he needed someone who knew the ropes. But from there I came straight here, to you.'

'You make it sound as though you were only up in Simla.'

'Just a little further, but just as easy.' He was dressed in a cream silk shirt with a silk cravat and light blazer, all beautifully made. No native tailoring for him.

'How long will you be . . . staying in Calcutta?'

'I've taken a house on Strand Road.'

'Strand Road!' It was the most elegant avenue in Calcutta. At the top stood the Governor's residence. 'Which house?'

'Sir William Beckett's. He's on home leave for a year and has rented it to me. Not a bad place.'

'Why, it's huge. It has a ballroom, a tennis court and goodness knows how many reception rooms and bedrooms.' The very size of Sir William Beckett's beautiful home stole her breath again. 'Are you living there alone?'

'What do you think?' He looked at her over his whisky and soda.

'So you've brought your wife and five children?'

'I left them all behind, my dear.' For a moment he looked deadly serious and Elizabeth's heart lurched. She could feel it bobbing up and down like an apple in a tub. Then he laughed out loud. 'I'm all alone there, silly.' He squeezed her hand. 'I would like you to come and visit me.'

'Are you giving a party? How exciting.'

'Yes, but you will be my only guest, dear . . . Elizabeth. I've been thinking about you constantly, ever since we met. I could hardly wait to come back to Calcutta. Will you visit me?'

'I . . . I . . .'

'Oh, I nearly forgot.' He drew a small packet from his coat pocket. It was wrapped in a square of brilliant silk. When she took hold of it, she felt the hard outlines of a box.

'What is it?'

'Open it. You'll see.'

She unwrapped the silk carefully. Inside lay a blue box of the kind made for jewellery, and though she had been given various presents before by her admirers, she was suddenly sure none would match the splendour of what lay inside this pretty casket. She hesitated, then undid the clasp. On a small satin cushion lay a gold brooch, set with several diamonds, in the form of a peacock. It had emerald eyes and was so exquisite that she felt afraid to remove it from the box.

'Here, let me do it for you.' Peter opened the pin and tenderly fixed it just above her left breast. He used both hands and unconsciously caressed the firm outline. He seemed unaware of her sudden blush, for he sat back and smiled. 'It looks perfect on you.'

'Peter! It's absolutely lovely. You shouldn't have. I've never been given anything so beautiful in my life.'

'The moment I saw it, I had a vision of your exquisite face before me, and I knew I had to get it for you.' He pulled out a gold hunter, its case intricately chased. 'I have to go now, my dear. I wasn't sure whether you would be at home, and stupidly I promised to dine with Harry Redgrave.'

Still holding her hand, which she no longer wanted him ever to release, he strolled out onto the porch. A coal-black gharri with two equally dark horses stood waiting in the drive. The footmen and driver also wore black, with white sashes.

'Is that Sir William's carriage?'

'No. I hired it for myself.' He kissed her once more. Not on the cheek, but lower down, his lips lingering at the corner of her mouth.

'Shall we say next Thursday?'

'Peter, I just don't know. It's not right . . .'

'Next Thursday. Lunch. Everyone will be asleep, so we'll have some peace and quiet. The servants will be in their quarters and it will be an empty afternoon, especially for us.'

Elizabeth dressed with great care for her seduction. She wore a coral-pink muslin frock which delineated her breasts, and she tied the sash tightly to emphasise her narrow waist. It was brand new and it had been difficult to find exactly the colour she wanted. There had been a boycott of English cotton cloth by the Indian merchants in Bengal, and she had no intention of buying the coarse Indian-manufactured cotton most of them now stocked. This swadesh was going too far, in Elizabeth's opinion. It was an inconvenience to her, but of course the people who suffered most were the merchants and the poor. Indian cotton was more expensive, but that didn't bother the mad Indian politicians who had called for the boycott. They argued that swadesh – the buying of only Indian goods – would break and bankrupt the great mills and factories in Manchester and Birmingham, would bring England to her knees. That was utter nonsense.

Indians *had* to buy English goods, as they had done for the last fifty years. The dreadful Indian-made cotton only served to prove the native incapable of producing anything decent himself.

So Elizabeth spent two frantic days looking in all the bigger native cloth shops, found what she wanted, and bullied Mrs Pereira into making the frock in only one day. It was an exact copy of the newest London fashion.

On the Thursday, Mary ayah was suspicious of all this mid-morning activity. Elizabeth had taken a second bath, which usually she took at night, and Mary could smell new perfume – French, she was told – around the room. Her baba had been restless and nervous all yesterday evening, and again this morning, flushed as if she had a fever. Mary ayah had checked her forehead. It was warm, but not hot enough to send her to bed. Elizabeth insisted that she was feeling quite well.

'Then why all this excitement? You will get ill.'

'But I *told* you! I'm having lunch with a friend from Bombay.'

'What friend?'

'You wouldn't know her. You don't know all my friends. Now, tell the gharri to come round to the front. Go on.' She pushed Mary ayah out of the room.

Mary ayah's hovering only increased her nervousness. The confounded woman seemed to be able to read her mind. Elizabeth opened her jewel box and took out the peacock brooch. She'd not worn it at all yet, and was now frightened to do so. If she managed to lose something as delicate and expensive as this, it would break her heart. Was it done to wear a man's gift when you were visiting him? She had looked it up in a book on etiquette, but the question hadn't been asked or answered there. That a single woman might visit a single man, and unchaperoned, hadn't occurred to the writer. Elizabeth boldly pinned the brooch above her heart.

She had been in a state of expectancy for so long that now she was eager to have it done with. In her mind, she could not describe the 'it', for she was quite ignorant of the actual facts. At school she had learned a little through giggling whispers about the terrible passion of two bodies fused together. Beyond that lay a gulf of ignorance.

If my mother were alive, I would at least have some idea of what to expect. Even Mary ayah refuses to discuss it with me, though I know she was married once. It is supposed to be horrible for women and enjoyable for men. That seems very unfair. To me, passion is breathless kisses rained down on my upturned face by a handsome man.

'What is that?' Mary ayah peered at the brooch and her eyes widened. Instinctively she knew its worth. 'I never seen it before.'

'A present.'

'Who gave you such a fine present?'

In reply, Elizabeth simply picked up her hat, marched past Mary ayah, and climbed into the gharri. She was leaving an hour early and had laid her plans with care. If she arrived in their gharri and stayed all afternoon with Peter, Sen the driver would immediately inform Mary ayah. He would also gossip with every other driver and soon the whole of Calcutta would know.

Instead, she told him to drive her over to Eden Gardens. The park had been built and donated to Calcutta by Lord Auckland's sisters, and was a huge expanse of shady walks, brilliantly coloured flower-beds, a lake, a pagoda brought from Prome, a cricket pitch, a tea-room and a dining-room. Calcutta's European society used Eden Gardens as a meeting place and to promenade. Elizabeth told Sen to wait at the East Gate, crossed the garden swiftly with her hat shading her features, hoping she would not see a familiar face at this time of day, and hired another gharri outside the West Gate.

Sir William's residence was an exact copy of a manor house in Somerset and had been built by a wealthy tea merchant, John Gibbs, in 1848. A long gravel drive flanked by eucalyptus trees led up to the wide front steps. On either side of the drive were carefully tended lawns. To the right of the house a tennis court had been laid. The house had been built of imported granite, so that it resembled the stone used to build the original in Somerset. It had many-paned windows and a huge oak entrance door. But in this setting its grandeur was diminished. It didn't look quite right in the harsh Indian sun with blood-red bougainvillea climbing up the front elevation.

Elizabeth didn't dismiss the gharri straight away. She looked nervously at the silent pile of stone. It seemed deserted, and now her boldness deserted her. She shouldn't have come here, and would have ordered the gharri to drive straight back to Eden Gardens if a bearer in black had not stepped out and started down the steps. He moved with a casual saunter, unlike the scurrying deference she might have expected.

'Is Bayley sahib in?'

'Yes.'

'Yes, "*memsahib*",' Elizabeth reproved him coolly.

'Yes, memsahib,' came the sullen reply.

He opened the gharri door and went back inside, not bothering to see if she followed. Peter would have to be told how to train a servant.

Elizabeth already knew the house. The interior was cool. The ballroom was on her left, she remembered, and in the hall was that great French chandelier, a mountain of inverted glass. She had visited the Becketts twice before, in the company of her father. The thought of her father made her hesitate once more, but now she was being led through a maze of corridors to a small, comfortable drawing-room. The french windows were open and led directly to a paved terrace.

Peter was waiting as though he had been standing there all day for her arrival. She had never seen such delight on his face as he came forward and embraced her.

'You look absolutely lovely, Elizabeth. Rao, bring two glasses of champagne.'

He led her to the sofa, caressing her arms as she sat beside him. He had a low, soothing voice, and she found herself calming down while she listened to him talk about a journey he'd made to Gaur to see the old Mughal ruins. He made it sound like a grand adventure, and he seemed to have noticed things she would never have considered of interest herself. Then he kissed her, not on the mouth, but on the tip of her nose, which she found to be gently intoxicating. She had been kissed before, by a boy crushing his mouth clumsily against her cheek, but never with such soft pleasure.

'I shouldn't be here, Peter. I just came to join you for lunch. I appreciate that you don't know many people here, so I thought we might go for a ride.' She tried to move away from him as Rao entered with the drinks, but Peter kept a firm grip on her. He seemed unconcerned at Rao's presence and continued to stroke her arm.

'Not in front of your bearer, please. He's so insolent,' she protested in a whisper, pulling away.

'Rao, were you insolent to memsahib?'

'No, sahib.' He bowed low and withdrew.

Peter reached for her hand again.

'You're here at last, my lovely Elizabeth. I've been waiting for you for two whole years. Haven't you been waiting for me?'

She was distracted by his hands which never remained still. They skimmed over her body and she felt his light touch on her thighs, her stomach, her neck. She tried to hold them away from her, but felt herself slowly losing control.

There was no hurry. They had the whole afternoon ahead of them. The glare outside was muted indoors and she felt her body become languid and heavy. She heard herself chattering about her own uneventful life, the death of her mother, Richard's imminent leave, times spent up in Simla, her longing to go back to England again. He seemed to pay attention to her, unlike other men. He was aware of her every little need, and even over the light lunch of salad and cold meats he made sure that her plate was filled, her glass never empty.

When they rose from the table, he took her hand and led her upstairs. They entered the main bedroom, which overlooked the front lawn. It was a huge room, containing an equally huge four-poster bed. The teak floor was covered with Kashmiri carpets and the furniture looked to be French. Peter picked up a silk dressing-gown and handed it to her.

'This is yours. Why don't you go and change in the bathroom?'

She stepped through into an expanse of white Rajputana marble and stood there, shaking.

I'm not really here. It is all a dream. I shouldn't allow myself to be seduced, and yet I want him. I'm in love with him and I've never experienced such a strong feeling before. This is only supposed to happen on my wedding night, and he hasn't even mentioned love. Or marriage. I can't even remember what we spoke about. I can feel a heat inside me, such a strange sensation. It's pleasurable, not painful. I expected . . . well, nothing at all. Only men are supposed to feel these passions. Something must be wrong with me. In London, where I was so much less circumscribed, and had so many admirers, I never felt like this.

Even as she talked to herself, she was undressing and putting on the dressing-gown. It was made of yellow Chinese silk, and felt light and cool against her skin. Her nipples were hard. She took a deep breath and left the bathroom. Peter was already lying in bed under the fine linen sheet. He held out a hand to her and she slipped in, and found him naked.

Peter gently removed the Chinese robe. She had a flawless body, he had imagined it perfectly. Round, firm breasts, high with large erect nipples, a deliciously flat stomach with a small triangle of soft, golden hair over her sex. Her legs were long and slim. He always enjoyed the sight of a beautiful woman; touching this one was as heady as wine. She was trying to remain unmoved, but he knew from the flush on her face and the dreamy look in her eyes that she would be responsive to his caresses.

He had not thought much about Elizabeth. But, once back in Calcutta, he had caught a glimpse of her in the club, and then he remembered his old lust. He remembered too the cool feel of her thigh against the back of his hand at that dinner, and how she'd not drawn back. Even then he'd guessed that this would be an easy and pleasurable seduction.

They entwined in the sweaty heat, and then she knew he was very experienced. His touch was sure and practised, but her own physical arousal frightened her somewhat. He whispered soft praises of her body into her ear, and she wanted so much to believe him. She was perfect, she really was. And when he knelt down between her legs, almost in worship, she was ready. She cried out once at the sharp pain, but then his gentleness eased it away and she forgot everything except the need to fill herself with this exquisite pleasure.

By tea-time, Elizabeth was demurely dressed in her coral-pink muslin once again. Peter held her hand on the way to the gharri and kissed her lightly on the tip of her nose.

'When shall I see you again?' she asked.

'Next Thursday.'

'Can't I see you sooner? Say, the day after tomorrow?'

'My darling, I have to go up to Shillong on business. I'm thinking of buying a tea plantation there. It must be Thursday.' He said this with a firmness that she knew she couldn't shake.

She wanted him. She had never before known such craving, and she felt guilty that she could feel no guilt. It was a peculiar emotion that worried her. Her heroines remained chaste, despite the heat of their bodies. She was now a fallen woman. She had discovered such pleasure that now she thought them all fools for having deceived her. She had spoken of love as well, it was true, but her whispers seemed to have gone unheard.

She thought she could never get through the long

week of separation and wandered about aimlessly, look-ing for any distraction. Then Richard came home, and she was swept off her feet.

Since her earliest years she had worshipped her brother, trotting behind him all over the compound, cheerfully suffering the indignities he put her through in his adventurous games. He would be Clive, she Hyder Ali; he would be General Lawrence, she a mutinous sepoy. He would ambush her, put her to the sword, tie her to trees, sometimes leave her tied up, but she never dared to complain in case he called her a cissy.

They were sent away to schools in England, she to Somerset, Richard to Norfolk. Despite the enforced separation they had remained close to each other. Though she was younger she had felt herself the senior and had, over the years, grown very protective of Rich-ard. He was her brother, but because they had no mother, she had always felt maternal towards him. She wrote to him at his school regularly and he would scribble a line in reply.

They had always looked forward to the summer holi-days, when they could spend time in each other's company. Their guardian, Mrs Bates, lived near Cirenc-ester: she was a plump woman with pretensions to gentility, and both children disliked her. She was stern and something of a tyrant, and as often as not Richard, for an unintended mischief, would be beaten. When she heard Mrs Bates' cane swishing down and Richard's stifled cry, Elizabeth would weep for him. Her own punishment was to be sent to bed early, without supper, though Richard would usually manage to smuggle some food up to her room. Quite suddenly, as though time had cheated her, Richard had grown up. He had gone to Sandhurst, and then joined his regiment and she felt herself losing him. They'd returned to India within a year of each other, but she'd seen little of him since, and wished time would not wreak such changes in people.

He had grown broader, become even more handsome. She kissed him and hugged him. Aunt Emma emerged from her sitting-room, and although she was not usually a demonstrative woman, flung her arms about his neck. The whole household, drowsy with the monotonous routine, suddenly came awake. They dashed here and there, fetching anything the chota sahib needed. The servants worshipped Richard baba, and came forward to receive his darshan. Mary ayah pinched both his clean-shaven cheeks and then kissed her own fingertips.

The Colonel shook Richard's hand firmly and felt the answering pressure. He too would have liked to have embraced his son: it had been a long time since he'd last seen him. But he couldn't. The emotional gesture would have embarrassed them both.

On the night of Richard's return they dined together for the first time as a complete family for more than two years. Aunt Emma had ordered the cook to make Richard's favourite dishes: onion soup, breaded veal cutlets with tomatoes, and a tipsy-cake.

'It's good to sit down to a decent meal again. The food in the mess is usually absolutely awful. Sometimes we have to sneak into Peshawar, to Greene's Hotel, to get some decent grub.' Richard ate heartily, his eyes alight with pleasure.

The Colonel couldn't help but smile at his own memories of being a young subaltern.

'In the old days we used to kidnap the best cooks in town. I remember once, Bob Lloyd and I were sent into Lahore to get hold of one. He was working for an English family at the time. What were their names now? Oh, the Altons, that's it. They had this Muslim cook, quite a young man, who would have put those jumped-up Frenchies at the Connaught to shame. Jack and I caught him up in the bazaar, gave him a hundred rupees, which was the entire mess kitty, and rode hell-for-leather back, with him in tow.' He looked with pleasure on his son. 'How do you get on with Dyer?'

'Oh, he's a grand chap, an excellent CO. Knows the natives, and has some pretty firm ideas how to deal with them. He's a good sport, too. Turns a blind eye when necessary. When we went over to show the flag to one of the tribal chiefs, Gulam, he . . .'

Elizabeth listened to them reminisce together. She had had no such glorious memories, no such adventures, no brushes with danger. It was a man's world that she inhabited, though she wished she could contribute something to their talk. Her only real adventure would have brought their combined wrath down on her head. Both of them would have probably horsewhipped Peter, though doubtless they indulged their own carnal appetites, either with chi-chi women or with natives. She couldn't bear such a vile thought.

'What are we going to do while Richard's here?' she asked over the pudding.

'Oh, I have all that planned,' the Colonel said. 'We're going on shikar. Remember how we bagged that panther up near Naini Tal, Richard? It was your first kill of big game. Did I tell you, Elizabeth, how we saw this panther, just a great shadow on the wall of this ruin and Richard was . . . how old were you then?'

'Seven, I think.' Richard and Elizabeth smiled conspiratorially at each other. Their father always told this story. Repeating it gave him a sense of closeness to Richard. There was little else.

'So young. I gave Richard first shot, and, calm as a real shikari, you just lifted your rifle, took aim, and got it straight in the shoulder. A perfect shot.'

'Yes . . . but, Father, I have done quite a bit of shikar up there since. Mostly small game, but some bear and sambar. I thought, while I was down here, I'd like to meet some of Elizabeth's friends. We don't get all that much feminine company up in Peshawar. Mostly wives, and everyone knows what kind of trouble you can get into with them!'

'Oh. I had especially taken some leave.'

And he had been so looking forward to spending it in the company of his son. They would pass the day shooting, and in the evening, drink a few chota pegs and talk around an open fire. The boy was now a man;

187

time was passing too swiftly. Elizabeth reminded him too much of her mother, so that he found himself putting an increasing distance between them.

'I'm sorry, Father.' Richard avoided having to see the disappointment on his father's face by turning to his sister. 'Well, Lil, you've got the prettiest friends. Charlie Hodges is down in Calcutta for a few days. He has a couple of girls lined up, but I told him Lil would have them even prettier. They'd have to be, I said, 'cos Lil is the prettiest of them all. You'd like Charlie. Jolly good fun.' They rose and went to sit out on the verandah with their brandies. Richard held Elizabeth's hand. She felt comforted by his affection.

'What about you, Lil? Not found the right fella yet? Thought you'd be engaged by now. What's wrong with the chaps here, then?'

'Oh, she does have her admirers.' The Colonel joined in their banter, 'One of them called the other day. Mr Bayley.'

'Who's he?'

'I met Peter in Bombay a couple of years ago – at dinner at the Rushtons. He's just arrived in Calcutta and came to say hello.' No doubt Mary ayah or Abdul had told the Colonel of Peter's visit.

Elizabeth assiduously mapped out a programme of visits and dances, knowing there would be new jealousies to contend with: girlfriends. They would all swoon the moment they clapped eyes on her beloved Richard. They would giggle and talk about him, breathless as the heroines in their silly romantic novels, begging Elizabeth to tell them everything about him. She was proud of their admiration, but still felt possessive towards her brother, and jealous. She wished she could be one of them, someone to be enchanted and bedazzled by this handsome man. She wished he wouldn't pay attention to their silly flirtations, but Richard was susceptible to a pretty face.

So his family saw little of him on his short leave. He would wake up late, gulp down his breakfast and then dash out to visit a new girl or else meet one of his fellow-officers at the club. Elizabeth and the Colonel felt themselves relegated to the edge of his life, when they both wanted to be its centre.

Kim stood at the entrance of the Bengal Club ballroom with Dr Malcolm. There was a humming mob at the door, waiting to go in, and the air within was filled with the loud music of a Goan orchestra hesitantly playing waltzes. There was a pianist, two violins, a bass, a trumpet and a drummer. Nobody minded their lack of melody. At least it was music, and they had all come to enjoy themselves this New Year's Eve. Dr Malcolm tossed a cigarette over his shoulder and they both heard the yelp, but neither bothered to turn round.

'Serves her damned well right,' Malcolm said. 'You'll enjoy yourself here. I think what you need is a young, plump partridge, warm and soft.' He shivered with delight at his own description. 'They're present in plenty tonight. I might even find myself a nice piece of muslin! Ah, but I prefer the native woman. She smells like a mysterious rose, and whenever I touch one of those dusky bodies, I almost burst with longing. Cucumbers, my boy. Think of cucumbers.'

They pushed their way deeper into the room, into the crush of people. The ballroom was gay with coloured streamers and Chinese lanterns hung from the ceiling. The air was thick with noise, and Kim could see the cardboard outlines of a model fort standing on display at the far end of the room. A Union Jack hung limply from a cardboard battlement. Beneath it were ranged a real cannon and a company of soldiers in full-dress uniform. The soldiers were all old, some infirm, but they sat proud and straight and their decorations vied with the colourful festoons of the ballroom itself. Yet they were like sad relics of a bygone age with their parchment-yellow skin and white beards.

'Mutiny veterans. They've been fêted all bloody year, but I bet they cut and ran at the time,' Malcolm said.

'We keep on remembering the damned Mutiny. All year we've been commemorating. No doubt in 1957 we'll be celebrating the centenary.'

Celebration was the theme of the ball, and the guests wore fancy-dress. There were faded uniforms of former regiments; some had come as natives – the evil Hyder Ali; the pitiless Rani of Jhansi; or in kurtas or achkans, or the vivid clothes of Rajput women. Kim wandered around with Dr Malcolm. In scraps of conversations he heard tales of bravery, of terrible cruelty too, but as with any gathering of people came the gathering of legends and myths. Stories told and re-told over those fifty years came together here, to change once more in the telling, as they would right across the country at similar parties and balls. There is a real fort here, Kim thought, not a cardboard one, and the walls and battlements are the memories of these people around me.

The bar was packed. It was a large, panelled room, decorated with ancient muskets, spears and animal heads. The deep leather armchairs were all taken by elderly men who demanded to be heard. The bar ran the length of the room and Dr Malcolm pushed and wriggled his way through, elbowing aside larger men, to emerge triumphant with two whisky-and-sodas.

'I just don't know why we glorify war and killing. I've seen enough of it to last me three incarnations, and so I suppose have most of these other chaps. But do you think for a moment it will stop them? Of course not. All this bloody talk of killing the natives only makes them drunk with their power to murder. Most of this lot weren't around in '57, but they honestly believe they were. They talk as though they speared a native, they blew him apart on a cannon, they hung him up by his balls.'

'And I think they want to do it again,' Kim said sadly. He knew that when men had such dreams, they could be made real.

'I think you're right. And God help us then. But before that happens, what about a partridge or two for us both,

Kim? Let them kill themselves, we'll die smothered in a woman's flesh.'

'Kim! Malcolm!' Before they could turn their attention to other, more pleasurable pursuits, the Colonel caught them by the elbow. He looked elegant in evening dress, and more animated than usual.

'I'm so glad you came, Kim. I'm sure you'll enjoy yourself. It's a good party.'

The Colonel was determinedly jovial, although generally he disliked these affairs. He had only accompanied Elizabeth and Richard because it would be the last chance for them all to spend a night out together. The next day Richard would be leaving to rejoin his regiment.

'I'd like you to meet my son and daughter. We have a table on the lawn.' He kept hold of Kim's elbow. 'I'm glad I caught up with you. This gives you a chance to see a little more of what we both serve, Kim. That's why I wanted you to work in the Department. When you go . . . native . . . you tend to lose touch with being an Englishman, knowing what it feels like to be English. I'm sure you never considered yourself anything but a native until now, did you?'

'No. I wasn't brought up in this . . . world of yours, Colonel. My friends don't remember the mutiny; they don't talk of killing with such pleasure.'

'Oh, I wouldn't pay any attention to all that nonsense. Still, I think it's a good thing that we do remember. The native doesn't. He can't remember his own history, which is why he repeats his mistakes. By remembering, we avoid the mistakes of our past. There will never be another mutiny in India.'

'But there will be more killing.'

'No. We shall make damned sure that we never lose control again.'

It was cooler out on the lawn, a welcome relief from the heat and press of bodies within, and quieter, too. The moon was full, but the lanterns threw a gentle yellow glow on the lawn. They threaded their way between the tables, stepping aside to avoid bearers rushing with drinks and young men who had already drunk too much and were now swaying like palm trees. Elizabeth was sitting alone at the table.

'Elizabeth, this is Mr O'Hara. And Dr Malcolm.'

Elizabeth barely looked up. A small smile hovered, quite mechanical, then vanished. She saw only an inconspicuous, good-looking man whom she took to be chi-chi from his complexion and the way he wore his suit, awkwardly, as though unused to the garment, and a small, older man with a cigarette dangling from his mouth in an uncouth fashion. She didn't associate the younger man with the native she'd seen two years ago in her father's office in Simla.

'Where's Richard?'

Elizabeth gestured tiredly towards the crush of people and again barely looked up.

She was sulking. She had wanted Peter to be her escort tonight. They had made love together that very afternoon, and she had thought she had the power to persuade him while he lay beside her, damp and exhausted.

'Lizzie darling, I don't think it would be a good idea for us to be seen together in public.'

'Why ever not? We'll have to at some time.'

'Not yet. Besides, I might not even come to the do. Can't stand them, actually.'

She had pouted at his reply, but when he began to caress her breasts again, the pout vanished and she lay back with a sigh of pleasure. Peter thought her delightfully greedy. Few women would have been so accommodating. Nevertheless, if she became too possessive, he would get rid of her.

Elizabeth now withdrew into the shadows of those pleasurable memories. She couldn't shake herself free from the longings of her body.

'Well, he'll turn up soon enough. You two will get on famously, O'Hara. I think you're both about the same age, and Richard knows the frontier as well as you do.'

Kim sat down beside Elizabeth. He noted the distant

look in her eyes, as though she had been hypnotised. She'd changed quite a bit since he'd last seen her, not much in age, but in the maturity of her face. She'd lost that girlish innocence, which was his clearest recollection of her on that afternoon. For a moment he wondered what it would be like to lie beside her. Would she smell the same as an Indian woman? And at night, would she whisper and giggle, and would her skin feel as smooth and silken?

'Are you enjoying yourself, Miss Creighton?'

'Yes, thank you,' Elizabeth replied in a soft voice that had been thoroughly trained to be polite to strangers.

Her solitude reminded him of his own. He still thought often of Parvati. She was alive, but where? Bombay? Or had she run away from that city, too, as she had run from Delhi, pursued by men who meant to cause her harm. He wanted to protect her, to be with her, instead of stuck here on the lawn with a young Englishwoman who had no interest in him.

They sat on at the table waiting for Richard. Without him there, they all seemed to be at a loss and the Colonel was distracted in his search for his son. He would peer this way, then that, and murmur an apology to no one in particular. He was acutely aware of the passage of time, the waste of an evening spent, like all the others, with Elizabeth instead of with Richard.

Kim saw the Colonel's lack of interest in his daughter, sensed his longing for his son, and wondered whether all families divided their children into the loved and the unloved. In a way it distressed him to see the Colonel so vulnerable to his son, and he wanted to help him. But no one could take Richard's place in his father's affection, making all others superfluous to him.

'I think we need another drink, Kim,' Malcolm said, and without apology rose and gestured for Kim to follow. It was a relief for them both to escape the oppressive impatience and sullen distance at the table.

'Now, where were we before the Colonel sahib so rudely interrupted us? Oh yes, in search of a brace of partridges. Though I must admit his pretty little miss sahib of a daughter is one woman I could sink into without trace. I wonder who's the lucky fella? Tally ho!'

Kim lost sight of Malcolm in the crowded ballroom. He slipped out of a side door and savoured the perfume of jasmine in the air. A gharri waited, but he chose instead to walk along the silent streets. Gradually the music faded into the distance. Men, women and children were sleeping out in the open, small bundles of shawls and blankets curled up against the chill of the night. He removed his jacket and draped it over a child which had rolled bare from the protection of its mother. He threw his tie away and felt for the first time that evening a sense of excitement and anticipation. Life lived without purpose, as it was here, and lived without companions, as it was here, was an empty and futile existence, and he had had enough of it.

16

On the banks of the fat and placid river Tapti, in the shadow of the ruined palace that tumbled down the slope like a flowing honeycomb of stone, and in which long ago the great Mughal Shah Jahan mourned the death of his wife Mumtaz Mahal, Kim met two blind boys who could see.

They were identical twins, physically mirrors of one another, with the soft, unformed features of the blind. The flesh appeared to be made of clay that had yet to harden. Both wore blue turbans; the one on the right carried a ravanhatta, while the other one held cymbals. When they played and sang, men and women prostrated themselves at their feet, serpents appeared from holes in the earth, birds fell from the sky and the river stopped flowing, for none had heard such clear, beautiful voices.

On this evening they sang the Gita in front of the small white shrine that stood on the riverbank and Kim saw with his own eyes the temple glow within and the idol rise up to dance in ecstasy at the marvellous sound of their singing. Nataraj's thunder shook the earth and the sky, and he danced for two days and two nights without stopping, for the boys sang all that time without pausing for food or drink or rest. And when they ended their music, the sky and the earth fell silent and all heard the enormous sigh that echoed across the universe.

When the twins left the town of Burhanpur their begging bowl was filled with food and money. They could have remained, for the whole town, including the munsiff and the seths, pleaded with them to make their home in their midst. To possess these young boys, who could sing for the gods, would have been a powerful attraction. They even offered to build them a special temple of marble, which would have been impossible since marble was virtually unobtainable, and to turn them into stone idols for people to worship when they came from all corners of India to hear them sing.

But it was their dharma to wander for ever.

They were not yet twelve years of age, and walked with Kim along the dusty road holding each other's hands. They were both named Bala, and Kim noticed that the one with the cymbals always walked on the left and the one with the ravanhatta on the right. They walked as confidently as Kim did with his good sight and his greater size.

'Our father too was a singer, and we were born in a village near Nyvelli.' They spoke in such perfect harmony that it was impossible to distinguish one voice from the other. 'He was a bhakta of the Lord Krishna. When we were born, he prayed to the Lord Krishna to grant us the boon of voices that would turn milk into honey and water into wine. Lord Krishna heard him and granted his boon. Our first cry turned the grinding stone in our hut to water, and the earth into rice. But, having granted the boon, Lord Krishna told our father that the whole world must hear us sing and that we must travel alone on this journey. Our father wept when he learnt this, so Lord Krishna relented and told him that when we reached the age of twenty-five years we would lose our voices and we could then return to our village. We left our home when we were five years old and, protected by the boon, we have travelled ever since. No one would dare harm us. Rajas must open their palaces, dacoits must give us free passage, the tiger must turn aside. To kill or harm either of us before the ending of this boon is to bring down the anger of Lord Krishna. He will destroy the men and destroy their households, and the kingdom from which they come will be shattered and will vanish from the face of the earth.'

'But you are blind. We have walked many miles now, and yet your feet are as sure as mine. You see the birds overhead, the changing colour of the sky, the distant hills, even as I do.'

'We were born without eyes, but we are not blind. Brahma, when he heard of the boon given by Lord Krishna, gave us sight. He did not open our eyes, but instead opened our minds. We can see as clearly as you do. For us, the world is divided into two, the right side and the left side. Bala walks to the right and Bala to the left. Bala sees only to the right, Bala only to the left. If we change positions, we cannot see. And what Bala sees, Bala also sees, when we keep our position.'

The three walked on through a landscape of despair. Gaunt trees extended gnarled roots that resembled claws, imploring sustenance; lantana bushes, unable to bear their suffering any longer, immolated themselves, spurting smoke and ash into air which was so still that the ash neither rose nor fell, but remained as a dense, grey mist. The earth would open parched lips to swallow air and anything else unfortunate enough to be standing nearby. Kim walked close to the boys, for even the earth knew of Lord Krishna's boon, and if it should accidentally swallow the boys, it would be evaporated by Lord Krishna's rage. Kim had never seen a sky so malevolent. It took joy in its destruction, at the fear it struck in the hearts of men, beasts and birds.

On the second night they rested below a great fort. They had seen it looming up from many miles away, and could not fathom its great size until they stood underneath it. The building rose straight up for half a mile, and the walls were black and fierce. Nothing moved within, and above it even the very hawks and kites avoided flying over that poisoned air. No other birds could even peep over the walls, for its height and dread had long been known to them. This was Asirgah, erected so long ago that men believed it to be older than the rivers and the mountains, and that the earth too had only been created to hold the fort up. It had no gate, it had no windows, and the black stone was smooth as glass. It was said to guard the entrance to Hell, but that was only legend. No one knew who had built it, or why it had been built.

As they slowly walked west (for the boys walked west, then east, then west, and at the point of each turn would walk north for two days. In this way they slowly climbed the inverted pyramid of India) Kim told them his own story. He told it from the very beginning, from his very first memory in Lahore, his journey with the Lama, his work for the Colonel, his boon from the dwarf, his meeting with Parvati, his wounding, and right up to this moment, when he had joined them. He had heard about them on the train, and had decided to alight at Indore to search for them.

In spite of their travels, the twins did not know that the land through which they moved was ruled by a race from across the kala pani. They had never even seen an Angrezi because they seldom went into a city, preferring to avoid them. Their singing was meant to be heard by the sky, the earth and the waters. In a city, this was not possible.

'And you are now searching for your Parvati?' They were delighted and clapped their hands.

'Yes. I am going first to Bombay, then wherever the trail leads me. Except that I don't know what she looks like now.'

'We will compose the poem of Kim and Parvati, and if you look closely at the space just between us, you will see her. She will appear, though only for a moment, from wherever she is, where we do not know, for the power of our singing can make men and gods materialise before us. We can summon thunder and lightning too.'

They began to sing the story of Kim and Parvati. First the campfire around which they sat was stilled. It didn't flicker or waver, and forgot to give off its heat. Then the wind came down to them, chilling the air, for it too wished to listen. And just beyond, in the night, Kim saw the glowing eyes of beasts ringing them and cobras and kraits uncoiling at their feet.

Kim concentrated on the narrow corridor of air between the boys. There was just enough space for a woman to stand, if she should appear. If he expected this materialisation to happen immediately, he was disappointed. They sang for an hour, then two, then three, and just as Kim began to doubt the power of their beautiful voices, he saw a tall, slim woman wearing a blue sari, with tendrils of jasmine wound in her hair, staring emptily out at him.

He was looking at Parvati, but she couldn't see him. She was sitting on a chair in a room. Her loveliness stopped his breath and once again he longed to caress the delicate contours of her face. Her amber eyes were sad, and even as he watched she suddenly roused herself and stared around her in fear. He wanted to cry out, to tell her not to be afraid, but then his face darkened. Her fear was the result of seeing someone else. Then a man stepped between Kim and Parvati and they vanished.

Kim continued to stare at the empty space, willing her to reappear, but he did not have the same power as the boys. And he too felt afraid of this man, who had frightened Parvati. If he was to save her, he must hurry, even though he dreaded that already he might be too late. The man who had been hunting her had obviously found her.

When the boys finished their singing, the fire sighed and remembered to burn again, giving off heat; the wind lifted to carry their song north for the Himalayas to hear, because they too had wanted to come, but Brahma forbade them to move. The animals and serpents wept dew and returned to their homes.

The following day Kim took blessings from Bala and Bala. They would be continuing west in a straight line until they reached the kala pani, then they would turn

and walk east. They hoped that, by their twenty-fifth
year, they would have been heard by the whole land.
He watched them for a long time as they dwindled to
dots in the distance, and then to nothing.

17

KIM'S VISION of Mohini had been true. On the day that she had felt the chill of being watched by unseen eyes, she had been sitting in Alice's drawing-room, wearing a blue sari. A vision is illusion, but her feeling had been physical. The weight of those unseen eyes had frightened her. Mohini believed in a malign universe, and believed too that men could summon up this malignant energy to obey their will. She dreaded lest those eyes had been sent by her husband and his mother to search for her and she imagined their evil was now in the room with her. So she was relieved and delighted then to see Romesh Nairoji enter the room, dispel superstition by his mere presence. A second later she felt the unseen eyes disappear.

Romesh was the only man who had any significance in their spinsterish lives. When he visited, both women came alive, alight like fire brought to candles. Mohini's feelings were only of affection and pleasure. But Romesh was Alice's lover and her financial supporter, a stocky, muscular man with the lithe movements of a ballet dancer. He appeared to walk on the tips of his toes.

He was a Parsi, a member of the large Zoroastrian community that had escaped Muslim persecution in their homeland of Persia eleven centuries ago. They had made their home in Bombay, and were known to be astute businessmen, scholars, intellectuals and sportsmen. Because they assiduously retained their identity and traditions in this land of Hindus, and were such a small minority that they posed no threat, they were deliberately cultivated as favourites by the British, and were encouraged in all their pursuits, including politics.

Romesh's uncle, Mr Daddhabhai Nairoji, had, partly to prove his people's ability to transcend the barrier of being of a subject race, already represented the London constituency of Bethnal Green in the British parliament. The irony of this achievement hadn't escaped Mr Daddhabhai Nairoji. As he often told his nephew, when he had resigned his seat after a five-year term in the House of Commons: 'The British are a peculiar race. They will permit me, a native of India, to represent a constituency composed entirely of Englishmen and situated almost within sight of Big Ben, but they consider me totally incapable of guiding the destiny of my own countrymen within the borders of my own homeland in which, by the way, we may be considered to be separate from the Hindu, but by no means equal to the British.'

Mr Daddhabhai Nairoji was an Indian nationalist, a breed that was becoming increasingly unpopular with the Indian government. Having represented an English constituency, he understood clearly the motives of his rulers. 'The early Mughal emperors knew that their power depended on the Hindus accepting their rule. The English have cleverly reversed this principle. They dislike the Hindu because they do not understand the religion. Instead, they have elevated communities like ours, minorities, Parsi, Muslim, Sikh, Buddhist, as a buffer between them and the majority. It is a simple and effective method of government: divide and rule. I admire them tremendously because they are truly the most devious people God ever invented. But I also believe that our own political and intellectual development depends totally on their rule.'

Although he believed in nationalism, like the majority of educated Indians, Romesh's uncle could not as yet conceive of or even imagine an independent India. He defined nationalism as Indians ruling India jointly with the British, a sharing of the cake, not owning the whole cake. He believed that Indians were incapable of ruling themselves without paternal guidance. And this belief rested on the foundations of trust. Mr Daddhabhai Nairoji trusted the Englishman implicitly, trusted him in knowing better his country's destiny.

Romesh had imbibed his uncle's wisdom and enjoyed his family's wealth: his uncle and father owned two cotton mills and a coastal shipping business. Alice had met him while interviewing his uncle on the subject of Indian politics. Their attraction had been immediate. At first there had been only sexual desire. She knew he was married to a Parsi girl, but as long as they could snatch a day or two a week to satisfy their passions, she was content. He had been the one to give her the bungalow out on Malabar Hill, only a small property, though his family owned large tracts in that area which was outside the city itself. The early lust had gradually developed into a secure relationship which had now continued for a satisfying four years. But it remained discreet, as it was unthinkable for an Indian to have a physical relationship with an Englishwoman. And Alice was wise enough to understand the consequences.

She had, by now, ceased to contribute to the *Manchester Guardian*, since the paper could not make up its mind whether it wanted to be Imperialist or not, and had changed tack so often that it annoyed her. It believed in certain gradual reforms for India, but none that would shake the foundations of the ruling empire. Alice had little patience for such dithering. She believed that her people had no right to rule in India, no right to exploit the nation. She now contributed to the *New York Herald Tribune* which, insulated by distance and indifference, allowed her the freedom to write exactly as she wanted. Besides, they paid her a lot better than the *Manchester Guardian*.

Neither Alice nor Romesh knew what to do with the waif who had appeared on their doorstep. Alice had cleared out the little bedroom on the other side of the bungalow, and had moved the camp-cot in there for Mohini. The room remained as simply furnished as it had been on that first day, for neither woman could think of any further additions. In one corner Mohini had installed an image of Lord Ganesh, the elephant god of learning and wealth. Each morning, after her bath, she would spend half an hour in prayer. This continuity of some part of her old life gave her a great sense of security.

Mohini had been extremely shy at first, and wary of Romesh. She had also been shocked to discover that he was Alice's lover. The shock came before the shyness, for one morning she'd found Romesh emerging from Alice's bedroom and had fled back to her own room. If Romesh had been an Englishman, or Alice an Indian, Mohini would not have been so upset. Alice had had to coax her out again that day, but gradually she'd grown to like Romesh, partly because he had the same easy swagger in his walk as Kim.

It was strange how, even after such a long time, Mohini could still remember Kim clearly. It was as if they had parted only the day before; his features could not have been more distinct in her mind's eye. She had often tried to erase from her heart and her memory those days they'd spent together, but in her newly-discovered loneliness she found herself thinking of him a great deal. His memory was a solace to her. But if Kim had the belief he would find her again, Mohini had none. She was convinced that he was gone for ever, even now dead, and the memories she cherished were like a brittle rose petal preserved between the pages of a book of poetry.

Whenever Alice went away on an assignment for a few days, Mohini would not stir from the four walls of the bungalow. Loneliness was a new experience for her. Since she was a baby, she had always had a set place in life. She had grown up as a part of a large family: parents, cousins, aunts, uncles, servants. Within that lively group her position was as fixed and assured as the moon's in the night sky. She had never had any reason to doubt who she was or where she belonged. Her day was ordered, from waking to sleeping, whether it was to study, to play, to attend the temple, to perform puja at home with her mother, to learn about the preparation of food. There were countless duties, each well ordered and from which she never had to stray, or even find the time to consider herself as a separate and individual person. Every action and thought was bound by the people whom she loved and cared for.

And later, when she had entered into the arranged marriage, she had moved from her father's household into her husband's, a chattel passed from one and to another, and in this new household she again had her place. It was neither comfortable nor happy – the daughter-in-law of a malignant woman, the wife of a cruel, elderly husband – but it was a definite place for her to occupy. She was basically the same person, but now with a new setting, a part of another group of human beings with different customs, different traditions, but nevertheless familiar to her. She had attained the status of a married woman.

All my life, [Mohini wrote in her diary, a notebook given to her by Alice] I have been a part of something living and familiar. Like an arm or a leg, or toes or fingers. Now that I have committed a form of self-amputation, I am lost. I was meant not for individualism, but duty. I have failed in my duty as a wife, as a daughter, as a possible mother. But how do I reconcile that duty with the unhappiness I felt? Should I have accepted it as a part of my fate, like the bullock accepts his driver's cruelty, or a beggar the deliberate twisting of his limbs? Or is duty more important than my private self? I cannot fulfil one without contentment in the other. But then, most women are not permitted such a luxury. We serve, like the bullock, the needs of our men, be they father or husband. In England, Alice tells me, women are not dissimilar in their plight, but they have begun to revolt against such indignities. But here, where all men and women are

205

suppressed, what is my small need in comparison with the larger one?

Mohini wrote only when depression swooped in on her, though she enjoyed writing prose. She sometimes wrote her poetry too, sad and full of heartbreak. These exercises were a welcome escape from the loneliness of her room.

Alice encouraged her writing, and Mohini could indulge in reading voraciously all Alice's books: novels by Dickens, the Brontës, Scott; political treatises by Marx and Hume and many others. Alice was able to watch a bud slowly blossom, an expanding mind. She would read Mohini's efforts – not those which were painful and personal, but her analyses of the writings of others – and would offer her opinion.

It was not a particularly satisfying life, but it hid her from her husband and from her future. She was dependent on Alice for all her needs, and though Alice found this burdensome at times she hadn't the heart to reject Mohini. If ever Mohini did venture away from the safe haven of the bungalow, she would don the Muslim woman's burkha, a forbidding black garment that shrouded her from head to toe, with only a narrow slit for her eyes. 'It feels,' she wrote, 'like walking around in a tomb. I become a spirit, seeing but unseen. It is my best protection against the eyes of my husband's men, who even now may not have given up their search.'

Mohini had not meant to interfere in the running of Alice's household. Alice had a careless arrangement with Munswamy, the boy, who cooked the meals and did all the shopping. Unfortunately, Mohini discovered that Munswamy was stealing both money and food from Alice, having long realised that Soames memsahib had too much on her mind to miss such paltry items. Mohini, with her inborn distrust of servants, had caught him at it. Munswamy immediately resigned and went in search of another European memsahib who would be as ignorant as Alice of the price of food in Crawford Market.

Mohini now took over these household duties, and found it most satisfying. Alice couldn't have cared less. They ate well and Mohini saved her some money. But she knew Mohini couldn't continue in this way for ever.

Alice does get impatient with me, [Mohini wrote. She was filling the books at an increasing rate as the months passed in self-exile.] She is quite right, too. She told me that this is not the life for me – a Hindu woman, married, living in seclusion and slowly fading away in bitter thoughts. But what am I to do? No doubt it was the thousandth time I had asked her, and asked myself. To return to that man, my husband, whose chill touch on my body made my hair stand on end, would be the end of me. I should be watched constantly, never permitted to escape. Who knows: I suspect he would even kill me. I am a minute particle in his life, an irritant. His mother would aid him in this matter, and to kill a woman, locked up in a house, is an easy matter. A taste of poison, I have heard, is sufficient.

'Well, you cannot go on like this indefinitely,' Alice said. She meant it kindly, but I felt as unwanted as a pi-pup, being pushed gently out. 'I can't return to my husband. When I first married him as a child and he used me at will, I would cry. And when I cried, he would threaten to give me to his two servants. They are brothers, black as devils, and do his every bidding. I believed him then, and believe he would do the same thing even now.'

'How horrible. No, dear, I certainly wouldn't want you to return to that evil man. God knows, I would never return to mine. Not that he would permit me to, actually. He would probably have me locked away, or worse. I really think he would physically harm me if I showed my face in his house. He hates me, though I don't feel the same towards him.'

'Why? What did you do?'

'I was unfaithful to him, my dear. The wrong was entirely mine, as it has always been for us women. Men may philander, we may not. I married too young; certainly not as a child, like you, but too young to know my own mind. He was a dashing officer and I was susceptible. I'd just come out to India to escape the stuffiness of English life, and I thought India would be a grand adventure. Instead, I found myself living in the company of narrow-minded men and women. They were worse than their equals in England, for these people fed their pretensions to grandeur by lording it over the natives. I didn't find adventure, only a hideous sort of sun-baked Surrey.'

'Did you have any children?' I asked.

'Two. And I still miss them terribly, but the pain has lessened over the years. I know women are supposed to have ineradicable maternal instincts, but I'm not sure whether those instincts were not invented by men to keep us safely at home. The children have been told I'm dead.' She fell silent and I saw her eyes darkening as though she was about to cry. I suspect she wept herself dry ages ago, but memories cannot be swept aside as easily as tears.

'The boy must be twenty-four by now, the girl twenty-three. I wonder what they look like? If I saw them in the street, I probably wouldn't recognise them. But then, we are not discussing my life, Mohini, but yours. We have to do something for you. And I think I have an idea. You are getting much better as a writer, and though I dislike competition in my chosen profession, I think you should enter employment.'

'Do you want me to write for the *New York Herald Tribune*?'

'I would certainly discourage you in that. They only have one contributor here, me, and they think I'm a man at that. Max Johnstone is my pen name. I've no intention of cutting my own throat.'

'Then what?'

'Romesh and I are going to start our own magazine.

It will be mainly political and nationalist and I know you could help us. You have a valuable skill with which you can earn a living – you can read and write English fluently.'

And thus I began my profession as a writer.

The next morning Mohini donned her burkha and they took a gharri to Romesh Nairoji's office. It was a large bungalow, set well back in a garden. A board outside the gate proclaimed the building as the office of Nairoji & Sons. A number of gharris and rickshaws were waiting in the street, and even as they walked up the short drive, Mohini noticed the constant activity, the coming and going of Indians in suits who doffed their hats courteously to Alice (Mohini was ignored). A few men waited on the verandah and leapt up to give their chairs to Alice, and then as an afterthought, to Mohini. It was strange how deferential they were to the European, but one of their own was seen only as an object. Their behaviour reminded her of the way her husband had treated her, with ill-concealed contempt.

Romesh didn't immediately leap to his feet either when the women were ushered in by a peon. He waited until the door closed behind them, and then came round his large desk to hug Alice and kiss her cheek. He peered into the slit shading Mohini's eyes.

'You are inside there, aren't you?'

'Yes,' Mohini whispered in reply. She wasn't sure how she should behave.

'Good. Well, if you want to work in that thing you can, but I doubt whether any of your husband's goondas will be prowling around Nairoji & Sons, and I think you should put it aside.' He waited, and slowly Mohini lifted off the black cloth.

'It must be hot in there, with a sari as well. Come. I have prepared an office for you.'

'I've never been in an office.'

'It's like any other room, my dear,' said Alice. 'It will

have a desk, a chair and will soon be overflowing with all your papers.'

'But what shall I do in it?'

'You'll be helping Alice to edit the magazine. She's not going to have time to sit here, day in and day out. Nor shall I. I think that the first issue, until we can drum up other contributors, will be composed of writings already published. You will choose extracts from the writings of men like Tilak, Hume and others. Then Alice and I – well, usually Alice – will sift through your selection and make the final choice.'

'What is the name of the magazine?'

'*Sher*. Tilak called his *Kesari*, but I believe the tiger is a fiercer beast than the lion.'

Mohini's office was just down the corridor from Romesh's, towards the rear of the bungalow. It was exactly as Alice had described it, except there were no papers yet, only piles of books.

'*Sher* will be issued as a monthly magazine, and our first issue will come out in about two months' time.' Romesh was as enthusiastic about this new venture as a child with a new toy. He could already imagine it influencing the minds, not only of Indians, but of the government itself. 'You will be paid twenty-five rupees a month to start with, and when the magazine has a steady circulation, we will raise your salary.'

'When am I supposed to start?'

'Now,' they both said, and closed the door on her firmly.

Mohini cautiously sat down in her chair behind her desk. She wasn't at all sure of what she should do next, and felt intimidated by her surroundings. For the first day she only stared at the closed door, hoping it would open and allow her to escape. She had a window, and spent some of her time watching a servant woman in the next bungalow scrub dekshis, wash clothes and care for three children. Her duties were endless. Peons would come out to smoke a beedi quickly and return to their work, but the woman continued her labours. In the

210

evening, Romesh opened the door and gratefully Mohini donned her burkha and went to the gharri which would take her home again.

On the second day, she opened a book by Hume and read:

There are aliens, like myself, who love India and her children. [He had written an open letter to all Indian university graduates, with the permission of the government.] But the real work must be done by the people of the country. If fifty men cannot be found with sufficient powers of self-sacrifice, sufficient love for and pride in their country, sufficient genuine and unselfish patriotism to take the initiative, and if needs be to devote the rest of their lives to the Cause – then there is no hope for India. Her sons will remain mere humble and helpless instruments in the hands of foreign rulers.

Mohini had not considered herself a revolutionary before, nor had she volunteered for this post of editor. She had been pushed into it by Alice, but she now experienced a tentative sense of elation.

She could not eat or sleep much for the first few days. It was difficult to decide whether she felt excited or terrified. What new disgrace was she now bringing upon her dead father and mother? No woman in her family, as far as she could remember, had ever worked. They had always led comfortable, if somewhat narrow lives. Only the poor worked, and her family had been, if not exceedingly wealthy, then at least comfortable. Apart from the practice of medicine, her father had owned good arable land which gave them a decent income. Her husband, also from a landowning family, was a lawyer by profession, though most of his income was derived from the paddy fields and cashew groves. He was wealthier than her family, a distant cousin of the Baroda Maharajah. The match, from her uncle and aunt's view, had been a good one, despite the great difference in their ages.

211

So Mohini wrote in her journal:

If only we had a heroine who worked for her living in our pantheon of goddesses and amongst our mythic heroines. If Sita or Draupadi had worked, receiving emoluments for their labour, in the field or in the administration of the kingdom, I would feel a certain ease at the prospect of this work. I have none to pray to for guidance, none to emulate. And yet, what I am about to do I find honourable. I am working in an honourable profession, for the cause of India. I should not be ashamed, yet I am, deeply so. I feel disgraced, I feel soiled, I feel terrible things I cannot even describe in these pages. I know how I could be looked upon by my family – as a fallen woman, no better than a nautch dancer. And now, as I write, I dream again of Kim. I had laughed with him about my aspirations to be a nautch dancer, lying, naturally, and he had good-humouredly explained my duties. I wish he were here now to guide me. He was a man filled with wisdom. He did not treat me cheaply, as other men have done, but as a companion and a friend. Oh, Kim! I shall never see you again, though you will always remain alive in my mind and in my heart. What should I do? Work. It is a strange word for one such as me. But I cannot remain in the house, husbandless, diminishing my life. I will work, and though I write this firmly, I know I shall constantly waver and want to run back into purdah. Oh God, why did you make me thus? Why did you not make me obedient? Why did you not make me subservient? Why did you not make me a good woman?

God remained silent. Mohini felt ill with each dawn, but resolutely dressed and, after a reassuring embrace from Alice, took a rickshaw (cheaper than a gharri) to her office. The men, writers who sat hunched over huge, leather-bound ledgers, and peons perched on stools, were quite baffled by Mohini. She would arrive in her

212

heavy burkha and disappear all day inside her office. They, naturally enough, believed her to be a Muslim, but the peon who took in her tea and tiffin swore she was Hindu, because she wore a sari. But she had no marriage thali.

'It will take the men a little while to get used to you,' said Romesh. 'You are a brave girl, Mohini.'

'I'm frightened.'

'You'll get over that. We also expect you to do some writing. Alice is absolutely confident in your abilities.'

'But I can't use my own name. My husband . . .'

'Call yourself Draupadi, or Padmini.'

'No, Parvati. I have used that name once before.' And, though she couldn't really admit it to herself, if Kim was still alive, he might by chance, the gamble of dice, glance at the magazine and see the name Parvati. He would not know it was she, but it might remind him of her.

What the three lacked in experience, they made up for in enthusiasm. Alice was the firm base of organisation upon which Mohini and Romesh anchored themselves. She was breathtakingly bold, while they were tentative, only because the laws of sedition hung more over their heads than Alice's. In their very first issue of *Sher* the masthead read – Publisher: Romesh Nairoji, Editor: Alice Soames, Assistant to Editor: Parvati. Alice printed an extract from Tilak on the front page, and the entire issue was dedicated to him. The extract was printed in bold type.

This alien government has ruined our country. In the beginning, all of us were taken by surprise. We were almost dazed. We thought that everything the ruler did was for our own good, and that this English government had descended from the clouds to save us from the invasions of Tamerlane and Genghis Khan, and, as they say, also from internecine warfare. We felt happy for a time, but soon it came to light that the peace which was established in this country did more. As Mr Daddhabhai has said, we were prevented from going at each other's throats so that a foreigner might go at the throats of us all. Pax Britannica has been established here in order that a foreign government may exploit our country.

Mohini's own contribution, sandwiched between a lengthy story on the exploitation of India by the British, written by Alice Soames, and an article on the last Congress Party meeting by a reporter on *The Hindu*, a Madras newspaper, was quite brief. It was her first effort, and she stared all day long at the name, Parvati, her name, in print.

I am a woman and history advances without our being aware of it. People like me have lived in all the dark, dim corners of the world, where the price of rice or envy for a piece of jewellery is of more importance than the efforts of men to change our lot in life. We are backward because we are incapable of dreaming of a future in which men and women are equal in their treatment of each other. A future in which caste is of no importance, and in which we take pride in ourselves as individuals, rather than as members of sects which define us so narrowly.

New ideas can frighten and exhilarate. We grow afraid, waiting for lightning to strike us dead, as if God were damning us for daring to question the traditions and practices of a thousand years. Yet it is these ancient ideas that now shackle India and its women in chains. If we escape our past, India too will escape this foreign domination. We, like India, must let go of the old and grasp the new. At this moment it is frightening for us all, as we sway between the two; teetering first on one side, clinging to our past, then the other. The old is comfortable, familiar; the new is unknown.

Yes, yes. What Mr Tilak says is true; we must practise swadeshi. We must fight for swaraj. I am breathless with excitement for such things. I, a Hindu woman long incarcerated in purdah, and now wishing to march with banners. I am truly a disgrace, but how can I not feel for my motherland? In England, I am told, they allow the common man to speak his mind, but Tilak, because he has called for swaraj, has been expelled from his own Congress Party and imprisoned by the British in Mandalay. Who else is there to lead us, now that he has gone? Gokhale is too friendly with the English. He believes in patience, but for how long must we be patient? We must force ourselves to change, hurry along this change, if we are ever to escape British rule.

The first issue of *Sher* sold 2,879 copies. It was a decent distribution and encouraged them. But the competition was fierce. All over India, magazines and newspapers, some in English, most in the vernacular–Gujerati, Maharati, Bengali, Tamil, Telegue – had begun to proliferate. It was as though writing and printing had been newly discovered and men (mostly men) found they had minds to use within their heads.

By the end of the first year of publication, *Sher* had a circulation of 5,000 copies per month. It didn't make Romesh rich, but nor did it bankrupt his family. *Sher* had the good fortune to have Romesh's wealth supporting it for the first few issues, while less fortunate publications folded. However, there were always others to take their place.

Mohini had less and less time for her own writing. She virtually became the publisher and editor, and though she was given a rise in pay to thirty-five rupees a month, her name wasn't moved up on the masthead. Her life had slipped into the routine of an employee, going every day from Malabar Hill into Bombay and gradually, as she began to feel more confident, she shed her burkha on these journeys. However, if she were to deviate from her routine, to the bazaar or to the printers, she would disappear once more under the black shroud.

Alice continued to write and report and published the

articles she wrote for the *New York Herald Tribune* in *Sher*, and *vice versa*. Occasionally, if time permitted, Mohini would accompany her on an assignment to cover a festival. They would travel by train, in third class, where Alice was looked upon in awe. But since Mohini would have felt awkward in a first-class carriage, Alice had no alternative. On these occasions, Mohini would travel in her disguise, for she always remembered the feeling of those watching eyes, and prayed that if she wore Muslim dress the eyes would never be able to find her.

So when Alice suggested that Mohini should accompany her to the annual Congress Meeting in Allahabad, and that she should write a separate article for *Sher*, Mohini was delighted. She was to be a 'correspondent', and though it wasn't for a grand American newspaper, she felt extremely pleased at the elevation from mere 'assistant-to-editor'.

18

KIM HAD forgotten the noise and smells and crowds in
Bombay. The city assaulted his senses, and, if he had
not known his search had to begin here, he would have
run away. The lane of jewellers had not changed at all
since his first visit. He climbed the stairs at the back and
entered Isaac Newton's room.

Newton sat engrossed with his stones. To one side,
in a rejected heap, lay a tall pile of drawings and calculations.

'Kim!' He jumped to his feet and embraced him. 'You
are well?'

'Yes, yes, I am well. You haven't changed.'

'How can I change? God has made me the way I am,
and I accept his will. I am close to success once more
with this new machine. Sit, sit.'

Kim sank to the floor. 'And how is Narain? Still
loafing?'

'Oh, yes.' Newton smiled. 'Always First Class BA in
that subject. He has loafed all over Bombay in search of
those two miscreants who did so much harm to you, but
they have long since vanished.' He wasn't sure how
much he could confide to Kim. He had received no
warning from the Colonel sahib about this visit.

'I came to the hospital, but every time I tried to visit
you, you were asleep. It was as if you had attained
moksha.'

'It felt like that, in a way,' said Kim. 'Even the police
cannot find those men?'

'No. They searched high and low.'

'The Colonel sahib told me he sent a sergeant and five constables, but they arrived too late.'

'I ran to the government bungalow myself and conveyed your message to him in person. He told me he would have the police sent immediately, and then I went home. It was much later when I got a message saying that you had been shot by those miscreants.'

'One of them I remember now. I broke his ankle. I heard the bone break. He could not have gone far.'

'He went very far. So far that no one found him at all.' Newton noticed Kim's preoccupation. 'But surely you have not come here in search of them?'

'No. I have come in search of the girl.'

'We have looked for her everywhere, and have given up.'

Newton spoke the truth. On the Colonel sahib's orders, his men had scoured Bombay from top to bottom, from one end to the other, but they had been unable to trace her. If that old rickshaw-wallah had lived a little longer, they would have eventually got round to questioning him, but disease had killed him a few days after he took Mohini to Malabar Hill. Newton had written his report for the Colonel and had then closed the file.

'I have seen her.'

'Here? Then we will find her.'

'I don't know where. I saw her in a vision. I must search for her. Can Narain help me?'

'The loafer is at your command.' He raised his voice and screamed, just as he had before. 'Narain! oh, Narain!' And, in due course, Narain appeared, rubbing sleep from his eyes and apparently wearing the same dhoti.

He was as delighted as Newton to see Kim again, and swore he would loaf with Kim all over Bombay in search of Parvati. But, even as he spoke, he caught Newton's eye and understood that he shouldn't be too diligent. The Colonel's orders remained: not to tell Kim anything about her.

He had tea and jelabis brought for Kim. Newton's tea

was served in a mug decorated with portraits of the Prince and Princess of Wales. He was inordinately proud of this souvenir, and told Kim he had personally seen them with his own two eyes.

'The visit was a great success, truly. Everywhere he went, we gave him a big Zindabad, and that pleased him a great deal.'

If Prince George had imparted such an impression to Newton, it was mistaken. Privately, he strongly disapproved of Lord Curzon's last act as Viceroy, the partition of Bengal, and thought even less of his English subjects in India. He wrote in his journal: 'Evidently we are too much inclined to look upon them [the natives] as a conquered and down-trodden race, and the native, who is becoming more and more educated, realises this.'

A city is not an easy place in which to find a woman. Many are hidden behind the walls of chastity, both Hindu and Muslim. Only the men of the household can look upon their faces and, for a stranger, it is impossible. The Hindu adopted the purdah from the Muslim, though once the Hindu woman of high caste moved about freely, without the imprisonment of the veil. She not only revealed her face, but in the courts and mansions she wore cotton so finely spun that men could also see the shape of her breasts and the colour of her nipples. But as a result of the constant invasion by Muslim conquerors, the freedom of the Hindu woman was greatly curtailed, and she too disappeared behind high walls and veils to protect her from ravishment.

But Kim was determined, and Newton ordered Narain to go with him on this impossible search for Parvati. But Narain was ordered that if he should find her before Kim, he was not to tell Kim, but send a message to the Colonel sahib. Newton was ignorant of the nature of the Colonel's interest in this female and, since he was a very small cog in the wheel, expected that he would continue to remain in ignorance.

Kim, in spite of his diligence, trod only the old paths of Newton's men. He questioned beggars, twisted and

219

demented in their poverty, rickshaw-wallahs, chowki-
dars, peons, bearers, bazaar women, fruit-sellers. By the
end of six months he had questioned half of Bombay but
no one knew of this woman who wore a blue sari. He
even asked prohits, enquiring whether any marriages
had been performed, for he'd not forgotten the man in
the vision. But they could not help him either.

Neither Newton nor Narain had seen their friend look
so bleak once he realised that his search was hopeless.
Parvati was embedded in his mind, a scar which could
never heal, and he would have to live with the memory
of her. Newton had, of course, reported Kim's presence
to the Colonel. The Colonel replied that Newton should
only keep an eye on Kim, and keep him regularly posted
on his progress. 'He needs,' he wrote, 'to get her out of
his system. He's young, and will eventually forget about
her.'

'We could try the brothels,' Narain suggested, and
received such a stare that he paled.

'She would never be there.'

'What woman wishes to be there? They are taken
against their will.'

'I saw her in . . . in a decent home, a room with . . .
chairs.' Now that this scrap of detail was remembered,
Kim tried to see again the setting of the vision, but he
had been looking so intently at her face, that even if she
had been sitting in front of a volcano he wouldn't have
noticed. He cursed himself. He had been trained to
remember even the minutest details in a room, and here,
smitten by love, he'd been blind.

The mention of brothels reminded Kim of another
time he had needed to visit one.

He remembered his long-ago promise. The prostitute
Lakshmi would still be waiting for him in her cell, waiting
for him to take her back to her village. He might have
forgotten many things, but the words spoken had been
his, and he knew he had to obey them. She would have
forgotten by now: the promises of men were lightly
made to her. They would not understand that she too

believed and loved, and could be hurt. Once they'd spent themselves, the men would not remember what she looked like, and to be forgotten so completely, after such intimacy, was the worst of all humiliations.

'You can make enquiries, but she will not be there. And, also enquire about the girl called Lakshmi. I promised to take her back to her village.'

Narain turned round in surprise. 'But she is a no-caste woman. Don't bother.'

'I made her a promise.'

'She will have forgotten by now. And even if you did take her to her village, her parents will refuse to allow her back into their house, and then what she will do? You tell me.'

'I know,' Kim said, 'but it is my duty to her. If she does not wish to return, then I shall be freed from my duty.'

'Ahre, duty to a whore. That doesn't count.'

'For me it does,' Kim said quietly. 'Find out if she still wants to return. I can do that one small thing for her.'

Narain grumbled and consulted his uncle. Newton was absorbed in inventing a steam engine to drive a cart. This, he reasoned, would be of great service to his countrymen. It would save them from feeding their bullocks. He had studied the steam engines in Victoria Terminus, and had read many books about them. His problem was to reduce them in size so they would fit beneath the cart and drive the wheels. However, he made time to listen to Narain.

'You will do what he asks, and you will keep me informed on the matter.' He shook his head. 'Women always cause troubles. The other one he searched for and couldn't find, and this one he can find but no man will want. You must not bring her to this household. I will not be able to rid myself of her untouchableness.'

'Am I a fool?'

'Yes. That, as well as being a loafer. Where is her village?'

'I don't know.'

'Find out, then. It could be nearby, or it could be on the other side of the damned country. These girls are brought in from all over the place.' He took out his notebook. 'I will send a message to the Colonel.'

'But it is a private matter.'

'For Kim, nothing can be private. He is a very important person. VIP, Colonel sahib tells me, and if he should even sneeze, I must inform him.'

'I shall need money for this, then,' said Narain. His uncle's brows drew together in disapproval. 'Research. How else can I discuss these matters with the nautch girls?'

'You will only *discuss* these matters, Narain. No hanky-panky with the girls. You will catch diseases. Your hair and your teeth will fall out.'

'No hanky-panky,' Narain promised, and took the money. He, too, had to sign in triplicate under the name of Agent No. 3. He knew his uncle was No. 1, but he'd never discovered the identity of No. 2.

Little had changed when Narain arrived at the brothel. Durga sat, malevolently indolent, on the same divan. A different boy was crouched behind now, making paan. The musicians were the same, playing the same ragas; a new note of melancholy had crept into their compositions, and the air was sadder, heavier. The girls, sitting bunched under the lamp, were fresh as fruits on display, sprinkled with the dew of baths, powder, perfume and silks. This time, Narain was not invited to sit beside Durga and receive paan, but instead he was waved over to another divan. She might have recognised him, but those sleepy eyes held no expression except for an empty smile. He was not with Ahmed Sait.

The girl, Lakshmi, did not recognise Narain. She sat cross-legged, chin on an upturned palm, concentrating on the music as if hearing it anew. She seemed not to have aged at all, but her shoulders were stooped and her eyes had become listless.

Narain admired such concentration. He lusted for

them all. Three were new, light-skinned, supple and young. The novices smiled and flirted with Narain, and he regretted that he could not choose one of them. Other men drifted in to sit beside him and, as the music faded, Narain signalled to Lakshmi.

She rose gracefully and they passed the smiling Durga to enter the gloomy corridor. The tiny, partitioned room was as spartan as before. She turned down the small lamp, lit incense and unwound her sari. Narain felt a momentary pang of guilt, watching her shape emerge from the cocoon of the sari, the curves and the swell of her firm breasts revealed in the shadowy light. He quashed guilt with the thought that she was not special to Kim, except as a promise.

When he had satisfied himself with her, while she slowly combed out her hair and tied it into a knot, he asked, 'Do you remember me?'

'No. Should I?'

'I came with two friends some years ago. One was Ahmed Sait.'

'Did you lie with me?'

'No.'

'Then how would I remember? Ahmed Sait brings many men here.'

'The man who lay with you was very fair. Like an Angrezi. He promised to help you to return to your village.'

She broke into a smile. 'Ah, *Keem*. He didn't lie with me, you know. We just talked, and he made me a promise.' She shrugged. 'I did not expect him to keep that promise. Why are you reminding me of him now?'

'He has been . . . ill. But he has not forgotten about you. If you still want to return to your village, he will help you. Where is your village?'

'It is near Rae Bareli.' Carefully she re-tied her sari.

Narain's heart sank. 'That's a very long way away. I don't know whether Kim will be able to make such a long journey for your sake.'

'I did not expect him to.' She accepted her rejection meekly. 'Thank him for remembering me.'

'Wait.' He pulled on his trousers as she moved to open the curtain. 'How would you escape from here?'

'Every Friday, at midday, we are allowed to visit the temple, the Meenakshi temple at the corner near the fort. If someone were there to help me, I could escape in the crowd.'

'Does someone go with you?'

'Yes, one. But he's only an old man.' She smiled sadly. 'We all know what would happen if we ran away. She'd send goondas after us and have us beaten and sold to Ahmed Sait.' The name made her shudder.

'Why should it be different with Kim, Lakshmi? He will get into trouble with these goondas as well.'

'But with his help, they won't find me.'

'They will wait for you in your village.'

'I lied to them about my village. I have not even told you. The people who kidnapped me have long gone. But tell Keem I am not important, and that I don't want to cause him all this trouble. It was just a dream I had, that is all.'

'Everyone dreams, except me,' Narain grumbled.

He had thought of lying, but Kim's steady gaze on his face, his intent way of listening, shook Narain's resolve. He reported the whole conversation and added darkly that Kim should not become enmeshed with this untouchable.

'But if she is untouchable,' Kim chuckled, 'why did you lie with her?'

'I did not,' Narain said hotly. 'That is different.' He avoided Kim's eyes. 'When will you go to the temple?'

'Next Friday. Maybe Parvati is no longer in Bombay. I must pursue the search in Delhi, where we first met.'

Above all, he needed solace. The years had depleted him. Physically he was as strong as ever, but inside he felt his vigour seeping away. The months in Calcutta still affected him. The men and women he had seen led lives which pivoted on their position, their ambitions, their contempt for a people, their loneliness in a land where a million friends waited, their longing for their homeland. Nothing existed for them beyond those small frontiers. He had felt excluded from such small longings.

He needed to seek his own destiny. He envied the Siddhartha and his Lama friend. They had been called to a spiritual way of life and had followed the true path. His own search was still a blind one, groping in the dark to find his own true path. He would deliver the girl to her village and then he would make a pilgrimage to Benares. Kim remembered the miracle of the Jat Sikh's son, and he believed another miracle could occur for him. It only happened to those who believed in such things; those who sought them, found them.

I am troubled by my duty. I know the charioteer Krishna said we must each perform our duty to our calling. A prince must rule wisely, a Brahmin must conduct puja correctly. I serve a prince, but I am not sure whether he is the right prince. Is he the one to whom I owe my duty? A prince must be just, he must love his people, or his throne will fall. I can hear already the rumble of the earth beneath the throne of the Kaiser-i-Hind. I have learnt a lot about the Angrezi, and I see they feel no sense of duty towards the people they rule. Yet I am one of them. I cannot betray their trust and loyalty, but I have a greater duty to the people to whom I belong. I must seek advice, find a guru who will guide me in these matters.

While he waited for Friday to come, Kim continued his search, even though it was now performed mechanically. It passed the time. He found himself in Crawford Market, and remembered another promise he had made, and quickened his step. He needed comfort, too.

The Excellent Madurai Hotel looked the same. Gopalan was still shouting at his chokra, but when Kim looked in he saw that it was a different boy now, even smaller and more bullied. The dye woman sat beneath lamplight and Kim went to sit on the step.

'Ah, my friend from Lahore, where the women are as

225

cold as the snow. How are you?' She cocked her head critically. 'You've grown lighter and thinner. You must eat, but keep that fairness. It will increase your value on the marriage market.'

'Maharani, I am pleased that you remember me. You have a very sharp mind. Your beauty is such that I have not been able to forget you, and have returned from my travels to sit once more at your feet.'

'Your tongue was truly dipped in honey.'

'But it has tasted things even more delicious than honey, Maharani. Will you be finished soon?'

She smiled. Without a word she rose and began to place the shutters over the entrance. They stood together in the glow of the lamplight, smelling the dyes and each other. She took his hand and led him to the rear of her shop where she had a small store-room, piled with empty gunny sacks.

'Ah, you're a strong man,' she whispered as they lay down together and he began to caress her body. She hurriedly untied his pi-jama. 'I had not forgotten you and thought often of this pleasure. And did you think of Rukmani?'

'Often, cursing myself for not having come to you before.'

She was as experienced and eager as Kim, and when they had sated their first appetite, they began again. They lay in the stuffy darkness lazily holding each other, exhausted by their activity.

'It was a long time ago now, but on the day the Kaiser-i-Hind's son came to Bombay, can you remember if any police came to the hotel?'

There was a pause. 'Yes. They came in search of you. They asked me too, and of course I lied. Why should I help those badmashes? What have you done?' There was no alarm in her voice, in fact just the opposite: eager curiosity.

'Nothing. I just wanted to know if they came.'

'The police come and go, useless fellows, and they call at the hotel for free food, and to lie with their women.'

226

She stroked his face tenderly. 'But that isn't what is worrying you. I see something else in your face. A woman.'

'Yes. I have searched for her, but I can't find her.'

'If it is your karma, you will find her.'

They made love once more. When they left the dye shop, the lane was deserted. It seemed strange after the busy activity of the day to come upon such emptiness.

'When shall I see you?'

'If I should return to Bombay, Maharani, I will come straight here.'

'I shall be eager even then,' she said, and laughed and walked away with the gait of a woman well satisfied with life.

It was hot and humid in the sanctum of the Meenakshi temple. A railing separated Kim from the idol, wrapped in silk, glittering with gold and diamonds, garlanded with flowers. She was made of black stone and barely visible. Tiny oil lamps flickered, changing the contours of her face and body, pleasing the worshipper with whomever he should imagine in these shadows. Men lined up on the left, women stood to the right, carrying offerings: coconut, plantains, camphor, paan, flowers. The floor was slippery with the milk of a hundred shattered coconuts, the air sweet with incense and camphor, the granite walls polished smooth as marble by the press of flesh over centuries. Kim gave his offerings to one of the priests.

'Namam?' he asked.

'Kim.'

'Kim,' the priest repeated, and entered the small chamber. He was an old man, balding, pot-bellied, shiny with sweat. He placed the flowers on the idol, lit the camphor, performed arthi and recited a sloka asking for blessings on the man 'Kim'. Blessings for guidance and good fortune. It was all over in a minute and the priest returned the offerings to Kim.

He went to sit against a pillar in the shade, legs

crossed, watching the devotees. Some showed fervour, prostrating themselves, others circled the shrine; some sat, like him, contemplative.

He saw the prostitutes enter in a group. They wore freshly ironed saris, with flowers in their hair and an aura of scrubbed innocence. But they walked with a disturbing boldness, a kind of defiance that marked them. Other women looked away. Kim doubted that God cared who worshipped. Eight girls were bunched together; a ninth walked a step apart, looking at the crowd. Kim stood up so that Lakshmi could see him, and her darting glances passed over him once, then twice. He saw the downward look of despair, and then another frantic effort. She saw him, and barely concealed her delight. Behind her walked an elderly man with a cane. He wore spectacles with soda-boodi lenses, but there was a keenness to his glances that warned of an alert man.

The girls passed by, intent on worship. Only once did Lakshmi look back, to reassure herself that her rescuer waited and was not just a dream. Kim thought then of the countless tragedies, small and overlooked, of people trapped in destinies not of their own making. A perverse demon twisted and dangled them, changing the course of their lives at whim, pushing them into pits from which there was no escape.

'I have a rickshaw waiting,' Narain whispered. 'A very swift man. I paid him extra. How will you get out of Bombay?'

'By train.'

He was not annoyed about Narain's presence. He had grown fond of the young man and he only wished he could have said goodbye to Newton, too. But Newton would report back to the Colonel and now, so would Narain. There was no escape from watching eyes in this land.

'Will you tell Newton?'

'Oh yes. He has to know everything, otherwise the Colonel will get damned mad.' He dug into his kurta pocket and pulled out a few rupees. He thrust them into Kim's hand. 'I know you are a man who does not believe in having possessions such as wealth, but a few rupees will be useful to you on your travels.'

Kim tucked the money into his pocket. 'I cannot promise to repay this. How far will you come with us?'

'To the station only. I cannot leave Bombay. The rest of India is jungley to me.'

They rose as the chanting of the priests increased, the bells rang and the crowd around the sanctum had swelled so that people were crushed against each other, all seeking to receive darshan from Meenakshi. The heat had become unbearable and Kim was drenched in sweat as he and Narain pushed their way through. They saw Lakshmi intent on prayer. The old man prayed too, but he would look up from time to time to see that his charges were still together.

The priest finished the prayers, and as the people pushed their way out, Narain slid in to 'accidentally' block the old man's passage. The girls had stepped across the threshold and Kim followed them out, took Lakshmi's hand and quickly pulled her away. If the other girls had noticed, they gave no sign, but instead started on their walk around the shrine. The lane outside the temple was crowded with beggars, rickshaws and tongas. Tightly packed stalls sold all the necessities for worship: fruit, kun-kum, camphor, incense.

They threaded their way through the crowds and at the corner found the young rickshaw-wallah.

'I didn't believe you would ever help me,' were Lakshmi's first words. Disbelief was still in her eyes, even as she looked back nervously. 'Why?'

'I helped someone else once, and lost her.'

Lakshmi expected Kim to continue but he fell silent. The rickshaw moved slowly, a snail crawling through the lanes, and she could not help looking back for pursuers. She caught a glimpse of a man running after them.

'Someone is coming after us,' she said to Kim, and then to the rickshaw-wallah: 'Jaldi! Jaldi!'

Kim turned and saw Narain. He caught up with the rickshaw and walked beside it, sweating and out of breath. This time Lakshmi recognised him and looked away.

'Did the old man notice that she had gone?'

'Not yet. I saw him talking to the girls but they were shaking their heads. He will look around a while longer before reporting her to Durga.' He grinned. 'Then all the goondas will be let loose.'

'They will recognise you, my friend.'

'But I do not have her. You have. And I have enough goonda friends in Bombay to look after me, should I get into trouble. At the station you must catch the first train, wherever it goes. To wait would be dangerous. They will check the station first.'

The first train to leave Victoria Terminus was the train to Nagpur, and while Narain bought the tickets, Kim and Lakshmi found two seats in the crowded third-class compartment. The train began to move immediately and Narain panted up and handed Kim the tickets as he stood on the steps.

'You will remember me, Kim?'

'Yes, always, my friend.'

'Good. To be remembered is all a man can ask of life. It proves he once lived. You will live in me as long as I have life.'

Kim saw his tears and clasped Narain's hand tightly before letting go. Narain stood waving until the train moved round the curve and he dropped out of Kim's sight.

It took them two days to reach Nagpur, and they waited there another day, sleeping on the platform, before they caught a train to Benares.

'You have said so little to me,' Lakshmi said as they neared the holy city. 'Are you angry with me?'

'No,' Kim said. 'I have been thinking that, once I have left you, I do not know where I want to go next. I cannot wander for ever, and what I am looking for I am not sure how to find. I shall stay in Benares for a time, and then I think I will go to Delhi.'

'Will you not spend time in my village? My family will care for you.'

'Will they care for you now?' Kim asked. 'They might not want you back.'

'If that happens,' she said equably, 'I shall leave and find some work in Calcutta or Delhi or another city. I will become a servant in a household and forget my past.'

But, in that past, Kim held a special place. Throughout the journey, looking on him while he slept, caring for his needs – she would buy the food and fresh fruit at every station – Lakshmi thought about him. In the brothel she had known she would meet a man who would love and care for her, and she would return this love a thousandfold. And so she dreamed of living her life with Kim. They would settle in a village, far from the big cities where temptation lay, and she would have children and they would grow old together. A whole life was lived in a few minutes but it ran continually in her mind. When he slept, she would hold his hand and brush his cheek with her lips, so lightly that he did not wake up. She knew Kim would not stay with her. He was the kind of man she had never known, who gave without asking for anything in return, and all he wished for, it seemed, was to be free to continue his search. She had not asked him about his illness as he had not mentioned it. If only he would rest and remain with her she would make him strong and fat. It hurt her to hear that he would leave her in her village and continue his wanderings.

When they looked out at dawn they saw the holy city. The skyline was spiked with the countless Vimanas of the temples along the ghats. The Ganges glittered, thronged with pilgrims immersing themselves; the light playing on the water was pink and gold. They could smell the smoke and bitter-sweet odour of the burning-ghats, mingled with ghee and rice and milk.

To approach such sanctity excited the whole train, and when it stopped, people pushed and shoved to get off.

They were eager to reach the river; they had come to pray for miracles, they had come to be saved from countless sins, they had come to be cured, they had come to give thanks. Here were the accumulated hopes of all the people; they contributed their tithe of belief to Benares, swelling it to a huge wellspring of religious fervour. They believed, and Kim envied them their simple faith. By their belief it was possible for the blind to see, the lame to walk, the old to attain solace, the incurable to be made whole. Yet was belief the sole cure? Or did the Ganges, did the temples, did the air vibrant with prayers and the presence of the holiest of sadhus, have their own miraculous powers?

Lakshmi's village was two weeks' journey north of the city and the only way of getting there was by bullock cart, tonga, or on foot. They were jostled and pushed, besieged by beggars and rickshaw-wallahs and vendors and guides, all wanting something. With the presence of God came the avarice of men to fatten on the believers.

Kim drove them all away and Lakshmi followed him down the narrow lanes. They passed temple upon temple, as closely packed as the houses in Bombay, and there seemed to be as many temples as there were avatars. The streets were filled with noise and colour and thousands of people bent on worship. The old and infirm, the young with parents; the whole dusty air was expectant. If as a child she had ever visited Benares with her family, Lakshmi couldn't remember. But Kim appeared to know his way, for he confidently twisted his way through the narrow lanes until he reached a temple set a little apart from the others. It was the temple his old friend the Lama had stayed in during his search for the mythical river.

Inside the high granite walls, the noise and crush of Benares faded. The stone floor was smooth and cool in the shade and the ancient carvings looked as worn as a tapestry. However, the temple had only recently been erected. The old one had been razed by the Emperor Shah Jahan, and when the Mughal empire fell the priests had rebuilt it. Still, it held a sense of tranquillity. The air was soft with the murmur of prayers and Kim felt it embrace him, soothing cares and worries.

'This is my own special pilgrimage,' he explained. 'We shall rest here and I will meditate.'

Lakshmi was content to do whatever Kim ordered. She watched him seat himself, facing the small room in which the Lama had once stayed all those years ago. Now it was occupied by a pilgrim who had been disturbed in prayer when Kim had nostalgically peeped into the small cell.

Kim began to cleanse his mind of all thought. It took time to shed the memories, the smell of the woman nearby watching over him, the discomfort of the train journey, all the various petty distractions with which the mind loves to occupy itself. Gradually, he felt his soul becoming still, the agitation of thought receding to the outer edges. Within, at the point of emptiness, he saw the first gentle glow of light. It began as a spot, a pinprick, seductive and small, like a flickering lamp. It would go out if he allowed it to. He concentrated all his energy on preserving the light and gradually it began to expand, filling his inner vision until it flowed through his mind and coursed through his whole body. He felt himself become as weightless as a leaf, afloat in the pure air. It was a state of bliss, filled with calm and surrounded by a pure light that cradled him as a mother would a child within her body.

19

MOHINI'S HUSBAND was waiting for the Colonel in the shade of a banyan tree at the Royal Calcutta Club. He had a special pink tag tied to the lapel of his silk jacket which permitted him to enter the 'Europeans Only' enclosure. The public stand was situated as far as possible from the finishing line. He revealed no unease as he sat watching the Europeans strolling back and forth between their boxes, the club house and the saddling enclosure. It was like watching a drama; they were the actors, unreal in their costumes on this humid stage. He considered himself the audience, interpreting their actions and giving them life by his presence. Their stares at this intruder were met by his own: they took him for a prince, who were considered honorary Europeans when they behaved as such. He had a face too finely aristocratic to be considered handsome, though when he smiled the sharp lines on either side of his mouth softened. He was clean shaven, a growing fashion in the country, and wore a solitary gold ring with a large rectangular diamond on the little finger of his left hand.

Bahadhur Ram Shanker considered this meeting-place quite appropriate. He would not be observed by any of his countrymen, although he sat out in the open. The ruler and the ruled seldom met socially; the separation between them was occasionally inconvenient, especially if the meeting were clandestine. He was amused by the Colonel's choice. If they had decided to meet in secret, it would have been difficult. A hotel? But the Colonel would have had to visit an Indian hotel, and would be immediately noticed. A garden party then; but other Indians, men of influence like himself, would be in attendance and would notice their tête-à-tête and, if they did not remark on it, at least remember it at a later and inconvenient time. He could not meet the Colonel in his home except at night, and the Bahadhur found such actions excessively dramatic. Yes, a racecourse, where men and women wagered on winners, was ideal.

The club was an elegant and fashionable place. A great deal of money was spent on maintaining it to standards matched only at Ascot or Goodwood. People dressed with care for the occasion, the men in morning coats and silk hats, the women in summery frocks, flowered hats and parasols. They drank tea (except those who preferred something stronger in the afternoon) served in their boxes by bearers in spotless uniforms. The place was run with military precision. The Secretary of the club was an ex-military man, and believed that the strictest order should be maintained.

The saddling enclosure and the racetrack were beautiful oases of green turf in the brown expanse of Calcutta, well watered and maintained, with coolies standing by to prod the dislodged turf back down once the horses had passed.

And this particular occasion was particularly appropriate for their meeting. It was the annual Gymkhana Races, where only amateurs competed. According to his race card, the Viceroy, Lord Minto, would be riding in the last race of the day. Lord Minto, Bahadhur sahib had heard, was an excellent horseman and steeplechaser, a gentleman jockey.

A race was about to start and he pulled out his gold watch. The Colonel was a few minutes late. Bahadhur sahib placed an English cigarette in his ivory and gold holder and lit it. He should have been smoking an Indian brand, as a true nationalist boycotting all English goods, but he found swadeshi tedious. He had been to England once, as a young man, and had enjoyed the luxury of ordering his clothes from London. His suit was made in

Savile Row, the silk woven in Manchester; his shoes were hand-stitched by Peal, and his shirts purchased at Turnbull and Asser. A bearer passed with a tray of cool drinks. Bahadhur sahib snapped his fingers and defiantly took one. The bearer hesitated, met his stare, and returned to the club house to fetch a fresh order. As he sipped the nimbu pani – though the English called it lime-juice – he studied the horses parading around the ring. They glistened with sweat and good health, jittering nervously at the watching crowd. He didn't care much about horses, and was amused that people could be so foolish as to wager their money on the speed of an animal and the corruption of men. He only gambled on certainties.

Both men saw each other almost simultaneously. As the Colonel approached, Bahadhur sahib thought wryly that for once he had the advantage. After all, his was the only brown face – he didn't count the servants – in this little England, while the Colonel was one of the crowd. It was a curious reversal, and he understood why the English clung so tightly together: to be part of the crowd in a way they could never be once they stepped out of these temporary preserves. He rose only when the Colonel stopped in front of him.

'Bahadhur sahib, I am sorry to have kept you waiting.'

'I have been enjoying myself watching the fillies,' Bahadhur sahib said. He noted the Colonel's frown as two young ladies walked past, deep in a soft, laughing conversation. 'I meant the horses.'

'Of course. Why don't we go for a walk and have our discussion?' They walked towards the saddling-enclosure. The Colonel studied his race card and appeared to be fairly knowledgeable about the animals and their amateur riders. 'Sun King's got a fair chance of winning. It's the right length for him and Henderson's an excellent rider. Do you want to place a bet? I can do it for you.'

'Thank you, no. I allow that pleasure to men more foolish than I. But please go ahead, Colonel.'

'Maybe I'll wait.' The Colonel never felt quite at ease with Bahadhur sahib. The man seemed to be hiding a constant smile, like a secretive cat. His affectation of an English gentleman in those expensively tailored suits the Colonel found unsettling. It gave him an air of defiance which was hard to explain. He was a man who enjoyed power and wanted more of it. The Colonel was in a position to advise him on his moves.

They walked a bit further along the railings. The green track curved round in a large oval and in the far distance stood the starting gate. The races were run in an anti-clockwise direction. The two men took their places about fifty yards past the finishing post. The horses were now being led slowly up the course towards the starting gate and the Colonel watched them through binoculars.

'I think it's time you made a decisive move. It would be a good idea if you joined the Congress Committee now. It's floundering and needs new leadership to take it in the right direction. We feel you would make an excellent leader.'

'It is possible that I could be found acceptable by the other Congressmen. In Surat I managed to keep in the background, so they still don't suspect me.'

'That was excellent work, Bahadhur sahib. And I've no wish to lose you as my Daddaji just yet. They will be meeting in Allahabad soon. You should lay the ground-work for your election immediately. Naturally, the government will support your claim. We would prefer someone like . . . you . . . rather than another Tilak.'

'Will you be releasing Tilak before his sentence ends? If he should return . . .'

'He won't be coming back,' the Colonel said firmly, and Bahadhur sahib wondered if Tilak would die in his Mandalay prison.

'Ever?'

'Of course I don't mean for ever. But for some years.'

Bahadhur sahib had few illusions about his rulers. They claimed civility, but could behave as savagely as any Timur if it was to their convenience. Their vengeance for 1857 had equalled Nazir Shah's savage butchery of Delhi's inhabitants, and their brutality in Afghanistan in 1879 had, he had been told, sickened London. The Colonel's denial merely meant that killing Tilak was inconvenient at the moment. That could change if it suited them, if they felt themselves truly threatened. Their position as rulers was unassailable by India. But it would change; the Indian air reverberated with the crash of a thousand empires and the deaths of a thousand kings. Each had been for a moment unassailable. Of course the moment could last through his own lifetime; it was not possible to be precise in calculating the end of 'a moment'. But his family had survived only by their skill in such calculations. His father, his grandfather, his great-grandfather, had all been prime ministers to one prince or another, and Bahadhur sahib had a fine instinct in making judgements on new princes.

'What advantage would there be for me?'

'Power.' The Colonel lingered over the word, allowing it to stroke Bahadhur sahib's ears, allowing him to feel the silken caress of promises. 'We would see to it that your viewpoint is listened to as often as possible. Yours would be a moderate voice, of course, in Congress's dealings with the government. And we would help you in other ways. We'd make certain you are nominated to the Legislative Council as an adviser, eventually possibly even becoming a member of the Executive Council.' He paused. 'The first Indian ever to have held such a privileged position.'

'The first Indian': the phrase tasted sweet. The English made it a race, and the winner would gain the purse and the honours. Yet it was still odd to hear these words spoken on Indian soil by a stranger. The Colonel had the power to promise such things in a land which was not his. He could grant the boon or deny it, and Bahadhur sahib knew the value of being 'the first Indian'. It had an even greater meaning among his own people, struck them with awe, for it would mean he had achieved something beyond their wildest imaginings. They did not have the confidence to believe in their own ability, except when it was acknowledged by their alien rulers. He wondered how the words 'the first Englishman' would have sounded in England.

'That would be very satisfying,' Bahadhur sahib said. 'But it would be an expense I am not sure I could afford to incur, Colonel sahib.'

'We would ensure that all your costs for campaigning, travelling and, let's say, baksheesh, would be reimbursed.'

In the distance, through the haze, they watched the flag drop and the horses leap forward. The cries of encouragement came mutedly from the Europeans' enclosure; in contrast, the Indians set up a dull roar. The Colonel watched the race through his binoculars while Bahadhur sahib studied the face beneath the glasses. It had strength and determination, revealing little emotion. 'Stiff upper lip,' he thought to himself. The horses swept past them and the ground shook.

'Good advice, Bahadhur sahib,' the Colonel said. 'I should have lost by a head. Next time he'll make it, I'm sure.'

'It would cost around fifty to sixty thousand. Possibly a lakh.'

They watched the horses being led back to the stables; the winner to the winner's enclosure, the 'first'. The horses were drenched with sweat. A delighted woman in a large pink hat and white gloves came forward to kiss the lathered neck of her horse.

'That sounds reasonable. Oh, there's Mrs Nesbitt. Her husband is in timber. Making an absolute fortune, some of it illegally, I suspect.' The Colonel's soft aside was weighted not with envy, but with puzzled contempt for the lady.

'Is it wealth you do not approve of? Or corruption?'

'The Nesbitts are less than desirable acquaintances. They've been here for three generations and I've never known more arrogant or tiresome people in my life. We might all look the same to you, Bahadhur sahib, but there are plenty of my own people I dislike. People such as the Nesbitts think they have every right to exploit India commercially, and they have nothing but contempt for the people.'

'I thought that a common bond, Colonel sahib.'

'Damn it, no. I love this country. I've worked hard for it and for its people. And there are many men like me who've devoted their lives to the welfare of the native. We've served in the districts and in the jungles, places you've never even been to, and been damned lonely out there, too. Go into any village and ask the villager what he feels about us, and they'll tell you we've always been fair and just in our treatment of them. But the Nesbitts are here solely to make money, as much as they can, and how they do it is supposed to be no concern of ours. We are here to protect the people from the likes of the Nesbitts. And then you get all these Returned From Abroad Indians who, because they went to Oxford or Cambridge and wear suits, think they can tell us what they feel about us and how we should run the country. We've run it a damned sight better than you people ever did.'

'I had not realised you felt such passion, Colonel sahib,' Bahadhur sahib murmured.

'It isn't passion. I was just trying to explain the attitudes of a person like Mrs Nesbitt to you,' the Colonel said abruptly. 'Shall we have tea?'

'Shall I be permitted to?'

'You are my guest.'

They passed a florid, elderly man who was beaming proudly at the lady leading the horse around the winner's circle. He tipped his hat to the Colonel, who ignored him. When Bahadhur sahib looked back, he saw a brief scowl flit over the man's face before it broke back into a grin.

'But,' Bahadhur sahib began while he waited for the Colonel to order tea and cucumber sandwiches from a bearer, 'they are the ones who brought the empire here: trade did not follow the flag, as you say, to this soil.

Now you have such a dislike for those same traders.'

'And what a mess John Company made of it. The Crown had to take over. Yet they still believe the country is run for their benefit, their business, their selfish interests.'

Though he behaved as though he was only mildly curious about the conflict within the people who ruled them, Bahadhur sahib was acutely interested. What he and every Indian saw as a monolithic force was actually much more diverse. The interests of administrators like the Colonel sahib were in conflict with the interests of the commercial Europeans. He was not sure how this could be exploited. Now was not the time to consider such things too deeply, but to keep them in the back of the mind. The nationalist call for swadeshi could, if the whole country were united, eventually deeply wound the commercial class so that it would not be worth their while to remain. He had no doubt that this would happen one day, but it would depend on whether India could find a man able to perform the miraculous act of uniting all India.

'Well, I think it is time I took over Congress. The party is becoming a popular movement among the people.'

'Only the middle class, and they have no influence on the mass of India. It will serve their purposes to talk and talk and talk.'

'You believe the mass will not join?'

'Oh, for God's sake, how can they?' the Colonel said impatiently. 'Congress is totally divorced from the reality of India and its people, the villagers who sweat and toil so desperately hard for sustenance. What can Congress promise the people that we can't give them?'

'Ah, yes, I had forgotten about your people's great love for the peasant,' Bahadhur sahib said. Tea was set down carefully, with two plates of sandwiches and a plate of cakes. He saw that – for the moment – the Colonel was correct. Congress was all wind, powerless. It had become increasingly critical of the government, but as a party in opposition, it had little hope of ever getting into power. 'I believe it will be possible to influence the party. I know a number of Congressmen, close friends of mine, and a number more inclined to patience than any firebrand actions. But the task would be made easier if there were certain compromises on the part of the government.'

'Such as?'

'As you suggested, expanding the Legislative Council and nominating an Indian on to the Viceroy's Council. That would at least give the impression of the native having some say in the governing of our country.'

'We'll see,' the Colonel said. 'Mr Morley, the Secretary of State for India, is at this very moment discussing new legislative reforms with Lord Minto. I will have a word with the Viceroy and pass on your suggestions.'

The Colonel flattered Bahadhur sahib by implying that they were his suggestions now. The man preened himself and sipped his tea delicately, already imagining himself ensconced in the Viceroy's Council, possibly with a title. Sir Bahadhur sahib Ram Shanker. It had a pleasant sound to it. Titles were clever touches to keep in check those who aspired too greatly, for they coveted them more than riches.

'Have you discovered the whereabouts of your wife, Bahadhur sahib?' the Colonel asked with consummate politeness, but watching the man intently, pleased to see him flinch at the memory.

'No.'

'I thought we should find her in Bombay, but she seems to have vanished into thin air. These things can happen in India.'

'What was the name of the agent who befriended her?'

'I didn't mention a name,' the Colonel replied.

He had not wanted to be reminded of Kim, who had also vanished from the face of the earth. His unreliability arose from a childhood spent among the natives. If he was not dead, he was possibly wandering in the company of another fakir, and no doubt if it ever occurred to him, he would send word to the Colonel.

The Colonel was most displeased at his lack of responsibility, angry in fact, but still he held his feelings in check. Kim was valuable just because of his ability to vanish into India. And it was because of this that the Colonel could not find him. Thinking back over the past year, his old anger with Newton surfaced again, even though he knew it wasn't the man's fault. How could he have known that Kim would disappear? When Kim left Calcutta, Newton had reported Kim's arrival in Bombay and his activities. Then when Kim left abruptly, unable to find Bahadhur sahib's wife, Newton wrote another letter. If he'd sent a telegram, the Colonel could have kept track of Kim's journeys by train, but by the time he had been able to relay messages to the station-masters and the police, Kim had gone.

'Have you questioned him again?'

'No. He didn't know where she went. Such foolhardiness: I hope she has not come to any harm.'

'She is . . . was . . . a very stubborn girl. I should have taught her a lesson, but I was lenient with her because she was young.'

'Indeed,' the Colonel said dryly. 'Has she made any contact with her uncle and aunt?'

'Not yet. They will let me know if she does. She is as much a disgrace to them as to me.'

'And if she should be returned to you?'

'I shall chastise her.' Bahadhur sahib spoke primly, but the Colonel had no doubt of the exact meaning of the biblical term.

'I hope there won't be a scandal. We couldn't have a possible member of the Imperial Council involved with anything unsavoury.'

'It will be very discreet. We cannot allow our women to behave in this way. For instance, if your wife had run away – for whatever reason . . . another gentleman maybe – and then had returned. Would you forgive her or punish her? I'm sure you understand my feelings, don't you, Colonel?'

Bahadhur sahib turned and smiled at the Colonel and

the Colonel felt a sudden chill. He saw a secret in that smile: his own, long-forgotten and buried, and now on the brink of being revealed. Yet it could not be. Hardly anyone knew about his private life. His past was as secret as his work, and what had happened so long ago had had no witnesses. The Colonel took his time, watching the horses parading for the next race, the jockeys mounting, before he decided to discover if Bahadhur sahib's little smile had meant anything or not.

'Why should I understand?'

'Colonel, you think you know India, yet you do not. Secrets can be discovered. Small people too know our secrets. My servants, your servants, they see and listen and we forget that they stand in our shadow in silence.' He nibbled on a cucumber sandwich, its taste evoking memories of a bad English hotel. 'We are two men in similar situations. My loss, admittedly, is a more recent one than yours. Therefore you have more experience than I in this matter of disappearing wives.'

'My wife died,' the Colonel said shortly. Bahadhur sahib didn't flinch at the cold stare. In fact, he responded with sly humour.

'Of course she did, Colonel.' He looked directly into the Colonel's eyes and they both recognised the lie.

'Did you hear differently then . . . from the servants?'

'Ah, you know how we natives love rumours. They are juicy as bones to a pi-dog. Rumours. Naturally we need not believe, now that you insist they are untrue, that your wife met another person and absconded.' Carefully he placed a cigarette in the holder. 'But of course that is only a rumour. Isn't it, Colonel Sahib?'

'It is. A cruel one, too.'

'And your children were too young to understand such things and then they were sent away to England. I am more fortunate. Or should I say, unfortunate. I have not been blessed with children.'

'I would like to know who spread such a rumour about me and my . . . wife.'

244

'No one person, I'm afraid, Colonel sahib. Just whispers on the wind, travelling all the way from the south to Delhi. It is only by chance that I caught them. You were posted near Bangalore in your early years of service, were you not, Colonel?'

'Yes. That's where she died. Cholera.'

'That terrible disease. Two of my brothers died from it. I wonder if we shall ever conquer such calamities? It travels in the air, I'm told. How tragic that your wife should also be struck down, leaving you with the burden of raising two small children. However, I can assure you with all my heart I will see to it personally that these rumours about your wife are never repeated.'

'I'll see to it as well,' the Colonel said, and both men rose. A bearer scurried over to place his chit-book for the Colonel to sign. He noted a lime juice added on and signed the chit.

The two men strolled to the exit, neither speaking, absorbed in their own thoughts. The Colonel stood a head taller than Bahadhur sahib. Both men walked erect, but the Englishman with an authority fuelled by the deference accorded him by all those who passed them. Bahadhur sahib was quick to note this difference and held himself straight, trying to inch upwards. He knew this was another kingdom in which he had no rights. The pink tag on his lapel was only a reminder that he was a stranger on his own soil. Their route to the exit was lined with police constables.

'These certainly are troubled times when a sahib cannot walk in peace in this land,' Bahadhur sahib said.

'It's only temporary,' the Colonel replied, but he did not believe it himself.

He had spoken reflexively, a polite response he had given often over the last three years. Ever since Curzon had partitioned Bengal into east and west, and then left the disastrous problem he had created to return safely to England. The Bengalis vehemently opposed the partition. As Eastern Bengal was predominantly Muslim and Western Bengal Hindu, Curzon had, to make

245

administrating the massive province less arduous, divided it with as little consultation as possible. Vocal opposition had turned to violence and young nationalist Bengalis had set up secret societies which threw bombs and murdered British officials.

Only a week before, Mrs and Miss Kennedy, harmless English ladies, had been murdered by a bomb thrown into their gharri. It had been a cruel mistake. The police had caught the killer, Khudiran Bose, who would be tried and hanged. He had confessed to the mistake. The gharri in which the ladies were travelling looked identical to the one owned by Magistrate Douglas Kingsford. The Bengalis hated Kingsford, an admirable disciplinarian. He believed in whippings (Khudiran Bose had been whipped for 'arrogance' towards a European policeman), and many a young Bengali brought up in front of Magistrate Kingsford, for whatever offence, was soundly thrashed as a part of his punishment. The whole European community in Calcutta had been outraged by the murder. In its editorial on the day following the killing of the two ladies, *The Pioneer* suggested that the government should hang ten natives for every European murdered. 'This will give due warning to the native that there will not be a repeat of 1857, when we Europeans treated them so leniently.' The other result of the bombing incident was that the police now protected all European homes.

'Divide and rule,' Bahadhur sahib said, as if he had not heard the Colonel. 'Every empire has an inbuilt wisdom, ways to perpetuate itself. Your military might can still hold India, but your political philosophy is to meet us not with brute strength, but with subtlety. We divide ourselves and you rule us. What would happen, I wonder, if one day we did not divide?'

'That is a day which will never come,' the Colonel said flatly.

At the arched gateway, woven with pink bougainvillea, they stopped in front of an armed constable who immediately presented arms. The road outside the race

246

club was sprinkled with a few army men, lounging touts and racegoers.

'Best of luck.'

'Thank you, Colonel sahib. I will keep you informed of progress in Allahabad.'

The Colonel didn't wait to see if Bahadhur sahib found a gharri to take him to the station. He was glad to get rid of him. Bahadhur sahib always unsettled him; the man wove a spell of deceit as good as his. We are alike, he told himself as he walked away. We spin tales to distract the mind from its real purpose, like the charmer weaving strange tunes on his flute. Except that I work for the greater good, while Bahadhur sahib strives only for his own advantage. He will remain loyal only as long as I can fulfil my promise to him, and we continue to hold the power to do so. The moment we lose that power, he will be gone. But that will never happen, and in that much I can trust Bahadhur sahib to do my bidding.

Bahadhur sahib didn't move far in his gharri. He climbed in and remained seated quietly. His two servants, the burly, dark men who had once frightened Mohini, waited poised for his order.

'Shouldn't we go?' one asked finally.

'No. I want to see who the Colonel is going to meet next. If I was invited to the privacy of the Angrezi racecourse for business, others will be as well.'

He waited an hour before another gharri pulled up at the entrance and two Indians climbed out. They too wore pink tags in the buttonholes of their long jackets. Bahadhur sahib, recognising them, smiled in pleasure at his own cleverness, and told his men to take him directly to the railway station.

The Colonel had returned to his table, satisfied at becoming ten rupees richer on a small bet. He was studying the race card when the two Muslim gentlemen came to stand in front of him.

'Mr Ali, Mr Khan! Delighted to see you. No trouble I hope for you to visit me.'

'None.' Mr Ali spoke for his companion. They both wore an air of apology, Mr Khan's the more pronounced. And when they sat, they only perched. They didn't feel the same confidence as Bahadhur sahib had, and when the Colonel's light conversation ended, the silence stretched between them. Tea was served once more, but neither the Colonel nor the two Muslims ate or drank.

'Well, I think it's time I introduced you both to His Excellency. He should be in the changing-room. We'll only take a minute. He has the last race of the day and hates discussing politics before he mounts up.'

'Then we shouldn't have troubled him today.'

'Oh, it's no trouble at all. It is a good opportunity for him to tell you how he feels about your forming the Muslim League. Congress, after all, is a Hindu party and it will only look after the interests of its own people. We believe the Muslim should be represented in government, too.'

'It was most encouraging for us that you should personally take such an interest in the Muslim League, Colonel sahib. Without your help, it would have taken us much longer to form the League, and years before we could have had an audience with the Viceroy. When we met him in Simla last year, he told us that the government would recognise us immediately, and ensure that the Muslim's rights would be protected.'

'To us,' the Colonel said as they strolled around the saddling enclosure to the changing-rooms, 'every Indian is important. We have to be sure that those with less power are not crushed by the Hindu majority.'

The Muslim League would be the counter-balance to the Congress party. While a number of Muslims still belonged to the Congress party, the government hoped the League would attract the majority of them. They had certainly succeeded, placing Congress in an uncomfortable position and undermining its claim to represent all Indians, whatever their religion. Congress had denied religious favouritism. But once the Muslims understood that the government would encourage them as separate from and equal to the Hindu-dominated Congress, they had insisted on forming their own political party. For the Crown's part, it was always easier to deal with two parties than with a united opposition. Neither party, however, truly represented the masses as they claimed. While Congress had somewhat widened its appeal to people other than the upper classes, the Muslim League represented the narrow interests of the wealthy Muslim landlord and the religious leaders.

The changing-room was in cheerful chaos. It smelt of sweat, leather, polish and dust. The men and boys, stripped to the waist, were exuberant as they prepared for their races or rested after finishing. In one corner, an elderly gentleman was weighing jockeys with their saddles and taking careful notes, and as they went out to their mounts there were calls of 'good luck'. The only furniture consisted of long benches and clothes hooks. On the other side of the room, two young ADCs, impeccably smart in uniforms, peaked caps and epaulettes, stood guard at the furthest door.

They immediately opened it for the Colonel and his two companions. The adjoining room was extremely large and comfortable. There were several leather arm-chairs, a dressing-table and even a bed. A small group of men stood with their backs to the door, facing the Viceroy. The Colonel recognised the Secretary and Steward of the race club and three of the Viceroy's cronies. The Viceroy was having his boots pulled on by two uniformed bearers. Two others waited with his colours, his riding whip and his saddle. A fifth held a silver tray with a pot of tea, while a sixth held a towel.

Lord Minto was a stocky man with a round, unmemorable face. It had the weatherbeaten and rusty hue of an English squire's, though a shade darker from the Indian sun, and had corroded from rich living. He sipped his tea, enjoying the services and attention of those who surrounded him.

'Come in, Colonel, come in.' He also had a country squire's booming voice. He didn't rise to shake hands with either the Colonel or the two Muslims who hovered near the door and had to be summoned forward. 'It's a pleasure, yes a great pleasure, to meet you, gentlemen.' The Colonel leant forward, softly reminded him of their names. 'Mr Ali, Mr Khan.' The Viceroy rose, soft-fleshed and stocky. He stamped his feet firmly into his boots. 'Why don't we take a turn in the garden?' He turned to the others. 'Gentlemen, you'll excuse us for a minute?'

The room led through french windows onto a porch and a lawn as green as the race track. It was screened off from the rest of the racecourse by a high hedge and patrolled by a dozen soldiers. The three men stood in the centre of the lawn, with the Viceroy facing them.

'I would like to say first of all that I am grateful to you for the opportunity you are affording me of expressing my appreciation of the just aims of the followers of Islam, and their determination to share in the political history of the empire. The essence of your request is that in any system of representation, whether it affects a municipality, a district board, or a legislative council, in which it is proposed to introduce or increase an electoral organisation, the Muhammadan community should be represented.' Lord Minto glanced up at the Colonel for approval and received a short, firm nod. He abruptly lost interest in the two Muslims, who looked like birds frozen in mid flight. 'Well, what do you think of my chances, Colonel?'

'I feel you've got a race on your hands. Young Scott is riding Prince Valiant, a most promising two-year-old.'

'I'll allow him a length or two at the start, but these young fellas push their mounts too hard.' He turned and began to wander back into the dressing-room, when suddenly he remembered the two Muslim gentlemen and thrust out his hand. They each shook it with fervour and hope.

The Colonel ushered the two men out of the Viceroy's presence and strolled with them to the gate.

'Will His Excellency keep these sentiments private, Colonel sahib?' asked Mr Ali.

'No. If you approve of what he has said to you both, he will make a similar statement at the next Executive Council meeting.'

'We approve.'

'Good.'

The Colonel waited until they had climbed into their gharri and driven off before he went in search of his own. He had no desire to watch His Excellency ride. Beneath the calm exterior he felt uneasy and wanted to escape.

'Home, sahib?' his coachman Sen called down, interrupting his thoughts.

'No . . .' He hesitated. The house would be empty. Emma was out visiting, and Elizabeth had gone to Simla to stay with friends; he didn't want to sit on the verandah staring out at the garden all by himself. There was work to be done in the office, drawing up a draft of proposals for Lord Minto.

He's such a change from Curzon, the Colonel thought. Minto was a bluff, good-natured man with none of the arrogance or the mercurial brilliance of Curzon. The Colonel believed he could be manipulated through his enjoyment of Viceregal office and pomp. It gave him a good income, and he could ride to his heart's content. He was also a man who had quickly grasped the reality of India, the need to crack down on seditionists and terrorists. In the Colonel's view, speech and action were as dangerous as each other, and he was relieved that Lord Minto shared the feeling. Mr Morley, sitting in London, had no idea of what was going on and, as Secretary of State for India, kept pressing to give the babus more say in local government. Mr Morley proposed that the Legislative Council in Calcutta be expanded to include thirty Indians, and those in the provinces to include fifty. The Colonel had no intention of letting such nonsense pass unopposed, nor had any other secretaries of the government departments in Calcutta. Lord Ripon in 1882 had suggested the creation of municipality councils with Indians, but the ICS had deftly sabotaged his proposals. They would do the same again.

'The office,' he ordered, hoping it would give him refuge from memories stirred up by Bahadhur sahib.

It is strange how the past can suddenly trap you. It waits, not in dark corners or on humid nights when you sleep in warped dreams, but in broad daylight, with the sun beating down, filtered by the delicate green leaves of a banyan tree, drinking tea and surrounded by a familiar world. Fear then feels unnatural because it is so unexpected. You meet it and pass it by, and only shiver long after at the thought of how closely the danger has brushed you.

I practised deception on myself, and have now become so used to it that I had forgotten Elizabeth's mother. Did she ever exist? Her image does, in Elizabeth. And now, on a sunny day, from the mouth of Bahadhur sahib, she emerges from the past like a demon out of the fire. A rumour that she did not die? The scoundrel knows that rumours come alive, they rise slowly, weaving and dancing, mesmerising the victim. It was our joint deceit that we pretended to believe it was only a rumour, but he is a man who will not let go of such power over me. He will track it down until he can pinpoint the moment of her death. Or disappearance. Oh God, sometimes death is such a convenience. It softens pain, gives reason to heartbreak. We can accept its finality, an ending which we cannot reverse. Even now I cannot think of her clearly, I cannot remember her features.

'Stop!' he called out, and the gharri halted. 'I'll walk the rest of the way.'

'But the heat, sahib, and all the dirt,' Sen said protectively. 'It would be better for you to remain inside. Office not far now.'

'Stop being a damned mother-hen, Sen,' the Colonel

252

scolded his old servant, though it cheered him that someone cared at least that much for him. 'A short walk will do me good. Just follow a little way behind.'

He got down and stretched, thinking he would escape the sense of claustrophobia, but instead found himself in a larger confinement – Calcutta. It teemed all around him: hawkers, chokras, beggars, the constant idle curiosity of men and women who would stand and stare as though they'd never seen a European. This, in spite of three centuries of their presence in this city which they had founded and built. He could not retreat, but grasped his cane and began to walk resolutely, the heat beating down on him, the dust settling on his polished shoes. The Colonel didn't consider this walk an act of bravery, though he was aware that out in the open he was an easy target for any hot-headed Bengali youth who carried a gun or a knife.

There had been another banyan tree, a long time ago, when he had been a young man. The memory reluctantly pushed into his mind from the far edges of forgetfulness. His mind had filed away the images and feelings and now, unexpectedly, that past was recalled. The pain still remained unbearable; time was no healer.

It had been a widespread banyan, two hundred years old if it was a day, on the stud farm in Hosur, a few miles out of Bangalore. He used to spend his weekend leave there with his friend Charles Redhead, the superintendent of the 2,500-acre farm. Charles always arranged a damned good hunt, and Europeans from a wide radius would leave their hunters stabled on the farm and come every weekend. Charles's bungalow, a cool, sprawling building set in a rose garden which he nurtured like a child, never had enough room for the gathering, but he arranged for tents and camp cots to be set up on the lawn. The Collector, the District Magistrate, the Police Commissioner and several army officers would gather on Saturday afternoon, with the memsahibs. Some of the ladies hunted, while others came just for the occasion. The Hosur Hunt Club had a hodge-podge of dogs

– setters, pi-dogs, labradors, alsatians. The farm and the surrounding country was perfect for riding, the land undulated gently and here and there were thickets of jungle. If you half-closed your eyes, it even resembled the English countryside in its contours, except that the grass was brown and coarse. But Hosur, because of its elevation, enjoyed a fine, sunny English summer most of the year round, cool and dry. In winter one needed a pullover and scarf in the mornings, and when the sun set, the nights were decidedly chilly. The farm also had a tennis court for those who didn't ride. It was laid out in the shade of three huge rain-trees.

He had owned a hundred-guinea hunter then, a damned good horse. They would gather under the banyan for a chota peg before the hunt moved off. It was on the third weekend – how damned precise memory can sometimes be – when she had arrived at the meet with an aunt in tow. Her hair, framed against a gap in the shade and lit by a beam of sunlight, had a reddish glow and the glow enveloped her face. It was a perfect face, with steady grey eyes and a firm chin. Even though he stood watching at some distance, he fancied he could smell English rain and the perfume of roses on her skin. He was drawn to her and soon found himself standing only a foot away, like a gawking schoolboy. She caught his stare; his intensity made her blush. During the hunt he kept a close eye on her. He had to admire her skill as a horsewoman, yet at times her recklessness made him wince. It seemed she wanted to match the men rather than following more cautiously with the other women. They got two jackals and she had been presented with one of the tails.

He went over to congratulate her later as they took refreshments. She was surrounded by admirers and he waited patiently. She slipped away from them and he quickly moved to her side.

But before he could speak, she said: 'Thank you for keeping an eye on me. It was grand fun. You must come and call on us in Bangalore.' She had a husky voice and when she smiled he felt blinded.

She lived with her aunt in the cantonment in Wellington Street. He called, had tea with her and was soon visiting her on every spare evening, accompanying her to dances at the Bangalore United Services Club and to dinner parties.

He could not help but lose his heart to Miss Soames. The intensity of his ardour outshone that of any other young man she knew. Oh, there were many others, but gradually, as word got around the mess and the club, they, grumbling with envy, turned their attention to other girls: there were plenty who had come out looking for husbands. He was attracted to her partly by her good looks, but also for her mind. He had never met a woman so widely read, who could speak intelligently on politics, history and science. Her father, he discovered, was a professor of history at Christ Church, Oxford, and her mother was a poet. Her aunt, Mrs Caxton, was a widow whose husband, a Chief Magistrate, had broken his neck out hunting. Their children in England were grown-up, and she had decided to remain in India among her friends, as a small number of Europeans were choosing to do, rather than return Home.

He could not clearly remember the courtship, except that he had never been more happy or more miserable in his whole life. Miss Soames was flirtatious, but quick to soothe his jealousies. She had a sharp, bright sense of humour, but didn't laugh or giggle as other girls did; instead she had a low, throaty chuckle which enchanted him. When she gave him her full attention, he would float on air, and love would sing in his heart. A small drawback was her informality towards the natives, but as she'd been out only six months, he was sure she would soon learn.

He had a small income besides his pay and was not as impecunious as many of his fellow-officers, which made him an attractive proposition for any young woman. She knew this, and appreciated the difference it could make for an army officer's wife in India. Before he could ask for her hand in marriage, though, he had first to obtain permission from his commanding officer. Colonel Waters frowned on his request, preferring young officers to put off marriage until they were thirty, and made him cool his heels for a few weeks. But he pleaded that private means did make marriage financially feasible for him, and how could he risk losing such a lovely woman? On the day Alice Soames accepted his proposal, he rode pell-mell all the way back to the barracks and bought the whole mess drinks until dawn. That was a hangover he never forgot.

They were married in St Andrew's Church, just off the South Parade, and spent their honeymoon in Ooty. On their return to Bangalore they found a small, pretty cottage in Langford Town, not far from the Club and the social life she enjoyed. He returned to duty a happy and contented man. But before long Alice was pregnant. It was not as pleasant a period as he had hoped. Alice resented her condition and sulked at its restrictions on her life. She couldn't ride or hunt or play tennis, and as her body rounded and thickened she became depressed, despite her aunt's support throughout.

At the same time, because of his fluency in Urdu and Hindi and his flair for Intelligence work, he found himself seconded from the army to work in the political and secret department. He might have left the glamour and dash of army life, but he enjoyed the independence and the demands of his new position. Once Richard was born, Alice regained her spirit and humour and her boundless energy for enjoyment. But, disturbingly, instead of returning to the social whirl, she began to take an even greater interest in the natives. She began to learn Hindustani, visited the mission hospital, talked with elders, and took what he considered an unnecessary interest in the private lives and problems of their servants. She would even argue quite heatedly against the English presence in the country. He had to admonish his wife, but she refused to listen, and his friends began to avoid him.

He was saved further embarrassment by being posted

to one of the Native States as an adviser and watchdog to the ruler. There was little left of the old kingdom, but it was an excellent training ground for intelligence work. They were the only Europeans there, except for a young Englishman commanding the army. Captain John Wood-ruff was extremely good company. He knew the surrounding countryside and its history well, and would take Alice out for long rides. Elizabeth had been born there.

'. . . Colonel . . . Colonel.'

He didn't hear the call the first time and started from his reverie and looked around. He saw no one he knew and just for one second believed he was a hair's breadth from an assassin's bullet. The assassin was calling to attract his attention; his last memory would be of a native's hatred. The moment passed. It was a woman's voice. A gharri had stopped on the opposite side of the road, with its curtains drawn. They parted a little, and a woman's hand beckoned him.

'Colonel Creighton?'

He crossed and peered into the shadows. The still air was perfumed with a French scent and he caught the glitter of jewellery and white teeth in a dark face. The hand drew the curtain further back and light fell on Mrs Basu's face.

'You do remember me, Colonel Creighton?'

'Of course. How are you, Mrs Basu?'

'I'm well, but it is difficult to carry on a polite English conversation in the middle of the road. May I offer you a lift?'

'I have my gharri, but . . .' It had been a long time since he'd dined with her at her father's house and, though he had not given her much further thought, her image had remained at the back of his mind. Was it prudence, or was it the gulf between the two races that had prevented him from dropping her a line? He had composed a thank-you note, but had never sent it. Among Indians, the thank-you note was not a part of the tradition. Once, a year before, when he was translating

Abu Talib Kalim, court poet to the Mughal Emperor
Shah Jahan, and he had had difficulty with a couple
of phrases, the memory of Mrs Basu had risen as a
temptation. He had mentally composed a request for
some help in the translation, but again he'd never written
it. So she was not forgotten, but held at bay.

The Colonel found himself opening the gharri door
and climbing in. He had, involuntarily, looked around
before doing so and the action immediately raised a
chuckle from Mrs Basu.

'Surely the Colonel sahib can ride with an Indian lady
without fearing comment?'

'I was thinking of your reputation, Mrs Basu.'

'You English are always so concerned for us poor
natives. You are even willing to consider my reputation,
as you do our well-being.'

'An English lady . . .'

'English ladies are so proper. Let's not discuss memsahibs. It will spoil the ride.'

The gharri was already moving. 'You don't know
where I'm going.'

'I do. It will be a surprise for you. Or don't you like
surprises, Colonel sahib? Here.' She pressed a white lace
handkerchief into his hand. 'It's too hot for a sahib to
walk.'

He dabbed the perspiration from his face and would
have returned the scented little square, but she waved
it away.

'How is your father?'

'All my family are well, Colonel. My husband is on
his estate. That will save so much endless politeness
enquiring about everyone's health. And I shan't enquire
about your daughter.'

'Were you at the races?'

'Native women are not allowed there. Only European
memsahibs can flaunt themselves. I was out shopping.'
He noted a pile of clothing on the opposite seat. 'As a
good Indian, I must buy swadesh. They're not as pretty
as the saris made in Manchester, nor as fine, but we

have to be patriotic. And I was just gazing out of the window when I saw a sahib striding through the streets of Calcutta as if he owned it. But, of course, you do. And did you win at the races, Colonel?'

'In a manner of speaking, yes. I had meant to drop you a note the other day,' he found himself confessing. Her proximity, the perfume and the warmth were disturbing and he wanted her to remain attentive. 'I was having problems with a translation.'

'I wish you had. I would have been glad to help. Which poet?'

'Kalim.'

Poetry provided neutral ground for conversation, and for the length of the ride – he still had no idea where she was taking him, but pride kept him silent – they discussed the various poets they loved. But she had also read others, and sang the praises of Tagore and Ganesh Damador Savarkar and Bankim Chandra Chatterji.

'I'm not familiar with Bengali,' the Colonel said, wishing to avoid the discussion. Could Mrs Basu be unaware that they were seditionists and that most of their writings had been banned? Chatterji was especially dangerous. His writings encouraged the bomb and pistol as a means to an end: the end of British rule. 'I was just wondering why you have given me a lift?'

'I find you an interesting man,' Mrs Basu said. 'You are not like most of the other Angrezis. I suspect there are a few like you, loving India, but hating Indians. You like to translate Urdu poetry, but if Kalim had written a single line against your rule, you would have no hesitation in imprisoning him. I also believe you are lonely, as I am. I was married very young to an indifferent husband who prefers to ruin his health drinking on his estate to being with his wife. No doubt he will kill himself soon. Then I shall be a widow, and God help me.'

In a flash of sunlight he saw her tears. Behind her gaiety there was the constant fear of widowhood, of the shaving of her hair and the white shroud of mourning. All colour would be removed from her life and she would be stripped of the jewellery she wore. It was the ultimate loneliness, the worst any woman could be subjected to. She would be an outcast, and in a country of deep superstition, the worst luck that could befall any man or woman was to cross the path of a widow. He did not comment on the savagery of the customs which kept India backward. The loneliness had already begun – with her marriage.

Hardly knowing what he did, he took her hand, needing the comfort of that small contact as much as she did. It had been years since he'd held a woman's hand intimately, and longings stirred within him. Her hand clasped his tightly. He was surprised at its softness, its warmth. He had long suppressed the memory of flesh, of the pleasure of lying with a woman. The thought of himself with Mrs Basu at first startled him. He could not imagine it, yet the need, once awakened, remained ravenous.

The gharri stopped and for a while neither moved. Finally the Colonel opened the door and found himself standing in a large garden, looking on a silent mansion. Both house and garden appeared to be deserted. He saw no malis, no servants, no children. Yet the gardens looked well maintained. The lawn was immaculate, the flower beds symmetrically arranged.

The mansion was shuttered. He thought of it as a kingdom cut off from the rest of the world, a secret place. Even the birds were silent and the air still, the sky boundless and watchful.

'Where are we?'

'My house. I live here.'

Quite naturally, he followed her up the steps into the drawing-room. It was shadowy, high-ceilinged and crammed with sofas, chairs, and cupboards filled with curios. Heavy blue-velvet curtains hung over the windows and the floor was covered with luxurious carpets. Dust lingered in the air, although he saw no traces of it on the marble table-tops or the mahogany cabinets.

'Are you alone here?' His voice echoed in the silence.

It hung there, mocking him, reflecting his longing. He had not meant to sound hopeful.

'Not always. My sisters-in-law stay here some of the time, but they are away at present. Once a year my husband comes to see people. However, they are ghosts passing through my life. Servants, too, who wait on me. I have every comfort. But yes, alone. I talk to myself at times, just to hear a voice.'

The Colonel would have taken his place politely on one of the chairs but she kept on moving, penetrating the quiet interior of the house, expecting him to follow. They passed into another room, equally crammed with furniture and, like the previous one, seeming to serve no purpose. They had been built and furnished and now waited for company, laughter. They went down a passage lined with swords and lances and a musket or two. Finally they came to a smaller room. It was lighter here, airy, and its furnishings were simple and worn. He noticed her perfume lingering in the air, and felt her presence. A large bookcase lined one wall, while books and newspapers lay carelessly on the table. There was a silver tray of fresh paan leaves. He had the uneasy feeling that someone had left the room a moment before they entered. It reminded him of a burning cigarette. Eyes might have watched from behind mirrors.

'Gin? Whisky? Brandy?'

'Whisky, please. With soda. Am I intruding?' In the fresh light he saw the red of her recent tears, little creases of sadness round her eyes and mouth. They diminished her, making her look lost.

'I hope you are.' She went to a cabinet, opened it and took out a bottle. 'I keep the drinks cupboard well supplied for my dear husband.'

'Is he here?'

'Don't sound worried, Colonel. No. This is only in case he should visit.' She took a glass and poured a little, holding it up for approval. There was soda water on another table and she added a splash.

'A little more, I think.'

When he took it, he took her hand too, and held it. She tugged but he kept hold, believing it a woman's wile to resist. Her head was averted and lowered. Her boldness had been a façade, a child strutting to show off. He wanted to protect her now, caress away those fears, tell her how much he needed her.

'How long has it been since . . . your husband stayed with you?'

'Our wedding night and one other: I am not much practised in these matters, I'm afraid.' He could scarcely hear her and, putting his drink down, turned her face to him. Her eyes were closed and he could not imagine a lovelier woman. She reminded him of a carving, silently sensual, waiting to come to life, to dance and sing.

'It's been many years for me,' the Colonel said. 'And I'm afraid I'm not much practised either.' He leant forward and kissed her cheek, lingering over the smoothness, wanting to inhale her completely. She turned her face and he kissed her on the mouth.

20

'WELL, ANIL RAY, how are we doing?' Inspector Goode enquired politely.

Goode's promotion was recent and a beam of sunlight filtering through the barred window glittered on his new decoration. It had been awarded for bravery above and beyond the call of duty. Such was the irony of life that Anil Ray's attack, which had left a faint scar on his belly, had been responsible for this elevation. He had felt relieved that the killing of Anil Ray's uncle had not been considered a blot on his career.

'Your use of the royal "we", Mr Goode, is most erroneous. I am in prison, while you have been commended for murder.'

'I'm sorry. I had no intention of making fun of you. I had meant it more as a friendly term of address. I spoke to Mr McKay, the prison superintendent, who informs me that, for a highly educated man, you have been quite a problem. I had hoped you would have behaved yourself.'

'Education, Mr Goode, does change men. And because of my high education, as Mr McKay calls it, I rail against the pricks and barbs of my gaolers.'

Anil Ray's hands were manacled, his legs chained. His beard reached down to his chest and its blackness darkened his face. His hair now grew down to his shoulders and with the fierce look in his eyes he looked like a mad fakir. In contrast, Goode looked sleek and young in his neatly pressed uniform and highly polished black shoes. He kept his swagger-stick tucked under his arm and Anil noted that the flap of his holster was tightly buttoned. One hand hovered protectively over it.

'If you behaved yourself, the treatment meted out to you would be much kinder.'

'There is no kindness in prison, Mr Goode, only cruelty, only injustice. I'm surprised that you've come to see me. Is it to gloat?'

'I wouldn't gloat,' Goode said indignantly. 'I went to a lot of trouble, coming all the way here to Delhi.'

'Ah, I'm expected to show gratitude, then, that the Goode sahib has made such an effort to save the miscreant.'

'You mistake my intentions. I had hoped my influence might make your stay here less uncomfortable, but you seem to persist in rejecting my efforts.'

'Like most Englishmen in my country, Mr Goode, you are well-meaning but stupid. It's your good intentions that keep us in chains for the present, but it will be your stupidity that will eventually break them.'

'I resent that remark,' Goode said. He was flushed and now tapped his swagger-stick against the side of his leg. They were gentle taps but there was no mistaking the flicks of anger. 'I came here out of kindness, but I could make your life most unpleasant here.'

'You couldn't,' said Anil Ray. 'Nothing can be worse than to be held here like an animal. And if you believe that kindness will eventually save you, Mr Goode, you're mistaken.'

'I've not forgotten your threat.'

'It's what keeps me alive.'

Goode saw that it was useless. Anil Ray was imprisoned not by walls, but by his hatred. His stare nearly made Goode flinch, but it didn't frighten him. He wasn't afraid of Anil's rage or his threat, instead he felt only a bleak helplessness at the situation. He had changed this man's life by accident, and hoped that he could somehow change it back, but knew it was now impossible. Tihar Gaol would have to hold Anil Ray as long as possible.

'I shall keep trying. Sethu!'

Anil's gaoler immediately entered and saluted. He was a dark, box-shaped, meticulously neat man, in a khaki uniform starched as stiff as cardboard. The creases of his trousers were sharp enough to cut skin. His moustache was oiled and waxed.

'You're not doing a good job, Sethu. He hasn't changed at all. Would you like to be transferred to Mandalay Prison?'

'No, sahib. I like it here.'

'Then make sure Mr Ray learns his manners, because if he hasn't by the next time I visit, you'll be sent away.'

'Yes, sahib.'

Goode left the sparsely furnished interrogation room and Sethu, who was carrying a thick, leather-bound cane, hit Anil twice on his back. They were not hard blows. If he had used all his compact, muscular strength, he would have broken Anil's spine.

'You are causing most unnecessary trouble. Do what he wishes. It is easier on you. Please, for my sake, otherwise I shall have to keep beating you daily. I enjoy it, admittedly, but it isn't good for a sahib like you to be beaten like a bullock. You are an educated man and you should know better. If the Angrezi wants you to do this, do it. Go, go . . .' He prodded Anil and kept prodding as Anil slowly shuffled down the long corridor back to his cell.

Anil had long discovered that Sethu had a wicked potential for patience. He could, with his casual cruelty, outlast any man's rage. Sethu was, Anil could tell from a glance, a sudra. Probably his ancestors too had been gaolers, and if he'd been asked, Sethu would have claimed one who'd been an executioner for the Mughals. There was always such continuity in India, not only of good men, but of bad as well. Here, Sethu's low caste made him superior to the Brahmin in chains, and he enjoyed this superiority. Where else would God allow him the privilege of treating a Brahmin like a bullock?

Anil shared a small cell with three other men. It was twice the size of a cabin-trunk and they took turns to eat, to sleep, to pace. They had one mattress, straw-stuffed and infested with lice and cockroaches. Three paces took them from one granite wall to another. A small barred window set high in the wall permitted air to enter, but very little light.

He was a C class prisoner. There were also A and B classes, who were allowed many more privileges than he since they were not considered dangerous. Goode had ensured that Anil Ray would always remember him, for as the arresting officer he had recommended the classification.

Once a week Anil was permitted an hour of exercise in the compound with the other prisoners. He would make use of the precious time by walking swiftly along the walls, like a rat exploring its cage. He felt a great hunger to stare up at the sky, the pattern of clouds moving over his cage, the heat of the sun against his body. He missed the simple magic of nature. Prisons separated men from the elements, isolated them from the natural order of the seasons. Anil envied the monkeys that played in the trees within the compound, leaping up over the high walls when they wanted to escape. At first, they were just monkeys. But over the weeks and months he grew to recognise each one in the tribe. The fierce, bad-tempered elder, the women, the younger males, the mischievous babies. The elder would prowl protectively around his tribe, sometimes patiently allowing a child to worry him, at other times cuffing it aside. He reminded Anil of Professor Timmins at Balliol, whose mood depended on the amount he had had to drink.

Anil found that by the end of each exercise period he was exhausted by this small exertion. Once he had had the ability to sprint a hundred yards in record time, to score a century with effortless ease. These accomplishments he only dimly remembered now, as though they belonged to someone else's life. Someone he had observed from afar, dreamt of; hero-worshipped with the other boys.

Tihar Gaol's superintendent, Mr Simon McKay, wasn't a cruel man, at least, not intentionally. He believed strongly in discipline, so misbehaviour was severely punished by whippings or incarcerations in a small, mud-lined heat box which baked men as swiftly as a tandoor oven did morsels of meat. He was certain that those days in England had had a civilising effect on Anil Ray, and the weekly exercise hour was an expression of his kindness and concern. Other C class prisoners were not permitted such luxuries.

One of his cell mates was Man Singh, the dacoit. He had bribed Sethu to allow him to share Anil's cell. Man Singh knew this young sahib was totally ignorant of the cruel world he'd been sent to. The other man, Jai Singh, had been adopted by Man Singh as his lieutenant. The third was a boy, Charan. He had no other name, no parents, no home. He'd survived on the Delhi streets. Supposedly he'd killed a man, but he denied it constantly. He could barely speak because of a cleft palate, but was eager to be liked and his three cell-mates took care of him.

Man Singh still plotted escape but Anil had little belief in his new-found friend's fantasy. Tihar was built to contain men for ever. It was made of granite and iron, with walls thirty feet high, their tops jagged with broken glass. Men were locked in their cells and lived only at the whim of their gaolers. If they were fortunate to have a family with means, the gaolers were bribed for small luxuries: cigarettes, soap, food. If not – and Tihar had many if-nots – the poor, swept in by circumstance, by the rage of a moment in their slum, survived by becoming the servants of the gaolers. A gaoler chose carefully and though the lucky man was kicked and beaten, he received some kindnesses – beedis, scraps of extra food.

Once a month Anil's father came to see him. With each visit, Anil saw him ageing more. His cheeks had grown hollow, his hair turned grey, then white, his shoulders round. Anil saw the shadow of death moving over his father and despite his love he knew that he was losing him. It was his own fault; he had betrayed his parents. A year after his imprisonment, his mother had died. He was told of this in a letter from his father, delivered two weeks after the event. He had mourned for days.

'I must escape, I must escape.'

'Sahib, that is what I have been planning all this time.'

'But it's impossible.'

'All things are possible to Man Singh, top dacoit. We need money first. You come from a rich family?'

'Yes. How much?'

'Two thousand rupees. Can you get that much money?'

'Yes. But what do we need so much for?'

'The prison sends some convicts out for work. They build roads, dig ditches. Cheap labour. The money will be a bribe for the superintendent's writer to put our names on the list. Once we are allowed to work outside, my second-in-command, Ranjit Lal, will have my men ready to attack the prison guards and we will escape.'

'It sounds too easy.'

'Only because it is. You get us the money for the bribe.'

On his father's next visit, Anil saw that he leaned heavily on a cane and shuffled as though his legs too were in chains. The sight frightened him, lent urgency to his escape plans. Father and son, in their own way, were gradually fading away in front of each other's eyes. He whispered his request to his father, and even such small hope lightened the burden. His father would have given all his wealth in exchange for his son's freedom.

'Once you are free, you must flee the country,' his father whispered. 'Go to America. The British cannot touch you there.'

'I will. But first I must kill Goode.'

'No, no, no. Leave him. God will take care of him.'

'As he has us? I couldn't live, knowing that he still lived.'

'You must promise not to harm him. Kill him, and the

British will kill you, then I shall have no son. They'll catch you – even in America – and hang you. No, it would be better for you to remain in here.'

'I promise.'

It wasn't a simple matter to bribe the superintendent's writer. Menon, a man from Cochin, slim as a reed, needed to consider the matter in depth. Man Singh wasn't a problem, but Anil Ray was. The superintendent took a personal interest in his welfare. The bribe was increased to three thousand rupees, and Menon's consideration ceased. He wouldn't accept half the money first and half after the escape. He insisted on having it all at once. Logically, once Anil escaped – the implication of the bribe was unspoken – there would be no necessity to pay the money. The bribe was paid in gold sovereigns. Anil, Man Singh, Jai Singh and Charan were transferred to a work party forthwith.

Anil, who had never done an hour of manual work in his life, now took pleasure in digging the earth. He attacked it with zest, exuberantly feeling the shock of the pick on the hard, brown crust. The earth fought him, giving up only crumbs. He was one of a gang of men digging a small canal to drain monsoon water from the moat of the Red Fort. Anil would pause occasionally to catch his breath, to stare at the marble palace seemingly afloat on the battlements of the fort. He had never been inside the walls, but knew that they too had once held a prisoner – an emperor.

The convicts had fifteen prison guards, eight armed with rifles, guarding them. As long as the men carried on working, they paid little attention to the prisoners. The day began at dawn and ended at dusk.

'When are your men going to come?' Anil asked at the end of one week. He had been patient. The work preoccupied him. He felt better, darkened by the sun, but wiry and muscled.

'Soon,' Man Singh said. 'I have sent word through one of the guards who is related to my village headman. Ranjit Lal must make plans and get arms before he can attack. I promise he will come. Otherwise, the chuthia knows I will slit his throat one day.'

It took a further three weeks before Ranjit Lal was spotted by Man Singh. Anil had worried he would never come. The canal was nearly completed and they might all be removed from the work detail. Ranjit Lal wore a flamboyant red turban and was older than Anil had expected. Man Singh was in his thirties and Anil thought his second-in-command would be a young man. Instead, he was old and scarred, badly shaven. He acknowledged Man Singh's signal with a curt nod and faded back into the crowd. They presumed he would follow them to the fort and arrange the attack there. All day they laboured expectantly, tensely waiting for gunfire, the need to sprint for cover and escape. At the end of the day, they were doubly exhausted from the tension.

'The chuthia,' Man Singh swore. 'I will certainly slit his throat when I escape. How dare he keep me waiting?'

'Maybe he's being careful and making plans.'

'Yes, yes. He always was a cautious type. I am the reckless one. You will have to come with us to the Chambal ravines. The police will never find us there. How many kings have sent their armies in to hunt us? Even Chandragupta sent soldiers a thousand years ago, but the ravines have hidden us well. There you'll be safe.'

'I'll follow you later.'

'Ah, you still want to kill the DI. If you do, the Angrezi will never stop searching for you and your presence will make our lives dangerous. But I am Man Singh, big dacoit, and I will defy even the Angrezi. We shall never have peace, but if I were to be afraid of the Angrezi soldiers and police, I wouldn't be Man Singh.'

'Thank you.' Anil knew it would be his only refuge until he could escape to America. He didn't want to think that far ahead. There were ways one could be smuggled onto a ship. Lajpat Rai, twenty years ago, had escaped to America, even though he had been hunted by the British.

They didn't see Ranjit Lal the next morning. There was no sign of his red turban, nor any sign of Man Singh's men. Man Singh was moody and angry, muttering threats under his breath. They worked until eleven. By evening, they would have completed the ditch and wouldn't be returning.

The midday meal consisted of cold chapatis, dhal and a few potatoes. They found shade under the walls of the Red Fort, but Man Singh sat separately, gazing at the passers-by, looking for signs and omens.

His men came, not from the road, but along the bank of the Jumna where they had been waiting in the high reeds. Just when the guards began their meal, they opened fire. People scattered, dropping their belongings. The armed guards immediately snatched up their rifles.

'Come! Run!' Man Singh shouted and, in a crouch, ran towards his men.

Jai Singh sprinted after his leader, but Anil hesitated a fraction. Something was wrong. The gunfire, the confusion of running people, puzzled him. But he had no time to consider. He pushed Charan ahead and they both followed behind Man Singh.

As they cleared the mound of freshly turned earth and were fifty yards from the reeds, Anil saw Man Singh suddenly stumble, twist and fall backwards. Jai Singh stopped to kneel by him and the force of the bullet half lifted him and flung him back. By this time Anil and Charan had covered a further twenty yards in their rush towards Man Singh.

'Stop, stop,' Anil shouted to Charan, but the boy, excited by the escape, ran like a child, laughing and shouting. 'Ranjit Lal is shooting at *us*. Stop!'

But it was too late for Charan to stop. He hadn't heard and was still laughing when the bullets hit him and he somersaulted backwards. Anil instinctively fell, feeling the earth around him come alive in small, vicious explosions. He rolled the last yards over to Man Singh and smelt the blood. It had the same odour as his uncle's blood. Sweet and sticky. He was vaguely aware that the firing had stopped and that the prison guards were running towards him.

'Betrayal,' Man Singh whispered. 'Betrayal. If kings are betrayed, why not the king of dacoits? The chuthia planned to kill me. He has taken over my gang.' He sighed, eyes glazing. 'Anil, you must promise me revenge. Man Singh cannot die without revenge. Promise.'

'I promise,' Anil whispered quickly, and wasn't sure he'd been heard.

21

IT WAS dark within him. Not an impenetrable blackness, but the darkness of chaos and distraction. Kim heard the voices of pilgrims, the murmur of sastras, a crow cawing as it flew east, the smells of incense and camphor. The stone beneath him was hard and uncomfortable and he felt an urgent need to rise and stretch his legs. Thoughts disrupted him. His mind scurried through the middle of his life, throwing up scraps for examination, piling them in untidy heaps: the moment he was shot, the incredible shock, yet no pain, only blackness; Parvati's laughter as she spun tales out of her vivid imagination, the light on her face at dusk; the Colonel's hand on his shoulder reminding him of his duty; the growl of his stomach for food and the hope Lakshmi would soon arrive with it. He prayed for control over his monkey-like mind that bounded from one thing to another.

His ritual had been the same now for many months. He woke in his monastic cell at the sound of the priests' early chanting. It would be dark and cool; the air would be clean, washed by the stars and the moon. He would breathe the pure air while walking down to the ghats to bathe in the river, passing the processions making their way to the burning-ghats carrying their dead. There would be thousands of other pilgrims like him, dipping themselves in Mother Ganges and turning east to pray as Surya sent the first beam of light to split the earth from the sky. The river would turn from black and silver to a fiery red as the sun touched it, and the temples would begin to glow, as though the ancient stone emitted light from within. The gods in their tiers moved in their eternal dance as the shadows softly flowed over them, changing an expression here, changing a movement there. When he had bathed, he would cup his hands and sip the sacred water, turning his face to the north, where the river rose high in the Himalayas. The Ganges was a celestial river, originating in the sky, and when it fell to earth its impact had been softened by Shiva's long hair.

Kim would then return to the temple and sit in the shade of a bhodi tree to begin his meditations. If the purification of his body was a simple act of immersion, that of his mind was a battle. The mind was the stone wall between him and his soul. At times, he would feel the bliss of nearing the central point of his conscience, where all thought fell away and he could experience a sense of lightness and calm. But these experiences lasted a matter of seconds before he wavered in his concentration and the light rushed backwards into the darkness of his mind.

He would wait then until the hardness of the stone numbed his limbs and the growl of his stomach could be heard by those who passed this sunyassi who could not control such physical longing. It would be noon when he caught a scent of jasmine and heard the sound of Lakshmi's anklets as she settled down to wait. She would sit opposite him, staring at every feature, at his nose, his mouth, the curve of his lips, the straightness of his shoulders. She absorbed him through those large, liquid eyes. When finally he opened his eyes, having made her wait a good half-hour, even though his mind was occupied with nothing more mundane than feeling a cooling breeze off the river, Lakshmi would smile in delight.

'Did you find what you seek?'

'No. I was disturbed by your presence.'

'But a true sunyassi would not be disturbed by me. He would not notice the passing of a woman or the passing of a tiger.'

'One and the same. Both are dangerous to a man.'

'Tomorrow then, you will find what you seek. I am sure.'

She was not despondent over his failure. It meant she could serve him longer, and immediately unrolled the plantain leaf that she had brought and spread it in front of him. Kim would wash his hands from the lota of water she poured for him and then, kneeling beside the leaf, she would heap it with rice and a vegetable curry from a clay pot. From another smaller pot she would scrape out mango pickle and a pinch of coarse salt. She also brought a sweet, either a ladoo or a jelabi.

While Kim ate, she would chatter away about the doings of the city. She gave him snippets of news and gossip, usually exaggerated and highly coloured. This priest was taking bribes for puja, that old man waiting to die was a rich landowner who hoped to attain moksha by his presence here, that sadhu could perform miracles, the police were searching for miscreants who had stolen an idol. Kim listened with half an ear, hoping she would eventually tire of her role and allow him to take her to her village. But she was a city woman and enjoyed wandering through the lanes and bazaars. She had little problem gathering their food; the temples and rich pilgrims fed the poor regularly and she would wait in line with the others. At night, she would sleep in a serai, another charity for pilgrims. It was a low building on the outskirts of the city with large rooms sectioned off for men and women. And each day, precisely at noon and at dusk, she would appear with Kim's meal. He had tried to persuade her to eat with him, but she refused. It was her duty to serve him and make sure he was well fed. When she left he would retire to a cool corner of the temple compound and go to sleep. The temple closed its doors and all activity, except the row of clerks counting the morning's donation into the temple hundi, temporarily ceased. The heat stilled the monkeys too, and they would doze in the shade of gods.

Once the sun dipped below the gopurams of the

temples, throwing lengthening shadows, Kim would wake and seek out Anand, the old head priest who was now eighty and spent his whole day reading newspapers. He read them in Urdu and English, in Bengali and Hindustani, in Maharati and Tamil. Old ones, new ones. They were all kept in his tiny room which had only enough space for him to stretch out at night. In the evenings, he could be found in the sunny west corner of the compound, near one of the small shrines.

Anand was bald, both his head and body, and satisfyingly rounded. He had few teeth in his head and those remaining were gold. He sat cross-legged, leaning against his usual pillar, with the newspapers piled on his right, held down by a rock. On his left were those he had finished reading. With his gold wire glasses perched on his nose he reminded Kim of a curious owl. They were not his glasses. A pilgrim had left them and Anand had adopted them as his own. He squinted to read. Anand could hold forth on any subject from the Gita to the latest cricket scores, yet to Kim's knowledge the man hadn't left the temple compound for forty years.

Kim wasn't the only one who would seek out Anand. Younger priests, pilgrims, beggars, servants when they had time, would sit around him and listen to his discourses. It saved them having to read (that is, those who could) and they could then speak with some authority from picking Anand's encyclopaedic memory. It was an awesome memory. Anand, as a small boy, and in the tradition of his ancestors, had learned by heart all the vedas, which had so many volumes that they filled a room, the puranas and the Gita, and anything else he turned that wondrous memory to. He spoke in a chant, being in the habit of performing prayers all his life. Now he was alone, *The Statesman* an inch from his face.

'I am,' he spoke without looking, 'reading about this one called Mohandas Gandhi. Have you heard of him?'

'No,' Kim said. 'Is he with Congress?'

'He is a strange young man. He comes from a small town near Bombay called Kathiawar. His ancestral duty is to serve as prime minister to one of the small rajas in that area, as did his father, grandfather and an uncle. But instead of following ancestral duty this Mohandas went to Great Britain to study law. Then he returned here the day after he joined the Bar and found nothing to do. Following a wasteful period, he went to South Africa. Now he is engaged with the Natal Indian Congress and is battling with the British government there over many bad legislations passed against our people. But it is strange that, unlike the young men in Bengal, he has not used violent methods to attain his goal, though he has spent many months in prison for burning passes. He believes in sticking to the law while achieving his ends. I believe he has understood the key to the empire. You see, it rules by force, and by force it inflicts pain and death. Now this strange man Gandhi has philosophised that by absorbing pain, he will prevail. It is very clever. Pain is the best method of controlling people. Once pain loses its ability to frighten people, it loses its power. And once power is lost, the empire is lost. Now, the question that arises is: how much pain? Is it a calculable sum? Three mangoes and two papayas make five. Pain cannot be so easily summed up. We all hate and fear pain, but Gandhi, like a true sunyassi, has overcome his abhorrence of pain. But one man, however strong, cannot absorb enough pain to bring down the master. There must be many and that is where the calculation enters the argument. How many men will stand beside him to absorb the pain?' Anand peered over the top of the paper.

'Is there a limit to this pain? I have suffered pain but know even when I am deep inside it that there will be an ending, a cure to the illness. If there is a limit, then men will be beside him in South Africa.'

'No, no. There can be no limit. If the master knows that there is this limit all he has to do is take a man to the limit. It is like the boundary to Ahodya. Rama, Sita and Arjuna were banished from their kingdom, which had boundaries. Once they crossed the line they were

277

in exile. But what if Ahodya had had no boundaries, if it had been as limitless as this earth, then where would they have gone? What would exile be then? Why, death, of course. How else can one be exiled from life than by dying? And so it must be with pain. Limitless.'

'What do the British think of him?'

'A nuisance who will go away, eventually. One man is mortal; empires are not. They will patiently await his departure and then continue in their old ways. Empires do not like new ways. New ways change people.'

'But when he leaves there, will he not come home?'

'Yes. It will be interesting to see what he will do here. And even more interesting to see what the government will do to him.'

Kim sat silent, thinking about Gandhi. In his mind he saw a balance. On one scale this Gandhi; on the other the government. The weight of one tipped the balance and he could not understand how Gandhi could achieve anything. The empire would remain, unperturbed. Hadn't other men tried to upset this balance of power? Gokhale, Lajpat Rai, Tilak, the countless seditionists who were regularly beaten, imprisoned or hanged. They were but tiny pricks on the hide of an elephant, and the great beast was not even aware of their presence or their efforts to make it change its course.

He was not a political man. He saw the permanence of the empire and the peace it had brought to a country which had for countless centuries warred within itself, one raja against another, and when the invader came – whether Babur or the British – they could not unite long enough to fight effectively. Instead they betrayed one another, not caring in their short-sightedness that they would be equally betrayed by the invader. No. He could not see this Gandhi having any effect on the government, not without weapons. Military might could only be overthrown by military might.

These thoughts swirled through his mind as he settled himself back in his usual place for meditation. The temple's doors had reopened and the pilgrims streamed in. They namasted him; one or two, in the mistaken belief that he was truly holy, even asked for darshan, which Kim gave. He knew that if people believed, their belief could not be shaken, and if they believed his blessing was beneficial he could not deny them.

It had become cool and in the shadows a faint breeze dried the perspiration on his face. He felt himself slowly entering a state of peace and tranquillity, the noise of the temple fading gradually as though it were moving further away from him. He experienced the first gentle glow, not of light, but of awareness, like the light of a candle whose flame was not visible. It could vanish in a second and he concentrated totally on preserving the light. Gradually it expanded, filling his inner mind and flowing out to encompass his whole body. He felt this lightness as though he were a leaf, afloat in crystal-clear air.

A vision took shape. A giant stood on a vast empty plain. He was huge as Trivakrama and he blotted out the light. His shadow stretched over the earth to the horizon. He held a bow the size of a deodar and arrows which gleamed like gold. Wordlessly, he fitted an arrow to the string, lifted the bow and shot the arrow high into the air. Kim followed the path of its flight as if he were flying alongside, and when it finally struck the earth, the arrow was transformed into a beautiful flowering tree. The single flower of that tree was a strange shape, and its perfume was delicate and sensual. He reached for it, marvelling at its delicate texture, and felt himself enveloped in a state of bliss. He turned to look back at the giant and saw him now fitting another arrow to the string. It flew an even greater distance and where it fell to earth, the ground exploded. Smoke and dust and dirt flew up, filling the air, choking Kim. Out of the dust came a fine red spray that soaked his clothes, burning his skin. It was suffocating and he experienced a tremendous pain. He could not pinpoint the pain, but it was all around him, in the very air itself. He stumbled out of the dust and darkness and saw the giant waiting for him. The giant fitted the third arrow. It did not arc down to the earth, but rose higher and higher and finally disappeared into a brilliant light. He looked again at the giant, but he had already disappeared.

Slowly, Kim began to return. He heard the murmur of voices growing louder, the chime of the temple bells and the familiar sense of Lakshmi's proximity. When he opened his eyes he peered into her face, which held a worried expression.

'You have had a vision?'

'Yes. How did you know?'

'Your face looked so remote and absorbed, like those of people who see God in a mehla. Will you go away now and leave me?'

'Is that all you are concerned about? Don't you want to know what I saw?'

'No. I can only be concerned about my own happiness. If you go away, I shall be alone again.' She sulked and didn't spread out the leaf. 'What was your vision, then?'

Kim told her and she listened carefully. 'Who was the man?'

'I don't know. What do you think it means?'

She shrugged and slowly unrolled the leaf. The joy had gone out of her movements now, and she felt heavy and tired. Lakshmi's visions were only concerned with Kim, and in his presence she felt herself come alive, felt her life gain a meaning. This vision threatened her. She had no idea what it meant, but the threat was in Kim's face. He had to discover the meaning, and that would mean making journeys. He would leave her, and she knew they would never meet again. She felt so miserable that she wished now she had stayed in the brothel. She had been cut off from such terrible pain in those small rooms. Where there was no hope, there was no expectation – and no pain. That numbness would be welcome. What would she do in the village which she'd nearly forgotten? Live like a peasant, labouring in the fields all day, suffering hunger and thirst, and with the expectation of little pleasure from this life?

280

'When will you leave me?'

'I must discover the meaning of the vision.'

'Well, it won't be in the newspapers,' she said shortly. 'Ask Anand, or that sunyassi in the ghat who performs miracles. He will be able to interpret it.'

'I shall ask Anand.'

Anand had moved from his usual position to one nearer the lamplight, though he was no longer reading. Kim sat in front of him, while Lakshmi kept her distance. Anand would never permit a woman near him. Women were unclean in his eyes. He listened to Kim carefully and then brooded for a long time, fingering the sacred thread.

'I see your vision in this way. Those three arrows point you on the path of your life. The first one, which you say blossomed into a tree, is your physical goal in life. It will give you enormous pleasure for the body. You understand? Then the second arrow points you towards danger. I am not sure whether it is a warning or whether harm will befall you. The red was blood, possibly your own. The pain was in the air, so all around you were dying men.'

'I dreamt once of being in smoke and blood.'

'Then it will happen.'

'Shall I live through it?'

'I cannot tell. I think you will, because you saw the flight of the third arrow. It is possible that you only saw it spiritually leading you up to Brahma. By this, I mean after your life has passed. You will attain ahimsa for your goodness during your life on earth. Or . . .' Anand paused, pursing his lips. 'Each arrow might represent a choice in life. You must follow one or the other. Each leads you to the goal.'

'How will I know which to choose?'

'Did you each time return to the point from which the arrows were shot?'

'No. I moved from one to the other without returning.'

'Then there is no choice of paths. One leads to the other.'

'How shall I know this tree? Is it to be found in the jungle or the desert?'

'The tree itself does not exist on earth. It is beyond seeing. You will know it when you find it.'

'How? I might search for ever unless I know what I am looking for.'

'These are the tribulations of one's destiny. To search.' Anand blinked benignly, his eyes large as brown moons, swollen by the spectacles. 'You are young and have many years in which to accomplish these things. But because of your youth you want life to be easy. You would like me to tell you that you will find a certain thing in a certain spot. Like a hidden treasure. Life is not precise, my young friend.' He sighed, a swift breath as though he had no time for a long-drawn-out one. 'You will be leaving very soon and I shall not see you again. I have derived great pleasure from your company because you listen well and you learn.'

'Please give me your darshan.'

Anand raised his hand, palm outwards and Kim touched the old priest's worn feet, tucked comfortably beneath him.

'What did he say?' Lakshmi asked.

'I must search.'

'I will go with you.'

'No. I will return you to your village. That was my promise.'

'You don't have to,' Lakshmi said petulantly. 'I can stay here just as well. What am I going to do in a stupid village?'

'That is your ancestral home.'

Kim recognised the stubborn tone. She sat looking at him angrily and he wished, just for a moment, that he had left her in that Bombay brothel. He had felt an urge to help and now her presence was like a yoke around his neck. He knew her dreams, though she'd never spoken them, for her eyes followed him with such hunger. If he stayed with her, she would walk beside him to the end of India should he ask it of her. Oh,

Narain, he thought, I should have listened to you. This woman will cause trouble because of her love for me, and I have no wish to hurt her. Her life has been unhappy for too long, but I cannot burden myself with unhappiness to erase hers.

'I shall return when I have found what I search for.'

'You promise?'

'Yes.'

And because she knew him to be a man of his word, she was content. If Kim said he would return, he would. Just as he had promised to help her escape the brothel, though even if he had never returned she would not have held it against him. She spread the leaf now, and gave him generous portions of food. A wealthy ghee merchant, fat as a ladoo, had distributed food for two hundred people at the Durga temple. His sins must have been great, for she'd heard too that he had given ten thousand rupees to the temple.

They left Benares before sunrise the next day. Neither possessed much. Lakshmi now had a second sari which she had received after a wealthy landowner's thread ceremony for his child; Kim an extra pi-jama and jiba. In the bazaar they found a caravan of bullock carts and camels preparing to travel along the same route as them. Kim found the leader, a sardar called Balbir Singh, who after a great deal of thought gave them permission to join his caravan. He and his camels planned to end their journey in Amritsar. They carried valuable silks from the handlooms of Benares. These saris were the finest in India, woven with gold and silver, and worth twice as much in Amritsar. He was naturally suspicious of a strong built man like Kim, who reminded him of a dacoit who'd once nearly cut his throat when he had been traversing the Chambal valley. Three of his sons travelled as bodyguards, armed with jezails. The youngest was only twelve, the eldest nearly thirty. The three were handsome men and very good-natured.

Apart from them, there were twenty-five bullock carts carrying cloth, spices, dekshis and other necessities for villagers. A wedding party accompanied them too, having made its pilgrimage to Benares. As they had a rath for the women of the party, Kim asked permission for Lakshmi to ride with them. A head peeped out and stared at Lakshmi for a long time, examining her from head to toe, before finally agreeing.

'Where will you be?' Lakshmi asked when he placed her bundle in the rath and helped her in. 'Will you go away?'

'No, I shall walk with the men. I promised to return you to your village, and I will keep my word.'

'Is she your wife?' the young bridegroom asked when Kim fell in beside him as the caravan began its journey.

'No. I am her cousin-brother. We were performing puja in Benares and I am returning with her to her village.' He lied only for Lakshmi's sake, for he did not want to sully her reputation. A lone woman travelling with a man was open to gossip and it was possible that some of these people came from her village, or knew people from it.

'Where is that?'

'Many kos from Rae Bareli. Just this side.' The direction was as imprecise as Lakshmi's memory of her home. Kim had no doubt such a place had existed, and only hoped it was still there. A village could disappear overnight if the rains had been bad. 'But I have not been there myself. I am from Calcutta.'

'I have never been to Calcutta,' the youth sighed. 'I'm told it is very huge and you can see the most wondrous sights. People with white skins, too.'

'The Angrezis are there. Do you not see them where you come from?'

'One or two. They own a lot of the land around us and our life is very difficult because of them. We used to grow wheat to feed our families and to sell, but now they insist that we grow indigo. They tell us it will make us a lot of money, but they do not pay us. And if the rains are bad, then we don't have enough food.'

He was a slim, pleasant youth, not yet twenty. He

had a dreamer's face and would often lapse into long silences and frequently glance back to the rath to reassure himself that his child-bride's party still followed. The youth's name was Rambaj and his family were tenant farmers. They cultivated one acre, which was now mostly planted with indigo. His father wanted to return to growing wheat but the Planters' Association in his district would not permit it.

'Your village panchayat should speak to the Collector about the problem. He will surely help you.'

'No. We are bound by tinkathia to grow indigo. At one time it was just. We planted three parts out of twenty with indigo, and then we could grow enough food for ourselves. Now it's ten out of twenty. The panchayat has spoken to the Collector sahib, but he will not help us. He tells us it is necessary to grow indigo.'

'Surely the sarkar will help you. They have great love and affection for you all.'

'Why should they?' said Rambaj bitterly. 'When have the sarkar ever helped us? This one is only a little different. We are treated like children, but they always stick on the side of the planters and once, when we protested, they even called the police. We are poor and easily frightened.'

Kim didn't quite believe Rambaj. He knew the English Collectors or Deputies or District Magistrates spent years of their lives in remote places such as Rae Bareli, building roads, dams and drainage systems so that the lot of the peasant gradually improved after centuries of neglect and exploitation. For Rambaj to complain that they were exploiting and threatening his people struck Kim as an exaggeration. But he made no further comment and listened quietly to the village gossip.

Rambaj's bride's father was a well-digger who had been too busy to accompany the pilgrimage. The wedding party consisted mostly of the women from both sides of the family. It was their one great adventure in narrow lives, and Kim hoped they had enjoyed themselves. The one other male in the party was an uncle, now a widower. His wife had died recently in childbirth. Suresh Lal was a short, cheerful man who certainly did not appear to be grieving. He had a pockmarked face and a fierce moustache that curled richly almost up into his turban. He had been a jawan with a Jat regiment, and with his savings had bought several acres of land, which were now let to a tenant farmer. He didn't approve of hard work; his days in the army had been exhausting. He had seen action on the North-West Frontier and was thankful he was still alive.

'The reason I left,' he told Kim, 'was that there was just too much fighting. Here, there, everywhere. I even went to Tibet six years ago to fight the Russians. I have never known such cold. One side of my moustache froze like a stick and snapped off. I knew then I would leave when my time was up.'

'Did you fight the Russians?' asked Kim.

'No. Only Buddhist priests whom we slaughtered because we were ordered to.' He twirled his moustache. 'That taught them a lesson, though what the lesson was, I am not sure.' He had something else on his mind, but didn't mention it until a day later, looking back at the rath. 'That is a very pretty cousin you have. Do you intend to marry her?'

'No,' Kim said. 'I am just taking her back to her village.' He saw the furtive parting of the curtain. Lakshmi's eyes constantly drilled into his back. 'She is a good, kind girl.'

'So was my wife, but she wasn't as pretty as your cousin. I like them fair and graceful like that.'

Kim expected him to continue but he fell silent and thoughtful, mulling over his longings. He may have been old to Kim's young eyes, but Suresh was only forty-five years of age. Kim couldn't help but hope that with a little encouragement there could be a match in the making. Suresh seemed well off; apart from his land he also had an army pension. He would look after Lakshmi well. A tremor of guilt at the relief of having Lakshmi taken off his hands passed through Kim. He had promised to rescue her; not to marry her off. Before the thought had even been completed, he found himself summoned to her side. Lakshmi had, with the intuition of a woman, sensed that something was afoot.

'What were you and that Suresh talking about?'

'This and that.'

'He keeps looking at me. Did you tell him what I am?'

'That is your past and it will always be my secret. You are now a free woman. You should look to the future.'

'But I do.'

'I must continue my search. And I cannot remain in a village for long.'

Her sniff and sulk were audible to all, but Kim hardened his heart and strode away quickly. He thought it wise to keep out of her sight for a few days.

At the head of the caravan, Balbir Singh strode with the same loping walk as his beast, and could tirelessly cover twenty or thirty miles a day. The land on either side of the narrow road was luxuriously rich. They were walking in the Gangetic plain; the soil here was the most fertile in India. As far as the eye could see on either side the land was covered with a carpet of crops: indigo, wheat, sugar cane, mango groves, mustard, pulses, chillies. The sun glittered on the Ganges and the small canals snaking away from it, beating down on the men and women as they cut and planted and drew water, on buffaloes and camels, ploughing and carrying.

'If I were to dig a hole in the earth and spill my seed in the ground, children would sprout,' Balbir Singh said. 'If I were a farmer, this is where I would buy land. But I have spent too many years travelling to stay in one place for more than a month. I would get restless. Think what it would be to live with but one woman all your days. Ahre, it would drive me insane. I have one wife in Benares, others in Lucknow, Delhi, Amritsar and Lahore. A month with each one is about the most I can take.'

'How many children do you have?'

'Many. As I grow older, I cannot remember.'

'Whose boys are with you?'

'Two are from the Amritsar wife. The other from Delhi. They are good boys. They don't tell their mothers about any of the other ones. Admittedly, I threatened to thrash them if they mentioned such things, but they are obedient. And you are not married?'

'No.'

'What is wrong with you? You look healthy and strong and passably attractive.' He peered at Kim, suspecting him of being a badmash who, like himself, took his pleasure where he could find it.

Balbir was tall and stately. He was dark from the sun and his beard had already grown white. One couldn't call him handsome – he had a bulb of a nose – but one could sense a delight for life there. He would travel all over the earth to trade or barter. Balbir had been across the mountains too, and as a boy had travelled the silk route to Samarkand, accompanying his father. He had seen the tomb of Timur-i-leng and described it as a great wonder, though not as beautiful or as delicate as the Taj Mahal. The women there were squat and strong and he swore one of them wrestled him to the mat thrice. And then pleasured him in such ways that he would have spent his life there, but she had exhausted him with her demands. He had only managed to escape her six brothers and her father by the skin of his teeth.

Each night, the men would play dice. Balbir, because they were his dice, always won, mostly from his sons. He explained that by cheating he taught the three a lesson on life. Though what lesson, he didn't elaborate. Kim suspected the sons knew of their father's habit and laughed each time they lost. The sons were obviously close to their father, and joked constantly with him.

Travellers left and others joined the caravan as it moved northwards along the Ganges. On some nights they would set up camp outside a village, if they were fortunate enough to find one; otherwise they settled out in the open with a fortification of thorn bushes to keep out jackals, tigers and dacoits. Those were rare nights. Because of the richness of the land there were many villages along their route. Balbir Singh was known in many of them, and if the women had the money they would look at his display of jewellery. It was all made of gold, richly decorated with emeralds and rubies, or else silver bangles and anklets and ear-rings. They would bargain and then buy. Kim knew that Balbir Singh made a healthy profit. The women would also finger the silk saris and sigh in wonder and envy. Few had the money to spend on such finery, but if there was to be a wedding soon, Balbir would do good business. It depended on who was getting married. If it were a vakil or thakur, they usually had money. But if they were only kissans, Balbir would swiftly wrap the silks back in their linen coverings. Kissans had no money at all.

'You should buy a sari for when the time comes,' Balbir coaxed Kim. 'Then you will be ready.'

'I have no desire to be ready. Like you, I enjoy moving from place to place. Women hate that.'

'Ahre, you are going to be travelling longer than I ever will. What is this flower you are seeking?'

'It is a tree, not a flower.' He was not surprised by the question. Lakshmi would have talked about him to the other women in the rath; then the women would have told their men. 'A kind I've never seen or touched, with a perfume as heady as wine.'

'Not a rose or a lotus then? I have seen so many different kinds of flowers in my life. In the mountains they grow as diamonds in the snow, white and delicate, and in the jungle they are as emeralds, rich and perfumed.'

'No. When I see it I shall know it.'

'If you should come to Amritsar, my friend, look for Balbir Singh. My shop is on the street north of the Golden Temple. Balbir and Sons. One of my other sons looks after the shop.'

About thirty miles from Rae Bareli, Kim reluctantly said goodbye to Balbir and his sons. They would continue on to Lucknow and then strike west for Delhi, while Kim, Lakshmi and the wedding party would travel west. Over the following days Kim missed Balbir and his sons; their talk had been entertaining, while the local people spoke only of their own small world. On the fourth day, they reached Rambaj's village.

It was quite small, surrounded by acre upon acre of indigo, here and there a little wheat and mustard. There was a main road lined with a few stores: a provisions merchant, a cloth shop and a tea shop. There were one or two single-storey brick buildings, but generally the homes were made of mud and thatch. The brick homes belonged to the local landlord. On the outskirts of the village were pitched four tents; one large with two rooms, the others smaller. A police sergeant, four constables, two peons and two bearers lounged in the shade of a mango tree.

'Collector sahib has come,' Rambaj whispered.

The village was unnaturally quiet. It was an hour before noon and the street, though not deserted, was empty of cart traffic. Men stood in twos and threes, conversing softly. No women could be seen. The air was full of whispers, the light breeze murmuring secrets in everyone's ear, nothing definable, yet chilling as though it carried a winter's warning.

'You must stay a while with us,' Rambaj said politely, but he too was aware of the mood, the waiting. The women got down from the rath and scurried out of sight.

Lakshmi squatted in the shade of a mango tree, preoccupied with her misery, and with a look of hopelessness about her. This was a large village; her own would be tiny. Yet, when locked up in the brothel all she could dream of and remember were the fields of wheat and mustard, the great blue sky above her head, the smell of the earth. The poverty now appalled her and she was determined to stay with Kim. Wherever he went, she would go. He needed her. Who would wash his clothes? Who would cook for him? A man was not expected to perform such menial tasks. She would persuade him and he would say 'yes'.

'We must try to reach my cousin's village by nightfall. It is only a few kos, isn't it?'

Rambaj hesitated, gazing at the endless horizon. Though he had travelled to Benares, he'd not moved more than a couple of miles in any direction from where he stood.

'I'm not certain. Wait, and I will ask.'

Kim squatted in the shade with Lakshmi while Rambaj hurried to find an elder who could direct them to her village. It was close to the Gomati river, by the hill rise. Beyond that, the village had no name.

While they waited, they saw the Collector returning from inspection. He was a slim, sunburnt Englishman, possibly the same age as Kim, his back straight with authority. The brim of his topi shaded the upper half of his face, while the lower part sported a neatly trimmed moustache and a firm chin. His khaki shirt stuck to his body. He acknowledged the salaams of the villagers with his riding whip. A bull-terrier trotted at his horse's heels. He stopped once to talk to an elderly villager, and Kim saw the deference in the elder as he stared up at the horseman. The Collector was giving the villager a scolding, which was received with a polite smile. When he had finished, he rode past Kim and looked at him, first casually, incuriously, then, possibly sensing something different about him, with a stare. Kim met his look without rising, and sensed Lakshmi's unease at his boldness. The Collector rode past and then, thinking again, turned his horse and reined in a foot from Kim. The sun was behind the Collector's back and Kim in his shade.

'Where are you from?'

'Benares.' Kim stared up at the Collector. The man had a round face and grey eyes lined with wrinkles. He tapped his riding crop against his boot steadily, as though keeping time with a tune running through his head.

'And why are you here?'

'I am taking my cousin to her village.'

'Stand up, damn it, when I'm talking to you,' he

shouted, startling the horse. Then to himself in English: 'You bloody wogs are getting too big for your boots.'

Kim rose, making no effort to smile or show deference. He still stared up and the Collector noted he had eyes the same colour as himself. They were quiet eyes, neither eager to please nor showing fear. This quality made him even more uneasy. If there had been even a glint of anger, he would have had him arrested. Instead, Kim was waiting patiently, appearing more amused than angry.

'Then what are you doing here?'

'We came with the wedding party just now. And we shall be leaving now.'

'Yes, I think it is a good idea that you leave here. Where is the village?'

'Near the Gomati. By the big hill.'

The Collector turned his horse and spurred, not looking back. Lakshmi, who had covered her face out of shyness and fear, peeked out from behind the sari.

'Why was he angry?'

'He is young and afraid.'

'Of what? Us?'

'The quiet.'

Lakshmi looked around. The men in their groups stared at them in silence. She couldn't understand why, and then realised that the whole village was unnaturally quiet. Children should be playing in the dusty street, women going about their labours, carts carrying produce. Even the pi-dogs, sitting in the shade, twitched uneasily.

'What is happening here?'

'I don't know. Let's ask Rambaj.'

Rambaj came swiftly, almost at a run. He pointed to the east even before he reached Kim's side.

'If you go that way, you will reach your village. It is a journey of about a day and a half. You should leave soon.'

'What is going on?'

'The Collector had the police arrest our sar-panch

yesterday. He and the panchayat went to petition the Collector to allow us to grow more wheat. Instead the sar-panch was arrested for causing trouble.'

Rambaj looked excited. His dreamy eyes sparkled with the drama, most of which he'd missed. He was also angry at this injustice and quivered with the indecision of a boy, uncertain of how to express himself. He was too docile to take to violence, and would probably, like the rest of the village, talk himself into calm acceptance of their lot. It would be a salutary lesson, and the village and district would return to normal.

'What should we do?'

'Nothing.'

'But we must. My father and the others are talking of asking the Collector to release our sar-panch.'

'Do nothing. He will be released soon. But if you approach in a crowd you will frighten the Collector and he will arrest more of you.'

'Why should he be frightened of us? He has the police.'

'He will still be frightened.'

Kim knew why. The ripple from Bengal was gradually spreading. There was a stirring, as though people were waking up from a long sleep. And this awakening disturbed the government. It had caught them by surprise; first Bengal and now, in this small village, a handful of men were unhappy at the crop they had to sow. A year ago they would have remained silent. Now, though in whispers, they questioned the authority of the Collector. He was not used to that.

Rambaj turned, barely saying goodbye, forgetting the invitation to stay with his family, and ran home.

'Come,' Kim said to Lakshmi, and began walking in the direction of her village. He could not hide his relief at nearing the end of this journey and swore to himself that he would never get involved with a woman again. He had only gone a few yards when he looked back. Lakshmi remained stubbornly in the shade of the tree, toes dug into the dust, eyes downcast.

'Are you coming?'

'No.'

'Why not? We are near your village now.'

'Because I am frightened. I shall be a stranger in my own home and God knows how I shall be treated. How can I say where I have been, what I have done?'

'Tell them you worked for a rich landowner as a domestic servant.'

'It's all right for you to say that,' Lakshmi said angrily. 'You'll just go away and leave me. Men are always so lucky. They can do what they please, but women can't. I shall come with you.'

'Lakshmi.' Kim squatted beside her. 'I cannot take you everywhere I go. I have my life, and you have yours. Listen. There is another person for whom I care deeply.'

At that Lakshmi burst into tears. Her shoulders shook while she sobbed bitterly into the hem of her sari. Kim waited until the crying ceased, not touching her, for that familiarity would tighten her hold on him. But he understood her heartbreak.

'Why did you not tell me before? We have spent so much time together, and now you tell me there is another woman.'

'I may never find her, but she remains alive in me and I cannot still the memory of her. She is my private grief, not to be spoken of to anyone.'

'That's because I'm a prostitute.'

'Do you think I care for what you were?'

'No,' Lakshmi sighed, abandoning, not hope, but her recourse to tears. He looked at her kindly, but the kindness wasn't going to dissolve into softness. Kim was too strong, and she wished he weren't.

'Go, then,' she said dramatically. 'I will remain here.'

'Doing what?'

'Working. I shall starve and be beaten like these people. Look at them.' She was angry with them, angry at herself too for having once been one of them and thinking that she wanted to return to such a life. 'They have nothing to eat and they are dirty.'

'Only because they are poor. And because they have no money to buy new clothes.'

'In Bombay I had a new sari every month.'

'Do you regret leaving Bombay?'

'No. If only I could have kept the good things without the bad things.'

Kim knew then that he had fulfilled his obligation. He had brought Lakshmi across India, to within a few miles of her home. Like a stubborn camel, she would move no further and it was not his fault. Duty had been done. Yet still he couldn't abandon her. He sat for a while listening to the hum of insects about them, the quiet of the village which on the surface remained placid. Yet he could feel the tension growing, men talking to each other, gathering faint courage like the pieces of a jigsaw being cautiously pieced together.

'Wait here,' he said. He went to the chai-shop and bought tea and biscuits. He also asked for directions to Suresh Lal's house and, after taking the tea to Lakshmi, went in search of Suresh Lal.

He was sitting on a charpoi outside his home, sucking on an unlit hookah. He was glad to see Kim.

'I feel very lonely now. The villagers are avoiding me. People are getting themselves worked up because the Collector sahib arrested the sar-panch. He deserved to be arrested. Why should he approach the Collector sahib and worry him about this indigo?'

'Doesn't it affect you?'

'I don't grow any indigo. Only wheat. I don't belong to the Planters' Association.' He smiled happily. 'My wheat is going up in price all the time. People need food more than dyes.'

'I have come to discuss another matter; about my cousin. Or have you forgotten?'

'No, I have been thinking about her constantly. I have no one to care for me, no one to cook, no one to light my hookah. Your cousin is fair and pretty, and she looks as though she could bear healthy sons for me. What will be her dowry?'

'None.' Kim had worried on that matter. 'Her family are poor. She was working for a landlord in Bombay and wanted to return home. You will have to marry her without a dowry.'

Suresh Lal knew his worth. He was a well-off man and any family would be pleased to pay a good dowry to marry off their daughter to him. He had a pension, a good chit from the sarkar for service in his army, several acres of land. But the village girls were not sophisticated. He had seen big cities, drunk with comrades, frozen a moustache. He would like a sophisticated girl for a wife. She would understand his needs better.

There was one other reason. If Kim's cousin didn't please him, he could always throw her out without having to worry about her family's wrath. He had no wish to have his throat cut in a feud over a woman.

'Very well,' he said. 'I always make up my mind quickly. I will marry her.'

'Good. Is there a prohit in the village?'

'Yes. A senile old man, but he performs all the marriages. I will talk to him.'

To Kim's amazement, Lakshmi didn't sulk, but seemed quite pleased at the prospect of marrying Suresh Lal. He didn't realise that she thought it would teach Kim a lesson. Once he left her, he would find out how much he wanted her, and would return to carry her off. She would spurn him at first, make him beg. And then she would relent. It was pleasant, dreaming of such sweet revenge against Kim, and this kept her cheerful.

The prohit pored over their horoscopes and decreed that a quarter past six the next morning would be the most propitious time for the marriage. He was a small old man, wrinkled and leathery as a skin left too long in the sun. Beneath the frail exterior lay a grasping mind. He lived well, accepting gifts and money for his services, and ate regularly, even though others hadn't enough food. He knew his worth; men and women consulted him on the many events that composed their daily lives: when to plant, when to sow, when to sell, when to buy, when to marry and, if it had been at all possible, the precise moment to die. Yet despite this influence, this power over a whole village, he was a sour man, secretive and cynical.

The women of Rambaj's family were delighted to help their travelling companion, even though they were suspicious of Lakshmi's past and her relationship with Kim. Still, the pair had behaved with decorum on the journey, and purchased all the necessities for the ceremony with money provided by Suresh Lal. He had hoped that Kim, as Lakshmi's cousin, would meet this expense, but Kim pleaded poverty.

As befitting a man of affluence, Suresh Lal was also expected to provide a wedding feast for the village. He did grumble at this but the women silenced him. They would willingly cook and serve the food.

Dawn broke on an auspicious day indeed, Kim thought, for a prostitute who was to marry a man of considerable respect in his village. If it had not been for Kim, Lakshmi would have languished and died in the dim rooms of the brothel, diseased and finally discarded as her beauty faded.

A small and simple pandal had been erected outside Suresh Lal's home, the beaten earth decorated with intricate drawings, hexagons, triangles within triangles and other imaginative patterns made in many colours. The prohit, meticulously checking to ensure he had everything he would need to conduct a wedding – rice, ghee, flowers, water, mango leaves, limes, camphor – set himself up in the centre. The women knew exactly what was fitting. Many of them had attended marriages from childhood on, and could even recite the sastras, though none could read or write. By chance, there were even two musicians in attendance; wandering minstrels, one with a tabla, the other playing a flute.

The guests settled themselves on the bare earth, women to the right, men to the left. The children ranged back and forth, thin and ragged, waiting like their elders for the breakfast feast that would be served. It was a diversion from the dullness of their lives, a simple means of entertainment and an excuse to gather.

However they still only had one topic of conversation – the arrest of their sar-panch and what, if any, action the village should take. Though they had all slept on the matter, they had reached no conclusion. There was no one to lead their thinking.

Kim heard their whispers as he sat by the prohit. As the male 'cousin', he had to give Lakshmi away. He would be asked for his consent by the prohit and would gladly give it. Suresh Lal, fresh from his bath and wearing new clothes, sat to the left of the prohit. His skin shone from scrubbing and, like Kim, his cheeks glowed from a fresh shave given by the village barber with an old cut-throat. He studied the gathering, sensing the unease, the distraction that kept the men whispering among themselves.

'They are fools,' Suresh Lal said. 'The more they whisper, the more agitated they make themselves. I have told them they can do nothing against the Collector. He has the police at his bidding, and will call in more if they should approach him. You should speak to them.'

Kim was surprised. 'But I am not from this village. The panchayat must do it.'

'They saw how you were not afraid of the Collector, even though he shouted at you. They will believe what you say.'

'I only wish to continue on my journey.'

Despite the small size of the village, not everyone knew of the wedding, nor were they all invited to attend. Those who did not know had gone off to work in the fields, or to the mela at a village further north. They attended it to trade what little produce they'd managed to save, or else to sell a buffalo calf, or buy one. Those who had not been invited lived on the edge of the village, like flotsam. They had their own separate well and did the most menial tasks. These untouchables remained beyond the pale of acceptance and could not acquire the services of the prohit for any of their ceremonies. They were even poorer than the rest of the village.

The police sergeant knew of the wedding, but kept silent. He had been invited, but since he was on duty, and the Collector was in an ugly mood, he failed to inform the Collector sahib that such an event was taking place. It was not the wedding season – that being June – and the marriage was unexpected.

The Collector did not ride on inspection that morning. Ralph Sparrow had expected a different life. His brilliance, and he had little modesty on that subject since he had achieved a First in Classics at Balliol and come first too in the ICS exams, was wasted in this miserable district. Sparrow believed that life was meant to be pleasurable; achievement and success had come easily to him. He was not a sportsman, and had devoted his life to his books. He expected academic brilliance to bring its own reward, and had not realised that in India he would have advanced more swiftly if he had been an asset to the Governor's cricket team, or rode well enough to be in demand for polo. As he could do neither, he had been posted out-station immediately, and less worthy men who could bowl devilish leg breaks remained in Lucknow or Calcutta.

Without his topi, which always left a livid division between his red face and the white of his forehead, he didn't look as authoritative. Close up, his face had taken on a peeled look. He had a nervous habit of not looking at the person to whom he was speaking, which often confused his bearers and the police constables. He would look away to the right, and even though they shifted themselves to get into his line of vision, they always found themselves just outside it.

Sparrow had expected a grand life. It had long been his ambition to serve in India. As a boy he had dreamed of one day being the Viceroy; he had seen paintings and photographs of burra sahibs dining with princes, mounted on elephants on shikar, lounging around clubs. Certainly he had servants and a bungalow but he lacked company, European company. At night, when the darkness closed in swiftly, so did the isolation and a sense of having been shoved out to sea with a boatload of strangers. He had to admit to himself that this outpost life terrified him. The worst was the lonely evenings. He would bathe and then sit outside, watching the flicker of the village lamps.

He was authoritarian and believed in firm control – these villagers were too damned casual and indisciplined. He was not sure why he had arrested the sar-panch, but both the Planters' Association and the government, sitting comfortably in Calcutta, had ordered him to deal with the situation firmly. His immediate superior had even suggested arrest and flogging if necessary. He had also warned Sparrow that outsiders, probably Tilak followers, would instigate trouble.

That morning Sparrow sat sullenly in his tent being shaved by a bearer. To make matters worse, he was suffering from a hangover. Before he'd come out to India three years previously he had avoided alcohol, but had found it increasingly difficult to keep to his resolve. He had begun cautiously, brandy and soda now and then to prove his good-fellowship with the other club members. Then it had increased; now alcohol was a friend who warded off loneliness.

He picked at his breakfast, soggy scrambled eggs, pale toast and awful tea. His cook seemed incapable of doing any better. Through the misery of a headache worsened by the splintering morning glare, he could hear the drumming of a tabla and the wail of a flute. It was too damned early in the morning for such festivity and he squinted suspiciously in the direction of the sound. The drumming seemed to be reaching a frenzy and it agitated Sparrow because he did not know the reason. It sounded to him like a signal, a rising. The villagers ought to be working in the fields.

'What's going on out there?' he asked his bearer.

'I do not know, sahib.' He listened to the tablas. 'It sounds like a wedding, possibly.'

'Well, who's getting married?'

'I do not know, sahib.'

'Do you know anything at all?'

'No, sahib.' The bearer cleared away the dishes and retreated, leaving Sparrow to brood by himself. Normally he would have known of a wedding. The villagers would, out of respect, have invited him to attend, but he had heard nothing.

The idea gradually took hold that it wasn't a wedding at all. It was an excuse to gather and conspire against him for having arrested the sar-panch. Sparrow had issued a prohibition on any gatherings the day before, under the Police Act of 1861 which banned political meetings for action against the government. It was under this same act that he had arrested the sar-panch. Now the law was being broken and he was determined to take action.

He had a sergeant and five constables under his authority and could send a telegram and summon reinforcements from Lucknow. Sparrow plucked at his lower lip, a schoolboy habit of pulling it out and then letting it snap back. That would take too long. He couldn't wait. He grabbed his topi and stalked out.

Sergeant Mohinder Singh, a Jat Sikh and a friend of Suresh Lal's, had been expecting Sparrow's appearance. He knew he should have warned Suresh Lal about the ban on gatherings, but he was not sure whether a wedding constituted a breach of the law.

He and the two constables on duty immediately snapped to attention and saluted Sparrow. They could sense his anger; his eyes were darting around as though there were some hidden danger in the shadowy corners. The sar-panch sat in the small tent, handcuffed.

'Where are Constables Jagit and Ramesh?'

'Off duty, sahib.'

'Who gave them permission?'

Sergeant Mohinder remained silent. He was cross with Sparrow. If he had been told the men were supposed to be on duty, they would have been. Sparrow paced, stopping to peer out every few moments, straining to look over the entire length of the village. The tablas were silent and the silence seemed to increase with the heat, oppressing him.

'Do you know of any wedding?'

'No, sahib,' he lied to protect Suresh Lal.

'Arm the constables, and yourself.'

The marriage ceremony was over in twenty minutes. If Suresh Lal had had his way, he would have shooed the guests out and taken Lakshmi straight off to bed. He had not lain with a woman since his last night in Benares. The guests remained, rearranged in orderly lines with leaf plates in front of them. Each was given two puris, dhal, subji and a jelabi. The food was served swiftly and eaten just as swiftly. Pi-dogs prowled the edges, snarling for morsels. It was eight o'clock when the feeding was over. By now the sun had become hot and uncomfortable. Normally the men would have hurried to their tasks in the fields; instead they remained squatting in the meagre shade, talking. Rambaj moved from group to group, listening eagerly to his elders, grizzled men, thin and dark, who took a protracted time to speak their thoughts. There was a durability about their features as though they had been fashioned from the very earth and rock.

'They have decided to petition the Collector now,' Rambaj reported. He was excited at the prospect of taking part in this with the older men, and Kim realised he had been carrying the news from one group to another. 'Sparrow sahib is a good man. He will understand us. We must be allowed to grow enough wheat to store for times of drought, otherwise we'll starve. And the sar-panch will be released once Sparrow sahib understands our plight. Will you come with us?'

'No. I am not of this village and I must be on my way.'

Rambaj looked crestfallen. He wanted his new friend to join them, to share their lives as he had done on the journey. 'But I am sure Sparrow sahib will listen to you,' Kim added.

Kim was not speaking idly. He believed the Collector

would, in the tradition of his office as father-figure and administrator, listen to his villagers and redress their grievances. Possibly he had acted hastily over the sar-panch, but two whole nights had passed and Kim was sure they would see the sar-panch sauntering down the street at any moment.

Rambaj rejoined a group of men as Kim went in search of Lakshmi. He felt relief and regret. She had been his companion for many months, caring for him. He was fond of her as a friend – except when she had exasperating sulks. Whether he would ever pass through this village again depended on the will of God. Kim found her giggling in the company of the other women. As was the custom, they had eaten apart at the rear of Suresh Lal's home. Now they sat in the shade of a peepul tree contentedly chewing paan and gossiping. He approached with deference.

'I have come to say goodbye to my cousin. Lakshmi, may you bear many children and be happy.'

Lakshmi had thought about this moment all night. She intended to remain aloof and, with a toss of her head, wish Kim goodbye. She had no need of him, ever. Instead, now that the time had come, she ran to him with tears in her eyes. She embraced him and cried on his shoulder.

'We are,' Kim explained to the women, 'very close, as cousins. You will look after her, will you not?'

'Oh yes, we will,' one of the women replied.

Lakshmi stepped back shyly, eyes downcast, toes digging into the crumbling earth. She still wore the mark of marriage and flowers in her hair. Her appearance had changed. She seemed more assured, now that she had an unquestioned position, and respect. Kim could see confidence already filling her face, glowing now with the excitement of the morning's events. She tilted her face away from the sun, and he couldn't but acknowledge her beauty. Women changed their faces as easily as masks; they drew on secret things that could alter their eyes and mouths.

'I love you,' she whispered. 'I always shall, and if you should need me, I will come to you, wherever you are.'

'I know, Lakshmi. But you will be happy here.'

'It is possible, but I would be still happier with you. Are you going in search of her now?'

'No. First I must discover the meaning of my vision.'

'Keem, you are a fool,' Lakshmi said. 'I am not a prohit, nor a seer, but even I know the meaning of the first arrow. What can be more beautiful and strange than love for a woman? She is the tree with the strange flower that does not grow on earth. I had hoped and prayed it would be me, but that is not so. You must search for her first.'

When he considered what Lakshmi had told him, Kim realised he was indeed a fool, and so was Anand. He had taken the tree too literally, and had meant to search the jungles and mountains, a task that made him quake. Now he saw its meaning, and when he looked at Lakshmi he saw that her eyes were glistening at having given up that secret so easily. She saw him fill with hope. If she had held her tongue, he might have returned to her side one day. But she could not have remained silent; she loved him too much.

'You are right.' He touched her cheek gently. 'All men are fools. I am not sure where to begin. I will go to Delhi first, and see if I can find her home.'

'Each morning when I do puja, I will pray for you.' She tried to smile mischievously. 'Pray you will return, pray that you will take me with you.'

Kim chuckled. 'When I return, you will be surrounded by children and will never want to leave. Suresh Lal is a good man.'

'Maybe.' Lakshmi was too knowledgeable about men to take one man's word as to the character of another. 'Good' had one meaning to a man, another for a woman. 'Give me your darshan, sadhu.'

She knelt and placed her forehead on Kim's feet, and the women were impressed by her respect for her cousin. Kim lifted her up.

'You must show the same respect for your husband, as you have for me.'

'In which case he will die happy. But my respect for you is more than any husband will ever receive from me.'

'Good . . .'

Kim never finished that 'goodbye'. The sound of rifle-fire startled him. The women had never heard such an extraordinary and frightening noise, and at first looked around them with puzzled eyes. Kim heard three shots sounding almost as one. Crows wheeled up in fright, cawing loudly, flapping away from the village like black thunderbolts. Beneath their noise was human silence. Kim strained, but heard no voices calling or crying. The village had fallen silent as though all had died in a space of seconds.

'What is it?' asked Lakshmi.

'Guns,' Kim replied and, hearing his concern, she felt afraid. The women too detected it and began to panic, not knowing whether to run towards the noise or stay sitting where they were. One or two scrambled to their feet and looked at Kim.

'Wait here.'

As he left them, he heard the men's voices, first a confused murmuring, then an indistinguishable gabble; then the voices stopped and there was only the sound of running. He turned a corner and saw men rushing towards him in a tight wedge which, as it neared, began to break up. Several of them ran into houses, down gullies, panting with fear. Many were old, stumbling to avoid being trampled by the younger ones. Children too darted wide-eyed like panicked colts, unable to choose their direction. What chilled Kim most was the silent intent of the men to escape whatever dread lay behind them. Their mouths were open as though to give warning, but no sound emerged.

Suresh Lal, who was straining to see beyond the crowd, was the only one not afraid. The sound of gunfire was familiar to him.

'What happened?' Kim asked.

'They went to see the Collector sahib. I think he was waiting for them and told the police to fire warning shots. Now look at them, running like camels in every direction.'

It was, admittedly, a comical sight. Turbans flew off and rolled in the dust, chapals were abandoned, kurtas flapped. Pi-dogs barked, partly in excitement, partly too in fear. Like the crows they had an intuition about the guns.

The street was suddenly entirely empty of villagers; the dust began to settle and Kim and Suresh Lal could see all the way to the Collector's tents. He and three policemen were moving about in a thin line.

'Someone is hurt,' Suresh Lal said softly.

It looked like a small bundle of clothing, on which the dust was settling. Kim waited for it to move but it remained very still. He walked towards it, hoping it would rise, brush itself down, and run to him, but it remained unmoving, very alone. The policemen stood at ease, rifle butts grounded.

He knew who it was without seeing its face. Death had already erased him as a man. Kim recognised the new, green turban that was now askew in the dust. He bent and turned Rambaj over. The face was still frozen in surprise, the mouth partly open, the pain cut off, still festering within the corpse. The freshly cleaned kurta was blood-stained around the chest, dirt clinging to the blood in small lumps; all red. Blood changed all things.

Kim was struck by an overwhelming sadness for his young friend. Rambaj had expected little from life, and it had been gorgeously rich only days ago. He had travelled to Benares with a young bride, had immersed himself in the holy Ganges, praying no doubt for longevity and many children. This incident had been a ridiculous tamasha, a small excitement in an otherwise dull and tedious life, a walk with his elders to see the Collector, and chance had it that a bullet caught him in

306

the chest. He had meant no harm and would have been a good man. But now that was never to be.

Kim brushed the dust from the dead face, the sweat still fresh and damp. He couldn't leave Rambaj lying here and knelt to lift him up in his arms. The youth was light as a child, but as Kim began to straighten, he felt a hard prod in his back.

'Leave him.'

Kim ignored the hectoring voice and felt a second prod, harder still.

'He cannot lie here like a pariah dog. I will take him home.'

'Don't you bloody well understand me? I said leave him.'

Sparrow rapped Kim sharply on the back with his riding whip. It wasn't a hard blow, but it stung. Kim turned around with Rambaj in his arms. Sparrow was flushed, partly with anger but partly too with excitement. The small world he inhabited now understood his power. His policemen stood behind. They had their rifles ready, pointed at Kim.

Sparrow immediately recognised Kim.

'What are you still doing here?'

'I stayed to attend my cousin's wedding.' He began to walk away from Sparrow, turning his back once more.

'Sergeant, stop that man!'

Three rifles, pointing in from three sides, stopped Kim. He didn't turn around and waited patiently for Sparrow to stalk around him and stare him in the face. Sparrow didn't like Kim. Kim was making him more nervous than any Indian he'd ever met. This native wasn't afraid of him; he had an intolerable arrogance, as though he believed he were meeting an equal.

'You're one of Tilak's lot, aren't you? You were sent here to stir up trouble. No doubt you planned all this agitation.'

'It was not an agitation. They only wanted to speak to you about their problems, and to obtain the release of their sar-panch.'

'You seem to know a lot about what's happening here. Well, since you seem to love the place so much, you can stay here. Sergeant, arrest this man immediately. If he tries to escape, shoot him.'

22

IF IT was the good fortune of a prostitute to marry a man she didn't love, it was Elizabeth's ill-luck to wait impatiently to be proposed to by a man she loved too much. She had imagined love would be easy; she would be swept up into strong arms and kissed fiercely. The heroines in the novels she devoured captivated their heroes through charm and flirtation and helplessness. They surrendered their bodies only at the end; she had done so at the beginning.

When she spoke of love, her whispers went unheard.

She had experienced many a heartache thinking about Peter. Sleepless nights had left circles beneath her eyes and put her in a bad temper. It was two years since they had met, yet she still knew little about him. What knowledge she had was scant, and this made him even more desirable. He had an element of mystery about him – how he lived and what he did. He was a subject of speculation in the tightly-knit European community, who lived constantly in the glare of each other's eyes. Elizabeth planned circuitous schemes for their love-making; they snatched at impossible hours and places.

Peter spoke of his own life airily, without conveying any definite information. For instance, he often mentioned his place in Hampshire, yet if she asked him precisely where it was he would become vague. She didn't want to ask, she didn't want to know. She wanted to believe him, not only about the house in the country but the flat in Half Moon Street and many, many other things.

She knew better than to harry him now. When first he disappeared for two months, without warning, she had worried herself ill. She thought he had left her and Calcutta for good. She had gone to Sir William's house and had found all Peter's things still stored in the bedroom. He owned so little, two cabin trunks. He had taken Rao, his bearer. When Peter returned she'd nagged him to find out where he'd been, but as always he waved over at the horizon, as though he had circled the globe.

'But where did you go?' Elizabeth had persisted.

'It's none of your damned business. My dear Elizabeth, we're not married and I'm not a husband you can nag to death. I'll go when I please and return when I please. If you don't like it, you don't have to see me again.'

'But I *do* want to see you. I love you.'

'We've been through all that before.' His caress was gentle, playing over her whole body. 'You are really beautiful and quite wanton. A perfect combination for me. I've no intention of marrying anyone yet. And you would probably make my life hell. Maybe one day . . . I don't know when. Now, let's make love before it gets too hot.'

Her discreet enquiries never led anywhere. He simply disappeared with Rao. She didn't like Rao. He was a silent, sulky man, too familiar with Peter. She had seen their heads bent together, whispering not as master and servant, but as conspirators. Rao was barely polite to her but now never failed to address her as memsahib. He tolerated her presence, but if one day he didn't, Peter would surely believe Rao before her. Rao's breath always stank of arrack, morning and night, and daily his eyes grew redder, becoming angry rubies by nightfall. Yet he was efficient. He looked after Peter excellently and was always immaculate himself in a freshly starched uniform with a red cummerbund and white turban.

At times, Elizabeth thought that Peter might have another woman. The thought arose from jealousy for she begrudged his sudden disappearances which left her stranded at home. A woman in a distant town, not Simla or Bombay or Delhi or Lucknow, but some mysterious place where no Europeans lived, in the jungle or the mountains. But she had no proof; only vivid imaginings. Time was passing; she felt herself ageing, the heat and the climate burned youth too swiftly into old age before its time. Wrinkles appeared, the skin sagged, the spirit waned.

'What did you tell your father?' Peter asked.

'I lied to him. I told him I was going to spend the night with the Hayeses. They live near Kufri. You don't like him, do you?'

'I don't like or dislike the Colonel. But, being your father, he's going to ask me one day, "M'boy, what are your intentions towards my daughter?" And when I say, "Lust, sir," he'll have me horse-whipped. The Colonel's the type.'

'You're exaggerating. He disturbs you. He does most people, you know. And he won't use a horse-whip. He'd most probably have you shot at dawn.'

They rode up the narrow bridle path. To the right, the hill sloped steeply down to a narrow mountain stream, and above them the deodars looked like giant burnt matches; winter had stripped them and the snow clung to their branches, covering the ground as far as the eye could see. Their breath was visible and it was good to feel the warmth of the ponies beneath them. The sky was an icy blue and the mountain wind blew down to cut at them. Their cheeks were pink from the cold and exertion. Behind them Rao and two porters led a hill pony laden with food and bedding.

The Colonel and Elizabeth had come up to Simla for the Christmas holidays. They expected Richard to join them on Christmas Eve, three days away. Elizabeth had bought her father an original painted manuscript of Mughal poetry, a beautiful and delicate work of art. It had been tucked away behind a stack of *Imperial Gazeteer*s in a bookshop in Calcutta, and it was by sheer chance that she'd come upon it. Though she couldn't understand a word of it, she knew her father would be delighted. For Richard, she'd bought a new saddle. The presents had been carefully wrapped and hidden under the bed.

Christmas was always very special. It evoked the past, especially here in Simla with the snow on the ground and the cold. Down on the plains, try as she might, Elizabeth couldn't imagine Christmas. She blotted out the many Christmases spent at boarding-school in England. Those were times of intense loneliness and despair, with not even Richard for comfort. He stayed at his school while she and other Anglo-Indian girls, like Sarah Rushton, stayed at theirs. They would cling together like waifs in the empty dormitory and dining-hall, spending Christmas Day huddled around the fire in the headmistress's room, recalling other days in India. As small children, she, Richard and their friends would have snowball fights and toboggan down the hill slopes. They would go to church in the morning, then sit down to a dinner of roast turkey with roast potatoes, carrots and beans. And afterwards a Christmas pudding, liberally soaked in brandy with twelve eight- and four-anna coins hidden inside. Aunt Emma also made four bottles of OT, a blend of lime juice, spices and a touch of brandy. When friends came to call, the ladies would drink the OT, while the men would take brandy.

Peter's presence had come as an unexpected bonus. He hadn't told her he would see her in Simla, and then out of the blue the day before she'd received a brief note: 'Why not come up to Kufri with me for the night?' Elizabeth couldn't resist it. Her father would never find out.

'We're not going all the way to Kufri,' Peter said. 'I've borrowed a bungalow a mile this side.'

'Whose?'

'The Godfreys'.'

'I thought they'd be back by now. I didn't know they were wintering down on the plain.'

'No, he took his home leave. I bumped into them in

Calcutta and they insisted I use their house when I told them I was coming up here.'

'That's rather sudden. I saw them, oh, two weeks ago, but they didn't mention any home leave. Their house is in a lovely place, you know, just on the side of a hill looking north. You can see Everest.'

'You can't.'

'Of course you can.'

'Elizabeth, you can see Everest from a place called Nagerkhot, which is just outside Katmandu. You can't see it from Simla.'

'I suppose you're right, and I suppose you've seen it from this Nagerkhot.'

'Not yet. Maybe I'll take you there one day and we'll make love in the shadow of Everest.'

They rode for a while in silence.

'Will you ever return to England?'

'Sometimes it's all I think of doing,' said Elizabeth. 'When I first came back to India, I hated everything. I felt my soul rotting away and I wanted to bolt. Then, at times like this, I'm so happy to be here. It can be beautiful and calm and all the people I love – Father, Richard, Aunt Emma, and you – are here. It's a comfortable life if you want it to be that way, as long as you don't look too hard and learn not to feel things. But sometimes I hate this place and want to leave for ever. Will you stay?'

'I don't know.'

'You're always so evasive.'

'Only because I live life by the day, not for a "for ever". You should know that by now.'

'Do you miss your mother?' he asked suddenly.

'What a strange question! No. But that's only because I never knew her.' She found him staring at her intently, trying to look beyond her words. 'What is it?'

He shook his head. 'Your father is a very secretive man.'

'And so are you. But then, that's his job. It seems so full of secrets I sometimes wonder whether his right hand knows what his left hand does.'

'Yes. It spills out into his own life.'

'He never talks about his work. I never ask.'

By tea-time they had reached the bungalow. It looked cold and abandoned, the garden piled with drifts of snow, the deodars stark, almost frightening in their blackness. Rao had a key and went round to the back to open the front door for them. It was even colder inside, and very dark.

The lamps were lit and in the gentle glow Elizabeth looked upon a room crowded with memories. There was so much bric-à-brac; it overflowed the shelves, tables and windowsills. Here were all the little bits of a life: English, Burmese, Rajput, Afghan. There were many exquisite sculptures and delicately detailed Mughal miniatures. On one wall was another collection of miniatures, these of Europeans painted by Indian artists in the last century.

She watched Peter walk all the way round the room with the lamp, stopping often to bring the light close to an object. He was like a boy in a treasure cave, fondling and caressing the things he liked. His hands were as expressive with a piece of bronze as they were with her body. She was fascinated by those delicate fingers stroking the voluptuous form of an Indian goddess.

'I wish I was her.'

She startled Peter. Quickly he put down the statue and came over to kiss her nose.

'You will be, tonight.'

Rao was efficient, as always. While making tea he also filled the stove with wood and soon had a fire going that gradually warmed the room. They drank their tea by the window, huddled together under a blanket, staring out at the slowly fading mountains.

'Who's your best friend, Peter?'

'Here, or in England?'

'In the world.'

'It's an odd question. I suppose I'd call Anthony Lawrence a close friend. I'm not sure about *best*. He was at

314

school with me. Now he's working at Lloyds in the City. And yours?'

'Richard. I tell him everything, or most things that a woman can tell a brother. And after him I suppose it would be you. I've told you just about everything about myself, and I do know you pretty well, don't I?'

'You know a lot. What about all the girls you know in Calcutta and up here?'

'We see one another because we have no one else to see. It's like being on an island. You take what you can get. They're nice, but I don't think they're my best friends.'

'Anywhere you live it will be the same. You make friends of the people you meet.'

'But in England you're not trapped.'

'And you feel trapped?'

'Sometimes. I see the same people day in, day out. In all the same places.'

'Well, this at least is a new place.'

In spite of her dislike for Rao, she had to admire his speed. He had their bath water ready just as it became dark, and by the time they'd finished and come back to sit under their blanket, looking out at the night, she could smell the food cooking. Peter had brought a bottle of whisky and, though she hated the taste, she had a couple of mouthfuls before dinner. It wasn't an elaborate meal, but it was certainly tasty. Rao had cooked pepper chops and a vegetable curry. He had also placed hotwater-bottles in the bed and had laid a blazing fire in the fireplace.

She had never made love in the cold before, and it was sheer luxury to feel the cool caress of dry skin and watch the firelight flickering over their bodies. The dancing shadows first hid and then revealed the twist and entwinement of their limbs, as though they were in constant movement. And when they were tired, she cuddled against Peter under the heavy blankets and fell asleep.

She awoke to bright sunlight and an empty bed. She

dressed quickly and found Peter in the drawing-room, studying the nineteenth-century miniatures of the Europeans.

'The Indian artist is the most adaptable creator in the world. Look, here they paint in the Mughal style because the Mughals are the rulers. And here, with such ease, they adopt the European style because the English are the rulers. What I mean is that they are eager to learn, to adapt, to blend. Their art is a synthesis of their past and the present.'

'I suppose so. But they'd never produce a . . . a Rembrandt or a Leonardo da Vinci.'

'They don't need to. Their art is different. It isn't attached to ego. See, none of them is signed. They never are. They are true artists. But you're a philistine and I'm boring you.'

'And I didn't know you were such an expert.'

'Not an expert. Just a passing acquaintance.'

He took her hand and they went out onto the verandah to look at the horizon of the awesome mountain peaks. They were shimmering white in the distance and, because of the air, appeared to be almost within reach.

They had breakfast on the verandah, and then it was time for Elizabeth to leave. She wanted to get to Simla before dusk.

Peter walked with her to the gate where the horse and porter were waiting. Elizabeth cried a little.

'Why don't you spend Christmas in Simla? Then I can see you.'

'I may do. But I do so hate Christmas. I want to spend it alone. Here.'

'Why "hate"?' She waited, but he only shrugged. 'I could come up here the day after Boxing Day.'

'Why don't you? I'll keep the bed warm.'

She thought about his remark a lot on the ride back. What would he do? Stare at the mountains all day? They were too perfect, too aloof. Silent and withdrawn, they never changed.

When she reached the outskirts of Simla she dismissed

the porter. The stables were below the Mall, so she handed her horse over to a syce and strolled home up the Mall. The shops were all open, crowded with people shopping for last-minute presents. There were many people she knew and it took her some time to reach home.

The moment she opened the door, she felt a prickly sensation on her skin, a chill that made her shiver, but not from the cold. The bungalow was absolutely quiet. She couldn't hear the servants at the back, and the dog lay watchful and sad on the rug. It wagged its tail once and lowered its head. Usually it leapt up to lick her hand.

'Aunt Emma?' Her voice sounded unnaturally loud in the silence. She went right through to the back. The servants sat under the apple tree, huddled together for comfort. 'Mary ayah?'

Mary ayah saw her but didn't acknowledge her. Instead, she scurried into her quarters, head covered by her sari. Suddenly Elizabeth was frightened. She ran to her father's room and when she opened the door, her heart sank. It was empty. Just as she was about to step back, she saw him sitting in his armchair by the window. He didn't move when she approached him, but remained staring out.

'Father, what's happened?' She knelt by him. He hadn't heard her whisper. 'Father, what's happened? Tell me.'

'Where in damnation have you been?' He did not raise his voice, but the whispered question was brutal and cold.

'I . . . I told you. The Hayeses'.'

'You're lying. I went there. The Hayeses haven't seen you.'

'I changed my mind. I went . . .'

For the first time in her life, she felt the hard sting of her father's hand against her cheek. The blow rocked her but she was too startled even to feel the pain.

'You spent the night with young Bayley! Just like that

317

harlot your mother, who'd climb into any man's bed.'

'My mother never did that.' She was so shocked, she had to defend the dead memory.

'Like mother, like daughter.' He leant forward and gripped her wrist so hard that he almost crushed the bones. Elizabeth cried out at the pain. '*You* should be dead, like her. Not Richard.'

Elizabeth didn't understand, couldn't understand. The assault on herself and on her mother confused her, but when finally she grasped his meaning, she began to cry.

'Richard! Dead? No, no, no. It can't be. You're just saying that because you're angry with me. Yes, I was with Peter, but that doesn't mean you can frighten me by saying Richard's dead. It's cruel and mean.'

'Read that.' He thrust the telegram at her as though it were proof of her sins.

REGRET TO INFORM YOU OF DEATH OF YOUR SON RICHARD CREIGHTON STOP KILLED IN ACTION YESTER-DAY STOP HE DIED A BRAVE SOLDIER FIGHTING FOR KING AND COUNTRY STOP DEEPEST CONDOLENCES STOP LETTER FOLLOWS STOP R DYER COLONEL

Elizabeth locked herself in her room. She couldn't stop crying all night and even at dawn the tears kept flowing. She wound herself tightly into a ball, hugging herself, rocking herself. She had no one else to hold her, to calm her. She had no thought except the agony in her heart. She didn't cry out aloud, although she wanted to scream, she wanted to wail, she wanted to hurt herself. She wanted her own death and hoped she would die from all her crying; if tears were blood, she would have done so.

In the morning she heard the door open. She thought it must be Mary ayah. The bed creaked as her father sat beside her. She felt his hand on her shoulder, but she didn't turn round.

318

'I'm sorry, Lil. I was terribly upset, and when I couldn't find you, I was worried. I shouldn't have been angry.'

'You were cruel. You've never talked about Mother, and then you say hurtful things about her.'

She turned her head and saw his face. It was grey and drawn; he had aged ten years. Carefully, she placed her own hand on his.

'Luckily, yesterday I had the presence of mind not to tell the Hayeses you had said you were spending the night with them. It was a childish lie. I should have found out eventually. And as kind as they are, they are dreadful gossips.'

'What did you tell them to save my reputation?' Elizabeth asked, knowing he was more concerned with propriety and his own reputation than hers.

'I just said you'd mentioned dropping in on them for tea. It was the best I could do under the terrible circumstances.'

'Thank you, Father.'

'We're going to 'Pindi. The train to Delhi leaves in an hour. We'll catch the Frontier Mail tomorrow.'

'I'm not going.'

'Don't you care for your brother?'

'He's dead, and I loved him more than you ever did. I don't want to see his grave. First Mother, now Richard. And he died a useless death. For what? India. Damn India. I hate this place. You go and look at his grave. It will look exactly like any other grave in any other cemetery.'

Her father gently shut the door. He hadn't even wept for his own son. They should have cried together, held each other.

Elizabeth knew that from now on, every time she saw an officer, Richard would come to mind. Already she hated the sight of a uniform. Richard was dead and she was alone. India was whittling down her family. She supposed all soldiers died useless deaths, capturing for a brief second the glory of bravery and then disappearing for ever into the endless stretch of painful memory for those left behind. Elizabeth heard only the stark echo of events in those rocky defiles, a rifle shot ricocheting on and on through eternity. A Great Game, her father called it. The loser – bad luck, old chap – was Richard.

In fifty, one hundred years, his headstone too would be worn by the weather, fading gradually like a painting left out in the sun.

. . . She had been seven years old, Richard eight. They were in a shooting camp with their father, near Naini Tal where Richard had shot his first panther. They sat on the ground together warming themselves around the fire, and stared into the flames.

– Do you remember a fire once? Richard asked.
– What fire? I've seen lots and lots.
– It was like in a dream when we were very young. It must have been only me who dreamed it, then. I thought you were beside me.
– No. I can't remember. How old was I?
– Just a baby.
– Then how would I remember? Babies can't remember anything. It must have been a dream, even for you.
– No. It was so clear. I was woken up by the firelight on the ceiling of our room. The punkah had stopped and the garden was glowing with flames. I got out of bed and went to stand at the window.
– What did you see then? Devils?
– No, silly. I think I saw Daddy, at least it looked like him. He was standing by the fire and there were a lot of things in a pile by his side and he was throwing them in one by one and poking them with a stick.
– What things?
– I couldn't see them clearly. They looked like . . . things. There were books and papers and lots of clothes. He poked them with a stick to make sure they burned right up, and he kept walking round and round the fire. Sometimes I saw his face, then he wouldn't have a face.
– Don't frighten me.
– I'm not. His face was black, like a native's. I think it was the smoke and the ash. So were his clothes. Then I

got tired and fell asleep. I always thought I fell asleep at
the window, but when I woke up I was in bed.
– See, it was a dream, then.
– I suppose it was. It's funny how you remember one
dream and then not another.
– What was I doing?
– You were sleeping, as usual. You always slept a lot.
But for some reason I thought you were beside me. I
was holding you up so you could see properly. You
don't remember?
– I was a baby, you just told me. How would I
remember? . . .

   It was peculiar how a conversation returned. The dead
stirred up old memories, the sediment of events that
were temporarily forgotten and lay at the bottom. What
brought it to the surface? She hadn't thought of it for
years. She suspected that in the future, each time she
thought of Richard, another trivial scrap would break to
the surface. Oh God, if only memory would not play
such evil tricks on her heart.

23

KIM WAS thrust handcuffed into a small tent standing behind Collector Sparrow's large one. A constable stood on guard outside, his body a silhouette against the side of the tent. The air was still and hot. Kim had fallen on his knees and awkwardly straightened to sit cross-legged. The sar-panch crouched in a corner, a thin bundle of clothes and a turban separated by a worried face. Bony wrists hung limply over bony knees; his thin face was hollow below the cheekbones, and shaded with white stubble.

'I heard shooting. What happened?'

'The village went to see the Collector sahib about you. He told the police to open fire. One man was killed.'

'Who?'

'Rambaj.'

'Ahre, ahre, ahre.' He rocked, clenched fists beating his temples, wanting to still the pain. Tears broke from his eyes and trickled down like an undernourished stream through the dust, to fall onto his kurta. The sharp mourning ran its course, then the sar-panch wiped his face, smearing the tears. 'He was my sister's daughter's son. He was only just married. They made the pilgrimage to Benares.'

'I came back with him.'

'Who are you? I've never seen you before.'

'Kim. I am from Lahore. I was accompanying my cousin to her village, but instead she got married here.'

'Who?'

'Suresh Lal.'

'Ah. What is her caste?'

'Kayasth.'

'That is good. Is she a good woman?'

'Yes.'

'Suresh Lal needs a good woman. My wife was thinking of a cousin of hers for him, but she might not have been suitable. One death, one marriage. Even in this little village things have changed which I have not witnessed. I do not know why the Collector sahib is treating me so unkindly. All we ask for is to grow enough wheat so that we won't starve if the rains fail. It is as though we had asked for all the land. What did you do to get yourself arrested?'

'Nothing, except try to carry Rambaj's body to his home.'

'Is that a crime?'

'I don't know. The Collector is young and frightened and believes we are all against him.'

'You are brave, then, to have defied him.'

'Your bravery is greater than mine. You tried to help your village get enough to eat. He will release you soon, if you agree to stop the agitation.'

'How can I? We are poor and grow poorer each day. I am not a man if I cannot help my village. If only I was braver and more clever. But I am neither. All we can hear is the cries of our children for food.'

'It is a good village.'

'What good is good if we cannot eat?'

They fell silent at the shrill cry of a woman weeping. The sound hung in the air like a kite, swooped to silence, then began again. Kim felt oppressed by the suffering in that cry. Rambaj's death had been pointless; his eagerness to prove that he was a man had robbed him of his chance of becoming one.

I could with the ease of a magician escape this suffering. I could escape these handcuffs. I could escape this tent. If I so desire, I need never see the faces of these villagers again. They are grains of sand in India, one already crushed, but thousands more too will be ground

323

to dust over the years. Gaunt men, thin women, starving children. They mean nothing in the scheme of empires. I do not need to care for them. I have been trained for greater things, but to what end? If what I do entails yet more killing, my own existence is diminished. I can escape this, but I cannot escape myself. I could call out to the constable and tell Collector Sparrow that I am an agent of the Colonel, an Imperial Agent. But I cannot ignore this suffering.

The flap opened and they were ordered out. They squinted in the glare. The village men had assembled beneath the bhodi tree. Collector Sparrow sat on a canvas stool at a portable table with papers in front of him. The constables frogmarched Kim and the sar-panch through a narrow gap between the squatting villagers. The women were hidden in the dark doorways of their huts, and children cried from within. Otherwise the silence was as heavy as the heat.

Sparrow read his papers, allowing the silence to draw out. He was calm, just as though he were sitting in an office. Finally, he lifted his head and stared at the sar-panch, ignoring Kim.

'Ajit Singh, you have been a very naughty man. Because of you, all this trouble has occurred and my men had to shoot one of the villagers. I am sorry it was Rambaj who died, but it was necessary in order for you all to understand that defying the sarkar will be severely punished. Do you understand?'

'Collector sahib,' the sar-panch said, 'I don't understand the need for you to kill one of us. We shall die anyway. I did not mean to defy the sarkar. All we wanted was permission to grow food to feed ourselves. Indigo is not food for our bellies, and if the rains do not come we shall have no food to spare and we shall all die. The death of Rambaj has deeply saddened me, sahib. If I am to blame for his death, I must be punished.'

'We've gone all through this before. The sarkar believes indigo is the best crop for this village to grow. If the rains fail, the sarkar will come to your aid, as it has done before. Is that not right?' Ajit Singh remained silent. 'I am going to release you on condition that you stop all this mischief. Do you agree?'

'If I disagree, shall I be punished further?'

'I've also decided that you should not be the sar-panch of this village any more.' The villagers drew in their breath noisily. Sparrow ignored them. 'Mohinder Kumar has been appointed sar-panch. You will obey him in all matters. Is that understood?'

'But the village must elect him, Collector sahib.'

'That isn't necessary. The sarkar has appointed him.'

Mohinder Kumar looked no different from the other villagers; a thin man, stubbled, with downcast eyes. It wasn't possible to tell whether he was pleased or unhappy at his sudden elevation. He wilted under Ajit Singh's stare. They were not to know that even the princes of huge states could be replaced as easily as the sar-panch should they cause problems to the government. A sar-panch was a mere mote. There was no doubt that Mohinder Kumar had been chosen because he would obey Collector Sparrow. As long as he did that, he would remain sar-panch. The villagers knew they had been betrayed, but were helpless to do anything other than accept Mohinder Kumar as their leader. He would do little to help them, and Kim saw the look of fear in their eyes. Many would die when the rains failed.

'You can join the others,' Sparrow dismissed Ajit Singh. Quietly, now bent with defeat, Ajit Singh took his place at the rear of the rows of men. Collector Sparrow turned his attention to Kim. 'And now you. You're a troublemaker.'

'I have caused no trouble here. It was here before I came, it will be here when I am gone.'

'I don't like you. You're too bloody bold.' Sparrow rose and came closer to inspect Kim. He was not sure whether he read contempt or defiance in Kim's eyes. They still made him uneasy. There was strength in the man, as though Sparrow could not hurt him. 'I'm going to teach you a lesson so that this village and all the others around here will know it is dangerous for them to bring in men like you.'

'They did not bring me here. I came with my cousin.'

'You're a cheeky bastard, too. You keep contradicting me.'

'If you make up lies about me, I have to correct them.'

Sparrow sensed the villagers stir. They had never heard a native reply so boldly to an Englishman before. The ripple could spread outwards, touching other villages as they repeated the story of this man who spoke so bravely to the Collector sahib. They were waiting to see how he would react. Sparrow knew his authority must not be undermined by this man.

'Sergeant.'

'Sahib?'

'Have this man thrashed. Then we will take him back to Rae Bareli and have him put on trial.'

'Yes, sahib.'

The constables unlocked Kim's handcuffs and, holding his arms tightly, marched him to the bhodi tree. There was an earth platform two feet high surrounding the base of the tree. It was used by the village panchayat for their meetings. Nearly every village had such a tree and such a custom. The constables hauled Kim onto the platform and forced him to embrace the trunk of the ancient tree. The bark scraped his face and broke the skin.

Kim smelt the innocence of the wood. He could see nothing except the dark tree-trunk. He closed his mind to the uneasy murmur of the villagers. Then the closing of his eyes and ears followed the closing of his mind. Detachment from the body would make pain bearable. The body was the source of all pain, and by withdrawing into the inner light of his mind, he would defeat pain.

Kim didn't hear the testing swish of the cane wielded by the sergeant. It was thin and springy, the kind used to cane schoolboys. The sergeant mounted the platform and spread his legs for balance and leverage. He looked down at the Collector. Sparrow had expected Kim to

weep and grovel; he wanted him to. This silent acceptance once more undermined him, robbed him of the
power to control the man, to diminish him in the eyes
of the villagers. Pain would soon make the fellow cry
out, show him to be as weak and malleable as the rest
of them. He would then forgive the man and take him
away from the village.

'Ten strokes should teach the beggar a lesson,
Sergeant.'

'Yes, sahib.'

The sergeant lifted the cane and brought it whistling
down on Kim's back. Another man would have flinched,
but Kim remained still. The whack of the stick on flesh
hung in the air for a moment, then the sergeant struck
again. Thrice, four times. Kim moaned. His body was
betraying him. He felt the last blow penetrating his
tightly shut mind. It stabbed in like lightning, hungrily
snatching at his strength. He closed his eyes tighter,
concentrating fiercely on the inner light, now fragment-
ing with each blow. He clenched his teeth and pressed
his face cruelly into the bark to create a different pain to
prevent him from screaming out. He knew Sparrow was
waiting to hear him. Tears ran down his face, but he
would not give the salah Sparrow the pleasure of gloat-
ing.

At last the beating stopped. Kim waited, tense, expecting a trick. The constables released his arms. He tried to
step away lightly, but his legs would not bear his weight.
He toppled from the platform, rolling once in the dust;
fading from the sunlight and the compassionate stares
of the villagers, falling away from Sparrow's voice.

'. . . you must be careful not to harbour troublemakers
like this man again. The next time, I will have you all
thrashed to teach you a lesson.'

Kim regained consciousness, staring up through the
branches of the tree at the empty blue sky. On the
periphery of his vision he saw Sparrow staring down at
him. His face looked swollen, a white ganesh. Then Kim
recognised the Collector's topi. He tried to sit up, but

327

felt as though his back had been tied in knots. It wouldn't straighten, so he remained lying down, patiently waiting for the nausea of pain to subside. He felt his kurta sticking to the bloody wounds.

'Well, you can't lie here for ever.' Sparrow moved out of his vision.

'Handcuff him, Constable, and bring him along.'

Kim was pulled to his feet. The villagers rose too and he saw the pity in their faces. Suresh Lal and Ajit Singh looked poised to rush forward and help him, but they were held back by their fear of Sparrow. He had made Kim untouchable. They would be beaten for aiding him. A woman ran out from one of the huts, weeping.

'How can you take him without letting us clean his wounds?' Lakshmi shouted at Sparrow.

'He won't die from a thrashing.'

Lakshmi pushed the constables away before they could handcuff Kim. She led him back to the platform and sat him down. With the edge of her sari, dipped in a lota of water, she wiped the dirt from his face and then turned him gently to inspect his back.

'Those salahs,' she whispered and he heard tears in her voice. 'They should all be killed.'

'Be careful of what you say. The Collector will have you arrested for sedition.'

'They can arrest me all they please.'

She took the lota and poured water carefully on his back.

'There is a lot of blood, but the wounds are not deep.' He felt her dab the broken flesh and the cool water loosened the knots in his muscles.

'Give me some to drink.' He tilted his head back while she poured water into his mouth. 'You had better treat your husband with the same kindness.'

'But I do not love him as I do you.'

'You will.'

'Get rid of that woman, Constable. We haven't got all day.'

Lakshmi was pushed aside and Kim pulled to his feet.

He winced when they handcuffed his arms behind his back. The iron rubbed against his bleeding back. One of the constables attached a short chain to the handcuffs and took a tight grip on it.

'I will come with you,' Lakshmi said.

'No. Stay here. I shall be all right.'

The villagers parted reluctantly and Kim passed through. He felt Suresh Lal's hand briefly touch his shoulder, and in his eyes read the farewell. Kim couldn't blame them for their reluctance to help him. Their lives were already hard enough. He was marched between the two constables out of the shade of the bhodi tree. Sparrow strode ahead, the sergeant behind. Sparrow's horse had been saddled and he mounted. Without looking back, he trotted out of the village.

It was a two-day march to Rae Bareli. Kim found it painful to walk with his hands behind his back. The two constables prodded him with their lathis if he stumbled or slowed. The small procession – the Collector on horseback, riding with the authority of a prince; a camel-drawn cart loaded with camping equipment; the sergeant, Kim, and the constables – passed through villages and, like a dancing bear or a performing monkey, Kim was the object of curiosity. He was put on show, an example of the sort of punishment to expect if one defied the sarkar. When Sparrow stopped in a village, he would parade Kim in front of the sar-panchs and other villagers, telling them how he had caught Kim, and what his punishment had been, and what it would be once they reached District Headquarters. Kim would be tried for sedition and sentenced to prison. If they did not heed his warning and prevent men like Kim from corrupting them, they too would end up in chains, end up lashed, end up in prison. The lesson was listened to carefully, and the villagers would shuffle away from Kim. Even to be seen within his shadow could bring down such a terrible punishment.

Kim would smile at them then, and see the doubt rise in their minds. It was a cheery smile, as though he was playing a game. It was, after all, a game for him, though a different one from the Great Game. He had been caught in the trap set for the natives, and if he was to be mistaken for one, he might as well be one.

To escape this punishment would be so ludicrously easy. He had only to open his mouth to Sparrow. But once more, he remained silent as to the matter of his identity.

They reached Rae Bareli at midday. It was a large village, nearly a small town. The two-storeyed brick buildings with red tiled roofs reflected its growing affluence. The main road was busy with traffic. The shops sold everything from basic provisions to silk and jewellery. Behind them, divided by teeming lanes, the houses shrank in size until, on the outskirts, they dwindled to mud and thatch.

The largest residential bungalow was set in a spacious compound at the far end of the village. High walls surrounded it. The garden, though brown and dusty, was neatly maintained. The gravel drive was swept of leaves and the flower beds had been planted with cannas, marigolds and roses, and looked freshly manured. However, it was a desolate place, withdrawn from the ebb and flow of the village. There were other small buildings within the compound wall. One was the dak bungalow for visiting government officials, another a cheerful red-painted cottage covered with bougainvillea, which served as the police station. The third was the District Magistrate's office.

Kim was marched into the police station. His handcuffs were removed and he was locked in a room with a barred window. There was a bed roll in one corner, but apart from that, nothing broke the monotony of the walls except glistening brown cockroaches the size of a finger. They ignored his presence, bustling along the corners of the walls. He was the visitor, they the permanent residents.

He accepted his continuing misfortune philosophically. Everything in life was of a temporary nature:

330

success, failure, pain, joy, anger, happiness, sadness: each came and went in an eternal cycle. One had to believe that nothing was ever permanent, to understand life was illusion, a magician's trick, a coin appearing and disappearing, a child vanishing in mid-air. He spread out the bedding, lay down and promptly went to sleep.

He was woken at dusk by a small chokra with round eyes and hair smelling of coconut oil. It glistened in the lamplight and filled the cell with a strong, sweet odour. The chokra warily unfurled a leaf plate on the floor, ducked out and returned with several small clay bowls containing food. He squatted by the doorway, ready to bolt, and watched Kim eat.

'Are you a dacoit?' asked the boy.

'Yes. And if you don't behave, I'll come and cut your ears off.'

'What for? I don't have any money. I thought dacoits only killed people for money. Have you killed many people?'

'Not many.'

'How many? Ten, twenty, a hundred? Did you cut their throats or use a silk cloth, like the thugs?'

'Not one,' Kim admitted. The boy looked annoyed. 'But I did once know some dacoits who have killed many people. They are my friends and prowl the Grand Trunk Road waiting for boys like you to come along. They steal you and sell you to Bombay merchants.'

'I wouldn't mind that. Anything would be better than here. All I do is work and work. If I am lucky, I might get an anna; if not, not. I get my food and the salah I work for doesn't beat me too much.'

He reminded Kim of the chokra in the Bombay hotel. Lost childhoods abounded in this country, and when he thought of his own, spent not working but wandering the great land, he could not help but feel sorry for others less fortunate.

'You should run away then.'

'Where? Everywhere is the same.' When Kim had finished his meal the boy carefully rolled up the leaf, meticulously picked up a shred of vegetable from the floor. 'Are they going to hang you?'

'I hope not. It would make life most difficult if you were dangling from a rope.'

The next day Kim woke at dawn. The air in the cell was pleasurably cool, giving him a brief sensation of delight. He knew that once the sun rose, the coolness would turn to malevolent heat. He was led out for his morning wash and saw the village stirring to life. Carts were wending their way slowly down tracks towards the fields, followed by a swaying, graceful line of men and women. The first smoke of cooking fires filled the air with a sweet smell of burning wood.

He returned to his cell and sat cross-legged to await the next event. With a forefinger he closed one nostril, breathed deeply through the other, held the prana to the beat of twenty, and slowly exhaled. He repeated the exercise, alternating nostrils, until he experienced a deep calm which rose from his mind, spreading down through his body. His blood ceased to pound, his heartbeat slowed.

He remained suspended in this state of calm until the chokra interrupted him with his morning meal, a thick piece of nan bread with a cup of hot sweet tea.

'In the village they are saying you are worse than a dacoit. You are a sed . . . seditionist. You are fighting the sarkar. Is that true?'

'I have harmed no one.'

'But I hear there are men who have killed Angrezis. I was told that in Calcutta a bomb killed two Angrezi women. It was meant for a man, but the men who threw the bomb made a mistake with the gharri. It was a Justice sahib they really wanted to kill.'

'You are better informed than I, then. These are changing times. Worse is still to come. An elephant is slowly awakening, and we do not know its mood yet. One part of it is angry, another part is placid. If the mahouts continue to prod it, it will become angry all over. Those who threw the bomb in Calcutta are the angry part, but

332

they are a very small part. The rest of the beast is still sleeping. We shall see what it does when it awakes.'

'Am I part of this elephant?'

'Yes. A hair on its behind.'

'Huh. I would prefer to be a tusk. I think you're making all this up. Anyway, I also heard that they're going to question you this morning. The police constable says the Superintendent Laird will be personally in charge of the enquiry.'

Kim wasn't surprised at this news. All the gossip would have flowed by the chokra's large ears as he went about his chores in the chai shop. He had to wait until midday, when the heat made breath difficult, for his questioning to take place. A chair was brought into his cell by the constable. Kim was made to sit on it with his hands handcuffed behind his back and his back to the door. Minutes, then an hour passed, and time became a quiet stream flowing around him. The light faded as the sun moved west and now only its yellow glow lit the room. He could hear the low voices of the villagers as they passed his window, the creak of wheels, the shrill cry of parrots. The cockroaches, aware that he was unable to move, left the sanctuary of the walls to explore his feet. He did not start or move at their dry whispery touch on his skin.

He heard the door open and felt a slight stir of cooler air. When it shut, he sensed the presence of men behind him, one to his left, the other to the right. They stood in silence, waiting for his unease to grow. He knew they expected him to turn, to desperately try and catch a glimpse of them as if to reassure himself that they were only men and not devils. But Kim stared straight ahead, smelling their odours. One was the constable who used the same hair oil as the chokra; the other had a distinctly European smell, cologne and polish and pomade.

Kim's turban was gently removed and he felt a fatherly hand placed on his head. The fingers spread through the thick black hair, snuggling in, and then the outspread fingers suddenly drew together to make a fist. His head was jerked back, and he stared up at the ceiling a moment before the face of the European moved into his vision.

Superintendent Laird had a thin face with a small clipped moustache. His eyes were shaded by the peak of his cap and his chin was pointed. He was not European, Kim could see that from the very tilt of the man's head and the pinch of his nostrils, but an Eurasian.

'Well?' he said softly, his accent confirming Kim's first thought. It was a hollow word, an expression which required no response, though it hung like a question over Kim's head. It was more of an observation, a discovery of something unpalatable.

'Sahib, I am an innocent man,' Kim said hoarsely in Urdu. His throat was stretched tight enough to split. 'I have done nothing.'

'Of course.'

The silence became oppressive. Kim heard their hearts beat and noted the pulse in the superintendent's throat. The face hovered above him, wavering as though he were under water, staring up through the distorted surface. 'I don't like you. I hate you people. You all say you are innocent, you have all done nothing. I will now ask you a few questions and I would like the answers. I don't suppose you understand a word of English either, do you?' Kim allowed incomprehension to slide over his face. 'Constable, translate.' The constable did.

Laird placed his baton across the bridge of Kim's nose. He rolled it first up, then down, as though testing the surface. He lifted it a little, not more than half an inch, and allowed it to drop back. Kim's eyes watered.

'What is your name?'

'Kimathchand.'

'Well, Kimathchand-wallah. Where do you come from?'

'Lahore.'

'You are Pathan?'

'No.'

'Now, what were you doing in that village?'

'I was taking my cousin to her own village which was

some . . .' The baton rose, poised and fell. The blow was harder.

'How can someone from Lahore have a cousin down in United Province?'

'Sahib, she is a distant cousin, for UP is distant. Her father's brother's wife's husband is my uncle's cousin's brother.'

Laird sighed. 'I haven't got the time to work that out. But you were there to cause trouble.'

'No, sahib.' The baton rose, paused longer and dropped, its weight heavier each time. Kim's eyes ran with tears. He could not move his head, the constable still gripped his hair tightly. The bridge of his nose felt as though it would break with the next tap. 'I swear, sahib.'

'Who sent you there?'

'No one, sahib.' The baton fell, this time it had moved further down his nose. Kim felt a sharp pain.

'Who sent you? Was it Tilak? Was it Bannerjee?'

'No one sent me. I am an ignorant man. I do not know this Tilak or this Bannerjee.'

'Do you believe we are the rightful rulers of this country?'

'Yes, sahib. Who else can rule?'

'Oh, I suppose one of you niggers would like to take over. You'd make a bloody mess of it, of course. Where were you coming from?'

'Benares, sahib. I went there on a pilgrimage. It is permitted, is it not?'

'I'm asking the bloody questions.' He dropped the baton from the height of an inch, precisely measured, and Kim felt the blood start to drip. He sniffed it in and struggled for breath. 'And where were you intending to go?'

'I was on my way back to Lahore, sahib.'

'Who sent you?'

'No one, sahib.'

'Have you ever been to Calcutta?'

'I have visited it, sahib. It is a great city.'

335

'Did you meet and discuss politics with the seditionists there?'

'I do not care for such things, sahib.'

'Did you meet any terrorists?'

'No, sahib.'

'I suppose you believe in swaraj?'

'What is that, sahib?'

The questions repeated themselves, as did the blows to his nose. There was no pattern, just a remorseless monotony. An hour passed and Kim felt his nose swelling. His eyes strained downward and the organ now appeared to be twice its normal size. The cruelty of it was so casual. The man who practised it was not really aware of him, not considering him worthy of compassion or concern. Like a bullock, he was prodded and expected to respond.

If he gave the answers that were expected of him the questioning and the baton falling like a hammer would stop. Superintendent Laird wanted Kim to be a dangerous terrorist, a man capable of throwing a bomb or firing a gun. This longing drove him. He needed proof to justify the punishment. He could not reason otherwise. Kim was in the cell, handcuffed; Laird stood over him. They were both present in the same cell for the same reason: Kim's guilt.

'You're a stubborn nigger. I'll break you yet. I'll try again later. Maybe I'll cut off your balls. I bet you wouldn't like that. Let him go, Constable.'

Kim's head fell forward. Blood dripped down his shirt, fell to the floor in a spreading pool, soaked into the earth. The constable unlocked his handcuffs and the chair was abruptly pulled out from under him, sending him sprawling. He lay there, carefully touching his nose. It was swollen beyond all proportion. Even the slightest contact made him wince. He wiped away some of the blood with the sleeve of his kurta and tried not to sniffle.

Superintendent Laird did not return the next day or the day after. Instead, on the fourth day, the constable handcuffed Kim and led him out of the police station.

They walked up the drive to the Collector's bungalow and waited in the shade of a rain-tree. Other men waited too, in ones and twos and small groups. Some were villagers, others bunias. They were all waiting for an audience with the District Magistrate.

Each was summoned by a peon and led into the DM's office. When his business was over the peon called another in. Then, at midday, the flow ceased. The DM was having lunch, and would sleep for a while before continuing work. The day passed with Kim watching the flow of petitioners. Now and then a vakil would represent a client, but for the most part the men were unaccompanied. Most could not afford the high fees for legal representation.

It was nearly dusk when the peon beckoned the constable, who prodded Kim to his feet and they entered the large, cool room. The District Magistrate sat behind a desk piled high with papers. A clerk sat at some distance from him, surrounded by an equally large mound of paper and files. Both men ignored Kim as they notated and scribbled away; their scratching steel pens the only sound in the room. Finally, the DM looked up. He was a round, small man and quite sallow in the subdued light. He snapped his fingers for the clerk to hand him the right papers. When he'd read them, he looked up again.

'Superintendent Laird thinks you are guilty. Have you anything to say?'

'Sahib, I am an innocent man.' Kim's voice sounded strangely nasal. His swollen nose had subsided, but it still distorted his voice.

'You all are. However, the Collector found you making trouble, and whether you belong to any group or groups is beside the point. I am sentencing you to six months RI.' He waved the constable away and Kim with him.

'Am I to stay here for six months?' Kim asked as the constable returned him to the cell.

'No. People like you are sent to Lucknow Prison. We have no money to feed you for six months.'

337

'When shall I be sent?'

'When Collector sahib signs the chit for your transportation. I suppose I shall have to accompany you.'

Now that Kim's guilt had been established by the Collector and the superintendent, the constable became friendlier. Guilt secured his position of authority and Kim had been reduced to a chattel. If he wished he could beat Kim or treat him kindly. He had chosen kindness for now, but a little power in the hands of such a man was an arbitrary thing. His attitude could change in the hour.

'Do you like mistreating men?' asked Kim.

'If it is part of my duty, I must do it. If Superintendent Laird orders me to hold you, I must hold you. If I disobey, he will sack me and then how shall I live? I have a wife, five children. Four boys,' he added proudly.

'Yes, but suppose the person you beat is innocent?'

'What difference does that make? By beating him we discover his innocence. If we did not, we would believe he was guilty.'

The logic is irrefutable. With hardly any effort a man can persuade himself that his dharma is to harm another man in the name of justice. The mind is a rocky bed with swift-flowing currents through which I must step carefully. My dharma is the same as this constable's: as an Imperial Agent I serve the very same authority with blind loyalty. Yet, if it permits him to commit such injustices, permits Superintendent Laird to hurt me in the pursuit of their version of truth, how can I continue to serve blindly? I saw a boy killed because he tried to complain about the hunger of his people. I saw the justice of their cause, I saw none in the Collector's. And he represents the very people I too serve. Out of common compassion I chose to lift the dead boy from the street where he lay like a pi-dog, and for this I was arrested. Now, by an inexplicable chain of circumstances, I find myself sentenced to prison. Somehow, even with such a small gesture, I have struck fear into them.

Kim sighed, troubled by these treacherous thoughts,

which had come unbidden. Doubt welled in him like bubbles rising in water. Whenever he pricked one, another took its place. If he was to be true to himself, as he had been until now, he foresaw a troubled and dangerous life ahead.

He had plenty of time to mull over his predicament in the police cell. Chit-signing was a ponderous process and he felt imprisoned not by walls but by paper; and the paper was stronger than walls or bars.

He whiled away the time sleeping or playing cards with his guards. The chokra entertained him with the gossip of the village, even though he was bitterly disappointed that Kim was not going to be hanged. He savoured the idea of having met a future dead man. Such opportunities were rare in his district.

While sleeping off his lunch in the same leisurely manner as his guards, Kim was woken by an irritable constable.

'Your brother wants to see you. I told him to return later, but he keeps insisting.' The constable did not bother to conceal the coin in his hand.

Narain poked his head into the cell and before Kim could rise, rushed to embrace him. He was weeping with genuine relief and Kim found it difficult to breathe with the pressure of the hug. Narain was in a sorry state: his clothes were grubby and dusty, and he looked even more underfed. Lines of exhaustion had aged him. Kim couldn't suppress his pleasure at seeing his old companion, when he'd recovered from the surprise. Once Narain released him, he did a little dance around the cell.

'How did you find me?'

'I have been looking high and low all over this jungley country for you, Kim. I went here, there, everywhere, making enquiries in bazaars, jungles – which is the whole land – temples, mosques, brothels. Then in Benares, where they have so many temples I got dizzy praying in each one for guidance, I was told of this man Kim, who spent some months there in the company of a woman. Even then, do you think it was easy for Narain? First I ask which direction, and they point to every corner of the land at the same time. But then I remember Lakshmi telling me that her village was to the north. But where in the north? A thousand villages lie north of Benares. So I ask every fool I meet, and finally I pass through a village and they said they saw you in the company of a sardar's caravan. I followed your footsteps and found Lakshmi. What joy! I had not had a woman for months. I offered her money but the woman has married some fool and now thinks herself chaste. She refused me but sent me on here. And here I am.'

'Why? I am all right.'

'All right? All right?' Narain wept. 'You are in a police lock-up and you say "All right". Just like that. Colonel sahib will fire another cannon ball at me. He fired one at my uncle, who fired one at me. It is my fault Kim has disappeared, they tell me. My own uncle tells me never to return without finding you.' He collapsed back against the wall, limp with relief. 'I thought I would never be able to return to my beautiful Bombay, ever. I thought I would have to wander in jungley exile for ever.'

'Now you will return?'

'How can I? I can't return and tell my uncle and Colonel sahib, "Yes, I found Kim in a police lock-up." I shall be hanged. No. I will immediately send a telegram to them both: "Kim found, stop. Narain." The Colonel sahib might give me a promotion, instead of me having to depend on the whims of my uncle.'

'How is Newton sahib?'

'He is extremely despondent. He has invented a new machine which nearly works, but we cannot puzzle out what it is supposed to do. One day I know he will be successful. But Kim, what I want to know is, why you did not tell the Collector sahib who you are? You just have to say to him, "I am Kim, and please verify with Colonel sahib", and you will be out of this place in a jiffy.'

'It is difficult to explain my reasons. I did nothing wrong, yet I was found guilty. I could have escaped, but if I were another man, an ordinary one who did not have the magic of my name, I could remain in this cell for years. I chose to be that other man.'

'Ahre, baba. You are a fool. If you have influence in this world you must use it. It makes life comfortable. It eases our way through, like the juices between a woman's legs. Use the baksheesh God gave you. If you behave like an ordinary man in this country, without the influence of uncles, fathers, cousins, you will surely lead a most miserable life and end up dead in some gully. If you are the friend of a prince, why spend time in his dungeons?'

'Unless the ruler knows how the ruled live, there will be no justice.'

'You speak as if you're the prince. Ahre bhai, Kim, you live in dreams. We must use every opportunity to escape pain. What are you? Like me, an agent, but you have a great deal of influence with our employer, I very little. I am down in the ranks, third-class loafer for His Imperial Majesty. When men like Tilak are arrested for speaking their thoughts and sent to Mandalay Prison, what are we? Nothing.'

'But what he spoke were his true feelings.'

'What difference does that make? He was another fool. He spoke once too often that the British must be driven out, and they shipped him off to Burma.'

'And you don't agree with Tilak?'

Narain cocked his head and glanced worriedly towards the open cell door. The corridor was empty. He didn't reply, but turned to study Kim, his worry openly changing to panic. He placed a finger to his lips.

'Please don't ask me questions like that. I can't answer you while we're sitting in a police lock-up. I am for the British,' he added, loudly enough so that should there be an eavesdropper, he would have been heard. Sweat popped from his forehead. 'This place must be driving you mad.'

'I am not going mad. But you must promise not to tell the police what I am.'

'You *are* mad. If you trust your life to these salahs, you deserve to climb into my uncle's flying machine. If I tell them, they will treat you like a prince.'

'No.'

Narain, shaking his head and giving the police constable a further rupee, went to send his telegram. Now that Narain had arrived, Kim's diet in the lock-up improved. The chokra brought him chicken and parathas, biryanis and mutton kormas. He was always accompanied by Narain, who sat over Kim and watched him eat. It was as though he wished to fatten Kim up before the Colonel's arrival.

The Colonel did not arrive, trailing power, as Narain had hoped. But finally the chit was signed by the Collector, the train tickets purchased. Kim was taken out in handcuffs by the constable to the railway station. He was followed by a solemn Narain, who was determined to travel on the train with Kim, and even accompany him into Lucknow Prison. He didn't dare lose sight of him now that he'd found him, and bribed the sergeant so that should a Colonel sahib from Calcutta arrive, he would be told that they were in Lucknow Prison.

Kim travelled in the guard's van of the Benares Passenger, his chain held by the constable. Narain rode in third class, and at each station he rushed around buying food and tea for the prison party. The constable, after all, needed baksheesh to treat Kim well.

On the second day, when Kim looked out of the window he saw the silhouette of Lucknow. The minarets and domes stood proud against the reddening evening sky, and as the train drew nearer, they grew to a magnificent size. He recognised the outlines of the Kaisarbagh and the Great Immanbara, and there behind was Satkhanda. Dhows moved slowly along the Gumti river which flows beside the palaces and mosques built by the Nawabs of Oudh. They were not as great architects as the Mughals, nor had they been such competent rulers.

They were only kept in a position of power at the whim of the British.

The sight of this great city filled Kim with nostalgia. It was years since he'd been to Lucknow and he wished he could be transported back to the past, his young mind unchanged by the events that had overtaken him. The train passed not far from the Residency in the centre of the cantonment. It was a carefully preserved ruin, not of a palace or a tomb, but of an ordinary, if rather grand, mansion. It was once the home of the British Resident and stood with broken walls as a reminder to all, both British and Indian, that here, in 1857, at the height of the Mutiny, the British had resisted the mutineers for eighty-seven days. It was a place of pilgrimage for the British. They would stand in the vast garden, the drive lined with palm trees, and look at the shell marks on the walls. Their eyes would mist with thoughts of past bravery. The British flag flew permanently above the shattered walls.

Not far from the Residency was his old school, and Kim caught a glimpse of the halls and playgrounds as the train slowly went round the curve into Lucknow Junction. The school was one part of his past Kim did not want to return to. He had not been happy there, forced into wearing uncomfortable English clothes, restrictive as armour, taught English manners by strict European elders who were determined to turn him into a gentleman. He had disliked his fellow-pupils intensely for bullying and mocking him for what he was. At every opportunity, he had escaped into Old Lucknow and India.

Kim could almost taste the city as it drifted by the train. It had its own special smells, its own character. The old bazaar where silks spilt out of shops like water, and jewels glittered like the stars at night. As a boy he had watched the nautch girls dancing in the homes of the wealthy merchants. Women so beautiful that even to catch a glimpse left an ache of desire in the loins to possess those sensual bodies and those rich, red mouths.

Ah, if I could be free, I would return to the bazaars. I would see my old friends again and meet the women I was too young to possess at the time. I would watch the magicians perform their tricks, and listen to the storytellers in the bazaars telling of the kings and queens who ruled Oudh.

He saw two policemen, one a superintendent, the other a sergeant, looking up and down the train as it pulled into Lucknow Junction. Immediately he knew they were watching for him. As soon as the train stopped with a great steamy sigh of relief and travellers began to explode out onto the platform, the guard's door was opened and the constable snapped to attention.

Kim was led down the platform to the first-class waiting-rooms. A constable stood on guard outside a door with a 'Europeans Only' sign. The room was cool and gloomy and silent, providing a relief from the noise and glare of the train, and was furnished with comfortable sofas, a writing-desk, a dining-table and chairs. A portrait of the King-Emperor and lithographs of Lucknow hung on the walls. Two doors led away from the high-ceilinged waiting-room. One was a bathroom for men, the other for women. His eyes took a moment to adjust to the dim light and catch a movement from one of the sofas.

'Kim,' the Colonel said, getting up. He seemed unaffected by the heat, and at first sight looked as fit as ever. He came forward quickly. 'I thought you too might be dead. You just disappeared. Oh God, the fools still have you handcuffed. Superintendent!'

The superintendent, a Eurasian as fair as the Colonel, stepped in smartly.

'You fool. Get rid of his handcuffs! Then bring in some khanna and make sure no one disturbs us.'

Kim rubbed his wrists as the superintendent retreated to his post outside the door. The Colonel remained standing by him, an arm still affectionately on his shoulder. At close quarters, Kim was shocked by the Colonel's appearance. Sadness had taken over those

344

chilling eyes. Kim remembered the photographs in the Colonel's office in Simla, showing him with his children. The sadness then had been contained within the gaze; now it had rippled out to touch the wrinkles at the edges of the eyes. His hair appeared whiter, too.

The Colonel read Kim's thoughts and went to a mirror and looked at himself.

'Yes. It shows, doesn't it? Death always puts its mark on those who are left. My son Richard was murdered by tribesmen up in the Khyber. You never knew him, did you?'

'No, Colonel sahib. I am very sorry.'

'That's why I was so concerned about you. You have always been a second son to me, and I was frantic in case this wretched country had taken your life as well. It's taken so many, needlessly.' Then in a determinedly changed voice: 'Why don't you have a wash in there?'

When Kim returned, a bearer was serving tea and cakes and sandwiches. The Colonel took his place at the dining-table and Kim joined him.

'Well, this is a pretty pickle. All I know is that you're on your way to prison. What happened?'

Kim broke his cakes into pieces as though they were roti and ate. He gave the Colonel the bare, factual details of his arrest and sentencing, but did not reveal any of his thoughts and feelings. He remained silent on this because he wanted the Colonel to reassure him that he felt the same sadness, felt the same revulsion at the needless killing of a boy. What Kim imagined, even as he spoke, was that the Colonel would say: 'Ghastly. We will punish Collector Sparrow.'

'It's unfortunate that you interfered,' was the Colonel's first comment, and then Kim felt a great despair. It was as though he had been pushed from a great height and had just begun to fall.

'He was a boy, dead, and I lifted him from the street.'

'You're a compassionate man, Kim. But Sparrow was trying to control a law-and-order situation. If he had to resort to firing, I am sure he had good reason to believe the situation could have deteriorated and affected other neighbouring villages. He had to display his authority. If he had been weak, he would have been overwhelmed.'

'But all the villagers wanted was permission to grow more wheat.'

'It isn't as simple as that. The government feels that indigo is an excellent cash-crop for the ryot. We pay him for his labours, naturally, but indigo fetches a high price in Europe. India has many debts and loans to pay off. Half our total budget is spent on defending the country alone, although we are at peace. And on top of that, we have had to borrow capital from England for many of the projects we are undertaking that will improve conditions – canals, roads, railways. I won't go into it all, but you must understand that Sparrow was acting in the best interests of the country.'

'But was not Rambaj too, and the other villagers? They don't understand why half of all that India earns is spent on the army. They think only of their empty bellies. They are poor and grow poorer.'

'Nonsense. Their lot has improved tremendously. Do you think the princes cared as much for their people as we do? Not a bit of it. This country was in total chaos until we took over.' Once more the Colonel read Kim's thoughts as though he had spoken aloud. 'All right. I am sorry the boy was killed. I shall instruct Sparrow to compensate the family, but I cannot reprimand him. If the demonstration had got out of hand, he would have been sent back to England. We have to keep control, Kim, you must try to understand that. Naturally enough, he mistook you for a seditionist. He wasn't to know you were English, one of my agents. The seditionists have been spreading their poison all over the country and all collectors, magistrates and commissioners have been ordered to take extreme measures against them. This swaraj nonsense must be stopped. We have no intention of quitting India. Ever.'

'Rambaj did not know the meaning of swaraj.'

'I'm sure he didn't.'

The Colonel studied Kim closely. He had changed a great deal from the boy he had once been. The man now appeared to have lost his zest for the Great Game. He had lost his capacity to believe. Belief was absolutely necessary to sustain a man. He could not function, could not commit himself loyally to a cause, without belief. The Colonel, mulling over their conversation, had detected a germ of doubt in Kim's voice. He had not spoken out, but this wretched Rambaj's death, one of those unavoidable lessons that the natives needed to be taught, had unsettled Kim. The Colonel sensed a shift in Kim's attitude. While he had been speaking and explaining the government's policy, Kim had shown a flicker of impatience, even a hint of anger. The Colonel had seen this in other men, those who wanted swaraj. He needed Kim even more now and yet he hesitated. He had to test Kim further before he could put complete trust in him.

'Remember that you are not an Indian, Kim,' the Colonel said quietly.

It was a warning, and he did not want to elaborate. Betrayal was always a two-edged weapon, and he wanted Kim to be reminded that the Colonel knew his ancestry.

'I will remember. But what is an Indian, Colonel sahib? There is no such person.'

'A native. Though I admit you were born here, like me.'

'Not quite like you, Colonel sahib. But I will remember who I am.'

The Colonel paused, unsure of his meaning, and then decided to continue. 'Now, as to this little pickle. I could easily have you released immediately.'

'Yes, I know.' The calm eyes watched, committing themselves to nothing, waiting for the Colonel's next move.

'But there might be a silver lining to this cloud. Many of the terrorists and seditionists, the ones we have caught, are in Tihar Gaol in Delhi. We do not know the full extent of their network. Who is financing them?

Who is harbouring them as fugitives? Who are their sympathisers? The few now in gaol are the tip, I believe, of an iceberg. Certainly not all India supports them. The villagers will always support us. It's these educated babus who are causing all the trouble. We must crush them.'

Kim nodded, sipping his tea, listening to the sounds of the station outside. The Benares Passenger still stood at the platform, though the clock above the mirror showed it was already ten minutes late in departing. The train was being held for him.

'You could refuse, Kim. I want you to know that. I should quite understand, and I would send you to another part of the country to continue your work. But this seems a golden opportunity for us to discover these men's contacts. As you will also be a prisoner in Tihar Gaol they will readily accept you as one of them. After all, the charges against you are of sedition.'

24

ALICE ROSE from her bed and sat down at her desk. She was surprised that she wept. She cried not so much for the death of a stranger but for the waste of life, her life and his. It could have been different. That was the worst of human existence – all the could-have-beens. If she had been a different sort of person, she could have known him. She could have seen her son grow up, have heard his laughter, wiped his tears, listened to his adventures: he could have known her love, even her anger or impatience. There was a whole gamut of experiences she had missed, he had missed. But there was one could-have-been which she would not have been able to prevent – his death.

She pulled a sheet of paper to her and sat staring for a long time out of the window at the mali watering her small garden. She had imagined, when the thought first came to her, that it would be an easy task to write a letter to her daughter. But she was not sure where to begin to tell of her life, a life that was a mystery to her daughter.

My dear daughter Elizabeth, [Alice began, after an hour of staring at the blank page.] I read today in the *Imperial Gazette* of Richard's death. He was your brother, and my son. I cannot help weeping, not for myself, but for him and for you. What would I have had him do with his life? Perhaps I could have prevented his dying. Richard could have gone to Oxford and, if he had still wanted to serve in India, he might have joined the ICS. Or even become a scholar, like my own father. Obviously that course was not in his nature. I know nothing of my own son, but I do know that the nature of a man is innate. He is born with his own rhythms, and like the seasons, they can be harsh or sunny. Maybe it was Richard's destiny to be a soldier, and his destiny to die so young.

This letter will come as a shock to you, I expect. Yes, I am alive. I am not sure what other feelings you will have; possibly you will be angry with me for never having written to you. I tried and tried. At our separation, I wrote to your father begging permission to visit you. At first he didn't reply. But I was persistent and even wrote letters to you both, though I am sure you never received them. Finally, your father wrote me a curt and cruel letter: 'I have told the children that you are dead. You are dead for me and for them. I shall deny that you are their mother should you ever dare to show your face here again.' Then he sent me a steamer ticket to England. I tore it up, and sent the pieces back.

But that was the ending. I must tell you now of the beginning.

I met your father under a banyan tree in Hosur. All the others rather took that tree for granted, but I had never seen such a magnificent sight. It was shaped like a huge umbrella and, standing in its shade, it seemed to me that it had been created especially for children. It was a mother tree, with low and comfortably ample branches. If only I'd had such a natural playground in England. As an only child in Oxford, my playground was not among trees and bushes, but in my father's study and libraries where he encouraged me to spend a great deal of my time. I met learned men who told me about India, not of her power and dominion and riches, but of her people, their languages and customs. It was then that I began to fall in love with India.

I remember, when I was still very young, meeting a former student of my father's, Sir Roger Chichester.

350

His great-grandfather had served with the East India Company as a clerk, his grandfather as a soldier. India had rewarded them with wealth and a title. Sir Roger's father had fought in the Indian Mutiny, and after the English victory served on the Tribunal. One of the men found guilty of treason and rebellion had been a nawab. He accepted his sentence of death calmly, even the manner of his dying – strapped to a cannon mouth. On the day of the execution, Major Chichester was one of the witnesses. The nawab, noting his presence, took a diamond from his turban and handed it to the major. A minute later he was blown to bloodied shreds.

Sir Roger showed me the diamond. It was cold in its beauty and when I held it, I could feel the spirit of the brave nawab. 'Why didn't the major return it to the nawab's family?' I asked. Sir Roger told me: 'My dear Alice, that diamond was the spoils of war. After the Mutiny we made a fortune confiscating treasures like this.'

I suppose it was an oddity of my nature that I sympathised so much with that nawab and despised the greed of Sir Roger's family. I thought the act of plunder no different from that of outright robbery. After that I read more avidly about India, and when I was nineteen years old I persuaded my parents to allow me to visit my aunt in Bangalore.

I loved India from the moment my foot touched her soil. The books had not told me of the vibrant colours, the rich odours, the beauty of this country, the splendour of her sky, the marvellous buildings and monuments, the friendliness of her people. I found my aunt to be a kindly woman but she, like all the other Europeans, lived so detached from her surroundings. I immediately began to learn the local languages, and in that found myself unique among the women.

It was strange, but I felt that somehow I had come home. England was forgotten. I could hardly remember home, such was the passion I had for India. And that passion was my downfall. I was steeped in it and, under that wonderful old banyan tree when I saw a handsome young man with piercing eyes, I felt India was to be my destiny. To complete this destiny, I would be married to an Indian Army officer. I had never known such determination in a man. He was single-minded in his pursuit, single-minded in his ardour and his wooing.

A woman is easily flattered by such attention. She cannot help but believe in love and the utter sincerity of the man who whispers of it to her. In the beginning I believed he felt the same love for this country that I did. He had been born and brought up here; his passion I believed was greater than mine. He knew the languages of India, her customs, her people. But I should have realised that he too kept his distance. India and all her riches were his possessions, even as I became one by becoming his wife. I was expected to feel as he did.

His detachment from the essence of things ran deeper than merely India. It was like an icy stream within him. I had mistaken intellect for passion, possessiveness for love, and I'd discovered, too late, that he found love-making embarrassing, almost unnecessary save for the procreation of the children he wanted. I was the vessel for his seed. When these truths dawned on me, how quickly love evaporated and another passion arose: hate.

But I couldn't escape. I was pregnant. When one is very young one doesn't know whether to run, even how to run. Then, when Richard was born and I did plan my escape, he had me watched constantly by the servants. They reported my every move. His greatest hold over me was through the purse-strings. Everything was on account, even my dressmaker. What chance had I of saving even a few rupees?

But, when he was seconded into Intelligence in one of the princely states, I did manage to escape, if not physically from his hold, then in spirit. You were born a few months later.

It was a relief to be free of the closed world of our own people and live away from gossip, away from the narrow confines of a disapproving society. And then I met John Woodruff. He was not handsome, not dashing. He rode badly, his uniform seemed to burst at the seams, but he did have a splendid rollicking laugh. I suppose it was my loneliness that led me to him, but he was so much like me. His passion for India was genuine. He was kind and gentle and didn't treat India as a possession or her people like pets. I learned so much about India from him, and I loved our daily rides. I began to love him too, first only as a companion, and then as a lover. Of course, I should have expected the resentment and rage of my husband. His informers were not only the servants now, but the countryside itself. When we rode together we were watched, and when we laughed and held hands he knew of it.

I was truly unaware of the violence contained in your father. It was hidden beneath that well-bred English calm. I had thought him passionless. Certainly he had no passion for love, but he had for anger. And in that miscalculation I brought about John Woodruff's death. Oh dear God, he deserved better.

We had planned our escape, not meticulously, but haphazardly. Lovers have no mind for intrigue; they are selfish and self-absorbed, besotted with each other. The plan was childishly simple: John would come for the three of us in a tonga a little after dawn at a time when my husband was away on duty. It was a day's drive to the railway station in Ranipet. We would catch the Madras Mail and disappear for ever. We were like two children planning an adventure.

I got you both dressed very early, and settled down to wait for John. You were restless and crying, partly because of the heat and partly because I believe you felt my desolation as the hours ebbed away and gradually shadows crept over the land. At last you were put to bed and I sat alone in the dark, unable now to escape my fears.

Finally a tonga came. I didn't get up, knowing by now that it couldn't be John. My husband came in silently, gripped my arm and led me out to the tonga. I couldn't put up any resistance; I had lost all my will. I could only just summon up the strength to walk. He whispered in my ear as he handed me onto the tonga: 'Your rail ticket,' and thrust the paper into my hand.

'My children?' I asked. I could not look into those dreadful eyes of his.

'They will remain with me. Don't you want to know about Woodruff? He changed his mind. You might hear from him eventually.'

I never did. He was already dead by then. I read in *The Hindu* two days later that he had died of snake bite.

I'm sure your father has not told you any of this. When he sent you both to school in England, I was never told where. Otherwise I would have written years ago to you at school, where my letters would not have been intercepted. But, whatever my faults, I have never forgotten you both, ever.

Your loving
Mother.

Even in the harsh morning light, memories and shadows lurked in the corners, clinging thick about Alice, until she felt she would never escape them. She could hear Mohini getting ready to leave for the office, and wanted to go to her but could not. She read her daughter's name again at the end of the *Gazette* announcement '. . . and his sister, Elizabeth Violet,' and stood up firmly. She folded the letter neatly, slipped it into an envelope and placed it in her drawer. She had to see her daughter again, hold her in her arms.

25

ALTHOUGH THE river was mythical, Mohini knew it existed in the form of a woman holding a manuscript in one hand with a vina lying across her lap. She imagined the river to be cool and sweet. To be immersed in the Saraswati would be to be washed in clouds, its touch healing the spirit, bringing bliss to a soul in turmoil. She wasn't sure of the river's exact path, except that, like the Ganges and Jumna, it had celestial origins and its bed was somewhere below the train.

Mohini was impatient to enter Allahabad, but the train had stood still, hissing, on Curzon Bridge for over half an hour. She sat looking down on one of the most sacred places in India, the confluence of the Ganges, the Jumna and the invisible river, the Saraswati. The sun glared down on the meeting of the waters, the Ganges swift and the colour of ochre, carrying rich silt down to the distant sea; the Jumna blue and calm, its flow imperceptible. Although the city of low white buildings stretching away into the distance was known as Allahabad, she knew it to be the city of Prayag, the ancient Vedic city The reason for its great sanctity was that where the rivers met, Brahma performed a horse sacrifice to commemorate his finding of the four lost Vedas.

'I must bathe in the Tribeni ghat,' said Mohini. 'I might never have the chance again.'

Romesh glanced up from his book, a recent edition of the collected poems of Shelley, then down at the two rivers below the window. He was amused by her fervour.

'You won't be permitted to in that costume.'

'I shall not be wearing this.' She plucked impatiently at her black shroud. The heat inside it was intolerable and she was tired of seeing the world through a glaze of fine black netting. 'I'll take it off before I enter the temple.'

'Is that wise? It is very possible that your husband will be attending this conference. He has become an important and powerful man in the Congress party these days.'

'No, it's not wise. Nothing I've ever done has been particularly wise. But I must bathe here. It is as sacred as Badrinath or Benares. I must also pray. I'll hide among the other women and keep my face covered. Anyway, he's not a religious man. He never went to the temple, never performed puja in the house. He doesn't believe in God, only in himself. He won't bother to visit the temple.'

'But he will visit the Nehrus' house.'

'And I shall be hidden in the women's quarters. Oh, why do I have to spend my whole life in hiding?'

Mohini was frightened. She had felt anxious from the moment they had boarded the train in Bombay five days before. Her palms were damp all the time and her eyes beneath the veil were hollow and black-ringed from lack of sleep. She forced herself to eat, though she felt ill with this fear. Once she had learnt of the possible presence of her husband in Allahabad, she had wanted to refuse the assignment, especially since this time she wouldn't have Alice's protection. Neither Romesh nor Alice would have forced her to go but Mohini knew she couldn't for ever live like a snail hidden in its shell. If she were cautious, he would never see her. No man would dare look behind the veil, no man would dare enter the women's quarters of the Nehru household. She would be invisible, and this was her sole comfort. Her desire to take part in this ancient ritual was, eventually, stronger than the fear of her husband. She'd lived too long in the sophisticated atmosphere of Alice's home, and now felt uncomfortably remote from her traditions. Immersion in these holy waters would be swift, and she would not be noticed in the crowds.

'You will look after me, won't you?'

'Of course. But I can't watch over you in the women's quarters. Nor will I go to the temple. Remember, too, that you're supposed to be a Muslim woman. Call yourself Banu, and avoid talking too much.'

'But how shall I be able to write anything? Alice said she wanted a long report on the Congress meeting.'

'There's a special section for women. Sit behind the screen and make your notes. I'll give you any additional reports you need.' Romesh stared glumly down at the river. 'I hope Alice is well.'

'But you did know she was married?'

'Yes, but I didn't expect that she would ever visit her husband and children. She never talked about them much. I'd ask her and she'd make a little joke and wave them away. I suppose you can't just wave away the past when you've lost a son you've hardly ever seen. I hope she'll be safe. It's strange how both of you are frightened of your husbands.'

'Can you blame us? The way you men behave would frighten any woman.'

'What do you mean – "you"? I haven't mistreated Alice.'

'And what about your wife, Romesh? What does she have to say about your friendship with Alice? She sits at home day and night while you enjoy yourself. But if she did the same thing, you would throw her out of your house.'

'That,' Romesh said loftily, 'is the way the world is. I don't beat her or harm her in any way. It was an arranged marriage, so I had little choice in the matter. Even men aren't as free as you think we are. We too must obey our parents and perform our duty to them.'

The train lurched forward. She watched its shadow ripple slowly over the Ganges, falling on small black islands of water buffaloes, on women washing clothes, children playing. Rice fields ran along the river's edge, a brilliant pure green as far as the eye could see.

She felt bitter about the good fortune of men, angry at her own dilemma. Though Romesh was always kind, she knew he disapproved of her. She should have stayed in her husband's household and borne that pain, even as his own wife did. In fact, she felt that his real sympathies lay with her husband, and not with her.

They took a tonga from the station to the Nehru house. Allahabad was the capital of the recently created United Province. Prior to 1902, it had been the headquarters of the North-West Provinces. Because of its recent elevation, it had also become the centre of the province's High Court, a large, white building, its entrance flanked by imposing pillars and set in a huge, dusty maidan. They passed by lawyers, English and Indian, garbed in their black gowns, and white-coated peons wearing bright red sashes. The lawyers reminded Mohini of menacing crows.

There were layers to this town that Mohini immediately noticed. The richest elements reflected the European influence, in the architecture of the houses and the administrative buildings, the cantonment and the names of the long avenues down which they were now travelling. Below the European was the layer the Muslim invaders had left: the Mughal King Akbar's fort on the banks of the Ganges, the Khusrau bagh, the mosques. And deep below, waiting to be reclaimed, was the forgotten city of Prayag, not visible to the eyes but, like the Saraswati, mythical, its influence stronger than the more recent additions. Those lay as dust on the surface of the earth and couldn't conceal the secret essence of Prayag.

The Nehru home, Ananda Bhavan, sat on a gentle hill surrounded by high walls. The tonga passed through the gates, which were guarded by Gurkhas, and up the gravel drive to the palatial mansion. It was very European in style, with a porch and a verandah encircling the house like a moat. There were two floors and the green shutters were closed against the morning heat and glare. On the roof was a kind of pavilion. The garden was carefully tended, and beyond the main house Mohini could see a smaller building for the guests. Against the far compound wall were the servants' quarters. She also caught a glimpse of a small rectangular body of water to one side, and at first thought it was an ornamental pond. Romesh told her it was a swimming pool. She could not swim, and found the idea of it extraordinary. A pond or even a fountain would have been expected, but a swimming pool, which had no decorative purpose, puzzled her.

They were not the only visitors. Men sat on the verandah in twos and threes, heads bent together in conversation, while others sat in the shade of the mango and tamarind trees. Her eyes darted in panic from man to man, straining through the netting to try to catch sight of her husband. Romesh felt her trembling and calmed her.

'I'll escort you to the women's quarters. Stay there for now. If you need anything, send a message out. Don't come out yourself. And for God's sake keep that veil on all the time.'

'You don't need to tell me that.'

A servant led them along the verandah at the rear of the house. They passed by reception rooms filled with men, and heard snatches of whispered conversation. They reached a door leading to a narrow staircase. At that point Romesh left her to find his own room, and Mohini experienced a moment of blind panic as she watched his retreating back. No matter what he thought of her, he was her only friend in this alien world. The servant ushered her up the stairs, and Mohini found herself in a cool, large room containing a number of women, sitting or lying down. There was little furniture, in contrast to the richly decorated rooms below. The walls were bare and rolls of matting had been stacked in one corner. Motilal Nehru's wife, Swaruprani, a small, round woman, namasted and drew her fully into the room. Because Mohini had only just arrived, a servant woman was ordered to fetch hot water for her bath. The women were the wives of the visiting Congress members, and also the women of the Nehru household. The Nehrus were Kashmiri brahmins, and Motilal was a wealthy lawyer. The family had originally moved from Kashmir to Delhi, and only in the last generation had they made their home in Allahabad.

In the room below, Motilal Nehru sat opposite Mohini's husband. They equalled each other in elegance. Both wore cream silk suits, silk shirts and ties. They lounged in their armchairs, calmly sipping tea as though enjoying the comforts of a London club. Although Nehru had spent little time in England, he was a great admirer of the British. He had sent his only son Jawarhalal to Harrow and Cambridge, for he wanted the very best education for his boy. It was rumoured, too, that he was so enamoured of English ways that he sent all his laundry to London. Even princes were not so imaginative in their extravagances. Motilal was a stocky, handsome man with a powerful voice. There was an air of confidence in the way he sat and moved and spoke. He was in his own kingdom, and Bahadhur sahib had to behave with due deference.

Nehru wasn't totally committed to the Congress party at the moment. He certainly supported them with financial contributions, but politically he still kept his distance.

'I consider myself to be an interested observer, Bahadhur sahib. I'm just not sure where you Congress-wallahs are going. What do you people mean by self-government?'

'Within the framework of the empire we would have a certain, small control over our lives.'

'No, no. What sort of political institution?'

'Parliamentary and democratic, naturally. But it would exist under the umbrella of British rule. We would simply share in their rule, not take it over. No, like you, I believe that we enjoy an unequalled peace and prosperity under the British, and should continue to do so.'

'I agree. I don't believe we can transplant a European form of government on to Indian soil. It won't unite us, probably the reverse.'

'I'm not asking for swadesh or swaraj. Those actions are utterly unnecessary to us. We should request some seats on the legislative councils in the provinces and in Calcutta. I do believe that in time the government would be amenable to such things. In fact, they suggested that as a Congress Party member, I should even join the Viceroy's Council to represent the native point of view. I am considering this, and will, naturally, consult other Congress Party members.'

'Oh-ho, a man with the government's ear? Excellent! And you'd like my support?'

'Yes. Do I have it?'

'A frank man. Yes, I could see myself supporting you.'

Bahadhur sahib solemnly inclined his head in thanks. Within he smiled broadly. It had all been easier than he'd expected. Nehru wasn't a political animal; he considered himself too grand for such petty ambitions. He was of some temporary use to Bahadhur sahib, only because of his influence. As a successful lawyer, with his grand house and his laundry sent to London, he could sway the thinking of jealous men wanting his favours.

Motilal watched the head incline in false humility and the long, delicate fingers holding the tea-cup. He didn't trust Bahadhur sahib, not because of the man's character, but because of his greed for power. No doubt the man would rise far, for his ambition was limitless. And if the government were offering him a seat on the Viceroy's Council, he would then be the most influential Indian in the whole country. For the present it was a pact of convenience to both men.

They talked a little longer, discussing which members to approach, whom they could depend on. When the meeting was over, Motilal walked with Bahadhur sahib out into the garden. They were both satisfied. Bahadhur

361

sahib's usual two servants waited by his gharri to drive him back to the house where he was staying for the duration of the Congress meeting. And when Nehru had shaken his acquaintance's hand, he stood watching the gharri rumble down the drive, and then turned to his next guest who had already been waiting for an hour on the verandah.

If Mohini had known her husband was so close, she would not have sat at ease with her back against the wall, chewing paan and gossiping with the other women. She felt much refreshed by her bath and she had temporarily discarded her disguise. The women were naturally astounded to discover beneath the burkha a Hindu woman, a lovely one, in a flame-yellow sari with a tilak mark on her forehead and her hair decorated with jasmine. Mohini was feeling much more confident now, and told them that the man who had brought her with him was her husband, a Muslim, so she had adopted the mode of dress but was not a convert. This was acceptable, for there were a few Hindu women married to Muslim princes. Her only wish, she told them, was to bathe at the Tribeni ghat as a true and devout Hindu should. Naturally, to comply with her husband's wishes, she would wear the burkha right up to the temple entrance.

There was to be a small mela at the ghat that very evening and all the women had planned to bathe there. The women were all from different parts of India and, though Hindu, were ignorant of each other's religious customs, for the complexity of the religion lay in its diverse methods of worship and its many gods. Even language separated them and, as Mohini knew none of the south Indian tongues, she and many of the others could not converse with the women from Bangalore or Madras. They whispered among themselves.

Just before dusk that evening the women ordered gharris to take them to the ghat. They carried fruit and flowers, camphor and incense, coconuts and betel leaves. It was a merry outing for them all and reminded

Mohini of her own childhood when she would accompany her mother to the temple each Friday.

Her companions conspired to shield her from evil eyes. In the gharri she sat in the centre, clad in black, almost invisible in the fading light. The pilgrimage, like any pilgrimage, was partly religious but also provided an amusement. After their worship, they would meet other women and pass the time in gossip, talking about their husbands, their children, the problems of maintaining a household, the cost of jewellery, the marriage prospects of their sons and daughters. Mohini, heeding Romesh's advice, kept silent for the most part. She knew that concocting too many lies would only ensnare her.

The Saraswati temple stood on the triangle of land exactly where the rivers met. There was a quarter moon and the night air was warm. Mohini took off her burkha and left it in the gharri and, closely surrounded by her companions, entered the temple. This was a welcome return to a familiar part of life – immersed in the mass of people, smelling incense and camphor, feeling the damp stone underfoot, hearing the mantras and bells. She was pushed and shoved and jostled, sublimely happy. It took a full hour for them to finally reach the sanctum, to gaze intently at Saraswati, glowing in the lamplight, wound in silk, glittering with diamonds, richly embellished with rose garlands.

'Oh, God,' Mohini prayed. 'Help me. My heart and soul are like a bird that can find no place to alight. Am I to spend the rest of my life in this state of suspension, fluttering above the ordinary life I yearn to lead, or will you guide me to some safe haven where I can settle down? I have, I know, neglected my duty as a wife. But should a wife's duty be placed above her happiness? Is it too selfish to want a reasonable existence? And is pain to be the permanent state of my life? Please guide me in these matters.'

She had no time for a lengthier discourse with God. The priest took her offerings, placed them briefly in front

363

of Saraswati, chanted the mantra of her name – Mohini – for she could not lie to God that she was called Parvati, and then returned her gifts. With her companions and a hundred other worshippers, both men and women, she made her way down the ghat to the water's edge. Slowly she stepped into the water, fully clothed, as did all the other women. She immersed herself completely three times, an act of self-baptism that renewed her faith in herself, and then rose dripping to sit on the steps to dry out.

Her total absorption in the act of worship took away her fear for the moment. It was replaced by a sense of calm and a feeling of having attained sanctuary. But even as Mohini sat on the step, waiting for the other women to join her, she was seen.

From the top step of the ghat her husband's servant, the younger of the two brothers who had always served their master faithfully and who had so frightened Mohini, looked down at her. It wasn't a coincidence that he should be where he was. He too was a religious man and, like Mohini, wanted to bathe in the ghat. He had recognised her in the crush of the sanctum, for the temple was also a place to look at women. They were usually hidden behind walls, and a man like him had little opportunity to cast his eyes on them. He was not an attractive man, but his lust was immense and if he were lucky, he might meet a woman who, with some persuasion, would lie with him. In his search he had thoroughly examined the women's side of the barrier. He couldn't believe his eyes when he saw Mohini's fine, beautiful profile. She'd been too intent on her prayers, the very prayer which asked for God's guidance and help. At that moment God had perversely revealed her identity to the very man she feared.

But she didn't look round, and even if she had, in the crowd and shadows, she would not have seen her husband's servant. Instead she looked up at the clear night sky and fixed her gaze on the north star, and wondered whether Kim, somewhere, might also be looking up at the same star. She drew a great triangle in her imagination, linking the three together, though she knew it was only a dream. He would have forgotten her by now; he was probably lying with another woman and they were both looking at the star. She saw her life stretching out, interminably alone, and whispered into the sacred air: Kim, Kim, Kim.

Bahadhur sahib too looked up at the dark sky, holding a whisky and soda. He was content with the world; those stars were under his control now. They were surely guiding his destiny to power. Two men sat by him, Rajender and Mahender.

They were brothers who had served his family for two generations. The relationship was feudal, their loyalty absolute. They could be familiar with their master, yet they knew never to overstep the boundary to intimacy. Rajender was the elder, but by how many years, neither knew any longer. He was the more loquacious of the two, and would spend the evenings squatting by Bahadhur sahib's chair, listening to him, offering advice, which was sometimes accepted. Mahender always stood a little apart, furiously silent. His anger could be felt, even at a distance. They were not quite servants for they were not paid, though they both cared for all Bahadhur sahib's needs: cooking, cleaning, fetching and carrying. They also kept an alert eye on his finances and ensured that his orders were carried out by the rest of the staff. They were his eyes and ears in the webs he wove.

Mahender was listening to his master telling them of that day's meeting with Motilal Nehru and the other Congressmen. Unlike his brother, who relished gossip and intrigue, Mahender preferred just to follow orders. If they involved physical action, so much the better. He waited impatiently for a break in the conversation.

'There are some ladies attending too,' he interrupted eventually.

'But they have nothing to do with politics,' Bahadhur sahib said. He knew Mahender could be a fool, and would have returned to his discourse. But he noticed that Mahender had not finished.

'I went to the temple tonight. It was an auspicious day for worship and there was a mela. I went to the ghat to have all my sins washed away.'

'Then the ocean would be a better place for all your sins, Mahender. What are you trying to tell me?'

'I was paying homage to Saraswati. The crowd was huge. A thousand people, maybe more. While I was praying, I asked for God's guidance, and when I opened my eyes, I saw her. She was standing but a few feet away. She didn't see me.'

'Whom did you see?'

'Mohini memsahib.'

His master's jolt satisfied Mahender. In the lamplight he could see Bahadhur sahib's features tighten. Her name alone caused him pain, and he sat so still that he didn't seem to be breathing.

Bahadhur sahib continued to listen, though Mahender had fallen silent. He could hear his heart, the quickening beat so loud in his ears that he wondered whether his servants could hear it as well.

'Mohini . . . Mohini.' His tongue coiled around her name.

The ache for her, long hidden by rage at her defiance and disappearance, returned strongly. Surprising him. He remembered the silken smoothness of her body, the perfume of her skin, the greed with which he had spent himself in her. She was the only woman for whom his appetite could never be sated. He would watch her as she bathed and dressed and combed her hair. Her coolness, her distance, her very hatred of him, goaded him to greater effort. And when she escaped, he had felt panic-stricken at the thought of not having her in his power. He understood his own obsession of her, as he did the obsession of other men for other women in the past. Muhammad Khilji for Padmini, Muhammad of Gaur for Rupmati. They hadn't had the luck to touch and hold and revel in those exquisite bodies, for the

366

women had denied them by killing themselves. But he had, and could never forget the pain of exquisite pleasure.

And she was here. He was sure Mahender wasn't mistaken. His whole body craved for her as never before. He would strip her and look on her, and watch that cold indifference that made it seem as though she didn't belong to the body he kissed and touched. She would moan when he hurt her, but she would never scream. Such an obsession could drive a man mad, like the longing of an addict for opium.

'She is here. I can feel it. She is in this town. I want her back. Mahender, you will find out where she is staying and report on her movements. Then, when the time is right, we will catch her like a bird, tightly, but not too tightly. We'll have a tonga waiting and carry her back to the fort. Not home: to the fort. I will come on by train.'

'I have already found out where she is staying. I waited at the ghat until she went home with her friends and followed her. She goes about disguised as a Muslim woman. If I had not been in the temple, and had only instead passed her on the street, I would not have recognised her.'

'Where is she staying, Mahender?'

'In the Nehru house. I spoke to one of the servants. He told me she came with a man, Romesh Nairoji, a Parsi. He owns a magazine in Bombay.'

'Then why is she here?'

'I'm told she writes for that magazine.'

'She cannot stay in the Nehrus' house for ever. If she is writing for this magazine, she will attend the Congress meetings. You and Rajender can get her then.'

'Yes, sahib.' Mahender rose, pleased with this duty but disappointed that he had to share such pleasure with his brother.

Bahadhur sahib had not actually said not to hurt her. He wanted to do her only a small hurt. A slap, a pinch, a tight rope to bind her. He could not touch her in any other way, though he would have liked to. The day might come when she would be tossed to him as a gift, if she should anger Bahadhur sahib enough. A man could suffer only so much from a woman.

'But if you lose her,' Bahadhur sahib said, 'you will both be killed. Take her back safely. Hire more men if you need to.'

The Congress meetings took place every day on the maidan behind the High Court. A huge pandal had been erected for this event and the ground was covered with dhurris. At one end was a raised platform on which the party leaders sat. They were all there: Gokhale, Valabhai Patel, Motilal Nehru, Mohammed Ali Jinnah who would soon join the newly formed Muslim League, and many others. Bahadhur sahib, who should have sat next to Gokhale, pleaded illness in order not to be seen by Mohini. He hoped that by the final day, when he was scheduled to speak, Mahender would have completed his task. They conducted all the proceedings in English, for it was the only language all the delegates could understand, and just as Bahadhur sahib had reported to the Colonel from Surat, the speeches were interminable. Some of the men droned on for four or five hours. There was a languid, indolent air in the pandal. Men listened or talked, came and went, clapped or fell silent and contemplative.

In the audience sat three police officers, carefully writing notes. They didn't bother to conceal themselves, but now with Tilak in prison and Congress split, little of any consequence was said against the British. There appeared to be a tacit consensus that freedom was unattainable. All they wanted now was to share in the ruling of their country.

Near the platform to the right side of the pandal was a partition. Behind it the women listened, but took no part. Mohini scribbled in her notebook, wishing she could write faster, and also wishing the speeches were not so long. She kept running out of paper, for she had not yet enough experience to know how to sum up a speech. In any case, most of the speakers repeated themselves endlessly.

Endless too was Mahender's and Rajender's watch on her. They had hired two goondas, recruited from among the loungers in the bazaar for two rupees a day. A tonga too was kept on permanent hire. Each morning they would follow Mohini's gharri from the Nehru house to the Congress ground in the tonga with the goondas. They would sit patiently in the shade of a tamarind tree at some distance from the entrance. Mahender and Rajender stayed in the tonga, because Mohini would recognise them. When the meeting was over they would follow her back. She travelled with the women, never leaving their company even for a minute. And once in the household, she never stepped out of the women's quarters.

As the days passed Mahender grew increasingly frustrated. He wasn't a patient man; waiting irked him. Rajender remained calm, knowing the right moment would come eventually. Each night they reported their lack of progress and saw their master's face become grim. He felt anxious, as the Congress meeting would end in another two days. Yet at the same time Bahadhur sahib urged caution. He had not forgotten the Colonel's warning, and didn't want a ghur-bhur which could upset his schemes.

'She must simply vanish,' Bahadhur sahib instructed. 'No one must see what has happened.'

This quashed Mahender's wilder plan to arrange an accident. The gharri would overturn – admittedly, some of the women would be hurt, but that didn't worry him – and they would snatch Mohini in the confusion. He had even considered starting a fight in the pandal, as he'd done at that Surat meeting, although there he'd been helped by forty other men. In the chaos he would swoop into the women's enclosure and snatch Mohini.

It was at noon, when it was so still and hot that even the shade seemed to be on fire. Rajender had the idea.

It was simple and deceptive. He considered running to Bahadhur sahib to tell him, but if it was to work then they would have to act immediately. The maidan was almost deserted except for a few scavenging pi-dogs and a couple of food-sellers sheltering in the shade of another tree. Rajender cautiously got down from the tonga and strolled over to them. Two were women holding baskets of fruit. They looked grubby and unkempt, but the younger one, a bold, buxom girl, would serve his purpose. He squatted down beside her and examined her mangoes. They haggled lazily over the price of one before he paid her the money.

'How much do you make in a day?'

'Why do you ask? Do you want to marry me for my dowry?'

'I just asked you a simple question.'

'No question is that simple. There must be a reason for it. You might be planning to rob me.'

'Woman, I have more money in my hand right now than you make in a month.' He pulled out a fistful of silver rupees. 'I could give you some of these.'

'I knew I shouldn't have sold the mango so cheap. You look like a poor man. Why would you give me money? Do you want the whole basket?'

'I don't want any more mangoes. I will pay you five rupees if you will carry a message for me to my mistress. She is in the women's enclosure in the pandal and I can't go in.'

'That's a lot of money for a message.'

'I'm feeling generous. Do you want it or not?'

She held out her hand and he placed two silver coins on the palm.

'You said five.'

'You'll get the rest when you've delivered the message. Do I look like a fool?'

'Most men are.' She rose and began to lift the basket on top of her head. 'Don't just sit there. Help me.'

'You can leave it here.'

'And who can I trust to look after it?'

370

But she noted his irritation and called out to the older woman to watch her mangoes. She took the added precaution of counting them loudly, a task that took an inordinate time. She wiped her face with the edge of her sari to make herself more presentable and followed Rajender to the pandal.

'My mistress is a Muslim lady. You will easily recognise her in her burkha. Tell her that Romesh Nairoji sahib wants to talk to her urgently, and that he is waiting just outside the tent, by the tonga. Can you remember the message?'

'I'm not stupid.'

'Repeat it.'

She did, and he pushed her towards the entrance to the women's section. As soon as she had gone in he summoned the tonga, along with Mahender and his goondas. He made the tonga wait to one side near the exit, and had his two helpers stand well back in the shade. He and Mahender crouched down in the tonga. If Mohini even glimpsed them, she would bolt.

The fruitseller stepped out of the pandal first and, a moment later, Mohini followed, wrapped in the black burkha. The young woman pointed to the tonga and led Mohini past the two goondas, who moved quickly behind them. Just as Mohini reached the tonga, they grabbed her round the waist and heaved her head first inside. Mahender clamped his hand over her mouth, while Rajender sat on her. 'Jaldi kharo, tonga-wallah. Jaldi!'

The fruitseller, seeing the abduction, didn't wait for her money but immediately ran away. She could have helped Mohini by screaming, but instead she ran back to her mango basket. She had no desire to get involved, no wish to talk to the police; it would only cause her trouble. When she turned to look back, the tonga pony was galloping out of the maidan, the tonga-wallah standing on the shafts, whipping it cruelly.

Mohini knew immediately what had happened. She was apprehensive and terrified, and angry with herself for having been so easily deceived. She kicked and bit. She clamped her teeth on Mahender's finger and crunched down with all her strength, but the cumbersome black veil blunted the venom of her rage. He jerked his hand away and, as she drew breath to scream, he struck her. The blow stunned her and the hand clamped down back on her mouth. She tried then to push off the man on her stomach, but didn't have the strength to shift him.

'Tie her up.'

She recognised Rajender's voice and began to weep silently. They turned her over onto her stomach, grabbed her hands and bound her wrists together, then her ankles. A dirty cloth which made her gag was tied over her mouth. The two brothers had come well prepared. They threw a blanket over her, and she was hidden from sight.

When her crying was done, Mohini prayed. She begged God to help her. Escape, escape, escape; the pony's hooves drummed a tattoo in her head, while the tonga swayed to the rhythm. She began to feel ill from the constant movement. The tonga never stopped, though the pony now moved at a steady trot. Each time she tried to stretch or turn, the brothers prodded her. The prods hurt and one of them – she knew it had to be Mahender – surreptitiously caressed her, not gently, but with enough intent. She thought that soon the pony would need to rest and she would somehow escape or call for help. They would have to let her up. She knew that her husband, whatever else he might do, would never allow any physical harm to befall her. But the tonga kept on moving.

Finally the pony slowed and the tonga came to a complete halt. The stillness was a relief. She felt the blanket removed and her legs untied.

'Get up. Relieve yourself. We shall be having food now.'

She was pulled out of the tonga but when she tried to stand, she fell over. Rajender helped her up, lifted the veil and undid the gag. It was dark. She had no idea where they were. There was no sign of life, and the land looked cold and ghostly in the moonlight.

'Untie my hands.'

'You'll run away.'

'How can I relieve myself? Untie my hands. Bahadhur sahib shall hear of your ill-treatment.'

Rajender undid the knot.

'You always did treat us like dirt,' Mahender said from the shadows.

'Because you are.' This she said imperiously as she moved past him towards the bushes. 'And don't follow me.'

She relieved herself and walked quickly towards a slope. There might be a village just beyond but when she came to the top she could still see nothing, not even a distant light. The sheer emptiness of the countryside hurt her more than the ropes or the humiliation. A shadow rose suddenly out of the ground and she caught a flash of white teeth.

'I thought you would try to run away,' said Mahender. He pushed her back towards the tonga.

'They'll be looking for me.'

'Who?'

'Nehru sahib. And Nairoji sahib.'

'Of course they'll look, but what can they do? No one saw us take you away, except that fruitseller, and she will be too frightened to talk. Besides, you are Bahadhur sahib's legal wife and we are only taking you to his ancestral home. They can't interfere. Now eat.'

He thrust a leaf packet of food at her, filled with cold chapatis and subji. In frustration she nearly threw it at the brothers, but the smell of even the cold food reminded her that she hadn't eaten all day.

They were telling her the truth. What could Romesh or Mr Nehru do? Send men in pursuit? Send the police to search Bahadhur sahib's home? Nothing, nothing, nothing. Besides, they had no right to do anything. She was his wife, his property to do with as he pleased. She shivered at the thought of what he would do to her. Her imagination shrank from envisioning the punishment awaiting her at his hands. The night could only partly reflect the dark misery within her. There would be no saviour. She would have to save herself; either by escaping, or with her death. Death. Other women had killed themselves rather than submit. Padmini of Chitor committed jauhar; Rupmati drank poison. History was littered with the corpses of brave queens. All dead by their own hands. Mohini tried to plot her own death, but the day's events had completely exhausted her, and when Rajender tied the rope around her ankle, and the other end to his wrist, she accepted this humiliation meekly.

She woke at dawn feeling more hopeful. The sky was a pale peach hue, streaked with bright gold, and the air was still cool and clean. She looked around eagerly for a village and saw one in the distance. Men and women were moving through the wheat fields, a camel pulled a plough, a man balanced on a beam drawing water from a well. They had slept in a hollow a few yards from the road and soon she heard the creak of a bullock cart. Mohini stood up, and then remembered the rope around her ankle. But even as she began to untie it, Rajender came awake with a grunt and gave it a vicious tug that brought her down again.

'Do you think some villager is going to come to your help? He won't. We shall tell them you are our master's wife and that you ran away. They will understand.' He laughed. 'They might even give us a stick to beat you with. They won't encourage such behaviour in case their own wives get the same idea.'

He took out a dagger and the blade flashed in the sunlight. She saw why she wouldn't be helped. The two brothers were small but strong, and their faces were menacing. Mahender's angry eyes would ensure that even the bravest villager would refrain from trying to free her. The bullock cart slowly came into view. It was packed with women and children and as it creaked past they waved cheerfully to her. It was a wedding party.

The tonga-wallah was her last hope. He was only a young man, with a soft beard. When he woke up he immediately went to tend to his pony. It was sturdy, though small, and looked decently fed. He brushed its brown coat and gave it oats and greens from a small supply kept beneath the rug of the tonga. His concern for the beast gave her a small hope. Surely he would also feel compassionate towards her. Who else was there?

'If you behave yourself, we shall be kind to you. You will be allowed to sit up in the tonga. But if you don't, we will tie you up and hide you under the blanket. It's up to you.'

'I'll behave,' Mohini said meekly.

This time Rajender went with her into the bushes, but remained at a discreet distance. There was a small ruin hidden in the tangle of bushes and vines, shadowed by a peepul tree, a forgotten temple. She considered offering up a brief prayer. But she was angry with God for having abandoned her so casually. She was given another chapati and made to don her burkha. But before she was rendered invisible again by the black garment, she managed to smile at the tonga-wallah. He didn't return the smile, but stared at her solemnly. He didn't seem as evil as the two brothers, yet he knew she had been abducted and had carried her this far with no protest.

She was placed in the middle. Mahender and the tonga-wallah sat in front, while at the back, with his legs dangling over the edge, sat Rajender. He was only half-turned and never quite took his eyes off her, while Mahender would swivel around from time to time to ensure she hadn't disappeared. She didn't know that their lives depended on her safe return. There was little she could see between the bodies of the two men in front, just a fleeting glimpse of trees and the sky. Villages passed slowly by like driftwood. Already they had forgotten about the tonga. She watched the shadows of the trees and the hills dully, her mind incapable of plotting further. Except that she thought about the knife. It be-

came the focus of her attention as she vividly remembered the sun glinting on that sharp blade. If she could
get at it, she would stab herself in the heart and, though
she experienced a flutter of fear, she was determined to
end her existence before she had to set eyes on her
husband again. But the knife remained hidden in the
folds of Rajender's clothes, and eventually her attention
returned to the journey.

'This isn't the way to Delhi.'

'We're not taking you to Delhi. You'd only run away
from there again.'

'Where then?'

'To a secret place.'

Rajender wouldn't tell her any more. She pestered
him, but he kept silent. She didn't know of any other
place that was south-west of Allahabad. Delhi lay to the
north-west. She tried to remember what properties her
husband had, but only knew they were vast and scattered. Delhi had been a little hope, a tiny prayer. If she'd
managed to escape once, there might come the chance
again. Now there was none. She wouldn't even know
where she was; there would be no familiar servants to
appeal to, and no Kim to rescue her, to lift her off her
feet, to calm her panic, to soothe her fear. He was the
past, long past and had forgotten her.

A little after midday the tonga halted briefly for
Rajender to buy food. They then drove on for a mile
and pulled up in the shade of a jamblam tree to eat. The
food was the same as the day before, simple and spare;
it was only a little warmer. The brothers wanted to go
on, but the tonga-wallah, who spoke only a little,
refused. He had to rest his pony until dusk when it
would be cooler to travel.

When the sun was setting and the sky had turned an
angry red, they came to a stream, a narrow, sluggish
tributary of the Jumna, brown with silt. There were high
reeds on either bank, and in the distance another small
village.

'I want to bathe. Stop.' To her surprise, the tonga

halted and she realised that, though a prisoner, she had the power to command these servants. It was a small power, but nonetheless she felt encouraged.

She found a secluded place in the reeds, undressed and slowly sank into the cool water. She shivered at its touch, but as it covered her, remembering the holy river, she felt herself revived after the exhaustion of the journey. She washed her body and hair as best she could. When she rose out of the water, Mahender was sitting on the bank beside her clothes. The light had turned her skin bronze and and the water gleamed on her like drops of honey. His eyes were wide and greedy, but if he expected Mohini to retreat, he was mistaken. She simply stepped up from the river, a figure as perfectly proportioned as a Saraswati, and came to stand but a foot away. There was nothing of her he couldn't see, but he had for so long imagined this. Then he knew why his master so wanted this woman. Her breasts were round and firm, with large dark nipples, while her waist was narrow enough for his hands to span. Her hips were lush as the land that ran along the Ganges, and her legs as lengthy and tapered as those of Nataraj, who dances eternally to save the world from conflagration.

Just as though he were not there, something less than a lump of rock or a tree stump, Mohini dressed herself, shook the water from her hair, bent to wring it dry and combed it with her fingers. She even hummed to herself. She could have been alone in her room, not surrounded by the darkening land or threatened by the glowering man crouched at her feet, coiled to spring on her.

As she stepped past Mahender, he grabbed her ankle. Not to pull her down but to hold her, to touch her. She stood perfectly still, waiting. She knew what he wanted; he ached, like her husband, with the same longing, as though the possession of her body could mean the possession of her spirit and heart.

'Do you want me? You can take me. Help me to escape and I will lie with you. You can touch me all over, do what you want with me.'

He was hoarse from his wanting, but when she looked down at him he could only shake his head helplessly. He calculated the pleasure of her body against the rage and revenge of Bahadhur sahib, and knew she wasn't worth his life. Yet she had made him aware of how insignificant he was in her eyes, and he wanted not only to take her, but to hurt her, to repay her for this moment of utter humiliation, though without any harm coming to himself. If he waited long enough, he would get his revenge. One day Bahadhur sahib would tire of her and then she would be his. And when she was, he would force her to remember this moment. He let go of her ankle and watched her saunter away provocatively.

26

ALTHOUGH HE knew he was privileged and protected, Kim couldn't contain his dread as he passed under the portals of Tihar Gaol along with ten other prisoners. The air felt murky and difficult to breathe, as though it only strained through the iron and mortar in small amounts. It was a fitting day for him to pass from freedom to prison. The sky was dark with monsoon clouds; the gloom exaggerated the brooding menace of the place. They had been caught out in a thunderstorm and were drenched through. Thunder rolled around the open cart that had transported them from the railway station to Tihar. Because of flooding, they'd twice had to push the cart when the wheels stuck in the mud. They now sat huddled under a thatch awning which dripped rain, waiting to be registered.

Kim finally shuffled across the stone floor to stand in front of Menon's desk. The writer didn't look up but continued with his paperwork. The ledger was moist and the ink had blurred. He blotted and blotted, but the blotter was moist as well. The walls of the room were damp, and trickles of water slid down to gather in puddles on the floor. Kim thought the walls must be weeping. Menon, who had disclaimed all responsibility for the clerical error of putting Anil Ray on a work party, finally turned to Kim's file. He glanced up and down at him, then primly entered Kim's name, his offence, his prison term and his privileges in the ledger. Menon didn't actually look at Kim. He was only another convict, another number, untouchable. He didn't address Kim either, and once the paper work was completed, indelibly a part of the Tihar records, he waved to the guard to bring in the next convict, having given Kim's status to a guard.

'You are more fortunate,' the guard said cheerfully as they trudged through the mud towards Kim's cell. 'A class prisoner. Very good. You will live very comfortably for six months.'

'Shall I be allowed to eat at Moti Mahal's in the Chandini Chowk each day?'

'Of course not.'

'Then how can I be fortunate? This is still a prison.'

'But if you were a C class prisoner, your life would be truly miserable. Life is made up of little advantages. For instance, I'm not permitted to beat you without permission from the superintendent. See what privileges you have?'

'That is like telling the bullock it will not be whipped, but only have its tail twisted.'

'And he is grateful for that, as you will be. Can you get hold of any money?'

'Why?'

'If you pay me five rupees a week, I guarantee that you will be treated well. It isn't much, is it? I will get you cigarettes, arrack, even a woman. That is what you will miss most. Are you married?'

'No.'

'I could have let your wife visit you, but I do know a good woman. She costs five rupees for each visit.'

'And what happens if I don't give you five rupees a week?'

'Oh, your food will be full of cockroaches. I shall forget to let you out for your exercise. Other things.'

Hari Das the guard reminded Kim of Nadir Shah's bear. They both shambled along and were matted with hair. Like Babur the bear, Hari's shoulders were rounded. Kim thought the man would probably be more comfortable if he went along on all fours. The regulation turban perched on his head gave him some semblance

380

of humanity, for most of his face was hidden by a heavy beard which sprayed out in every direction. He was shaped somewhat like Babur, too. The round shoulders ballooned into a round gut and even rounder backside. All the flesh was stuffed into a sweaty khaki uniform.

Did God create a man like Hari Das to ease our suffering? Hari is more concerned with my comfort – at a price, which is naturally right, for men cannot be expected to do favours without appropriate baksheesh – than with my imprisonment. This ridiculous guard doesn't care about why I am in here. I represent an opportunity for him to increase his meagre wage by a modest five rupees a week. I can refuse and suffer, or comply and live in comfort. What am I supposed to do? If I were a true sunyassi, I should suffer. But God has created Hari for a purpose, and he loyally serves that purpose to ease his convicts' lives through this prison term. I am sure he finds making us suffer unrewarding. He must gain greater pleasure from spending the five rupees than from gathering up cockroaches to put in my food. I should be enraged that I am asked for the money, but why? Doesn't the priest ask for money for offering his mantras and slokas? All this ordinary man wants is to get a just reward for my privileges.

'I will pay you.'

'Good, good. Here.' He gave Kim a packet of beedis to seal their bargain. They were soggy and unsmokable.

Kim's cell was in a row facing the compound, which for the present had turned into a muddy lake. The building was long and low, and should have been white, but the walls were yellow and streaked black by the rains. There were twelve cells in the building; each had an iron door on one side, a barred window on the other. The roof was made of red tile and, in another setting, the cellblock would have made a passable cottage.

'A through breeze,' Hari announced, undoing the heavy lock that held the door. 'And dry, I think.' Kim peered inside. The walls looked dry, though the wind had driven the rain across the floor and soaked the charpoi. Apart from the rope bed, there was a desk, a chair and a chamber-pot. The cell was about ten feet by six.

'Are there any other prisoners in this building?'

'All the cells are full. Tihar is never empty. Never. We do good business. Scoundrels, badmashes, dacoits, seditionists like you, all take lodging here. Tomorrow I will show you where we hang them.'

'I've no desire to see that place.'

'There's nothing there but a beam and a rope.' He carefully read out his orders. 'You are permitted newspapers, magazines and books. I will bring you some with your midday meal.'

At midday, which didn't look that time of the day for the sky was still the same ashen colour it had been at dawn, Hari delivered his meal, two old newspapers, a magazine and a book. The newspapers and magazine were scrupulously censored, with neat rectangular holes cut into the pages. The book from the prison library was *The Flora and Fauna of the Lower Himalayan Foothills* by Sir Reginald Whittaker, ICS Ret'd. It was illustrated with line drawings, and Kim spent his first afternoon learning the Latin names for a world that was familiar to him in another language.

At five o'clock, Hari opened his cell door again. Kim stepped out warily and, looking down the row of cells, saw other men who all turned to study the newcomer. The man in the next cell was a young Muslim. He wore a khadi kurta and pi-jama and a fur karakuli on his head. He was pleasantly plump with rosy cheeks. Prison fare had yet to drain him.

'I am Jahangir Alam, from Delhi. And may I know your good name?'

'Kim, from Lahore.'

'Kim. An odd name.' They shook hands and Jahangir Alam took him to meet the others. 'We are, as you can see, men of all ages and creeds. We are united by the misfortune of having big mouths.'

They were a mixed bag, yet all seemed middle-class

382

and well educated. Three were elderly men who received great respect from the other prisoners, most of whom were the same age as Kim and Jahangir. The elders were followers of Tilak and, when he had been sent to Mandalay, they had been sent to Tihar. One of them, Mr Joshi, who was a slim, proud man, took his sentence as an insult to his status as a politician. He would have preferred Mandalay, with his friend and leader Tilak. Subash Bhattacharjee was there, elderly and myopic with spectacles as thick as soda-bottle glass. He had been arrested for his efforts to introduce swadesh to his district in West Bengal. He had personally led a raid on a merchant who continued to stock English-manufactured cotton cloth in his shop. They had thrown the bales on to a bonfire. Before he could set fire to the actual shop as well he had been arrested by the police. The third was a Lucknow lawyer, a cheerful tub of a man, as round as he was tall. Mr Akbar, while cross-examining a witness in a case involving certain property, had inadvertently accused the law of being an ass on a particular matter. As the magistrate, Justice Richard Lacey, hearing the case, had in fact been the one to introduce the law, Mr Akbar had found himself accusing the honourable gentlemen of being an ass, and had been sent to prison for six months on the charge of undermining the authority of a government official.

There were five Sikhs, all members of the same gurudwar in Delhi. They'd been imprisoned for demonstrating against the arrest of their head priest. The priest had protested against the beating of a boy by a police constable and had insulted a thanedar by calling him a lackey of the British. The Sikhs came originally from Amritsar and had moved to Delhi to set up a business importing Hindu religious brass statues made in Birmingham.

Three Panjabis were Congress Party members, arrested in Surat for causing a public nuisance, and given stiff sentences of three years apiece. Kim sensed that these imprisoned men, instead of being ashamed, were

cautiously proud of their sojourn in Tihar Gaol. Though
their causes were diverse, imprisonment seemed in a
strange way to fulfil the same purpose – it was an act of
defiance and martyrdom.

They all milled around Kim, introducing themselves
and explaining their offences while they commenced a
squelching perambulation around the compound. They
were watched over by a sodden tribe of monkeys sitting
in a tree. The three elderly men led this small delegation
on its exercise route. Behind them came the Congressmen, then the Sikhs. Jahangir trailed behind with Kim.

'What was your offence?'

Kim told them and gained an appreciative audience.

'And your offence?' he asked Jahangir.

'I am a journalist. I reported a meeting of the Muslim
League with the government, believing it to be my duty
to report on these things. There should be no such
organisation as the Muslim League. We are all Indians,
but the British have encouraged – no, frightened – the
Muslims into believing that Congress is concerned only
with the Hindu. I know this is wrong. I was arrested the
next day and bundled into this place with a nine-month
sentence. Seven months to go. My editor, Mr Ashok
Dass, absconded before the police could arrest him. He
is now hiding out in Meerut, staying with his uncle.
When I am released, I shall write your story. We are so
badly informed about the problems out in the country.
Now, how was I to know about that village being forced
to grow indigo, if you hadn't told me? When we can
communicate swiftly, this nation will be bound up as
one instead of being a thousand little tribes occupying a
peninsula called India.'

At five-thirty, they were made to return to their cells.
Kim sat on the charpoi. If he was to fulfil his duty to the
Colonel, it would mean the betrayal of these men. They
would, in the course of the next few months, innocently
pass him many such small pieces of information. All he
had to report was that Mr Ashok Dass, wanted for
publishing seditious material, was now hiding at his

uncle's home in Meerut. It seemed a simple duty for him to perform, but he was coming to understand the complexities of betrayal. The betrayer, and he could not refer to himself by any other word, had to betray these men for gain. He couldn't calculate his gain, only his deep unease.

The dull monsoon light faded swiftly and a fresh storm broke, the wind gusting more rain through the bars. He saw lanterns being carried to some of the other cells and waited for one to be brought to him. When it didn't arrive and an hour later his rain-soaked evening meal did, he asked Hari for one.

'I can't give you one. It isn't written in your file.'

'If I am to be given other privileges, surely I can have a light to read these newspapers?'

'It isn't in your file. Without orders I cannot give you a lamp.'

'Do you expect me to sit in the dark all evening?'

'Why not? Villagers do. Before we invented fire, so did we all.'

Kim went to sleep early. His routine became as monastic as it had been during the time he spent in the temple at Benares. His life was regulated by the sound of a bell – not the sweet chime of a temple bell, but the bitter angry beating of a stick on a rail. He woke to it, ate to it, exercised to it. Instead of a feeling of sanctity, however, the air was filled with the violence of men contained. Though distant from the darker labyrinth of Tihar, Kim could feel the vibrations of pain and despair, rippling like heat rising off the desert.

Every Sunday morning the A class prisoners were permitted visitors. The presence of unfamiliar faces, the bright flash of saris, was a welcome diversion. Kim, who had resented being confined to his boarding-school, already found imprisonment intolerable. He longed to climb the wall and continue his search for Parvati. She came from so close to where he sat, her home could even be within sight of this place. He wondered where she had played as a child, where she'd walked as a woman.

Surely someone would know her? But Delhi and Parvati were beyond his reach. He prowled his cell in frustration.

Narain brought up the rear of the procession of visitors. He staggered under the weight of a wicker basket and dropped it heavily at Kim's cell door.

'It's like entering hell. I had to give the guard two packets of cigarettes and a mango before he would let me in. You should tell Colonel sahib you want to leave.'

'I can't. I am being punished for an offence.'

'You're a man with too much honour. This will cause you great suffering. You should be more like me, corrupt about escaping the consequences of one's actions.'

'And if you become a cockroach in your next life?'

'Someone will stamp on me and end my misery. How would a cockroach understand reincarnation? Does it sit and think philosophical thoughts? That it has the soul of Narain who was as slippery as any cockroach in escaping retribution? As a cockroach, I shall be ignorant of myself as Narain. You should insist on getting out of this place damn quick.'

'We shall see. What did you bring?'

'Colonel sahib told me to look after you.' He opened the basket and out tumbled cigarettes, fruit, sweetmeats from Moti Mahal's, a new kurta and pi-jama, soap, towels, paan. 'I also have some money for baksheesh. How much do you need?'

'Five rupees.'

'Take ten.' He thrust the coins through the bars. 'What do you do here all day?'

'Nothing. We exercise once a day and the rest of the time I sit here and read or meditate. The others here are also on sedition charges. I talk with the Muslim in the next cell about the world outside; what he'd be doing at that time of day, what I'd be doing. He's married, misses his wife. She's expecting a child very soon and he won't be present for the birth.'

'I think you should get married soon. Forget this Parvati. God alone knows where she's disappeared to.'

'If God has made her disappear, and if it is my karma, he will let me find her too.'

'By then you will be an old man. Your linga will have forgotten how to grow hard and long. Ahre, Kim, forget about her. See, I never remember a woman for long. I found a place in the chowk where they have the most beautiful Panjabis I've ever seen. As a people they are usually the ugliest. Very cheap, less than Bombay.'

'All this talk of women doesn't do me any good sitting in this gaol cell. But while I am stuck here, you could search for Parvati's home. She told me that from her window she could look out on the south walls of the Purana Qila. Not really close but enough to catch a glimpse. It's a big house set in a huge garden. There will be a chowkidar at the gate and on either side of the gate are gold muhar trees. Opposite the gate is a small chatri. It should be easy enough to find out where it is.'

'And then what am I to do?'

'Ask who she is and, if possible, where she is. She might have returned, though I doubt it.'

Narain sighed at his friend's foolishness. 'I'll try. I have made friends with a smuggler. He should be able to help me find that home. Pah. Delhi has nothing, it's a village. Ruins everywhere. In Bombay we'd knock them down damn quick.'

They were interrupted by the harsh beating of the rail and the guards coming to round up the visitors.

'What have you learnt? Colonel sahib said you would tell me things and that I should send him this information immediately.'

'Nothing so far.'

Kim's tone was stubborn and Narain worried about it as he hurried out of the prison. He sensed that Kim had discovered something, but was refusing to divulge it to the Colonel sahib. Narain didn't like trouble. He wanted to send the Colonel sahib whatever he wanted. If Kim would not cooperate, Narain sensed trouble looming for him. He could send a report to the Colonel sahib stating: 'No information yet.' Or else: 'Kim will not tell.' But that would cause Kim trouble. He wished he could discuss the problem with his uncle Isaac Newton. He was more experienced in the business of reporting to the Colonel sahib. What to do?

Kim's response, 'Nothing,' echoed into the brooding evening. The air was electric, still. The sky was black with heavy clouds massing to strike, and the sky was lit by flashes of lightning.

Nothing. I have, by uttering this word, altered my duty towards the man I have served for so many years. I have denied him not just the information he wanted – a scrap in the total sum which he collects daily – but my allegiance. Could I have acted differently and still remained at peace within myself? I have betrayed one, and not the others. One has been like a father to me, the man who has loved and nurtured me. The other is a group of strangers to whom I owe no loyalty, no duty, no love: but they are my people. I am the same as the Muslim and the Sikh and the Panjabi. I am a part of them and out of this my duty must arise. If I am a part of something, then I owe my duty to the whole. I am not a part of the Colonel, even though we have similar blood. I am a European, but I am not a stranger, as he is. I'm not the ruler, but the ruled, because of what I am within.

I felt the pain of Rambaj's death, the laughter of Narain, the pleasure of Lakshmi, the love of Parvati, the companionship of Nadir Shah and Bala, the affection of Isaac Newton, the wisdom of my Lama. To shed them from my life would be to shed life itself. To betray them, and they are one and the same, is to betray myself. And on the other side of the scale stands a man, an empire. It is the weight of life against the weight of power. I have chosen life, not power. It would have been the choice of my teacher.

These thoughts ran through his mind on that fateful night when once more the rain was driven through the barred window. He huddled in a corner. The next day was no different, and the rain continued. The compound seemed to creep into his cell, and with it frogs and centipedes. Two snakes, flushed out of their holes, rippled through the muddy water in pursuit of frogs. They left blurred patterns in the wet earth.

When finally the rain eased, the air smelt of decay; of the rot of wood, chunam, cloth, small animals, mud. Even the fresh rainwater had an odour of rot about it. Magazines and newspapers fell apart in his hands. The compound was littered with broken branches, and when the sun broke through briefly, Kim hung up his clothes to dry. The non-privileged C class prisoners were brought out to clean up after the storm, and two were detailed to sweep the cells. Each carried a reed broom and a wicker scoop. The guard Hari opened Kim's door and a prisoner waited quietly for him to step out. Kim never forgot a face. This one had aged and deep lines masked its youth; the eyes had dulled and the body was emaciated from neglect. Anil Ray entered the cell to sweep out the mud and rainwater.

'Are you Anil Ray?' Kim asked from the door.

Anil Ray blinked up at Kim, but showed no recognition.

'Am I so famous?'

'No. I saw you once years ago in the Simla police lock-up. I gave you water. The police had beaten you.'

'That was nothing to what I get here.' He went on sweeping, trying to recall the one kindness he'd received since his arrest. 'I had . . . I had always thought that the man who gave me that water was only a dream. But then, I can't tell what is real any more. Your kindness seemed only something I'd invented.' He paused to move the book and held it as though it were a crown. He opened it, turned a page, and his fingers caressed the words. 'It's years since I read anything. I used to compose poetry in English. It's a language I hate now, but I cannot escape it.'

'Keep the book. It's only on the fauna and flora of the Lower Himalayas.'

'Even that is more than I have read in all these years. No. It will be missed. You keep it.'

'I'll tell the guard it rotted away in the rain. Hide it under your kurta.'

They both looked around. Hari was some way away. Anil tucked the book under his voluminous shirt and continued his sweeping.

'It's my fault that life has treated you so cruelly.'

'You gave me water.'

'That was later,' Kim said. 'I sent in a report saying that two men were planning an assassination in Simla. I had heard a rumour in the bazaar. Apparently one of them was carrying a jezail. They had gone into the hills above the railway line. This information I passed on to the police, and by a terrible mischance they came upon you and your uncle. When I found out that the two men I was really looking for had gone to Bombay, I tried to right the wrong I had done to you. I sent this new information to the government, but by then you had stabbed a Deputy Inspector of police. I am sorry.'

'What good is that now? At the trial I was told of this witness who'd reported the presence of a weapon, but the magistrate wouldn't permit me to call him. It was you. What is your name?'

'Kim.'

'That's not an Indian name.' Anil Ray examined Kim closely. 'Are you Eurasian?'

'No. Irish.'

'You look Indian.'

'I am Indian. I grew up in the Lahore bazaar, like any other chokra.'

'What an ideal weapon for the British! One of them, who is also one of us. Which one are you? From what you've said, you're an agent for the government. What are you doing here? Were you placed here? You're in a very dangerous predicament, having told me all this.'

'I was arrested by the Collector at Rae Bareli on charges of sedition. He didn't know who I was. I got a prison sentence from the magistrate under the same circumstances.'

'But . . .'

'My superior sent me to this prison and I am supposed to pass on information. But I have not, and will not. I am Indian.'

'Is that lip service for the moment?'

'No.'

'I'm not sure whether or not to believe you. I'm not sure yet how I feel towards you. I was grateful for the water; angry at the betrayal. Indirectly you were responsible for my uncle's death even though it was Goode who pulled the trigger. I should feel the same about you as I do about him. But at least you have been honest when you didn't need to be. You could have just given me the book and I would have been grateful for this small mercy. I need never have known anything more about you. I shall have to think about what to do next.'

'Chulo . . . chulo . . . chulo . . .' Hari shouted, banging the bars with his cane. 'Does it take half an hour to clean out one small room? There are others.' He prodded Anil, ushered Kim back into the cell and locked it.

Kim, who believed in the pursuit of truth, knew he must now accept the consequences of that truth. It couldn't be evaded. Anil Ray had every right to understand the exact reasons why misfortune had struck him so boldly and cruelly. It was Kim's mistake that, in this country of rumour, where illusion rather than reality was believed, where myth became history, he should have believed the rumour and reported it as a fact. The burden of Anil Ray's karma was now his. If Ray wanted to take revenge, he could pass on the information that Kim was an agent, a European.

Anil Ray lived without light. His cell did not have a window and the only light came from a lantern in the corridor, a faint yellow beam that barely reached into his tiny cell. It was large enough for him to sit in, legs outstretched to the opposite wall. He slept curled up. Since the escape attempt he had been beaten and put in solitary confinement. It could have been worse, but by fervently denying all knowledge of the escape – and claiming he'd run to aid the wounded men – he managed to wriggle out of having his sentence extended. He had betrayed himself and Man Singh and Chandra, but they were dead now, while he still lived.

He took out the book, a gift from the man who'd betrayed him to the police, and held it. It wouldn't be possible to read it but just to hold it was a comfort. He recalled the other works he'd read and loved: *A Tale of Two Cities, Ivanhoe, Macbeth, Wuthering Heights, The Count of Monte Cristo, Don Quixote, A Latin Grammar, A History of the British Empire*, law books bound in leather. They all tumbled through his mind, whole pages returning to memory, breaking through the barrier of his bitterness. The weight, the texture of these pages softened him, reminded him that outside lay a civilised world where words had value.

Kim! Fate had chosen to have the very man who'd been responsible for his own tragedy, put in the same prison. By telling the truth, Kim had put himself at Anil's mercy. He didn't, in all honesty, know what to do. Betray Kim's identity? Betray his calling? Swear vengeance, as he had on Goode? What happened in those hills above Simla had happened because of Goode, not Kim. If Goode had not killed his uncle, but merely placed them under arrest, the consequences would have been far different. Yet Kim had mistakenly reported as a jezail, that shooting-stick which his uncle carried with such pride, and it was that mistake which had killed his uncle. What should he do? Kill everyone, including the judge, Sethu, Ranjit Lal – he'd not forgotten his promise, and it hung on his heart like a meat hook – Kim. The list was endless and he was weary of his own hatred. Goode would be at the end no matter how many years he had to wait.

The next time Anil came to sweep out his cell, Kim

left out the box of sweets, a mango and a packet of cigarettes.

'Are these bribes to make me forgive you?'

'No. I would do the same for any man. Take them if you wish, or leave them.'

'I could make good use of you,' Anil said cynically, eating a sweet and pocketing the cigarettes. 'I have suffered enough because of the karma you set in motion.'

'No. You set it in motion yourself. You stabbed Inspector Goode. The action arose from within you, although my action presented you with the cause to stab him. We must both share the guilt. You cannot continually blame others for what happened.'

'What are you, a sunyassi?'

'Once I was the chela of a Lama. He taught me the consequences of action and inaction.'

On the next Sunday, Narain once more presented himself with a basket of food and clothes. He was subdued and avoided Kim's eyes.

'What is it?'

'Colonel sahib is insisting on information as regards the people here. He wants to know their secrets, the secrets they have told you. He sent me a letter to that effect. I have kept silent, but I know that in the next letter I shall get a cannon-ball from the Colonel sahib. He will blame me.'

'Tell him I have heard nothing.'

'He won't believe me. We Indians are notorious talkers. Nothing remains a secret with us for long. He will surely know that these men have confided in you. Give me one name, one morsel to feed the Colonel sahib.'

'There is nothing.'

'Nothing. Don't you understand the consequences of such a word for Colonel sahib? He will forget that you are his special agent. He will keep you imprisoned here for ever.' Narain gripped Kim's hand through the bars. 'Think about it, please, Kim. I too shall lose my job because of my incompetence.'

'Then you can return to Bombay.'

'That is true. But I would have to leave you and I don't want to do that. I am your friend.'

Kim laughed at the sentimentality. Narain's affection for him had always been obvious and he loved him for it.

'Now, what have you discovered about Parvati? Did she ever live near that house I described?'

'Yes.'

Kim waited, but Narain said nothing. Kim sensed that there was more.

'What else?'

'Kim, she is the wife of Bahadhur Ram Shanker. She ran away from him and has not been seen since. If she is his wife, he has all rights to her, no matter how you feel. You must forget her.'

It wasn't as much of a shock as Narain had expected. Kim remembered the gaiety of her stories about her betrothal, and knew she'd evaded the fact of her marriage. But he'd known, when on that first night in the cold he'd lain next to her and she'd pushed him away in her sleep, that she was pushing away a husband she hated. Bahadhur Ram Shanker. Kim remembered the report from Surat. He was the Colonel's agent, Daddaji.

27

SHE WAS imprisoned in melancholy and no one held the key to her escape. Every morning Elizabeth sat at her bedroom window, making no pretence of reading, no pretence of occupying herself with her hair or studying the fashions in *The Illustrated London News*. She made no pretence of eating either, although Mary ayah tried to coax her with rumble-tumble, her favourite – scrambled egg with chopped tomatoes, onions, green chillies and fresh coriander – bacon, hot toast and tea. Elizabeth would push the fork away, shutting her mouth tightly, just as she had as a child. Then it had been a game, Mary ayah's patience outlasting the child's hunger. Now there was no hunger to outlast and her baba was wasting away. Her hair had become stringy and lank, those lovely grey eyes had sunk into even greyer hollows around them. Elizabeth had always been slim and Mary ayah, ignorant of fashion, disapproved of thinness. A plump woman spoke of prosperity and contentment. Now Elizabeth was skinny.

The Colonel watched them from the bedroom door, as he did each morning. Elizabeth's stooped back seemed almost defiant in her misery. He approached her, kissed the top of her head and took her hand. It felt cold and still and fragile. Oh God, how he regretted that moment of rage. Words that never should have been spoken. His anger hadn't been directed at her, but at the past. He'd been so overcome by his own memories and misery that he'd confused the present with the past. Elizabeth's transgressions had reminded him of her mother's.

He'd gone to see Richard's grave, up in the Rawalpindi cemetery. The sun glistened on the new marble. The legend was simple: 'Killed In Action'. He didn't want more. And, remembering Elizabeth's words, he'd looked at most of the other graves, worn, faded, grey with lichen. Soldiers, women, children. Babies, babies, babies. Most were old; only a few were as new as Richard's.

Elizabeth also lay in a grave. In a way she too had died to the Colonel on the same day as Richard. Richard was gone, vanished for ever, but he remained pure and honourable in his father's heart. Elizabeth stained it. She remained stubbornly present, a constant reminder of her sins. The loss felt almost unbearable and he found he wanted to weep for both his children.

'Well, I'm off now,' he said with forced cheerfulness. 'Is there anything you need?'

'Will you find out today?'

'I'm still trying, but Bayley seems to have disappeared off the face of the earth. He didn't leave from any of the ports or by any of the steamship companies.'

'Then he's dead,' she said dully.

'Of course not, my dear. I should have heard if a European had been killed in the country. I'm sure you'll get a letter from him today.'

The Colonel watched her mail as closely as he watched the ports and the silk routes and the passes. He wanted that letter as badly as Elizabeth, but only to discover Bayley's whereabouts. Bayley disturbed him. The wispy rumours had taken time to reach him, but it seemed that wherever Bayley travelled, especially to the remote areas of this vast land, trouble occurred. It could have been coincidence but the Colonel distrusted such simple answers. He had tried to discover more about this man who had lived so boldly, so arrogantly, in Calcutta and seduced his daughter, but Bayley seemed to have an insubstantial past. His life was fading away into confusion as the Colonel tried to unravel it through telegrams to London.

He cared little for Elizabeth's heartache. She was young, it would heal. But while she still pined and yearned, like the she-tiger growling for a mate, he had to use her to draw Bayley from hiding, to bring him within his sights.

He kissed her again. 'You will come to the Viceroy's reception this evening?'

'Yes, I will, thank you.' She'd not been cold or hateful towards him since the outburst. She had withdrawn, and it was that scoundrel Bayley's fault.

'It will make a nice change for you. The Viceroy always asks after you.'

'I'm broken-hearted, Father. You can tell him that.'

Elizabeth watched her father climb into the gharri and wave in her direction. She didn't return the wave. In another place, another country, at home, they would have grown apart after Richard's death and his rage at her. But where could she go? To whom? To what? She couldn't leave for England without knowing what had happened to Peter. Suppose he were to walk up the drive with that sunny smile on his face, and she had missed him for ever. She had to wait here. Two months had passed with no word from him. The bungalow he had taken in Dufferin Street was inhabited only by his spirit. His clothes still hung in the almirah, his polished shoes filled the rack, the bed was neatly made for him. But he'd never returned from Kufri. Her father, with all his resources, could find no trace of him. No one had seen them. Peter and Rao had vanished. It was as if the earth had swallowed them both up. She imagined Peter dead, lost in a snowdrift or buried in a shallow grave. She'd wanted his comfort on Richard's death and had ridden back to see him on Christmas Day. The house had been empty and cold and the lovely miniatures had disappeared as well. What else? She was unsure. She had never told her father this, but kept it as her secret. Peter must have purchased them himself. There could be no other explanation.

Mary ayah removed the breakfast tray, leaving an

orange and plantain as a forlorn temptation. Elizabeth continued to sit at the window, waiting for the postman. She was sure that today she would receive a letter from Peter. He would write, reassure her: he was on some madcap adventure in Burma or Tibet or Siam. And of course he loved her.

Instead of the postman, a gharri turned into the drive, as though it had been waiting just down the road for her father to leave. The timing was too opportune. Yes, it would be Peter. Elizabeth leapt up, excited. She looked dreadful. Her hair hadn't been washed, she was wearing an old dressing-gown, she'd not had her morning bath, she'd not . . . There were countless rituals unfinished and she was unprepared for her lover's return.

She would have rushed to the bathroom, but the hunger to see Peter again, to watch him get down from the gharri, left her poised for flight. She sat down heavily, bitterly disappointed, when a woman climbed down. Elizabeth glared at the stranger. The woman didn't come to the house, but stood holding the gharri door as though for support. Under her shady hat Elizabeth could only see the lower half of her face. The woman looked vaguely familiar, not a total stranger, but was no one she could recall immediately. The woman looked at the house, then straight up at Elizabeth's bedroom, though she couldn't have seen Elizabeth sitting in the shadows.

Elizabeth hadn't heard Mary ayah approach with a glass of warm milk. Mary ayah looked out and saw the woman. The butler would announce her soon enough, and she would have to make excuses for Elizabeth. It was only when the woman strode towards the front step that Mary ayah became alert, worried. As a child she'd seen that stride, and for a moment couldn't remember, although intuitively she felt fear. It was the stride of a bold woman, full of life . . . Elizabeth's mother.

'You must stay here, Elizabeth baba. Don't come out. I'll send her away.'

'Who is she?'

'I . . . I don't know.' Mary ayah spilt the milk as she ran from the room. Elizabeth had never seen her so distraught, almost in panic. The visitor had climbed the steps, greeted by the Labradors. She bent to pat them. As watchdogs they were quite useless. Then the woman moved on to the verandah and was lost to sight.

Elizabeth waited. She heard the murmur of voices. Mary ayah's; the woman's. Both sounded abrupt, even angry. Her Mary ayah was shrill. Never before had she heard Mary raise her voice to a European. Now she was arguing with the same rage as she did with the mali or the sweepers. In spite of herself, Elizabeth was intrigued. She tied her dressing-gown firmly and went to stand by the door to listen.

'. . . No . . . no. Elizabeth miss sahib isn't at home. I keep telling you. Elizabeth miss sahib in Simla. And she will not wish to see you.'

'I'm reaching the end of my patience with you. I haven't come all the way to Calcutta to be lied to. The chowkidar said she was here. Now, will you please take me to her?'

'The chowkidar . . . damn fool . . . is lying to you. Not me, memsahib. Elizabeth miss sahib is in Simla. If you wish to see the Colonel sahib, he is at his office. I will tell the gharri how to get there.'

'I've no wish to see him, ever,' Alice said, wanting to strangle the woman. She didn't remember the little servant girl who'd looked after Elizabeth and Richard. That was too long ago, but Alice suspected this ayah had been with the family since then, for there was no doubt that she'd been recognised. The stubborn, protective stance angered her. 'Who are you?'

'Mary ayah. I look after Elizabeth miss sahib.'

'In that case you too would be in Simla. Now, I'm going to sit down and you, Mary ayah, are going to tell Elizabeth that I'm here. Please go.'

Elizabeth heard the creak of a rattan chair. Mary ayah hadn't moved and Elizabeth, knowing it was going to be impossible to avoid this insistent woman, opened her door and stepped into the drawing-room just as Alice was taking off her hat.

Elizabeth was struck once more by the familiarity of the face. It had strong lines, a firm jaw, high cheekbones. The hair was the colour of her own, though peppered with some grey. The woman sat very straight, and in the shape of her back Elizabeth saw anger, and something else. Nervousness. Her hands plucked at the straw hat, pulling the ribbons and flowers. They were delicate hands, like her face, yet not fragile. Because the sun was behind her, pouring through the verandah into the room, the woman appeared to be surrounded by a glowing halo.

'How can I help you?' Elizabeth asked.

Alice turned to look at her daughter. Though so many years had passed, she could only think of the baby she had had to leave. Her imagination had been unable to make the leap to womanhood, and she had not expected to see a reflection of herself. Where were the words she'd prepared, the scenes she'd rehearsed, even though she had known that her imagination could never encompass reality? She wanted to be simple and direct.

Alice rose, stepped forward and swept a startled Elizabeth into her arms. She hugged her daughter with all her strength. Elizabeth finally managed to break free from the smothering embrace. She felt overwhelmed, though in her misery she was momentarily comforted by the warmth of this strange woman. When she stepped back, she saw that the woman was crying, not in pain but out of a strange sort of happiness that Elizabeth didn't understand.

'Forgive me. Do I know you?'

'No . . . yes . . . no. I suppose you don't. Elizabeth, I'm your mother.'

Elizabeth sat down slowly, staring up at the woman. She knew that sometimes the heat, the loneliness, could turn some Europeans quite mad.

Only this woman didn't have that look.

'I don't think I understand you.'

400

'Your mother. Alice Creighton. I read of Richard's death, and then I knew I had to come and see you, whatever your father might have done to prevent me.'

Elizabeth felt a wave of hysteria roll over her, like the giddiness that sometimes overcame her if she was out in the sun too long. The woman's figure seemed to waver as she quietly sat down opposite Elizabeth.

'But my mother is dead,' Elizabeth said, and saw the woman begin to shake her head. 'She died when I was a baby.'

'That's what your father told you. He wanted you to believe it. I think he believes it himself now. If you want proof, ask your ayah. She recognised me immediately.'

Mary ayah stood by the door. Her face was rigid with fear, also hatred. Clearly Mary believed that this woman *was* her mother. Elizabeth stared. She did look like the woman in the photograph by her bed. But that picture had become so familiar that she hadn't really looked at it for years, even though she kissed it like an icon. So she wasn't sure. There was a certain likeness in those direct eyes, in the shape of her face. The hair was different; the body had thickened a little. What else? What else? Elizabeth couldn't respond.

'But you're supposed to be dead.'

'Yes, but I didn't die, I ran away. No. That's not true. Your father sent me away.'

'You've been alive for all these years?'

'Yes. All these years. But then I read about Richard's death, my son's death, and I had to find you again.'

'Of course, you're Richard's mother, too,' Elizabeth said tonelessly. She felt she had moved from one dream to another. In both she was helpless, tossed around by a great storm.

'I used to write to you. The letters were sent back unopened. You never saw them. Your father sent them all back. He wouldn't let me see either of you. And I was afraid.' Alice knew she was talking too fast. Elizabeth was still struggling to accept her. 'I had no money, so I became governess to an Indian family. Then you

401

were both sent away and I couldn't discover where. I had no friends here, because I didn't belong. I never expected you to return to India.'

Elizabeth listened to her mother, but didn't hear her. She tried to sort out her own emotions. The surprise had begun to die away and in its wake came anger. Anger for all these years she'd been cheated, been deprived of a mother. A mother who could have loved her, guided her, written to her, cared for her. A mother who was not the figment of a child's imagination, but a real mother. And now it was too late.

'Is that why you came? Only because of Richard's death? If he hadn't died, I should never have met you?'

'No. I didn't mean it like that, Elizabeth. I told you, I had no idea you had both returned to India. I thought I'd lost you both for ever, in England. You're angry with me. I don't blame you, but please try to remember that your father had a great deal to do with what happened. When I read of Richard's death, I sat down and wrote you a letter. And then I decided to come.'

'To be my mother? It's a bit late, isn't it. There must have been a way for you to have found out where we were.'

'No. Only through your father. I agree it's too late to be your mother, my dear child, but I would at least like to be your friend.'

The word 'friend' stirred Elizabeth's memory. She remembered herself and Peter riding in the foothills. Peter had asked about her mother, and then she heard him say faintly: 'Your father is full of secrets.'

He had kept this secret to himself and she was furious with him, furious with the others for not having told her about her mother. Had Peter somehow known of this?

'I suppose everybody knows, except me.'

'Very few,' said Alice. 'I went back to using my maiden name and, although it may seem a small society, I have lived quite outside it. I hope you'll forgive me. I pray that you will. I can't expect you to welcome me immediately, but eventually, once you've got over the anger and shock, you may come to think of me more kindly. Perhaps we could begin again, as friends?'

'Didn't you ever feel that Richard and I were worth your love?' Elizabeth asked, close to tears.

'It wasn't only you and Richard, my dear. You were only babies then. There was a fourth person involved, your father.We came to hate each other, and when that happens there's little room for love. Only self-preservation. I did love you both terribly, but I was given no choice. Women have to accept their destiny as it is fashioned for us by men. Legally, I had no rights to you. I had wronged your father. I was involved with someone else. I was going to take you both and run away with this man. He died, supposedly by accident though I've never been sure. And I was sent away.'

'That's why . . .' Elizabeth stopped, clamping her mouth shut. She had wanted to say 'That's why he was angry, because he thought I'd behaved like you.' But she wouldn't allow this woman to know anything of that. 'Do you expect me to forgive you now, to throw myself into your arms and cry "Mother!"'?'

'You really are like me. No, I don't expect that. I only came to see you, to say that I too have mourned for Richard. I wish I'd been braver. I wish I could have seen him, but we can't have what we want, by wishing. No. I only wanted you to know that I am not dead. That one day, when you feel ready, we might be friends. I certainly don't expect it immediately.'

'I doubt it will ever happen.'

'Nothing is for ever.'

The room was silent. Mother and daughter sat apart, the distance between them immeasurable. Alice looked weary, her face drained and sallow, while Elizabeth looked stubborn and uneasy. She seemed an instant away from tears.

Alice felt drained. She would have to be patient, to give her daughter time. She rose, crossed the room and kissed Elizabeth on the top of her head. She caressed

her face, but Elizabeth drew back as though stung. Alice
realised then that her dream had been false. She'd hoped
for warmth, for immediate forgiveness, for her daughter's love. But her child was angry and confused, and she
couldn't blame her. She'd also imagined her daughter
would be beautiful, for it was the common wish of a
mother, but Elizabeth was haggard and pale.

'You look dreadful. Are you ill?'

'No, I'm quite well, thank you.'

'Elizabeth, I shall be staying for a few days at the Great
Eastern Hotel before returning to Bombay. Will you
come and see me?' She took out a card. 'This is my
address in Bombay, in case you would rather write to
me.'

Elizabeth watched Alice stride out into the sunlight,
hat in hand. There seemed no remorse, no regret. How
dared she come back from the dead? How dared she
announce herself as her mother? Elizabeth ran back into
her room and snatched up the photograph from her
bedside table. She meant to smash it against the wall,
but instead held it to the light. If she'd had any doubt,
there could be none now. Elizabeth lay down and wept,
clutching the picture. She wept in confusion, wept for
all that lost love. The touch of those hands, long forgotten, the eternal void in her life. It couldn't be filled
by any stranger. Her love was for the woman in this
photograph, not for the flesh-and-blood supplanter she
had just seen. Oh God, Richard . . . Richard. She desperately wanted to talk to him. Ask him how they should
decipher the puzzle.

Strangely, Alice's sudden visit stirred Elizabeth from
the languor of mourning and heartbreak. She was angry
with Alice, but above all she was angry with herself.
Alice had stung her pride. Alice had seen Elizabeth
looking wan and dishevelled. Elizabeth, who took pride
in her appearance, was ashamed that she should be
thought of as ill. Elizabeth looked at herself in the ivory-
framed mirror: it reflected weeks of neglect, her assured
beauty was fading to the same sepia colour as the photo-

graph. Elizabeth looked as old as her 'mother' did now, not as she did then.

'Mary ayah, fill my bath. Quickly. Then I want to talk to you.' Elizabeth removed her dressing-gown. Naked, she was skin and bone, though her breasts were firm. But the flesh on her belly sagged a little. Mary ayah sidled in from the bathroom, face determinedly averted from Elizabeth's glare. 'Did you know she was alive?'

'Baba, I didn't know. She went away. Burra sahib told me never to tell you this. If I did, he said he would punish me.'

'Did she go away, or was she sent away?'

Mary ayah remained silent.

'Tell me, confound you!'

'Baba, she was a bad woman. Truly bad. She went with another man. She would spend all day with him. She never cared for you and Richard baba. Burra sahib sent her away because of her badness.'

'You're making up stories.'

'Baba, it's true. Why else would burra sahib not tell you about . . . memsahib?'

'I'm going to find out. Is Parkhurst memsahib at home?'

'No, baba. Memsahib gone to the club.'

Elizabeth bathed and dressed and tried to repair the damage of her self-neglect. She wished now she had been more presentable for her mother. She needed to calm the turmoil inside her. It was the loss of love that so angered her, the loss of a real mother. Elizabeth sat down at her desk. She had to confide in someone, otherwise she would burst with conflicting emotions. But just as she began a letter to Sarah Rushton, she heard Aunt Emma return home.

Aunt Emma had a private domain that Elizabeth rarely entered. It was a large room set at the rear of the bunga-low, and the door was always shut. Elizabeth called out and it took a moment for her aunt to answer, 'Come in.' The shady room was heavy with the smell of an old woman living alone, crowded with memories and furniture. The walls were cluttered with photographs and paintings.

Aunt Emma sat at the window with her playing cards. Elizabeth carefully threaded her way over to the table, but had to remain standing as her aunt sat in the only empty chair; the others were piled with magazines and newspapers. Aunt Emma looked up with some surprise. She'd expected the cook or the bearer coming for instructions.

'What is it, Elizabeth?' A card hovered in her hand.

'Aunt Emma, did you know my mother was alive?'

'Yes.'

'Why didn't you tell me?'

'It wasn't my business, my dear. I'm sure if your father had thought it necessary, he would have mentioned it.'

'I'm talking about something terribly important, Aunt Emma.'

'I know, but it isn't my place to interfere in family matters. How did you find out?' Carefully she placed the card down and took up another.

'She came here this morning.'

'Oh. I wondered why Mary ayah was running around looking like a wet hen. How is your mother? I never met her myself.'

'Mary ayah tells me she was . . . is . . . a bad woman.'

'I suppose she would. Elizabeth, I think you should discuss this matter with your father rather than with me. What would you like for dinner?'

Elizabeth wanted to slam Aunt Emma's door, but instead closed it softly and returned to her letter.

That afternoon, stung by her mother's implied criticism, Elizabeth dressed very carefully for the visit. Her cheeks had taken on a little colour, she did her hair neatly, and wore a dress that she knew made her look younger than her years.

The Great Eastern Hotel was a large, rambling, white building that much resembled a wedding cake. It was the smartest hotel in Calcutta, and had a ballroom on the second floor. The staircase leading up to the ballroom was a magnificent sweep of mahogany with elaborately carved banisters.

Elizabeth took a deep breath, hoping no one would recognise her, and approached the reception clerk, holding the card her mother had given her.

'I've come to visit Miss Soames, please,' she told the elderly man behind the desk.

'I'm afraid Miss Soames is no longer staying here, Madam. She received a telegram and left just an hour ago, on urgent business.'

'Are you sure?'

'Yes, Madam.'

Elizabeth was bitterly disappointed and angry at her mother for having vanished once more. For a moment she thought she must have imagined the morning's visit, since she really had no proof even now that her mother had ever appeared in her life. But at least the reception clerk had known of her existence. All the questions she had wanted to ask her mother now boiled within her, and in her frustration she snapped at the gharri-wallah and then immediately felt ashamed for her rude behaviour.

What on earth, she wondered, could be more important than seeing me?

She returned home, and by the evening, she was prepared for her father. She told the bearer to put out the drinks on the lawn and she determinedly tried to read while waiting for his return from the office. She poured herself a glass of sherry. The shock of her mother's visit had worn off. She wanted to talk to him, calmly, coolly, discover the real reason for his deception. He was never an easy man to talk to. If Richard had been alive, they could have talked man to man and Richard would have told her everything afterwards. Now she had to confront her father alone, and she couldn't quell her unease. Finally she saw his gharri turn into the drive and stop under the porch. He climbed down, patted the dogs and waved to her. He was followed into the bungalow by a peon carrying files.

He knows, thought Elizabeth. He knows that his wife, my mother, came here today. I don't know why I feel he knows, but then, so little escapes him. The chowkidar may have told him, or Abdul, the bearer. Perhaps she even went to see him. No, she wouldn't have done that. He went to see her, then? No. They hate each other too deeply, and the cost of that hatred is my life without a mother. I'm trapped, not in my own life, but in theirs.

By the time her father had bathed and changed, Elizabeth was seething with impatience. Her father returned to the lawn and stooped to kiss the top of her head before taking his place opposite her. She felt like judge and jury, studying the lined face, the expressionless eyes, the steady hand lifting the glass to his lips.

'You're looking much perkier, my dear. Almost your old self. I'm glad. I was worried about you. Richard's death and young Bayley disappearing like that must have been hard on you. But the young are resilient.' He lit a cigarette. The familiar pungent odour drifted across to her. She had loved that smell as a child; it had meant her father was at home. Now she wrinkled her nose in distaste. He went on speaking. 'I think it is time you went Home for a while. I have made a booking for you on the *Stratheden*. You'll be in excellent company. Lady Minto promised to keep an eye on you during the voyage.'

She thought, how clever he is. He had not quite said he loved her, but had implied it with his care and concern. And then, casually, he had altered her life once more. She could go Home for a visit. Escape the dreadful coils of this country to a simpler life. Far from her 'mother'.

'Do you know that she came here?'

'Yes.'

Elizabeth waited, expecting an explanation. He merely flicked ash from his cigarette.

408

'Is that all. "Yes"? Don't you want to know what sh
said, what I said?'

'I already know what was said. I'm sorry she came.'

'Sorry! But you lied to us all our lives. You told us
she was dead. And whenever we asked questions, you
wouldn't tell us any more. If you'd told us she was alive,
we still wouldn't have seen her, but there would have
been some comfort in the thought that at least we *had* a
mother.'

'And some shame. I wanted to protect you. She was
a bad woman and I didn't want her to influence you
both.'

What was it that her mother had said? 'Women have
to accept their destiny as it is fashioned for us by men.'
He had deliberately fashioned theirs. Altered it to his
convenience.

'You're feeling angry now, my dear, but I did it for
the best at the time. She did try to write to you both, but
I forbade it. It was better she be dead than a nuisance.'

'Father, it was important that we should know, that
we could make a decision as to whether we should meet
her, when we were old enough. We wouldn't have left
you for her.'

'I wasn't sure. I did the best I could for you both. Do
you intend to see her again?'

'Is that what is worrying you? That I'll run away to
her?'

'That would be extremely foolish. No. I just asked if
you intend to see her.'

'I'd like to.'

The Colonel paused, searching for the correct expression. 'I'd be . . . hurt . . . if you did.'

'But I'm curious about her.'

'Why? She's a complete stranger to you.'

'Father, she is my mother. Richard's mother, too. I
know he would have wanted to see her. Not that we'd
become close, just to find out about her. What did she
do that was so terrible?'

'She betrayed us.'

He wouldn't explain it further. Stubbornly, he re-reated behind his will, his authority as her father, as a man. He couldn't confess to the passion of loving and the bitter taste of rejection. He took her acceptance of his love as a victory, her defection as his defeat. He couldn't think of it in any other terms, except those of war. Now, he couldn't tell his daughter how much he'd loved this woman, how headstrong and foolish he'd been.

'But to know that we *had* a mother would have made such a difference to Richard and me.'

'Nonsense. Both my parents died when I was very young, and I grew up perfectly happily. I admit, if they had lived, I might have known a different home life. But, as it is, I've done extremely well.' He rose, ending the conversation, dismissing her emotional pain. 'I think we should go in to dinner. Come.'

He waited for her to rise. It was dark, and lights from the house cast a welcoming glow on the lawn. Elizabeth felt weary, baffled. She'd asked questions; as always he'd avoided answering them. It was not the loss of his wife which had so wounded him, but that by her adultery she had betrayed him. He would never forgive anyone who betrayed him. He would hate them all his life.

'Is that why you never married again? You would have had to get a divorce, and we would have found out.'

'I found no one suitable to be your stepmother.'

Aunt Emma was already seated at the table. The Colonel drew his daughter's chair out courteously and sat down opposite her. It seemed to Elizabeth that all her life she had faced her father and been defeated. She spooned her soup in silence, a silence she allowed to shroud the table. She did not want to forgive him. Ever.

28

ALL WOMEN, Mohini thought, lead identical lives. We believe ourselves to be different, but through tradition, through custom, even history, we are all alike: prisoners. Here I am now – one thousand years later – another Sita. Carried away, not by Ravana, but by my own husband. And again, like her, I find myself trapped on an island from which there is no escape.

Mohini looked out at the water. She was in a mansion built on an island in the middle of a lake. It wasn't as magnificent as Jagmandir, the lake palace in Udaipur. This one was made of pink stone, with balconies overlooking the water and an interior garden. Her balcony in the women's quarters had a jali which prevented her from jumping into the lake and drowning. The shores were not far away, but the land beyond was matted with jungle and rose up steeply on all sides. The jungle was a vibrant green, countless delicate shades of the colour. On the crown of the eastern hill she could see the silhouette of a ruined fortress, its walls had been breached by time and neglect.

Her room was almost bare. The floor was covered with silk Kashmiri carpets and in one corner was a divan. That was all. The door leading to the inner garden was locked; another led to a bathroom and the servant's entrance leading out was also locked. If she'd had any furniture, curtains, she would have built a pyre for herself, only she had no matches. She couldn't even hang herself. Not that she would have had an opportunity: a servantwoman remained in the room at all times. Still and silent and watchful. She was guarded by three women in all. They performed their duties warily; as though she might bite. She tried talking to them, but they wouldn't answer. Their loyalty lay with Bahadhur sahib.

She spent the first two days in such bare splendour. The rest of the mansion seemed to be deserted. She heard no voices, saw no movement, apart from the servants coming and going.

Then, what she had dreaded most, materialised one morning. Her mother-in-law, Gitabhai. She awoke to find Gitabhai staring down at her. Mohini rolled off the divan in fright. Venom glittered in those brown eyes. Gitabhai laughed in delight at Mohini's fear. There would have been some comfort for Mohini if this woman had been ugly, deformed, dark. Instead she had a lovely oval face, fair and ageless. It was hard to believe that a woman with such an unlined face and such a firm belly could have been the mother of Bahadhur sahib. This was why Mohini believed in the malign power of the universe. There was a power that preserved this woman perfectly, erasing wrinkles, holding age at bay.

'I don't know why my son is so obsessed with you. You're skinny and ugly. Truly ugly. And instead of being grateful, you run away. Huh, look at you. A real pariah. Ram sent me here to keep watch over you. If I were him, I'd throw you to the tigers.'

As always, Gitabhai wore a silk sari. This one was dark green embroidered with gold thread. In each nostril was an emerald stud, and emerald ear-rings hung from her lobes. She wore a matching emerald necklace and eight gold and emerald bangles on each wrist. Around her waist was a golden mesh belt. Her mouth was lasciviously red from paan. Incongruously, she carried a newspaper.

'It would be easier to poison you. I believe you're bad luck for Ram. Come and sit down.'

'No.'

'Oh, you've grown bold since you've been away. How

did you live? Did you sell your body? But I doubt any man would pay good money for such scrawniness. Come.' She patted the divan.

'I will not move from here until you leave the room.'

Gitabhai moved surprisingly quickly to stand in front of Mohini. Her head only reached Mohini's shoulder. For a moment she said nothing, then, without warning, she slapped Mohini very hard. As a child bride, when Bahadhur sahib wasn't at home, Mohini had often been slapped and pinched by her.

'When I tell you to do something, do it. Will you never learn?'

She was just turning away when Mohini, amazed at herself, struck Gitabhai a great whack across the side of her head, sending her sprawling on to the divan. The older woman lay there for a moment, stunned, rubbing her face.

'I have learned.'

'Is that what you learned, living with that European whore? To treat your mother-in-law so cruelly?' And she actually allowed tears to form in her eyes. Mohini felt no remorse. She knew Gitabhai would now work even harder to kill her, but not until he'd come. And gone. It made no difference now that he wanted her alive. Gitabhai would kill her for that blow. She could perform the deed with poison, a snake, a scorpion, or even a mantra.

'Get out of my room.'

'Your room? This whole house is my son's. I'll go when I please, you ungrateful pariah. We've fed you and clothed you. Just look at the way you treated us – running away and mixing with those dirty Angrezis. Here, you read English, read this.'

She thrust the newspaper at Mohini. A column on the front page of *The Statesman* was marked out in ink.

'Read. Out loud, you fool.'

This morning, Bahadhur Ram Shanker, a leading member of the Indian National Congress Party, was welcomed into the Viceroy's Executive Council.

413

Bahadhur Ram Shanker is the first Indian national to be so honoured as to attend the deliberations of our august ruling body. The Viceroy, Lord Minto, welcomed the new member to his Council, saying that Bahadhur Ram Shanker would attend the Council's meetings in an advisory capacity. He will not have a vote on any matters. The power of the Council will remain entirely in the hands of the Viceroy and its European members. At some future date, additional Indians will be appointed to the Council to comply with the reforms suggested by Mr Morley, the Secretary of State for India. Half of these additional Indian members will be voted in to their seats, the remainder will be appointed by the Viceroy. The reforms proposed by Mr Morley and Lord Minto will also extend to the provincial councils. In replying to questions from newspaper reporters, Bahadhur Ram Shanker stated: 'I am deeply honoured to have been chosen by the Viceroy to join the Council. I represent the aspirations not only of the Indian National Congress, but all India. And I firmly believe that India should continue to be ruled by the British Crown.'

Gitabhai clapped in satisfaction when Mohini finished. 'See what an important man my son is? The first Indian ever to sit with the Viceroy. He will be soon the most powerful national in all India. And then he will get rid of you. I'll tell him you will disgrace him. Perhaps an accident will befall you.' She snatched the newspaper from Mohini and left the room, locking the door behind her.

The report depressed Mohini. It had happened since the meeting in Allahabad. She should have written the story for *Sher*. She tried to distract herself by thinking about how she would have composed her version of the story. There was no doubt Bahadhur sahib had manoeuvred his way to such a powerful position. The souls he had destroyed and betrayed would never be known. She had no doubt the British had chosen him only because of his duplicity. He was their puppet. He would say only what they told him to say, not what India wanted.

She realised he had arrived when the servantwomen came in the next evening. They carried a silk sari and a choli, perfumes, oils, flowers for her hair. They pushed her into the bathroom, where a servant had left buckets of hot water for her bath. She tried to escape, but two of them held her while the third unwrapped her old yellow sari and ripped off her blouse. Still holding her, they roughly bathed her. The water was scalding hot and she got soap in her eyes. They dried and perfumed her body and rubbed scented oil in her hair, making it glisten. While one woman decorated her hair with flowers, another applied kohl to her eyes and then they dressed her in silk. She sat quietly now, withdrawn from these efforts to make her beautiful for her husband. Their final touch was the red tilak mark on her forehead.

She sat in the gloom, numb and exhausted. She felt like a doll, all made up, soon to be pulled apart. She barely heard the rain outside, plinking musically on the water, the wind humming a mysterious tune through the jali. She no longer prayed, for she'd given up hope. There would be no salvation, no saviour, no miracles. Not even welcoming death.

Bahadhur sahib, the first Indian ever to sit on the Viceroy's Council and for whom the world was now his oyster, was dressed as splendidly as a bridegroom. He had discarded European clothes now that he was far from the eyes of the Council members. He wore a long jodhpuri coat that fell to his knees, with tight jodhpur trousers, both made of yellow silk. In the gloomy light he seemed to glow. Mohini smelt the attar of roses, strong as a woman's perfume, wafting ahead of him. But neither the perfume nor the clothes could disguise his age. Bahadhur sahib called for a lamp and when it came the servant held it above Mohini. She didn't look up, but instead stared dully at her feet, feeling loathing and fear.

'My dear wife, you have no idea what pleasure I derive from seeing you again.' His voice was soft, silken, kind. 'I've missed you. I've missed your coldness, your anger. Missed too that beautiful body which feels like satin.' He stroked her cheek and when she turned away, the hand persistently followed, the caress becoming a soft slap. 'I like wilful women. I know you have little affection for me, which is most unfortunate because I have a constant longing for you. I love to look on your beauty, to possess it, to caress it, to hear it cry out. These things give me deep pleasure, and life without pleasure and challenge is empty. Yes, my life has been empty without you. Perhaps, if you'd stayed, I should have tired of you and given you to the servants. But your escaping has only whetted my appetite. I've dreamt of my revenge all these years.' He gripped her chin and lifted her head. The light shone on her tears. 'Oh, you are being melodramatic again. I imagine you have cast yourself as one of our heroines. You always had such a vivid imagination. Padmini or Rupmati. See, there is nothing in this room that will rob me of you. Don't you have anything to say to your husband? Even a hello?'

'Nothing. All I want is to kill myself rather than to feel your hands on me.'

Gripping her shoulders, he forced her to stand, and with the servantwoman holding up the lantern, he slowly undressed her. She could feel his breath on her face, panting against her ears, his hands sliding and slipping over her body. Then the lamp was removed and all she felt and saw was the blackness of the room and her own despair.

Now that he was home, she was allowed out of her room in the evening. The interior garden had a central lawn, surrounded by rose and canna trees. Bougainvillea climbed up one wall, a swathe of red. A lotus-shaped marble fountain played at one end, and a marble pool carried the water the length of the garden beneath a wide marble bench. Bahadhur sahib, reclining on a divan supported by bolsters, held his evening court enthroned

416

on this bench. Mohini had to sit beside him, always glittering in silks and now, jewellery, reluctantly given in loan by Gitabhai. As a daughter-in-law, Mohini should have received it as a gift, but Gitabhai was too mean for that. She would have preferred to see Mohini stripped of all finery.

'I found out that you were employed by Romesh Nairoji to work on his magazine, *Sher*. He only survives on the memory of his uncle. I read your writings. I am proud of you. You are intelligent and talented, disturbing flaws in a woman, but unfortunately talent has not necessarily given you wisdom. Your friends, including that clown, Mr Nehru, are trying to find you, but they never will. No one knows where you are, except for myself and my mother. There will be no rescuer this time. You are my wife, mine to do with as I want. You should accept your life here with me. It will make things easier. I shall not be taking you back to Delhi because I'm sure you will do something foolish. A pity. As the first Indian to become a member of the Viceroy's Council I would have found you a valuable possession to flaunt. Still, the European wouldn't expect ever to see an Indian's wife. Gokhale never shows his, so why should I? But it would have been good to see the envy in other men's eyes. An old man possessing young flesh. Well, aren't you proud of my achievement?'

'I'm sure you did it for your own reasons. Self-aggrandisement. Not for India, not for the Indian people. You will destroy us before you ever achieve anything for our country.'

'You're an extremist like my old friend Tilak. But he's in gaol, and so are you.'

One evening, while they were sitting outside in the gathering dusk, Rajender approached Bahadhur sahib and whispered in his ear.

'Bring them . . . send the boat quickly,' he ordered, and when Rajender had scurried away, Bahadhur sahib turned to Mohini. 'We are going to enjoy a little entertainment tonight. It will be a most amusing experience for us all.'

From the far end of the garden, Rajender eventually ushered in two boys, holding hands. One carried cymbals, the other a ravanhatta. They appeared to be asleep. Their eyes were tightly closed, but still they walked forward with absolute confidence.

'Namaskaar,' they said in perfect unison. Mohini had never heard such sweet, clear voices.

'Namaskaar,' Bahadhur sahib replied. 'Come, sing for us. I will reward you richly. Your fame is widespread.'

'For your generosity, Brahma will bless you.'

'What are your names?' asked Mohini.

'Bala,' they said with one voice.

They sat down in front of Mohini. The water in the fountain dimly reflected them, while above the sky was pale grey with a waning moon. The boys began to sing, and as soon as the first notes struck the air, the wind ceased to sigh. The water in the fountain became still and the flowers opened their petals and turned their heads towards the sound of the pure, clear voices. The moon sank lower in the sky, casting its full light on the two boys. Mohini was mesmerised, soothed. She only half listened to the words, the sheer beauty of their voices was pleasure enough. They sang first a few bhajans to Lord Krishna and then, as the hours passed, they began to sing of their travels across the land. She listened to them tell her of the jungles and the mountains, the princes and the people they met. And woven through the song, she suddenly heard them singing about Kim and Parvati, of lovers separated from each other, of Kim's search throughout the land for Parvati.

Her heart ached with its frantic beating. She couldn't interrupt them and she was afraid she had not heard then correctly. It *had* been Kim, *had* been Parvati. Or was the longing to hear those names so great that she had come to believe in the illusion they created by the sound of their lovely voices? She glanced at Bahadhur sahib, but his eyes were closed in pleasure. Besides, he would not know of Kim, or Parvati. Finally at midnight they stopped. The breeze blew stronger and the water in the fountain flowed again. The flowers closed their petals and turned their heads away.

'Shabash . . . shabash.' Bahadhur sahib clapped and took a large handful of gold coins from his pocket, passing them to the boys. 'Please rest for the night here in my home before you continue on your travels.'

The boys bowed and rose, and Mohini waited until they'd moved beyond Bahadhur sahib's hearing.

'I would like their darshan,' she said, and hurried after them.

They stopped when she bowed to them and whispered: 'In your song you sang of Kim and Parvati. How do you know about them?'

'Kim travelled with us for several days. He told us the story.'

'I am his Parvati. Can you find him? Do you know where he is? Can you send him to me?' The questions tumbled out, she couldn't control the flood of hope. Kim was alive and had told these boys about her. She touched their hands, for they had touched Kim.

'We do not know where he is. It has been a long time since we parted. But it is possible that we could send a message to him. What do you want us to tell him?'

'Tell him . . . tell him . . .' She faltered. What could they tell him? How would they find him? They were only innocent children, gifted with beautiful voices. How would Kim find her? She didn't know where she was. And by the time the boys reached Kim, she would, by God's grace, be dead. She had already decided on that. 'Tell him that you met his Parvati, and that she loves him and wishes him farewell.'

She felt their sightless eyes settle on her face, and knew that even in the blackness of night they would see the tears sliding down her cheeks.

'We will tell him.'

She wanted to ask how and when, but she hadn't the spirit to pursue her questions. One day in the future, in

419

their travels, they might meet Kim again. They would tell him how they met his Parvati in the middle of a lake in the shadow of a great ruined fortress and that she had said she loved him. It would be a cruel reminder that it hadn't been their destiny to see each other ever again. And he would live on with only the memory of her love.

Bala and Bala came upon a black panther lying on the battlements of the fortress where, three centuries before, a Rajput soldier had stood guard, and looked down on the might of the Mughal Akbar's army. The panther's coat glistened in the sunlight, full of secret colours. One paw hung lazily over the edge of the wall and its tail coiled back and forth, like a snake dancing. Its eyes were full and yellow as moons. Then the panther rose gracefully, picking its way down the shattered steps, and sniffed at the boys. They paid no attention to it and, full of curiosity, it padded behind them into the ruin. What had once been a magnificent palace was now filled with lantana bushes and scrub grass. The pink sandstone durbar hall, a large rectangular roofless building, stood in the centre. The wooden doors had been eaten away by white ants, and pigeons strutted where kings and ministers had once held court. One wall of the women's quarters had fallen into the jungle, the remaining were rain-stained and the pink stone had turned the colour of dried blood. The ground sloped up and the three of them passed the temple. It was set near the water tank which was still full of pure, cool water. The temple itself, the carvings intact though now dark and indecipherable, had been perfectly preserved. The idol within was missing. They walked by the palace of the king, its grandeur and dignity still holding it aloof from the other ruins, but this building too was roofless and in the lower chambers clustered the black drip of countless bats.

When they reached the highest point on the high cliff, where beyond the mist loomed the edges of the horizon, Bala and Bala sat down. The panther took its place in front of them. When the boys began to sing, it lay down and began to purr softly. First the pigeons came, a whirr of wings and cooings, to settle themselves in the trees and on the ground around the boys; then came the crows, the sky darkening with their massed arrival. Thousands flew out of the jungle, cawing excitedly, circling the boys, turning sunlight to shadow before swooping to find perches. And then came the parrots and peacocks, the partridges and pea-hens, sand-birds and sparrows, hawks and herons. They settled themselves on the ramparts and on the temple and on the palaces, heads cocked to the voices of the boys. The ruined fort city came alive with the flutter and movement of the birds. Bala and Bala continued to sing. The sun was high and the mist had burned off the lake.

At noon, when there was no shadow to be seen, they were aware of the slow approach of Jatayu. As the eagle came lower its shadow rippled over the jungle and its wings spanned the valley from hilltop to hilltop. It glided over the fort, and when it beat its wings once, the smaller birds were blown off their perches, the larger ones flapped frantically to keep their balance. The air was in uproar, with irate calls and the beating of wings. The panther's coat was ruffled as though unseen fingers stroked the fur. There was no room for Jatayu to settle, and although the birds shifted around to make a small space, none of them wanted to miss a single note from the boys' singing. To their disappointment Bala and Bala stopped singing and namasted the circling eagle.

'Namaskaar.'

'Namaskaar. I heard your voices at dawn when I was high above the abode of Siva. Never before have I listened to such wondrous singing. Your voices are as beautiful as the dance of Lord Nataraj. The Lord Krishna could not have granted a greater boon.'

'We would like a boon from you, Lord Jatayu. We have a message for you to carry to Kim. We met his Parvati down by the lake. She is being held against her will by her husband. You must tell Kim soon, for we fear for her life.'

'How much time do I have?'

'Very little. She is in despair.'

'It will not be easy. He is a wanderer, a friend of all the people. I shall have to search the hills, the deserts, the valleys, the mountains, the cities, the villages. It took me long enough to find him the first time. I shall have to ask the Lord Vamana to aid me. But I will find Kim and tell him that his Parvati is below on the lake. Namaskaar.'

29

KIM CAME to know the secrets of all his companions. As the Colonel had predicted, men believe that secrets spoken within prison walls are safe. While his companions exercised, they let slip names and places, incidents and events. He learnt that Mr Bhattacharjee's co-conspirators, who'd helped to burn Manchester-made cotton in his district, were hiding in Dakha with relatives; that the Sikh's gurudwar had a stock of twenty-one small-arms, stolen from an army depot in Ajmer; that Mr Akbar was writing a highly seditious article on the law which would be published under a pseudonym by a magazine in Madras. Mr Joshi, the Congressman, claimed to be the ringleader of a secret society of terrorists in Bombay, but Kim suspected he was making this up to maintain his status. His only glory came from being Tilak's friend. Kim also knew that Anil Ray obsessively planned the assassination of Inspector Goode.

In all, these secrets were minor scraps of information, except for Anil Ray's murderous intent. Not one would topple an empire. These men were dreamers, and their dreams were disparate; nothing bound one dream to another. They discussed freedom, but had no vision of it; they couldn't imagine what lay beyond a vague self-rule. They had no practical idea of how they would run the country. Before that dream, they dreamt of driving out the British, though none knew how to defeat such a superior military power. Empires were held by weapons and broken by weapons. If words were bullets, these men would have conquered the world.

Kim heard all these secrets and said nothing, though he knew they could be the threads that would unravel larger conspiracies. If he expected the Colonel, far away in Calcutta, to bear his silence patiently, Kim was reminded gently of his power. One morning when Hari brought his morning tea, he did not leave Kim a censored newspaper, and would have gone on down the row if Kim hadn't reminded him.

'No, no. You are no longer to receive any reading matter. I have new orders.' He peered at Kim suspiciously. 'What have you done to deserve this? Is it going to make troubles for me?'

'I've done nothing, and for that I am being punished.'

'Nothing is inaction. The Gita says you must act, for inaction is bad. "To action alone has thou the right, not inaction. And not to the fruits of thy action." But don't take any action that will cause me troubles. I have enough already.'

'Who gave the order?'

'The head clerk, Menon. Only he gives orders, in triplicate, given in turn from the Superintendent. Who tells him, God knows.'

Kim knew. He was reminded again of his inaction when Narain came to visit on Sunday, empty-handed. His brow was tight with worry and he sat outside Kim's cell, fretting.

'You must tell me something. Lie. Just lie. At least then the Colonel might believe you. He will say Kim is trying. Otherwise, he will think his Imperial Agent Kim is betraying him and God knows what will happen then. He has ordered me not to bring you any more fruit and sweets. No expenses for such luxuries. I have cigarettes for you, and Hari's baksheesh, but this is my own money.' He thrust the money and cigarettes through the bars.

Kim took them. 'He's already withdrawn my reading privileges.'

'See, next he will withdraw your food. Then he will

change you from A class to B class, and then to C class. You cannot escape him here.'

'He imprisons only my body.'

'Ahre, Kim. The body is everything. Without it how would you have a soul? It would be wandering all over the universe, homeless, not causing us trouble with all this religious nonsense.'

'I should become your chela. You would lead me straight to hell.'

'Of course,' Narain laughed. 'That's where the body enjoys itself most, I'm told. All bad people go there. All women, too.' He became serious. 'Tell me something.'

'I can't betray these men. I am one of them now.'

Kim was sad that this worried Narain. Narain would have to report the continued silence, and the Colonel would have to go on reminding Kim of his power over him. He would teach Kim a lesson: loyalty would be rewarded, betrayal would be punished.

'What? No metai, no fruit, no reading?' Anil Ray mocked Kim when he came to sweep his cell.

'The consequences of inaction, my friend. Or perhaps I should describe my inaction as an action that is displeasing the authorities.'

'You're a fool. Here you are, a member of the privileged race in this land. The colour of your skin, which strikes such awe into us natives because it is the mark of your superiority, ensures your freedom. Mine will keep me here for years to come. What difference does it make if you betray us? You can return to your homeland, live splendidly as a gentleman on your plunder. Great English fortunes were once made from the rape of this country. Once I spent a weekend with a friend from Oxford, the Honourable John Sutcliffe. He had inherited thousands of acres and countless servants and tenants, all from his great-grandfather, who spent a few years here. You could go there, once you've passed on our secrets to your master.'

'My home is here. And the privilege of my colouring is an empty one. My guru was a dark man, and wiser than the collected wisdom of the European, and because he shunned power, he was the mightier. Kyha rhe, you are more of an Englishman than I am. The way you speak, the way you dressed once, the way you think. I cannot speak English as you do; I have never worn the fine clothes you have worn; I have never been a guest of the Honourable John Sutcliffe. I have no desire to do or be any of these things.'

'It's true. I was once like that. That was what my father dreamed for me, and I too wanted that dream. But it is no longer my life. It could be yours, while I can never return to it. We are like two opposite lines crossing. I am going downwards. You?'

'Perhaps we shall not cross or cut, but run along beside each other?'

'It is possible. If only I could walk beside you when you leave this prison. Oh, to breathe a different air, to walk without coming up against walls, to look without seeing bars, not to be beaten at the whim of that ape Sethu.'

'And for how long would you be free if you should kill Goode?'

'They will never catch me again.'

'You trust me enough to tell me that you will kill Inspector Goode.'

'He knows. I know. You know. God knows. Who else is there? You won't tell because you are partly responsible – and you know you are – for my being here.' He gripped Kim's hand. 'Help me escape, and I will forgive you.'

'No. Only if you promise not to harm Inspector Goode. He was carrying out his duty.'

'But duty doesn't comprise cruelty. He comes here to torment me, torture me. He will come suddenly, as though I am his conscience, to goad me. He wishes I were dead too, and not witness to his murdering. How can I make such a promise? My father, dying now, has also begged for this promise from me. If I see my father before he dies, I might be swayed. If not, never. Goode

426

has destroyed my whole family. The repercussions of one shot echo on and on until we're all shattered. You speak as though you plan to escape. Do you?'

'No. I shall serve my sentence. I'm in no hurry.'

'Why should you be, when you have only a few months? I have years and I may not live to see the end of my term.' He went to the door to see if Hari was within earshot. 'If you help me to escape, I'll tell you the names of the two men for whom my uncle and I were mistaken.'

Kim didn't reply. He could not trust Anil Ray. The man had a crafty look of despair, even of insanity.

'How would you know that?'

'This is a prison, and in prisons one becomes a master of peculiar knowledge. Secrets are spoken to the walls. One of the men has a broken ankle. His cousin-brother told me this man killed a British police officer in Bombay. And that he was paid a lot of money for doing it.'

'By whom?'

'He doesn't know. But if you help me, I will tell you where to find these two men.'

'I will think about it.'

Kim had not forgotten those two men. The information seemed to be correct. One man indeed had a broken ankle. He knew they'd been paid, and if he could discover who their paymaster was, the Colonel would be delighted with him.

The rains had begun to ease and the sun broke through with a watery glare when the old monkey climbed down the prison wall and stalked nervously on all fours across the compound. Kim watched it advance, chattering with anxiety, and wondered where it was going with such determination. A guard threw a stone at it and the old monkey dodged and scolded him, but instead of scampering back up the tree to safety, it continued its progress to the row of cells. Kim lost sight of it and gave it no further thought. Half an hour later two more monkeys followed the old one's route. This time, even though they were as jittery as the old one, they went unmolested. The guard, preoccupied in talking to a companion, stood in the shade of the tamarind tree, not noticing the quiet gathering of the rest of the tribe. Kim thought it strange. Until now they'd remained on the perimeter of the prison, only using the high walls to cross from one tree to another. They'd never once stepped inside the compound, seeming humanly aware of the purpose of this place. Now they were all in the prison compound. One of the monkeys in the tree cautiously slid down the trunk, peeped at the guards, then scampered to the prison wall, fifty yards from Kim's cell. When it reached the wall, instead of climbing, it stretched up its arms. Kim saw that the older monkeys had been sitting quietly waiting for their companion and now, holding on to the top of the wall, they came halfway down to catch hold of their companion and haul him up. A little later, another monkey slid down the tree and the whole manoeuvre was repeated. It was a game for them, and after the fourth time they tired of it and moved out of view.

During that night, in his deepest sleep, Kim's dreams were filled with talons and the beating of wings. He saw the speckled plumage so clearly that he could count each individual feather and touch the soft white down beneath. Its musty odour almost overwhelmed him, and the fierce golden eyes fixed him with such intensity that he felt pinned to the ground. He knew he shouldn't be afraid, but the strength and size of Jatayu at such close proximity made him shiver and cry out in his sleep.

'Namaskaar . . . namaskaar.' The eagle's greeting vibrated through his sleep, expanding to fill the dark sky overhead. 'Do not awake, but listen to me. I have searched for you for many days. The bandar told me you were here in this prison. I have been sent by the brothers whose voices enchant the gods and can even still the wind Vayu and stop the fire Agni. They have spoken to Parvati, and she sends a message for you. She says she loves you and bids you farewell. She has been imprisoned by her husband on a lake in the Aravalli hills near the ancient fortress of Ranthambor and is in great danger. Namaskaar.'

'Wait . . . wait . . .' Kim cried out in his sleep. 'How much time do I have? How can I escape? Will you tell me more?'

But in his dream Jatayu made no reply, and the dark mist swirled with the beating of his wings. Kim ran forward to catch the rising eagle. He held onto a feather and was lifted up a few feet before the feather came away and he tumbled back to earth.

He awoke abruptly, jumping to catch Jatayu, wanting to be carried out of prison. His hand struck the wall painfully. It was only a dream, yet he could still smell Jatayu. He was clutching something in his hand, and held up a grey feather to the pale moonlight. It was real, the size of his palm, but even as he stared at it, the feather vanished.

'Are dreams real or do they come into existence through our cravings? I dreamt of Jatayu and he came to me with a message from Parvati. She loves me and I'm elated. But is that news only a reflection of my longing to know it? I must believe the dream is true. I held Jatayu's feather, briefly, as proof that illusion and reality are the same. We pass effortlessly from one to another. She is alive, but she is in danger, and I am dark with despair. She wished me farewell with such finality that I sense the ending of her. That cannot happen. I must escape, find her. It won't be easy; this isn't like St Xavier's school where I could climb over the wall. Narain will help me. He'll be coming tomorrow morning. But to whom is Narain more loyal? Me? The Colonel? The Colonel is his employer; I am a friend with no money. To hold a Government job is the desire of every ambitious Indian and I can't ask Narain to risk such good opportunity. But how will I escape? How?'

He had no one else to turn to. Kim was impatient now, prowling his cell, his mind agitated. How had Jatayu found him? Through the dwarf? And would he help? Kim took the pebble from the leather pouch around his neck. It was now a faint yellow colour, not yet as bright as when he'd first been given it.

'Will you help me? Help me,' he whispered.

Did the dwarf believe in love? Love was the passion of men, not gods. He hadn't helped when Kim had asked his guidance to find Parvati before. Why should he now? No one answered his prayer. The stone lay in his palm like any other pebble. He slipped it back into the pouch. Each passing moment was time squandered. Parvati could even now be near death. How long had Jatayu searched for him? How long, how long, how long?

Kim couldn't sleep. He waited impatiently for Narain the next morning, and in the perverse manner of such things, Narain was late. He was dishevelled and his eyes were red from arrack. He passed the cigarettes and money to Kim in silence.

'I have to escape,' Kim said. 'I had a message that Parvati is alive but in danger. You must help me.'

'Escape! Don't be foolish. If you escape, the Colonel sahib will have me hanged in this very prison for dereliction of my duty. You shouldn't tell me such things, Kim.'

Narain broke into a sweat. His friend was deadly serious. The Colonel sahib would never accept protestations of ignorance. His only duty was to watch Kim, be with Kim, relay information from Kim. Kim was his security, his emolument, his career. If Kim escaped, Narain knew he too would have to flee the Colonel sahib's wrath. Where could he run? Back to his uncle, who would throw him out for having made a mess of the job? Isaac Newton would fear his presence because it would jeopardise his own comfortable position. No. He would have to run and hide in the hope that the Colonel sahib would eventually forget about him. God only knew when.

'Kim, it's too dangerous. You only have three months to go. Serve the time and then I will personally accompany you to find your Parvati. I always knew she would cause troubles. What troubles, too! It's all very well for her to send you a message, but does she know the consequences of her actions? Of course not.'

'Can you arrange a tonga and train tickets?' Kim ignored Narain's panic. 'Tomorrow, have the tonga waiting outside the wall from early morning. Pay him well. I'll repay you.'

'With what?' Narain asked bitterly. 'You have no money. I must think about all this.'

'No. There isn't time. You must help me, Narain.'

Narain sighed. Some men were fortunate enough to lead undramatic lives. They ate, worked, lay with women, drank and died. Now he was responsible for this friend who was leading him into a precarious future.

'I will hire the tonga. But no more than that. How will you get out of here?'

'That's my business. I'll find a way. If I do not tell you, you will never be burdened with the knowledge.'

'I have a constant wish to be ignorant, but that isn't usually my good fortune.'

That evening, even before Narain had had time to write his report, let alone post it, the Colonel withdrew another small privilege. Kim was kept locked in his cell while the other prisoners were released for exercise. It was a game, a small one, which at another time might have amused Kim. Now it frustrated him. He'd planned to make his escape at exercise time.

Jahangir peeped into his cell before joining the others.

'What have you done?'

'Nothing,' Kim replied truthfully.

'We will protest to the Superintendent about this mal-treatment of prisoners. Mr Akbar will draw up a brief on your behalf.'

'We're not in a court of law. We are beyond the law. But I thank you for your concern.'

He watched the procession make its way slowly and solemnly around the compound. The precedence had remained the same as on that first day, the elders in front, the youngest at the rear. Jahangir now walked alone.

'Am I permitted any exercise at all?' Kim called out to Hari.

'Yes. Alone.' He peered at Kim and examined the cell suspiciously. 'You're doing something I can't see. What?'

'What can I do in this cave except sit and think?'

'Ah. That is the problem you are giving someone. You are thinking too much. You must stop that, otherwise I can see big troubles for myself. Next I shall be given permission to beat you, which I won't like much, but will have to do. I like you.'

'What time will I go for my exercise?'

'Morning only. Fifteen minutes.'

'But I didn't get any exercise this morning.'

'Then, you were under the old orders. The new orders came after this morning. So now you will only exercise tomorrow morning.'

All the rest of that day, Kim prowled around his cell, his mind entirely concentrated on Parvati. He had to get out, had to save her. But he was trapped by walls and bars and guards. The other convicts had finished their exercise and returned to their cells. The compound was deserted, even of guards. Vaguely he watched the monkeys at play. Once more they had ventured into the compound, sliding down the tamarind tree and loping over to the wall, to be helped up by their companions. It seemed to him a silly game, and he returned to his brooding. He'd never felt so desperate and dark. Already a whole day had been wasted; he'd travelled no further than the length and breadth of his cell.

He couldn't contain a sigh of melancholy. He languished in one prison, Parvati in another. Both were alone, both were afraid. He considered whether, if he couldn't escape, he would appeal to the Colonel sahib. In exchange for his freedom, he would have to betray the secrets he'd heard. The price would be the arrest of all the co-conspirators, now hiding with uncles and cousins, against Parvati's certain death. The choice was stark, and in the despair of night Kim chose betrayal.

Her life was too important to lose for honour. Where did his duty lie now? To save her life, he argued to himself persuasively. And in the darkness he found himself persuaded. But, as the morning light gently filtered into his cell and he slowly emerged from that darkness, he became more realistic again, a man instilled with a sense of duty, to himself and to others. Was love worth the freedom of other men; was her life? He was confused. How could he live with betrayal? Yet how could he live, knowing he'd allowed her to die?

He sat up and stared at the delicate dawn light. The words spoken by Jatayu echoed again, as though whispered anew in his ears. 'I have searched for you for many days. The bandar . . .' Kim stood up excitedly and peered out. The trees were empty of monkeys, but he couldn't stifle hope. '. . . the bandar told me.' The *monkeys* had told Jatayu where he was. Jatayu knew Hanuman. In the Ramayana, the monkey king and his army had helped Rama to defeat Ravana. This old leader of this tribe who played silly games wasn't Hanuman, but he had spoken to Jatayu. He had been playing the game for a purpose, and finally Kim understood it.

In his preoccupation with escape, Kim had forgotten about Anil Ray. He came at his usual time to clean the cells. Hari unlocked the door and Anil slipped in. He only nodded to Kim and moved around in a daze.

'What's happened? No talk, no discourse?'

'I heard that my father is very near death. He has not left his bed for days. The doctor says he hasn't much time to live. A day, two days. The news came yesterday and even as I speak he might be dead. I asked for permission to visit him, but the Superintendent refused. I'm classified as a dangerous prisoner. No privileges.'

'I'm sorry.' Kim laid his hand comfortingly on Anil's shoulder. He saw the hardness, the rage, dissolve. The bravado was gone. Anil Ray was close to tears and looked like a small boy, lost and alone.

'If you see your father before he dies, will you keep your word and not kill Goode?'

'I will. I swear it. Who cares for that chuthia? All I want is to see my father once more, and I know if he sees me, he will regain his will to live.'

Kim looked out to where Hari stood some distance away, smoking a cigarette and talking to another guard. The monkeys were peacefully foraging in the tamarind tree over their heads. Three of them sat on the prison wall, picking fleas off each other. They seemed unconcerned with the world. Perhaps he'd imagined the escape plan; the bandar had only been playing a game. If he ran to the wall and they didn't pull him up he would be trapped by the guards. Kim had no doubt he'd be beaten, not severely, but punishment enough. The Colonel would be told and he would become a C class prisoner for disobedience.

'Something should happen when I step out of this cell. I hope and pray it does. Stay close to me.'

Although it wasn't his exercise period and he was meant to remain in his cell, Kim cautiously stepped out. Hari hadn't noticed him but the monkeys had. They stopped foraging and looked up at their old chief. He climbed down from the higher branches of the tamarind tree and quietly the tribe gathered above the heads of the guards. Kim took another step away from the door, Anil a pace behind him.

Suddenly, the monkeys erupted into piercing screams. Some leapt down, surrounding the guards and rushing at them in mock attack. The others shook the branches, raining ripe tamarinds down on the ground. The guards were startled and began to run for the protection of the guardhouse with the monkeys in pursuit, spitting and snarling at their heels.

Kim and Anil raced for the wall where the three monkeys were sitting. He saw them staring down at him and he expected that at any moment they would run away. Instead, just as in the game they'd played, two held on to the top of the wall and lowered themselves down. Kim pushed Anil ahead of him.

'Take hold of their hands. Quickly.'

Anil was too surprised to move until Kim pushed him against the wall. He lifted his hands and the monkeys grabbed hold and heaved him to the top. They lowered themselves again. Kim looked back. The guards had regrouped. The monkeys were retreating from the flailing lathis. Kim grabbed the hands stretched down to him and was astonished at the strength of their grip. Almost without effort they lifted him off the ground and up to the top of the wall. Anil was sprawled in a ditch on the other side. The three monkeys loped away along the wall. The guards were now running towards him, waving their lathis, while others ran to the distant gate. Someone began to beat the rail, setting up a deafening clang. Kim dropped down to the other side and rolled into the filthy ditch.

There was no sign of Narain, no tonga. They stood, undecided.

'What now?' Anil was still dazed by the swiftness of his escape and, like any prisoner, was wary of the world outside. He had lived too long in confinement.

'Run. What else?'

They tore up the road, scattering passers-by, knocking over women carrying firewood, trampling fresh vegetables ranged on the ground for sale. They could hear pursuit behind them, the nearing drum of a pony's hooves. Kim glanced back. Narain was leaning out of a tonga, yelling at him, and behind him came the guards, two of them carrying rifles. The tonga didn't slow down when it drew level with Kim and Anil. Kim fell back a step to allow Narain to grab Anil's hand and haul him into the tonga. The gap began to widen and Kim ran harder, first touching Narain's fingers, then managing to grasp his wrist. He was dragged a few feet, then felt himself pulled in. Two shots whined past and the tonga careened around a curve in the road.

'You didn't tell me which wall,' Narain grumbled,

almost as breathless as Kim. He looked down at Anil. 'Who is he?'

'Anil Ray.'

'Ahre . . . ahre. A terrorist. Now when the Colonel sahib catches us he'll hang us all.'

30

ELIZABETH KNEW this might be the last time she saw the sea from an Indian shore. The natives called it kala pani. Black water. It was a strange description of something that was many shades of blue; almost pale green near the shoreline, darker further out, and in between, the gradual variations which could be seen clearly even from the beach. Each shade of blue had a boundary straight as a drawn line, and on a calm day the colours stayed within these borders. At night the sea glowed with phosphorescence and turned a silvery green. Elizabeth supposed that on a moonless night the sea could look black, but one had to squint to imagine midnight-blue as black. For a people with such a riotous sense of colour on land, in their dress and in the natural vegetation, they were oddly colour-blind about the sea. To her English eyes it was never black. Black implied evil. Death and plague were black. The low castes were black. Then she thought: because we came across the sea, to their eyes our touch has turned the water black. Also because their sons have crossed it and returned changed. The sea transformed old to new and filled them with a sense of dread.

The gharri moved at a stately pace around the curve of the bay towards Malabar Hill. The beach was achingly white, dotted here and there with fishermen mending frail nets and boats. Thatched huts huddled at the far corner of the bay, and children and women trudged towards them along the sand with empty fish baskets, having sold the morning catch in Crawford Market.

She'd not realised that Malabar Hill was this far from Bombay proper. Each time she looked out from under her parasol the green hill, dotted with white bungalows, seemed just as far away. But eventually they were creeping up the winding slopes in the shade, and the sea was hidden from view by banyans and peepuls, mango groves and tamarind trees. She wasn't sure what to expect of her mother's home. Probably a kutcha building, like the railway quarters of the chi-chis. She imagined grubby children and old servants and tinder on the drive, and felt almost disappointed when the gharri drew to a halt in front of a neat little bungalow set in a cool garden, shaded by a rain-tree that had scattered a carpet of pink flowers along the path. Her arrival had been noticed. A servant woman opened the door at the first knock and Elizabeth was ushered into a drawing-room. The walls were lined with books; newspapers and magazines lay scattered on tables and chairs. A busy place that looked lived in, with a bustle of intellect that felt alien to Elizabeth. She'd not yet thought about Alice's work. No woman she knew in India worked for a living. She couldn't imagine herself working at anything. Elizabeth sat sullenly, showing little curiosity for the books. She flicked through unfamiliar periodicals – the *Manchester Guardian*, the *New York Herald Tribune*, *The Spectator*, the *New Yorker* – and tossed them aside. They smelt musty.

'What a lovely surprise.' Alice swept in, spectacles perched on her nose, shapeless in a working frock. She immediately hugged Elizabeth, thawing the shyness a bit. 'I thought I'd never see you again.'

'I did go to the Great Eastern Hotel that day, but you'd gone.'

'A dear friend of mine is missing. She used to live here with me and it was my fault that she had to go to Allahabad instead of me. I rushed there to try to find her.'

Alice was deeply worried about Mohini. She'd received a telegram from Romesh – MOHINI DISAPPEARED

STOP SUSPECT HUSBAND STOP – and had immediately left Calcutta for Allahabad, though there was little she could do. Romesh and Motilal Nehru had filed a complaint with the police about Mohini's disappearance, but no one had seen her leave the Congress meeting. Being a woman, the English superintendent suggested, Mohini had probably decided to return to her lawful husband. Alice and Romesh had taken the train to Delhi and Bahadhur sahib's house, where Alice left a note asking Bahadhur sahib to get in touch with her immediately. She never received a reply. The Inspector General of Police acknowledged her enquiry curtly and promised an investigation. Since then, silence. Alice wished she could tell her daughter about Mohini, but suspected Elizabeth would not be sympathetic. She was too distant from the natives to feel any compassion.

'I came because I'm leaving for home tomorrow.'

'I'm sorry. I'd hoped we could have come to know each other better. There is something I must give you.' Alice left the room, returned with the letter she'd written to her daughter and gave it to her. 'I'd like you to read this. I've tried to explain as best I can what happened in the past.'

Elizabeth held the letter, feeling the weight of it.

'Can I read it now?'

'It can wait. I'd prefer just to talk now. Would you like a cup of tea first?'

'No, thank you . . .' Elizabeth still wasn't sure how she should address Alice, and let the sentence hang in the air.

'I know,' Alice said intuitively. 'What can you call me? Try "Alice", if you like. Did you talk to your father after my visit?'

'Yes.'

'And?' Alice prompted. 'I don't want you to condemn him in front of me. That would be unfair. All I want to know is whether he explained anything.'

'He said you betrayed him, betrayed us.'

'Yes, I suppose he would see it in that light, rather

than a question of happiness or sadness. Very military, very imperial. Loyalty and betrayal.'

'But in the beginning did you love each other? He wouldn't say. He treats me as though I'm still a child and can't understand these things.'

'I believe we did. We had certain passions in common, I thought. He was young and handsome and loved this country and I fell in love with the romance in him. Do you understand? I had come out to India full of excitement, but then he drained it out of me. I explained all this in my letter. As a woman, he expected me to have no sexual longings either, and after your birth he wouldn't come near me. I turned to another man for comfort, and in that comfort I found love.'

'I think I understand,' Elizabeth said slowly. 'I have these feelings sometimes, but I also feel they're wrong.'

'They're not wrong. They're natural, but we have to smother them. Just as we've been made to believe that marriage and a husband are necessary for our existence and fulfilment. Without them, we're told, we're useless. What they don't tell us is that we lose our own lives in husbands and marriages. I learned that I can live alone and be content. Most women can't.'

'I wish . . . I wish I'd known you earlier.'

'It's not too late.'

'It is. I'm leaving.' She wanted to bare her heart to her mother but she didn't know how. On the one hand, she felt the warm affection, the intellect, the fierce independence that would certainly have estranged Alice from her husband. On the other, Alice was a stranger, a stranger she'd possibly never see again unless she returned to India. Yet there is sometimes comfort in strangers.

'There is a man I'm in love with,' said Elizabeth. 'We've been conducting a love affair. Quite suddenly he disappeared and I don't know where he is now. Oh God, I miss him so much.'

Elizabeth began to cry and felt Alice's arms around her and found her head resting on Alice's shoulder. She had needed this comforting all her life, and she wished she could drown in Alice's warmth. Finally she sat up straight, dabbing at her eyes and blowing her nose.

'I'm sorry about that.'

'No. I am,' Alice said bitterly. 'Deeply sorry. Who is he? Is he kind to you?'

Elizabeth couldn't answer truthfully. Were men expected to be kind? Her father could be, but only in such an impersonal way.

'Sometimes. He has money of his own. I don't know who his people are or what he does, but I feel I'll find him in England. I know I will.'

'Write to me then, and tell me. I'll wait for your letters. And if there's anything I can do, just ask me. When will you come back again?'

'I'm not sure that I want to. With Richard dead, I can't live with Father any more, not after his deception.'

'He is a master at that.' Alice studied her daughter, the mirror of her own youth. 'I think you will return. You're like me in many ways, though I think you'll discover that for yourself. Will you visit my parents? My father's retired now, but he'd love to meet his granddaughter.' When Elizabeth nodded, Alice scribbled her father's address on the envelope. 'Give him my love.'

'Won't you ever go home?'

'No. This is where I want to die, and once you know that, you know where home really is.' She patted Elizabeth's hand and held on to it. 'Tell me all about this man you're in love with.'

The dusty sunlight fell between them, and as Elizabeth talked the room grew dimmer. Alice's heart sank as she heard about Peter Bayley and she wanted to cry out a warning. She saw the elation in her daughter's eyes, but felt in her heart the doom of Elizabeth's loving this man. And when Elizabeth fell silent, Alice kept hold of her daughter's hand, trying to communicate her fears.

'Be careful,' she began.

'Everyone says that. But he's so exciting and I love him. Please don't spoil it by telling me to stop loving him. I can't. You should understand that.'

'I do understand, but I also know the pain.'

'I must go now,' Elizabeth said. 'Will you come to see the boat off?'

'I don't think that would be wise.'

They walked out into the warm evening with the sea breeze ruffling the branches of the trees and the smell of the sea strong in their nostrils. The gharri waited. Alice hugged Elizabeth and kissed her before helping her in.

'Promise me you will write.'

'I promise . . . Mother.'

Alice watched the gharri until it was out of sight, nearly overcome by the sadness of this parting. Alice wasn't a believer in God, but she prayed mightily that God would guide her daughter in this search for her lover and bring her back to India one day.

The Colonel listened to Isaac Newton's report. Newton wore the same best suit and tie, the same shoes, carried the same briefcase. He felt, as usual, uncomfortable in his clothing, and clutched at an ebony walking-stick. The Colonel's unblinking stare never left his face. It was difficult to avoid the look since Newton had to stand at the door of the gharri, looking in. The Colonel was resplendent in full mess kit this evening, with a starched white shirt, and all his decorations.

'She went to see a memsahib. Soames memsahib,' Newton said. 'Then she went back to Government House, and since has stayed in her room.'

'I want you to keep an eye on this memsahib. Can you get anyone into her house?'

'She has a very poor household, Colonel sahib. One servant to cook and clean, one mali. The mali is an old man. Possibly he will fall ill and I could get a new one to work there.'

'What about the Nairoji organisation?'

'There is a writer working there who has been of great help to me.'

'In which case that should be enough. But I want regular reports on Soames memsahib, whom she sees, her friends, visitors? Do you understand?'

'Yes, Colonel sahib.' Newton slowly exhaled. The Colonel had fallen silent. It was time for Newton to go. There was important work to be done on his new invention. It was nearly perfect: a bicycle with a motor. It would be cheap to make, cheap to run, and it would benefit his countrymen who had to walk everywhere.

'Have you heard from Narain?'

'No, Colonel sahib.' Newton squirmed. It was the one question he'd wanted to avoid. He felt stripped by those eyes; they were cold, angry.

'He has disappeared. The police have been told to watch for him.'

'Colonel sahib, Narain is a very trustworthy man. He will tell me where Kim and that badmash are at the earliest opportunity. I would stake my life on his loyalty.'

'A reckless bet, Newton. Never gamble on a man. Or a woman. You'll always lose. Where would he go?'

'Where Kim goes, Narain will go. He is a true friend to the "friend of all the world".'

'I believe I know where Kim will make for,' the Colonel said, and Newton heard an edge in his voice that was sharp enough to cut a throat.

Newton salaam'd the Colonel, lifting his pressed palms above his head so that the Colonel could see the gesture. He picked up his briefcase and his ebony cane and purposefully strode down Church Gate Street towards the railway station and the rickshaw rank. However, once he turned round the corner, Newton peeped back. The gharri hadn't moved and Newton took up a position in the shadow of a paan-wallah.

He was intensely worried about Narain and Kim. They'd made the Colonel sahib angry and that was dangerous. If only he knew where they were, then he could warn them. The Colonel seemed to know, and

Newton, in spite of his worry, marvelled at the Colonel's ability to unearth all secrets. Newton wasn't sure why he was skulking there, spying on his revered superior who, should he be aware of this insubordination, would undoubtedly sack him without notice – or pension. The Colonel had, unusually for him, asked Newton to meet his gharri at Church Gate. Normally Newton reported to him in Government House. *Ipso facto*, Newton reasoned, Colonel sahib plans to meet another person. But curiosity can also kill the cat, and since I suspect hanky-panky, this cat must be extremely cautious, Colonel sahib being a tiger.

The man for whom the Colonel waited passed within a foot of Newton as he was stuffing a pinch of snuff up his right nostril. Newton had seen him cross the street, moving in the shadows, giving the impression of a man on an evening stroll. But before he crossed he glanced briefly at the gharri. Newton, whose eyes could spot a tiny flaw in a diamond, noticed. The man was middle-aged, stocky yet quick. He pads like a cat, Newton thought. Head turning this way, then that. He saw him halt by the gharri, exactly where he himself had stood. The conversation was brief. The man withdrew, not salaaming in the same obsequious manner as Newton, and joined the flow of people to the railway station. Newton gripped his ebony cane and followed him.

The gharri took the Colonel to the Viceroy's residence. It glowed with lights and the warm air was filled with the soft strains of music. Carriages lined the long drive, waiting to deposit their occupants. At the wrought-iron gates stood Imperial bodyguards, two on foot, two on horseback. The residence was a huge neo-classical house with four massive pillars flanking the stately entrance. The Colonel moved quickly through the elegant crowd, mostly Europeans with a sprinkling of Indians. The reception-rooms were all lit and bearers passed through the crowd with silver trays of drinks.

The Viceroy's ADC opened the door to a private reception-room and the Colonel joined the other guests.

444

The farewell dinner was less grand than Lord Curzon's had been: Minto had never been as formal as his predecessor. Lord Minto sat at the head of the table, Lady Minto at the foot, and all round the table the men who ran the country expressed their regret at the departure of the Viceroy, in marked contrast to their delight at Curzon's going. Although Lord Minto had allowed through just a few reforms, forced down his throat by the Secretary of State for India in London, Mr Morley, no power had changed hands. He had ranged with the men who ruled India and opposed as subtly as possible the demands of London. Minto was delighted to have fulfilled his ambition to be Viceroy of India. His ambition had also been to leave the country in a peaceful and stable state, and, with the help of men like the Colonel, he had succeeded.

'Be damned dull back in England, I tell you. I've had a splendid time out here. I'm going to leave this country and all of you with deep, deep regret. We've all worked well together as a team and because of you all, and your advice and help, I shall be leaving a part of the Empire that hasn't changed. I'm sure you will keep India loyal to the Crown as long as you live. I want to thank everyone for making my term of office such a pleasure.' He stood up and raised his glass to the portrait of the King. A new portrait. Edward VII had died in May that year, and Prince George was king. The others rose too, and turned to face the dark oil-painting framed in heavy gilt. 'The King-Emperor.'

When the ladies left the gentlemen to their brandy and cigars, the men drew up their chairs close to Lord Minto. A bearer remained standing behind each chair and the conversation became softly reminiscent. They talked of the past five years, the pleasure of serving the Viceroy, the steeplechases, the balls, the shooting-camps. There was an atmosphere of satisfaction in the elegant, high-ceilinged dining-room.

Lord Minto rose and beckoned the Colonel to join him away from the others. They stood at the window, looking out at the lights of Bombay glowing along the shoreline, and the ships looked like a chain of lights on the horizon.

'Colonel, I must thank you especially for your help and guidance during my term. Without you, I might have bungled a few things. We might have opened a Pandora's box if too many of London's reforms had been pushed through at once.'

'I quite agree, Your Excellency. They don't understand India in London, and I have indeed been fortunate to serve a man who does. The native isn't ready for political power yet. That's going to take many, many years. Congress will soon disintegrate. It's leaderless, rudderless. It's only a matter of time before it dissolves completely.'

'Thanks to you. Just between ourselves – I have strongly recommended you for a knighthood in the next Birthday Honours List. I can't guarantee it, mind, but usually the Palace does follow up these suggestions.'

The Colonel bowed with pleasure. He had long contemplated this award. Now it was definite. His eyes were moist. He would readily have given his life for the Empire.

'Thank you, Your Excellency. I have served India and the Crown as loyally as any man could. It would indeed be an honour to receive a knighthood, but it has been satisfaction enough just to serve the Empire.'

'Good, good. You deserve it. Well, we'd better rejoin the others. I must make my farewells.' He blew his nose. 'I hate goodbyes. Hate them.'

Elizabeth made an effort to appear her usual self at the Viceroy's farewell. She was excited and impatient, though a little sad at leaving. By this time tomorrow she would be far out to sea, watching the lights of Bombay fade away. Her high emotional state had lent her beauty an added lustre, and most of the men paid her effusive compliments. They kissed her hand, one or two even her cheek. She laughed in delight. The party was a whirl of familiar faces, hugs and kisses. Promises to write, promises to visit those who'd soon be home, promises

446

to look up friends and relations. Never, however, a promise to return. The farewell was exactly as she'd imagined it would be. She wore a silk ball dress, the last to be made by Mrs Pereira in Calcutta, who would sorely miss her patronage. The frothy dress just revealed the tops of her breasts. It was a delicate shade of eau-de-nil, with a bow at the back. Her only jewellery was a pearl necklace which had once belonged to the Rani of Jhansi, and the peacock brooch which Peter had given her. She wore it on every possible occasion. With the intuition of a lover, she knew she would see him again soon. He would find her, and she him.

She looked for her father, but couldn't see him in the crowd and so joined a line waiting to say goodbye to the Viceroy, who stood at the far end of the room. She chatted to Mrs Mitford and her daughter as they inched along. She felt a real end had come. Viceroy after Viceroy had been welcomed to India and been wished farewell on his departure. They were the power of England, but still only temporary figures who sailed away again. It seemed only yesterday that she'd danced at the farewell ball for Lord Curzon in Simla, and had then met Peter in Bombay on the day Lord Minto became Viceroy. Now she too was leaving.

When she finally reached the Viceroy and Vicereine, Lady Minto pecked her cheek and the Viceroy shook her hand warmly.

'You're looking exceptionally lovely, my dear, exceptionally.'

'Thank you, Your Excellency.'

'I believe we're sailing on the same boat. Your father asked me to keep an eye on you, m'dear, so I've arranged for you to sit at our table.'

'Thank you, Your Excellency. I look forward to that. May I wish you *bon voyage*?'

'We will wish each other *bon voyage*, Miss Creighton.'

Elizabeth could have talked and danced until her boat sailed. Familiar faces swam out of the crowd. She hadn't seen the Bowens for years, not since her childhood.

They were down on leave from Kashmir and were most disappointed that Elizabeth was leaving India just as they renewed their acquaintance. They introduced her to Sir Reginald Whittaker, an authority on the flora and fauna of the Lower Himalayas. He took up her precious time droning on about his next volume, this one on the middle Himalayan regions.

She was suddenly distracted by a glimpse of her father in the huge gilt-framed mirror hanging on the wall. He had his back to a pillar and was watching her. No, not watching, Elizabeth realised. He was studying her intently as though . . . as though she were a total stranger, someone under suspicion. His hooded eyes looked calculating, weighing her up, and she felt a faint shiver. She turned rudely away from Sir Reginald to face her father, but even in that swift movement his face had changed. He smiled at her and at this distance she wasn't sure whether it rose from affection or to conceal his thoughts.

Elizabeth crossed the floor to him and the smile broadened and she was grateful now to see that it was affectionate. He put out his hands and took hers.

'Had enough?'

'I could spend all night here but I think you must be tired. We'll go home.'

It was much cooler outside and she draped her wrap loosely around her shoulders. The lights reflected like tiny stars on the shining buckles and buttons and lance tips of the Imperial bodyguards. They were still as statues, tall and muscular with their neatly trimmed black beards and curling moustaches. She took a last lingering look at these men, drawn from the remote villages of India and trained to be soldiers for the Empire.

Elizabeth and her father would have swept down the broad steps but two men moved out of the shadows. Their clothes were slightly crumpled, and they gave the impression they'd been waiting for some time. One was an Englishman with a shiny bald head that gleamed in the harsh verandah lights, the other an Indian, a young man, slim and whippy. She knew instinctively they were policemen. They had that patient air of authority, and secretive eyes, bland yet watchful. The Englishman's eyes flicked down to her breast and back up to her face. It was not meant to be noticed but Elizabeth knew it had been a deliberate movement and raised her hand protectively. Her fingers touched Peter's brooch.

'Excuse me, my dear,' her father said and left her side to join the two men. All three now moved back into the shadows and their whispers sounded like the splash of a distant stream. Then her father's voice became distinct. 'Are you sure?' A murmured reply. 'Then I would like to meet him. Of course.'

Her father rejoined her as the two men walked quickly down the steps. He took her arm and followed them.

'What do they want?'

The Colonel immediately noted Elizabeth hadn't asked the natural question 'Who are they?' She knew that and he grudgingly admired her acute observation.

'They think they might have some clue as to the whereabouts of your friend, Mr Bayley.'

'They do?' Elizabeth couldn't disguise her excitement. 'Where is he?'

'Well, not him specifically,' the Colonel said. 'His bearer, Rao. He was arrested for possessing stolen property.'

'Ohh!'

Her flush subsided and he heard the tiny sigh of disappointment. She was transparent, innocently vulnerable, and he felt a pang of remorse that he planned to use her to find Peter Bayley. The man was under suspicion although as yet the Colonel wasn't certain for what. Bayley made him uneasy, his past was too vague and uncertain, as though it had been conjured up out of books. Once Elizabeth reached England, either she would find him or Bayley would find her. The Colonel had deliberately requested Superintendent Mitchell of the CID to await them on the verandah. He'd wanted Elizabeth to witness their conversation.

'Can I meet Rao?'

'He's in Central Gaol and I wouldn't advise it.' He paused as though a thought had occurred to him, but he kept her waiting until they were seated in their carriage. 'If you like I could question the man. He may possibly have some word on Mr Bayley.'

'Could you please, Father.' Elizabeth hadn't ever wanted to ask her father a favour but she couldn't help herself. This was an exception in their relationship. She had to find some clue whether Peter was alive. Or dead.

They followed the superintendent's carriage through the dark and almost deserted streets. There was a three-quarter moon, fixed like a lamp in the clear sky, and the city was brushed with pale silver. She was glad of this moon. She remembered in England she scarcely ever saw it, but this memory, of the light on the buildings and trees, and the people sleeping on the streets, would always be with her. The air was still perfumed with lingering wood-smoke blended with the odour of the sea. They stopped finally and Elizabeth peered out at a high white wall bright enough to dazzle her eyes. Beyond lay the prison.

'I'll be back in five minutes, my dear,' the Colonel said and followed the policemen through the small door inset into the massive wooden gate.

The Colonel did want to meet Rao and he waited in the interview room with Superintendent Mitchell while his assistant went to fetch the man from the cells. Mitchell offered a cigarette to the Colonel, who refused and gave him permission to light up. The room smelt, not of damp, but of suspicion – an odour of sweat and blood and cigarette smoke. It was badly lit and full of shadows. The only furnishings were a table, two chairs and a stained bench.

'He's a stubborn fellow. We've questioned him and I think he's protecting this Mr Bayley.'

'I'm sure you've done a good job,' the Colonel placated the superintendent. 'I'd just like to ask him a question

or two. You have sent the telegram to London for someone to meet the boat?'

'Yes, sir. I included a detailed description of the young
lady as well.' He wondered whether the daughter knew
she was to be the stalking-horse. He doubted it. She
would be the tethered goat, awaiting the predator, while
the Colonel hid above in the trees waiting to take a shot.
The superintendent had never been on a tiger-hunt but
he knew for certain he wouldn't want to be hunted by
the Colonel. The man was a chilling force, cruel in his
own way. Always calculating.

Rao was escorted by two gaolers. His hands were
manacled and he stood stoically in the room, looking at
neither man but at a point somewhere behind them. The
ruby in his eyes had faded and he shivered, not from
the cold but from his need for arrack.

'Rao, do you know a Miss Creighton?' the Colonel
asked.

Those faded red eyes focused gradually on the
Colonel's face, seeing it for the first time.

'Yes, sahib.'

'She visited Mr Bayley?'

'Yes, sahib.' Rao smiled maliciously. 'Often.'

'I see.' The Colonel ignored Mitchell's unease at
this revelation. He was more interested in establishing
the truth than shielding his daughter's reputation. It
was already tarnished. 'And when they talked, you
would probably hear them while you were serving
them.'

'Yes, sahib.'

'Did he ever mention meeting Miss Creighton in
London?'

'I didn't hear everything they said, sahib. I wasn't
present all of the time. Not when they withdrew.'

'But while you were there?'

'No, sahib. I never heard them mentioning any place
in London.'

'What did Mr Bayley do to earn his living?'

'I do not know, sahib.'

451

'You must have some idea, Rao,' the Colonel said softly. 'After all, you travelled with him around the country. Have a guess.'

'Business,' Rao said. 'He met men on business.'

'What business?'

'I don't know, sahib. He never talked to me about his business. He did once say he came from a rich family and that it amused him to do this business.'

'Did he buy and sell? Did he fill an order book?'

'I don't know, sahib.' Rao stared the Colonel in the eye and didn't flinch. There was a strange courage in the man. He wasn't afraid of any consequences and the Colonel knew it wouldn't be possible to break him down. His loyalty to Bayley was almost admirable. The Colonel waved him away and the warders marched Rao out of the interview room.

Elizabeth allowed her father to settle back in his seat in the carriage. She knew better than to press him. He would choose his time to speak. Her father always knew the right time to utter a word. Or not. They drove along in this expectant silence and Elizabeth wanted to scream at him. She clenched her fists to control the impulse. If she spoke first, it gave her father the advantage in this game.

'Rao mentioned that Mr Bayley has returned to London and that he's staying at . . .' The Colonel tapped his temple in forgetfulness.

Elizabeth knew her father never forgot. Except when it was convenient, and she waited. She smiled then.

'Dover Street?'

'That's it,' her father said. 'Dover Street.'

And Elizabeth knew that whatever her father now said would be fabricated for her deception. But he had confirmed her belief that Peter Bayley was alive.

Now that Elizabeth was certain she would find Peter, she was even more impatient. She couldn't sleep at all for the excitement and rose in the pre-dawn gloom to stand on the balcony. The city was quiet and still, the air cool, and the sea was as dark as the land. Both gradually lightened into blue and brown as the sky turned a delicate yellow colour. This would be her last Indian dawn and she was suddenly flooded by memories of dawns in the mountains, on the plains and deserts, in the jungles and villages and cities. Her life rushed past, woven round Richard, her father, countless friends, Peter . . . She would miss . . . she would miss it all.

Mary ayah had got her bath ready. Mary ayah's eyes were red and her face drawn. She'd wept almost continually since hearing that her baba was leaving her again. Not India: *her*. She pleaded, begged, to be allowed to go with her across the kala pani, not understanding the distance or the different life in England. Elizabeth had first been kind, then impatient at her endless tears. Her father had promised to keep Mary ayah in employ until she returned, as they all believed she would. They held on to that hope, but Elizabeth avoided making any promise. If Mary ayah wanted to take up another position looking after a European child, the Colonel had promised her an excellent chit, and so did Elizabeth. But Mary ayah swore she'd never leave.

Elizabeth joined her father for breakfast on the lawn. He looked resolutely cheerful, but she noted a tinge of sadness in his eyes. Even though she'd vowed not to say much, she did bend to kiss him, savouring his familiar smell. He clutched her hand for a moment, and released it.

'All packed?'

'Yes. They took the heavy luggage yesterday. There's only the cabin trunk and a dressing-case.' She felt a surge of affection. With goodbye came forgiveness. He would be alone now. 'You'll be all right, won't you, Father?'

'Of course. Always busy. Have you got all the papers for the bank, about your allowance?'

'They're in my dressing-case. You ought to take your Home leave, Father. Everybody else does.'

'They have people to go to, homes, too. I've none. This is my home. When I retire, I might go then.'

His words reminded her of Alice's. Wherever you wanted to die was home. Her father would die here, go to another grave, a thousand miles from Rawalpindi and Richard. Ironically, so would Alice. They were bound by their love for India, though the love was different. Where would she be in death?

The dock was crowded. The P&O liner *Stratheden* towered above them, its sheer sides white as the beach. There were three gangplanks. The special one for the Viceroy was flanked by a Guard of Honour. A massed band of the Indian Army was playing, adding to the noise and confusion. Elizabeth mounted the second gangplank, accompanied by her father, her friend Sarah, Mary ayah and two coolies. The third gangplank was for the third-class and steerage passengers, a few of whom were young Indians going abroad to study, followed by weeping relatives and smothered with rose garlands.

A helpful steward led them along corridors which smelled of paint and seawater and varnish, past ball-rooms, dining-rooms, card-rooms and bars. Her cabin was on the starboard side.

'Oh, Lil. This is super!' Sarah said, and she laughed, rushing to look out of the porthole. The cabin was simply furnished, with a bed and a dressing-table, and had its own bathroom. It was cosy and compact. The steward was impressed when he discovered that she would be sitting at Lord Minto's table, though Minto, the moment he stepped on board, would be shorn of all prestige. He was no longer Viceroy of India, but merely another Englishman.

As noon approached, the first bell sounded for visitors to go ashore. Sarah said goodbye, and Elizabeth clung to her and heard her whisper, 'I pray you will see him again.'

'I must, now,' Elizabeth whispered back.

Then only her father and Mary ayah were left. He sat

in silence; Mary ayah wept, squatting on the floor.

'Why don't we go up on deck? Come on, Mary ayah.'

She followed them mutely. Elizabeth hardly noticed her misery, there were so many people to meet, things to see. Above all, she would be travelling towards Peter. When the final bell rang, she hugged and kissed her father and Mary ayah who, as she feared, broke into a fresh paroxysm of tears and prostrated herself on the deck to lay her head on Elizabeth's feet. Elizabeth was embarrassed. Her father gently lifted Mary ayah up and, after giving Elizabeth one last peck, they slowly made their way down the gangplank.

Tugs pulled the liner away from the dock and Elizabeth could see her father and Mary ayah gradually diminish until they became part of a blur of waving people. The band played 'Auld Lang Syne', and soon the notes faded. She saw Malabar Hill and the white homes in between the trees. She wondered whether her mother was standing in the garden to watch the ship depart. Elizabeth remained at the rail until the brown coastline sank from sight and suddenly felt a strange certainty that she would one day return to India.

31

THE POLICE watched Anil Ray's home. They weren't
visible; five men in plain clothes who came as mourners.
Two were armed with revolvers hidden beneath their
kurtas. Freshly bathed, wearing new clothes, they sat
with the others in the wood-panelled hall. A chandelier
hung from the ceiling, but otherwise it was bare of
furnishing. The floor was covered with dharris. Mr Ray's
wife's brother, now the male elder of the Ray household,
received them, not knowing who they were. They took
his offering of fruit juice and metais, and settled themselves on the dharri. The house felt as though the death
had taken place a long time ago. It was silent, unused
to movement. The mourners felt as though they had
entered a recently excavated tomb where life had once
been vibrant.

Many of the relations had come from in and around
Calcutta, a few from further away. The men gathered in
the main hall; the female relatives and friends in other
rooms. Children played in the garden. No one mentioned Anil's name, though he lingered like dust in their
memories. He too was dead, though in a different way.
Mr Ray had died of a wasting illness, life had become
pointless. It was a broken heart, they all murmured to
each other, knowing how unbearable this pain could be.
The policemen also wisely agreed, though they scrutinised every male who came to pay his last respects.

Anil Ray sat in the dust outside his own home and
watched the five policemen walk past him without a
glance. His home was near, yet he hovered outside in a

dream. He knew he couldn't enter. He could never walk up the drive, never stroll in the garden, never lie in his own room, never be embraced by his father. He had sensed death in the silence of the house even as he'd approached, and had immediately prostrated himself in front of his home, as he would have done at his father's feet. Then he'd smeared his face and body with the dust of the street his father usually walked on. He had no tears. He kept his vigil, knowing he'd failed in his duty as a son. As a son, he should have received the mourners. As a son, he should have poured a handful of Ganges water into his dead father's parched mouth. As a son, he should have lit the funeral pyre. As a son, he should have recited the vedas while the flames consumed his father's body. Now his father's atman would have no peace.

His appearance was appropriate to his sad thoughts. He had been shaved bald and his face was smooth. Even as the disguise had been fashioned by a roadside barber in Delhi, Anil had had a premonition of death. It was an act of penitence among Hindus for the son to be shorn, laying aside vanity in the face of death. He wore an ochre robe and carried a begging bowl and staff. His own servants, his own cousins whom he'd played with as children in that garden, had passed and not recognised the emaciated pilgrim.

Anil stayed in a squatting position all day, facing the house. He watched the comings and goings, old friends moving about on the lawn deep in conversation, their lives so normal. He saw also the five policemen come out and, seeing their searching looks at all the men, knew who they were. They came to stand near him on the roadside, consulted among themselves for a minute, then three left. The remaining two faded back into the shadows of a mango tree.

He ignored them, as they did him. Instead, he concentrated on recalling the happy days of his childhood. He'd had his very own small gharri and pony, and had raced it in the garden. Beyond that hedge was a cricket pitch, where he'd first learned to play the game, coached by his uncle. There, on that bench, he'd sat in his father's lap and had listened to stories. There, on the terrace, his mother had placed him as a baby, out in the warm sun, shiny with mustard oil after his bath. He was comforted by those memories. Countless little images jostled in his mind like the shreds of a woman's colourful sari.

Suddenly he saw Sushila, walking with the other women in the garden. How graceful and beautiful she looked. He wanted to call out to his cousin, but clenched his teeth. As children, Sushila and he had built a tree-house and had spent hours playing contentedly together. She'd visited him at school in England, with her brother, and he'd been proud of her beauty. He remembered promising to marry her, but because she was a little older than him she'd been married off before he went to Oxford. When he returned home, his mother had already chosen his bride. He wondered vaguely what had happened to that girl. Doubtless her parents had hastily chosen a more eligible groom.

Then what he'd feared most, happened. He was recognised, not by a servant, not even by Sushila Basu who rode past him in her gharri without giving the pilgrim a glance. Bhima recognised him. The old dog, a cross between a fox-terrier and a pi, its muzzle almost white, shuffled out of the garden to explore the street and caught his scent. He growled first, and then, tail wagging furiously, came running over to lick Anil's face. Five years earlier, when he'd returned from abroad, the dog had remembered him immediately and raced around the garden in delirious joy.

'Go away, Bhima. Go. Go.'

But the dog didn't understand and licked the dust from his master's face, rolling over to have his belly scratched. Anil had meant to keep his vigil all night, but now he hastily rose and, without looking in the direction of the policemen, strode down the road with Bhima at his heels. He walked quickly until he was out of sight and then knelt down to hug the dog. In all his years in prison he'd not thought once of Bhima, but now he wet the dog's head with tears.

'Go now, go home. I'll come back. One day. Go, Bhima.'

Bhima was reluctant to move and whined plaintively. Anil turned away, picked up a pebble and threw it at the dog. When he looked back, Bhima was still sitting there.

Anil waited outside Sushila's house until nightfall. It looked deserted except for a solitary glow from a side window. He would have expected her to be away if he hadn't seen her at his house. He had not noticed her husband, but could have missed him among the mourners. They'd met once, at his welcome-home party, which more than three hundred friends and cousins had attended. Anil could not remember him well.

Anil crept along the shadows towards the window. It was as silent as his own home and he strained for the sound of voices: children, servants, Sushila herself, but heard only crickets and cicadas so loud that they deafened him. He glanced through the lit window and thought the room empty, then saw Sushila lying on the divan, reading. There wasn't a servant in sight, or a child. He had thought by now that she would have been a mother.

'Sushila.' His whisper wasn't heard, and he repeated her name a little louder. She dropped her book and looked at the window.

'Who is it?'

'Sushila. Come here.'

She hesitated, then came forward cautiously.

'Who is it?'

'Anil.'

'Anil! Are you all right? My God, what are you doing here? The police told us you had escaped.'

'Stop talking and please let me in. Where's the door?'

'At the side.'

Wisely, she didn't put on any more lights. He slipped past her and waited until she had re-bolted the door, then followed her back to the room. She drew the curtains, and Anil stepped into the light.

'Oh God, what have they done to you?'

She began to cry and he stood for a while awkwardly, before putting down his begging bowl on the table and comforting her. She couldn't stop her tears and, as though he were her father, he stroked her head. How long was it since he'd last held a woman in his arms? He had only dim memories of his days in England and of girls in Oxford, could scarcely remember Mavis, his landlady's daughter who would creep up to his rooms at night. Sushila was supple, warm, real, not a ghostly memory. Abruptly he stepped back.

'You must be hungry, and here I am, crying away.' She wiped her face with the edge of her sari.

'Where is your husband?'

'Where he always is, on his estate. Drunk, no doubt. I'll get you some food. There's no hot water, I'm afraid, and the servants have gone to bed.'

'Hot water is a luxury I've long forgotten about. Do you have any whisky?'

'Yes. My husband always leaves an ample supply.' He heard bitterness in her tone. 'You should be able to wear his clothes, too, though they'll be loose on you.'

Anil washed himself in cold water and put on her husband's pi-jama and kurta. The good sensation of clean clothes was another long-ago memory. Sushila had left the whisky and a glass on the table. It burnt his throat, bringing tears to his eyes. The first glass made him light-headed and he poured another. He was tired and longed for a deep sleep from which he need never wake. Sushila returned with a cold meal and fruit. He ate ravenously.

'I'm sorry you came too late. Your father died calling for you, I'm told. I wasn't there.'

'When was the funeral?'

'Only yesterday evening. How did you escape from the prison?'

460

'Ironically, it was an Angrezi who helped me. This disguise was his suggestion. He was in prison too, but much more privileged. He was an Imperial Agent, turning, I suspect, against his masters. We were helped by a tribe of monkeys. I'm still not sure whether it was by accident. And now here I am.'

Sushila couldn't believe his casual tone. He was thin as a stick, and he'd changed in another way too. Beneath that skin and bone, she could sense a terrible force – rage. He was capable of killing.

'I wish you could stay but you can't. The police will be questioning all of us soon.'

'I know. I just needed a little food, some rest and . . . If I could . . . to borrow some money. I've none. God knows when I'll be able to repay you.'

'Anil, I'll give you a slap! You can have everything I've got. What are you going to do now?'

'I have plans. Father wanted me to escape to America. I'll be safe there, far away from the British.'

'Yes, yes. You must go there at once.'

'But how long can I live in exile? Is it to be for ever? Must I die in a country not of my birth?'

'It is better to live in exile than to die in a prison here. Things will change one day.'

'When? They have an iron grip on India. We don't have the strength of mind or the strength of purpose to pry their fingers away.'

Only guns could conquer guns. His hands itched to hold one. Strangely, he remembered mocking his uncle for killing animals; now he wanted to do worse – to kill men. How could he have prevented this terrible change in himself? Life had long since spun out of control, and it was his karma to live with death. At the moment he felt too tired to get up and start his search for Goode. He had to rest, to sleep.

When he woke, refreshed from a deep sleep, he first thought he must be back in prison. The morning sun was a blur of light. He put out his hand and felt the reassuring touch of mosquito netting. The bed was in-

461

credibly soft and he wallowed in the luxury of a pillow and clean sheets before turning on his side. To his surprise, he saw Sushila asleep beside him, still in her sari. Her mass of black hair, redolent of jasmine, partly covered her face. He could only see the curve of her cheek, one closed eye, the corner of her mouth, but it was enough. He examined her minutely, taking pleasure at the serenity of a woman, and then looked down at the rise and fall of her breasts and the curve of her hip. He wanted to touch her, just to feel under his hands the sensation of a woman's skin again. His palms were damp, and the long-dormant need for a woman was bursting in his loins. He slowly, gently, turned over and away, unable to control the shiver of wanting. But he was also frightened. For five years he'd suppressed all thought of women, and now, with one so close, he couldn't imagine the intimacy. He'd been broken by prison, reduced to something less than human, and didn't believe he would ever be a man again. What woman, especially Sushila, would want him, want this wreck? Bald, emaciated, scarred. Her body would also give him false comfort, the illusion of hope when there was none for him in this world.

'Did you tire of looking at me?' Sushila whispered.

'I didn't realise you were awake. No. I could have stared at you all day.'

'It's been a long time for you, hasn't it?'

'Over five years. I'm too afraid to even try.'

'How can you be afraid of me? Turn around.'

Anil did, slowly, his heart fluttering as though a small frantic bird was trapped inside trying to escape. Sushila had brushed her hair back and a gentle smile rippled over her features. It spread down from her eyes and finally touched her mouth. She took his hand and placed the palm against her cheek, and then kissed it.

'I don't want pity.'

'It's not pity. We should have been lovers long ago. Remember when you were at Eton and I came to see you? You promised to marry me. You looked so strange

462

and foreign in those funny clothes. I said "yes" then, but we didn't really believe each other.'

'I meant it, Sushila. I was heartbroken when I heard you were married. Though I suppose our parents wouldn't have given permission anyway.'

'But we weren't determined enough. We didn't have enough strength of purpose.'

He leaned over and kissed her mouth, shocked by the incredible sweetness. The bird in him beat frantically. For a brief instant, he felt cleansed of the years of pain, the lack of love. She undid her choli and he cupped her breasts, firm and perfectly round, burying his face between them. He wanted to become a child again, sucking safely on those erect nipples. Most of all he wished to escape the world, to hide inside her. She removed his kurta and he heard her sharp intake of breath and felt her hands gently explore the scars of his beatings, now dark stains just below the surface of his skin.

She caressed him, stroked him, soothing his fears with her mouth. He began to believe in his strength, in his power as a man. The first time, their lovemaking was brief and frantic. Then they began again, more gently and calmly. He couldn't stop touching her, his bony hands trying to retain the sensation for ever. Sushila found touching Anil painful. His wounds burned her hands. He was so thin that her legs enfolded him easily. She thought of how all the promise of their young lives had gone unfulfilled. Anil was to have been brilliant and successful; she, happy and contented as a wife and mother. They'd both been cheated and there was no recompense. It was too late.

The servants never saw Anil. Sushila brought food from the kitchen and they ate like children out at a picnic. They dozed in the afternoon heat, wrapped in each other's arms. But as evening slowly drew in they became sadder and quieter. Anil knew he couldn't hide even in this vast house for much longer. The police would come eventually, a servant would talk.

He took another bath, a last glass of whisky. Sushila opened her safe and poured gold sovereigns and silver rupees into his hands. He took only enough to pay for his immediate needs.

'What about money for your passage to America?'

'I'll come back for that later.'

'You must leave now,' Sushila insisted. 'The longer you stay here, the more chance they have of finding you.'

'I can't leave until one other thing has been done.'

'Inspector Goode! Oh Anil, forget him. Your life is more precious than his. Go to America. Today.' She forced him to take the sovereigns again. 'Go overland through China and get on a boat there to America. Please listen to me, Anil. Please.'

'I can't leave. I promised Kim only that if I saw my father alive, I would spare Goode. Now I must kill him. He's the one responsible for all this misery.'

Sushila wept in frustration. Men had such stupid notions of honour and duty, even when it meant their destruction. Killing Goode wouldn't resurrect the dead, wouldn't change the past. Goode's death would only bring about Anil's own, eventually. The British would hunt him down, even in America.

When he left her that night, sliding back into the shadowy outside world, Sushila locked herself in her prayer room, lit camphor and incense, poured oil into the prayer lamp and lit the cotton wick. She performed arthi in front of Durga. She prostrated herself and passed the whole night begging God to take care of Anil.

Even if he had not known through the prison grapevine where Inspector Goode was posted, it would have been an easy matter to discover. All government appointments, whether in the IPS or the ICS, were published regularly in the *Imperial Gazette*. Inspector Goode was stationed at the police headquarters in Lucknow.

Anil went from Calcutta to Delhi. First he had to buy a gun, and he knew where to go. There was a grain

464

merchant in Chandini Chowk, opposite a metai shop on the third lane from the main road, who sold weapons. Anil had heard of him in prison. He was a thin, suspicious man and Anil had to spend an hour convincing him that he'd received the information from another convict in Tihar Gaol. At last, he was taken out to the back of the shop, and from a sack of wheat the merchant pulled out an army revolver. They bargained and in the end it cost Anil two gold sovereigns for the revolver and five rounds of ammunition. It was a service revolver; black and heavy, the butt grooved with a square pattern. Anil hid it in his begging bowl, covering it with a cloth.

He'd never been to Lucknow, and as the train approached he looked out on a low skyline punctuated by the glistening domes of mosques and palaces, and was reminded of Alexandria and Cairo. On his way home he'd disembarked at Port Said and taken the train to Cairo. For a wishful moment, he longed to be once again that formal, well-bred young man in his very British suit out sightseeing and looking with wonder at the unfamiliar skyline. Even the dhows on this river looked exactly like those on the Nile, and on the opposite bank from the train a camel caravan moved gracefully along.

He asked for directions to the police headquarters, a spacious, cream-coloured building in a large, well maintained garden. The British flag hung from a mast. Pillars flanked the doorway and an open verandah ran the whole length of the two floors. Behind them were the offices. On the ground floor, Anil could watch the comings and goings of policemen, lawyers, criminals, peons. He settled himself in the dusty street, beside a chai-wallah's hut. Constables came to lounge around the chai-wallah, not more than a few feet from Anil, taking tea and smoking beedis. One or two of them even threw a paisa into his begging bowl and he raised his hand in darshan while the other remained in the bowl, gripping the revolver.

Even though he'd learnt patience in prison, he knew he had very little time. It wouldn't take Goode long to notice the bald sunyassi. He saw Inspector Goode arrive for work. He hadn't changed much, apart from a little thickening at the waist, making his uniform tighter. Anil saw the material strain around his belly and under his arms. His moustache was still the same carroty red and he sat arrogantly upright, like a Roman general returning from conquest. His swagger-stick was tucked under his right armpit. Anil had expected him to be well guarded, but an unarmed constable drove the gharri.

Goode did not see Anil Ray on the roadside. He had received a telegram informing him of Anil Ray's escape, and his superior had suggested a guard. Goode had laughed at the idea. If Ray had been a Sikh, a Pathan, a Muslim, one of the races defined as martial by the British only because these men willingly fought in their army and died for them, he would have taken some precautions. But Ray was a Bengali babu, a cowardly race. Like most Hindus they never joined the army or fought for the empire. Goode didn't believe he would be attacked. Anil Ray would probably be cowering in some hole. And even if he did attempt to kill him, Goode was confident that he could handle him as before.

Goode left the building at noon for lunch and Anil followed him to the Gymkhana Club. He waited in the shade, some distance from the gharri. Goode was safe inside such an island of superiority. At three-thirty, flushed from lunch and a few beers, Goode returned to his office. He remained there until six-thirty, and Anil followed him home.

Anil felt quite calm. He had no rage left. It had seeped out of him in prison. Instead there was only a coldness of purpose. He could lift his gun and fire into the open gharri but then Goode would never know who killed him. Goode must be killed, even at the cost of his own life, but Anil had to see him, hear him, beg for his life. What did Anil have to live for now? His parents were dead, his inheritance beyond reach, a peaceful existence impossible. He could only live the life of a criminal. If they caught him before he could kill Goode, he would be returned to prison, his sentence extended another few dreary, ugly years. If caught afterwards, he'd be hanged. No longer did they strap one to a cannon to be blown to pieces.

Compared to Old Lucknow, the part of the city where Goode lived was a model of European neatness. The streets and roads had been named after English generals and viceroys; bungalows stood in spacious, well-tended gardens. Little shops sold English food and drink, clothes. Only a few natives could be seen in this orderly district, and were for the most part servants. Anil stopped at the corner of Clive Street and Bentinck Road. Halfway down Wellington Street was Inspector Goode's home, a modest bungalow with a trellis porch. There was a small lawn in front and, in the shade of a drumstick tree, a well. It had a neat gravel drive, lined with white-painted bricks. A wooden plaque on the gate gave his name: 'Inspector R. F. Goode, IPS'. The name of the bungalow was 'Scotland Yard'. Inspector Goode was a bachelor and, apart from his servants, lived alone.

Anil walked around until he found another street, Richmond Lane, which ran past the rear of Goode's bungalow. There were houses in between, so to reach Goode's place Anil saw that he would have to cross one compound, now occupied by a couple sitting out on their lawn. It wasn't going to be easy watching Inspector Goode's home.

He spent that night sleeping on the pavement, dreaming of Sushila, of luxuriating in her bed, and most of all, her flesh. When Goode set out for work the next morning at seven-thirty, Anil trailed behind.

Goode kept to a strict routine. He lunched at the club and went home at precisely the same time. One evening, some friends came to call and towards nine Anil saw them stagger out and weave down the street back to their own homes.

That night Anil, curled tightly in a ball beneath a gold mohur tree, dreamt of his uncle. It wasn't a true dream, but an invention of his sleeping mind. With great clarity he recalled those last fateful hours on the sloping hill above Simla. Except that now they were not picnicking but hunting, and the deodars had turned into jungle. He was unarmed, but his uncle was holding his shooting-stick as though it was a rifle. The jungle was silent and they watched the shadows intently until at last they saw the animal padding towards them. His uncle raised his stick and, in the patch of moonlight, Anil saw that the creature was a man on all-fours with reddish hair covering his entire body. Before his uncle could aim the stick, the beast rose to its full height and attacked his uncle. Because he was unarmed, Anil stood by helplessly while they struggled for possession of the stick. The beast suddenly stepped back, clear of his fallen uncle, and fired the stick at the prone man.

Anil awoke to find himself covered with red flowers. They resembled a great splash of blood, and as he brushed them off, he thought of the bitter irony that he didn't even know how to use the revolver in his begging bowl. Keeping it well hidden, he gripped the butt and curled his finger round the trigger. It was stiff and he was surprised at how much strength was required to kill a man. All the power lay in one finger.

On the third day of his vigil, Anil kept even further out of sight. He chose a position at the far corner of the road, a little way down from police headquarters. Goode didn't leave for lunch and Anil worried in case he had slipped out of the back of the building. He might have gone on official business to inspect police lines, gone to conduct an investigation. Anil paced the road, wondering what he should do. Further delays would only make him more vulnerable. At half past six, an hour which he had felt in his impatience and worry would never arrive, he saw Goode climb into his gharri and drive away from headquarters. However, the gharri didn't set off in the usual direction, but instead drove towards the railway station. Anil stayed fifty yards behind, threading his way through the evening crowds. The gharri passed the station and turned under the railway bridge. On the other side, set half a mile back from the line, was the railway colony, houses and bungalows nominally rented to the employees of the railway company. On the main road stood the larger houses of the administrators, and behind them, in descending order of size and rank, were the bungalows. The colony was neat and orderly, the fencing surrounding it was made of newly painted railway sleepers, the gravel lanes were swept, the gardens watered and tended. The tenants paid none of the costs of this maintenance; it was part of their subsidy.

Goode's gharri stopped and he climbed down. The constable took up his position at the gate, standing stiffly to attention while Goode walked slowly out of sight down the road. Then the man relaxed. Anil ran parallel to Goode outside the fencing until he saw an opening which led onto a narrow path. The servants probably used it as a short-cut to go to the bazaar, instead of walking all the way round. He ducked through and stood in the shadow of a tree. Ahead he saw Goode pass, waited for a minute, and quickly moved to the lane. Goode was now fifty yards down the street, carrying a prettily wrapped package. At a cross-road, he opened a garden gate, marched confidently up the gravel path and knocked on the door. It opened almost immediately.

Anil crept past the house. There was a painted nameplate: P. N. Nailer, Travelling Ticket Inspector. Beyond was another similar bungalow, and Anil retraced his steps and went up the side lane. The lights were on in the bungalow, the curtains tightly drawn. Anil wondered why Goode hadn't driven right up to the door in the gharri. The fence dividing the gardens was about four feet high and, quickly looking around to ensure that nobody was watching him, he clambered over the fence and dropped to the ground.

He heard voices: men's, women's, Goode's. They sounded happy, congratulatory. Anil half rose and spied through the window. Goode was standing in the middle of a room, surrounded by the family. A man shook his hand heartily; a woman stepped forward and laughingly planted a kiss on his cheek. Anil finally understood the reason for the gaiety when he saw a slim young girl move into the group and Goode shyly take her hand. Anil couldn't see her face but he hoped she was ugly. Goode deserved an ugly woman for a wife. Beyond them he heard the voices of several others. This was not a place for killing; there were too many people.

Anil made his way back to the main road. Goode would no doubt remain for some hours with his betrothed's family. The only place to kill him was at his home, where he would be alone. Anil walked back to Goode's bachelor bungalow as fast as he could. He had seen two servants, both men, the previous day, and now he stole cautiously into the garden. He circled the house. There were servants' quarters at the rear and it seemed the servants were asleep. Goode, he suspected, like all Europeans, would leave the keys to his home with his servants. Anil tested the back door. It was set in a trellis so it was easy to slip his hand through an opening and draw back the bolt. He crouched down in the dark, waiting for his eyes to adjust to the gloom, and then he crept silently into the drawing-room. It was sparsely furnished with wicker chairs, a carved teak table and a drinks tray. Against one wall stood a bookcase, full of police manuals and adventure stories. On either side of the drawing-room were bedrooms. In one the bed was neatly turned down, the mosquito netting tucked in. A fresh uniform was folded on a chair and underneath it brightly polished shoes were lined up. On a small side-table lay a pair of handcuffs, a swagger-stick and an empty holster. On the dressing-table was a jumble of silver-framed photographs of Goode's family and friends, and a neat stack of letters. Anil wandered into the second bedroom. It was crowded with Goode's sporting impedimenta: polo sticks, cricket bats, fishing rods, rifles in their cases. He picked up a polo stick. It was well balanced.

He settled himself into a rattan chair facing the front door, wincing at the creak which seemed unnaturally

470

loud in the silence. He took the revolver from his begging bowl and held it on his lap, pointing it at the front door. He laid the polo stick down on the floor beside him, and waited.

He would not kill Goode in the darkness. He would wait for him to light the lamp, to see him. Goode had to look at him, recognise him. The killing would be meaningless if he hid behind the anonymity of night. This was the revenge that Anil Ray needed to experience. He could feel it already, coursing through his limbs, the exuberance of omnipotence. Five years of waiting for retribution were nearly at an end. He remembered again with utter clarity the beginning of this nightmare, the moment this terrible sleep had befallen him. He could still savour the clear, cold air of the hills, hear the sighing of the breeze through the deodars, and the sound of the shot, how it lingered on in the thin air and how the breeze fell silent and the birds flapped and flew in panic. And how swiftly the flies were drawn to the bloodied little hole in his uncle's chest. Like a jeweller carefully balancing the scales, the revolver would be the delicate weight which would counter the death of his uncle and the years lost in prison. He imagined Goode's horror, and could feel already the joy when the bullet would strike Goode. He saw him falling and falling, even as his uncle had been thrown backwards by the shot. He would fire again and then . . . and then . . .

An hour passed, then another, but he remained alert, often getting up to stretch his legs or to examine the curios lying on the tables. He would have taken a drink from the tray but he needed a clear head. He felt that he could see everything with a heightened perception now; his vision pierced the dark with such clarity that he could even distinguish the delicate lines of a painting.

It must have been nearly midnight when he heard the solitary clopping of a gharri horse approaching. He heard it stop, the murmur of voices, the garden gate opening and shutting. Anil hurried back to take his place in the chair. The front door opened and he could hear Goode humming as he stepped into the drawing-room and lit the lamp.

Anil thrust the gun forward so Goode could not be mistaken. He expected to see open terror in Goode's face, but saw only the last vestiges of happiness and innocence draining away before rigid shock took hold of his features. It was a glimpse of the innocence in the man that shook Anil. He had just left the woman he was to marry and was still bathed in the enchantment of loving her. Anil felt bitter he had never been given such an opportunity to be happy.

Without any hesitation, Goode reached for the flap of his holster. In the same instant Anil swung the polo stick with all his might. It smashed into Goode's arm and he heard the bone crack. Goode yelped and sagged to his knees. Anil swung again and drove the head into Goode's side, cracking two ribs.

'What do you want?' Goode whispered. His face was drawn with the pain. He still wasn't afraid and now peered at Anil as though they were separated by a great distance. It took several moments for Goode to penetrate the simple guise of the shaven head and face. 'Anil Ray,' he said, and sighed, a sigh of inevitability, of regret that the time had come when he least wanted it, when life was just promising him fulfilment.

'Yes, Mr Goode.' Anil stepped around him and took his revolver. He raked the barrel down the side of Goode's head, ripping his ear. Goode fainted and Anil waited patiently until his eyes flickered open again.

'Kill me, then, damn you. Kill me.'

'No, Mr Goode. Why should I kill you? You did not kill me. You killed my father and mother. You had me imprisoned, and watched over me. I rotted alive in gaol. I do not have the power to imprison you, but you will rot in your own soul. See.' Anil took out the photographs and letters. 'I know where your mother and father live. They lead such unblemished lives. I know of your fiancée, Mr Goode. Does she love you because you're handsome? Maybe she'd turn away in disgust as people turn away from me, Mr Goode.' Anil smashed the barrel down on the bridge of his nose. Blood seeped down Goode's chin. His eyes were dulled but Anil could see the hatred there.

'I'll kill you,' Goode whispered. 'I swear that. Kill me now.'

'Ah, see the kind Mr Goode changing character. Pain and suffering corrupt a man, Mr Goode. The natives are not the only savages. Beneath your genteel veneer, I can see your savagery, Mr Goode. I want you to live, so never be afraid of my killing you. Think about your mother and father, worry yourself ill about that girl you want to marry one day.' Anil thrust the barrel into Goode's mouth, shattering teeth and splitting the lip. Goode gagged up bits of teeth and bloodied saliva. 'Already you are beginning to rot, Mr Goode. You thought naturally that, being a Bengali, I wouldn't have the courage. I have the courage, Mr Goode. I am as brave as you. I have suffered more than you and that has made me stronger than you. I can pull this trigger, something you did so thoughtlessly five years ago, and you, like my uncle, would cease to be a human being. There is no one to prevent me, Mr Goode. Not you, not the great British government. We are alone here.' Anil brought the barrel down on a hand that lay open, breaking the fingers. Goode howled and cradled his hand.

'You're a fool. Leave me alive and I will hunt you down like a dog.'

'Of course you will. But the hunter and the hunted both suffer from the same sickness. Besides, you would have to find me. India is a labyrinth and she is my home. You will always be the stranger.'

Goode managed to sit up and Anil waited until he'd propped himself up on his good arm, and then slammed the revolver into Goode's face. When he slumped back, choking on his blood, Anil hit him over the head. Goode fell unconscious. The shadows of the lamp flickered on his bloody face. Anil fetched the handcuffs and hand-cuffed Goode's arms behind his back. Then, methodically, he gathered the photographs and letters and uniforms and clothes in a heap and poured oil from the lamp over them. He sprinkled oil on the bed and on the curtains, then returned to squat beside Goode and wait for him to regain consciousness.

'Oh God, my arm,' were Goode's first words.

'Your face too, Mr Goode. Will she still love you, I wonder, the way I wonder whether I shall ever be loved?'

'You bastard. You nigger bastard.'

'An inaccuracy, Mr Goode. But let it pass. I want you to look around at all your possessions, all your carefully collected memories.'

Goode craned his head and saw the untidy heap. Anil brought the lamp and carefully placed the flame to a twist of paper. The paper caught, flared and he dropped it on the heap. It smouldered for a moment and then burst into a merry orange flame.

'Come, we must leave. You will not become a martyr for an unjust government.'

Anil dragged Goode out by his ankles as the fire caught hold, racing up the cotton curtains and leaping across to the books. The heat was unbearable and the night air was a cooling relief. Anil pulled Goode down the driveway and out to the road. From behind the bungalow he heard the calls of the servants. Goode began screaming now. He was afraid of pain, more afraid of the humiliation of knowing he would be found out in the road, exposed to strangers' eyes.

'Goodbye, Mr Goode.' Anil walked away. He wouldn't run.

'I'll kill you, Anil Ray. The last thing . . .' Goode screamed after him.

32

THERE HAD been three of them once; now only one was left. The Colonel knew eventually he'd grow accustomed to the vacant dining chair opposite him. The boy lay in a grave, already dust, and his chair stood against the wall. But his daughter was impressed in his memory; her voice and movements still lingered, a fading echo of her, and her chair was still drawn up to the table, although no place was laid.

An office peon came in with a telegram and laid the buff envelope reverently on the table. Breakfast was served on the verandah with the chics down and already the Colonel could feel the threat of the day's heat. The perfection of the blue sky hurt his eyes and the air was still and humid. He ignored the message and went on with his breakfast, the dogs lying by his side, Abdul behind his chair. *The Statesman* was propped against the tea pot.

'Take that chair away, Abdul.'

The bearer moved it, tenderly placing it against the wall alongside the other.

'Where will Elizabeth miss sahib be by now, sahib?'

'On the high seas.' But Abdul wouldn't understand the distance or the sea. The sea changed people, like a baptism. It would change her. She wouldn't return the same person. Nothing else remained the same, only India.

The change in Kim baffled him. He had shaped, created, that boy, that man, given him shelter when he had none, educated him when he had been roaming the

Grand Trunk Road, illiterate as a native, then employment – a good government job, with a pension. But Kim had destroyed it all, crushed his own love, also. Kim was his creation, his weapon, but he had loved Kim too. He couldn't deny it, and what had happened was his fault. Kim had lived too far removed from the European and now no longer thought of himself as one. He had reverted to the native, even as a tame animal will when let loose in the wild. India had absorbed him; he was hers now, not his. The Colonel realised he should have understood what was happening to Kim after Rae Bareli, when he had stoically accepted imprisonment instead of revealing his identity. The Colonel had made a mistake; he'd thought then only of the convenience of having Kim in Tihar Gaol, with a reputation which, like a brand, would have made him acceptable to the seditionist and terrorist. It would have given him . . . authenticity. But his silence was a symbol of his change. He could have saved Kim, sent him to England, the heart of the empire. The sea might have changed him, saved him from damnation, but now it was too late, too late.

The Colonel had been gentle. Kim had to understand his power. Like pulling away toy bricks, he had hoped to bring Kim to his senses. His was the power in India; not the native's. He could grant boons, be lavish in his reward of loyalty, cruel in punishment. But Kim hadn't understood.

Would England have had the desired effect? In Calcutta, Kim had been uneasy with the English. If only he'd understood his own superiority, the advantages of his race. The memory of Kim in Calcutta disturbed the Colonel. Kim had read all the files. The Colonel had intended this job to be another step in his education, apart from wanting Kim to understand more about the people he served. Everything in those files, those codes, every agent the Colonel had, was now lodged in Kim's memory. He had been trained to note every possible detail at a glance. Now that Kim had proved false to his bread and salt, he had become dangerous. He could jeopardise the lives of the Colonel's agents, or worse, undermine his plans. If Kim were to uncover them, would he be able to recruit equally loyal men? It would take time, even years, and the Colonel didn't trust time. Time changed, spun out of control. He was sure Kim knew that Bahadhur Ram Shanker – 'Daddaji' – was in his pay. There were others, men in the provincial councils, princes, sar-panchs. It would mean new agents, new codes, and the Colonel disliked change. He would have to abandon his intelligence network and start again from scratch.

It would be easier to eliminate Kim.

That was the answer. He saw no alternative. Kim was free and had helped the terrorist Anil Ray to escape too.

To kill a son, and I have always thought of Kim as one, not in blood but in spirit, is a burden I can hardly bear. But how can I avoid my responsibility? A king must punish a treacherous son. Didn't Arthur take up arms against Mordred; didn't King Charles have Monmouth executed, to keep the throne secure? Kim has become dangerous, the weapon I have forged will now turn on us all. I can destroy him, yet I cannot betray the Crown which I have served all my life.

If any doubt still lingered, any reluctance to act, it was dispelled when he read the telegram.

INSPECTOR GOODE ATTACKED AND INJURED AT LUCKNOW STOP CULPRIT ANIL RAY STOP DETAILS FOLLOW STOP

The news had reached the Viceroy's Council. The members of all the departments had gathered in the chamber, the centre of power in India. The wood panelling was a mellowed brown. The room was on the top floor and the Council members could look out over the rooftops of Calcutta. Bearers in scarlet kurtas stood ready to serve tea and biscuits. Others carried the files the members would need to consult. When the Colonel came in he heard the uneasy, angry murmur.

They took their places at the long polished table which reflected their faces and hands clearly. The Viceroy's seat was vacant, for Lord Hardinge had not yet taken office, and the senior Council Member chaired the meeting. These men ruled India in the name of the King-Emperor. They were all friends, they knew each other well. Lord Curzon had tried to break their power, suggesting that after a brief tenure they should return to their provinces and districts, but he'd not managed to bring about the change. They loved Calcutta, and had long lost touch with the outposts they'd once known as Collectors and District Magistrates.

'Well, Colonel. You heard the news?' the Viceroy's secretary asked.

'Yes.'

'A frightful business. I gather Goode was beaten unmercifully and his house set on fire. The absolute . . . *gall* of this Anil Ray, to think he can thrash a British police inspector.'

'I hope the details won't reach the newspapers,' the Member for Opium and Salt murmured. 'It wouldn't be advisable to let the natives read about it.'

'Half the neighbourhood, I gather, saw Inspector Goode's condition,' said the Inspector General of Police, who'd been especially invited to attend this meeting. 'Anil Ray left Goode in the street and the servants all saw the state he was in. And you know how they talk. By tomorrow the news will have reached every corner of the country.'

The senior member studied his report. 'Was the man who escaped with him, Kimathchand, an accomplice of Anil Ray's in this assault?'

'I'm not sure yet,' the IG said. 'A witness claims to have seen only one man walking away from Goode.'

'Walking! The bloody arrogance of the man.'

'This Kimathchand might have been lurking in the background. He had been arrested as a seditionist and I suspect that he too is dangerous. The police are looking for him.'

The Colonel scribbled on the blotter in front of him and remained silent. He hoped his own man would reach

Kim before the police did. It would be embarrassing if Kim were to be identified as an Englishman, and one of his agents.

'The European population will want us to meet ruthlessness with ruthlessness, don't you agree, Colonel? They'll renew the cry that for every European killed we should execute ten natives.'

'I can't agree with that,' the Colonel said, looking up from his blotter, 'even though some newspaper editors howl for it every time something like this happens. If we were to agree to their demands and condemn nine innocent men for every guilty one, the natives would cease to believe in us as fair and just rulers. They are like children and look to us for guidance. We embody the principles of European civilisation and even-handed justice. Such draconian measures are barbaric, and belong to the days when we first conquered this continent. We are the caretakers of India now and at some very distant point in the future, through our example, the Indian will eventually learn to rule himself – but with our continued guidance. There will always be extremists in India who believe that only through terrorism will we be driven out. But we shall never leave. I know we can control these men, track them down and punish them. However, I believe that instead of merely reacting to events, as we are doing now, we should act first. Prevention is far better than cure. If we can crush rebellion before it manifests itself, then we can stifle these cries for the execution of innocent men. But our masters in London must be made to realise that they cannot judge India as they do England. We have introduced the concept of justice to the Indian, and due process of law continues to tie our hands in dealing with terrorists. We must be enabled to catch and imprison these men *before* they can do any harm. We are dealing with terrorists, and they must be imprisoned immediately. And to do this we can't have trials by judge and jury, defence lawyers and all the other trappings they have in England. They only delay justice. The temporary powers granted to the police are inadequate, and must be reinforced. Once these seditionists realise we will deal harshly with them, India will be at peace within her borders.'

'Hear, hear, Colonel Creighton.'

'Well. Now we have to introduce our new member,' said the chairman, 'an Indian gentleman who will become a member of the Council, though solely in an advisory capacity. Peon, ask Mr Bahadhur Ram Shanker to join us.' When the peon had left the room, the chairman added: 'I don't think we should make any further comment on this matter of Inspector Goode.'

Bahadhur Ram Shanker entered behind the peon and bowed stiffly to the table. The chairman immediately rose and waited for Bahadhur sahib to reach him.

'Mr Bahadhur Ram Shanker, I would like to welcome you as a new member of the Viceroy's Council. We look forward to your advice in our future deliberations.'

'Thank you very much for your welcome,' said Bahadhur sahib, looking around and noting the silent reception. He had been stuffed down their throats, but was considered the most palatable of the natives to sit with them. If they expected him to retreat now, they were mistaken. He was here to stay. In his determination to be accepted, he had dressed too formally for the occasion. His suit was too new and too elegant, his shirt was of silk and his cufflinks too heavy. He glowed in this room, when he should have looked as understated as they. He made a note to imitate them, for he understood power and knew how to flatter. 'May I address the Council?'

'Of course.'

'I would like to condemn most strongly the dastardly attack on Inspector Goode.' He paused for the murmur. 'I know I speak for every Indian and for India, when I say that we must exact retribution for this humiliation. The Crown cannot tolerate such evil in our midst. We must close ranks against terrorists and murderers and do everything within our power to bring these men to justice. Thank you.'

When Bahadhur sahib sat down, the members thumped the table in appreciation. Though a native, he was a good chap and his sentiments echoed their feelings. He looked replete, lazily confident. He didn't know that the man who'd rescued his wife on the train so long ago, was, even now, on his way to the hunting lodge in the Aravalli hills. But the Colonel knew. The trap was set. The perfect bait – love; the hunter – his man. By now the trap might even have been sprung. He was expecting another telegram – KIM CAUGHT.

'I would like,' Bahadhur sahib continued when the applause faded, 'to personally offer a reward of twenty-five thousand rupees for the apprehension and chastisement of the criminals.'

'Hear, hear!'

The Government of India immediately matched this sum of money until the price on Anil Ray's head was fifty thousand rupees. Fifty thousand! A fortune which would easily purchase his betrayal. One-twentieth of that, they knew, could purchase any Indian soul. Life was as cheap as shoe-leather and corruption would deliver Anil Ray to judgment. The Colonel was pleased with Bahadhur sahib's offer and his echoing of their sentiments.

At the end of the meeting, the Colonel accompanied Bahadhur sahib out of the chamber. They walked in silence down the corridors to the wide teak staircase.

'That was a stirring speech, Bahadhur sahib. We appreciate it greatly.'

'Thank you, Colonel. We must stamp out terrorism if we are to remain in power.'

'You're quite a cynical man.'

'Pragmatic, let us say. We both understand each other's needs. Sometimes I am startled at the similarity in our lives. Even our wives have returned to us at the same time. Or, should I say, your wife returned but didn't remain.'

The Colonel stopped short. His fierce stare was deflected by a mocking glance as Bahadhur sahib continued down the stairs. He stood waiting for the Colonel under the porch, then signalled for his driver.

'How did you know?'

'Information, as you well know, Colonel sahib, is the most valuable tool of any civilisation. Unless we keep abreast of . . . events . . . we lose control. A little bird told me.'

'Your wife, I gather, is at home. It was fortunate that your rather drastic action to win her back wasn't witnessed by Mr Nehru or the other Congressmen.'

'Even if it had been, Colonel, I'm sure you would have helped me to smooth any ruffled feathers. Yes, my wife is delighted to be back in her husband's arms. It's strange how obsessive we can become over the female of our species, is it not, Colonel? We become reckless for love, for the sensual pleasures of the flesh. Ah, how many kings have fallen from their thrones for the love of a woman!'

The Colonel expected a gharri to arrive for Bahadhur sahib. Instead, a monstrous, long, glittering motor-car pulled up. The Colonel saw his own stare reflected in the huge round brass headlights. He could smell its newness.

'A Daimler. I'm told it's the very best. May I offer you a lift?'

'No, thank you.'

The chauffeur was an Englishman. He wore a white uniform with highly polished black boots and a white peaked cap. He opened the door for Bahadhur sahib, who sank into the leather unholstery.

'Colonel sahib, I must recommend the motor-car. It moves far more swiftly than the gharri, and in these times we must keep pace with change. If you should ever require one, please don't hesitate to let me know. It would be a pleasure for me to make one available to you. On a long-term basis, naturally.'

'Naturally.'

The Colonel's home was in silence. Even the many lights could not dispel its emptiness. The Colonel took his whisky out into the garden, and sat for a while fondling the ears of his dogs. The silence was oppressive. There was no one to break it, like a prison sentence it was now interminable. No one waited for him, nor did he wait for them to come home, to swoop in, to kiss his cheek. Even though he and Elizabeth didn't spend whole evenings together, at least she provided company over their meal. He missed her deeply. He had meant to tell her how much he would miss her, but the words had stuck in his throat.

He was disturbed by Bahadhur sahib's knowledge. Information was the Colonel's trade; he constantly weighed its worth, thought about how it came to him. How had Bahadhur sahib known of Alice's visit? It had been sudden and brief, and she had not been back again. Who had seen her come? Who had told Bahadhur sahib? Elizabeth? She didn't know Bahadhur sahib, except in passing. Alice herself? But she had harboured Bahadhur sahib's wife and was still trying to stir up a hornet's nest about her disappearance.

He knew about her enquiries, her requests for an investigation, her visit with Romesh Nairoji to Bahadhur sahib's residence in Delhi. She was becoming a nuisance, not only in the matter of Bahadhur sahib's wife, but also through her writings in *Sher* and her foreign reporting. What a tragic error he'd made in his youth! How on earth could he have loved such a woman, who now brought discredit on herself. He would have to take action against her soon . . . if she continued her seditionist activities.

Would she have told Bahadhur sahib of her visit to her daughter? No. They were enemies because of the abducted wife. That left the servants. Bahadhur sahib had known about Alice years ago. The Colonel remembered their meeting at the racecourse. What had he said? 'Servants whom we don't notice.' Which one had been in his employ when his wife left? Abdul, who'd served him so devotedly all these years? Surely not! Abdul had grown up with him. They'd weathered the years together, were growing old together. Though they were about the same age, Abdul looked old enough to be the Colonel's father. Mary ayah? How could he question her loyalty to the family? He'd never seen such devotion. She'd wept for days since Elizabeth left, and he still saw her wandering through the bungalow like a rudderless ship, in search of her baba. There was another possibility, that Bahadhur sahib had had the bungalow watched, the Colonel followed. This made the Colonel distinctly uneasy. It undermined his power, his control over events.

Well, he'd test it this evening. He had not planned to go out, but the silence overwhelmed him, adding unpleasantly to his feeling of powerlessness. The gharri was brought round to the front and the Colonel smiled at the memory of the subtle bribe offered by Bahadhur sahib. A motor-car! He wondered how much it cost; certainly more than he could afford.

He told the driver to go at a leisurely pace and frequently looked behind to see if anyone were following. The streets were crowded and in the gloom it was impossible to distinguish a familiar face. He gave his driver new instructions and sat back as the gharri moved faster. Tomorrow he'd have one of his own men keep watch.

The house looked as deserted as his own bungalow. A solitary window was lit, like a beacon in a sea of darkness. The Colonel strode up the gravel drive and, when he looked into the room, saw that she was alone. He knocked once sharply with his cane against the shutter and saw her rise quickly.

'Who is it?'

'Jack.'

He waited by the side door, his starched shirtfront a triangle of white in the dark. When the light spilled on him, he heard her low chuckle.

'Have I invited you for dinner and forgotten?'

'No, Sushila. I just . . . thought I'd call in. If you're busy . . .'

'Oh, the formality of you Englishmen.' She pulled him in, pleased at his intrusion. He stood as awkwardly as a schoolboy. 'Aren't you going to kiss me?' He pecked at her. 'Is that all? I thought we were lovers?'

This time he kissed her mouth and followed her into the room. Sushila took his jacket and hung it up neatly. Then she knelt and removed his shoes. She placed a bottle of whisky on the table, with the soda-water, and curled up on the divan. He lounged beside her, stroking her silken black hair, feeling himself soothed. He was constantly mesmerised by her clear, simple beauty. There were no imperfections in her face, the features were sketched so deftly and clearly.

He enjoyed talking to her. She listened attentively and didn't sit in judgment on his past. Nor did she weigh his words, seeking favour, probing for weaknesses. She made him feel manly.

'I'll miss Elizabeth very much. I didn't mean to come here, but I needed to get out of the house. I suppose I'll get used to the emptiness, but at the moment it's too full of memories. I found myself thinking about Richard. You never really accept that you could lose a son so young, and you store up things for the future instead of doing them immediately. Foolish of me. It's difficult to be a friend to one's children. Recently, Elizabeth and I haven't been getting on too well, but now she is all I have.'

'Can you blame her for being angry?' Sushila said. 'It must have come as a great shock to learn that her mother was alive. You ought to have told them earlier.'

'I was afraid they'd run to her. It gave them an alternative. God, how I hate her. She shouldn't ever have come. She had no right!'

'She had every right, as a mother. Her son had been killed. I would have done the same.'

Gently, Sushila smoothed the creases on his brow. He was still an attractive man, controlled and powerful. His dark hair was touched with white at the temples. He was her solace, and she wished he'd visit more often. He was also, in a strange way, her future. By his discretion, he kept her reputation unsullied, and when her husband drank himself to death on his estate, she wouldn't shave her head and drape herself in the white shroud of eternal mourning. He could help her to escape the cruel restrictions of her religion. She wasn't sure she wanted marriage from him. He was too much an Englishman. Two hundred years ago, of course, he wouldn't have hesitated. Nor would she. From being friends, the English had become rulers, now nearly enemies. She wanted to ask him for news about Anil Ray, but she held her tongue. She didn't want to think about Anil because all her thoughts were bleak and dark.

'Do you know Bahadhur Ram Shanker?'

'Of course I do.' Sushila laughed and took a sip of his whisky. She grimaced and kissed him. 'Don't look at me so suspiciously. I'm not an ignorant Hindu woman. His name is always in the newspapers. The first Indian to be elected to the Viceroy's Council.'

'But you've never met him?'

'No. You sound relieved. Why?'

'Oh . . . he's a scoundrel.'

'Let's stop talking about scoundrels and partings and death.' She lay back, closed her eyes and recited in Urdu:

> 'The Spring, the Cup, and thy Beloved's face
> Suffice to make the earth a pleasant place;
> And therefore, – Jack –, when the shadows fall,
> Drink deep and seal thy passion with a kiss:
> Until Tomorrow thou needst not recall
> That there is any other World than this.'

33

On the evening of his escape from Tihar Gaol, Kim managed only by stubborn and loud insistence, which attracted the attention of Police Superintendent Ivor Bradley, to obtain a first-class sleeper on the passenger train leaving Delhi at 8.45 P.M. It would stop at Mathura, Agra, Sawai Madhapur, Gwalior, Jhansi and Nagpur. He bought a single ticket to Nagpur and berated the clerk behind the barred window for not serving him promptly. Superintendent Bradley watched Kim push his way through the crowds, followed by a coolie staggering under the weight of a leather suitcase, much battered and stuck with labels. He paid them no further attention and returned to his assignment. His men were closely examining every passenger who passed the ticket barrier, while other constables patrolled the platforms, ready to catch any one who tried to jump the fence or cross the tracks.

Kim smiled broadly at the superintendent and, trapped in the press of people, was swept past, towards the scrutiny of a sergeant who glanced down frequently at a sheet of paper he held. Behind Kim, the coolie struggled to keep pace. The sergeant glanced at Kim and immediately cleared a path, driving aside the natives who were waiting impatiently to board the train and now blocked the way for the sahib. He took note of the neatly-pressed linen suit and the Wyke-hamist tie. It looked shabby, a much-worn favourite, quite appropriate for an ex-public schoolboy. A white topi shaded the sahib's eyes but the sergeant glimpsed a firm mouth with a neatly clipped military moustache.

Once clear of the barrier, Kim strode down the platform, passing a policeman posted every ten yards. He peered into a vacant first-class coupé with a small bathroom attached.

'Jaldi . . . jaldi . . .' he ordered the coolie and stepped aside to allow him to heave the suitcase into the carriage. It was 8.40 by the station clock and the guard kept anxiously glancing at the crowded barrier. Only a thin trickle passed. The train wouldn't wait a minute after 8.45, and already his whistle hovered at his mouth. The ticket collector was slowly moving down the platform, file in hand, checking carriages and passengers. Kim jumped into the empty compartment and sat by the window.

'Did anyone see us?' Narain whispered from the darkened bathroom.

'No. The TC's coming. Stay hidden until the train moves off.'

'What if another European gets on? It's all very well for you, being the sahib. You didn't have to carry a suitcase full of rocks. And if a sahib comes I'll get booted out into the arms of the police and be hanged tomorrow morning.'

'At least that would keep you quiet. Shh.'

The ticket collector poked his head in, examined Kim from head to toe to reassure himself that this really was a European and not a chi-chi behaving like one. The tie, which he didn't recognise, convinced him. Only an Englishman would wear one so frayed and faded. He clipped Kim's ticket and moved on.

'What tie am I wearing?' Kim asked.

'How should I know? It cost me one rupee in the bazaar. It looked proper British. The topi cost me one rupee fifty, made in Army and Navy Stores, but the suit was stitched by one Lalchand and Sons in Meerut. It cost . . .'

'Shh.'

It was unsettling, trying to talk to the darkened bath-room without attracting attention. Kim watched a Euro-pean slowly making his way down the platform. He was an overweight man, his paunch straining under his suit. He was muttering about the delays and the dirtiness of the carriages. Kim had, briefly, behaved like one of these and it had left a bitter taste in his mouth. If it hadn't been the only way that they could have escaped by train, he would never have posed as an Englishman. The topi, the suit, the tie were constricting.

'Is that berth taken?' The Englishman peered in, ask-ing the air and not directly addressing Kim. 'Damn train's run like a bloody bazaar. Never enough decent compartments for us. Too many given to the damn wogs.'

'It's taken,' Kim said coldly. 'My uncle is in the bath-room.'

The Englishman sniffed haughtily and strode on, prodding the coolie with his cane to move ahead faster. The guard waved his green flag, ignoring the panicky cries of those passengers still trapped by the police behind the barrier. His piercing whistle and the answer-ing scream of the engine silenced all of them. Kim looked down the train and saw the fat Englishman leap through an open door. The coolie hurriedly threw in the baggage and, in return, was thrown a handful of coins that rolled and scattered over the platform. The coolie scrambled to pick up the coins; now that the train was moving it was too late to haggle for more. This petty insult angered Kim. The power to humiliate was so easily conferred by the colour of a skin. His own had granted him the invisibility required to pass the police barriers.

Narain cautiously emerged once the train was clear of the platform. Gingerly, he sat down on the bunk, then bounced twice on the padded leather and stretched out in unaccustomed luxury. In third class, the seats were wooden slats.

'You are a fool for wanting to be Indian in India. Look at the advantages you have as a European – salaams by the police, great luxury carriages and the opportunity to be superior. Men kill for such privileges.'

'Ahre, Narain, you envy only the skin and not what's inside. Like all the others, you look at the exterior of the man and make your judgment on that. What have I done to earn such privileges? I came from the womb of an Angrezi woman whom I never knew. And the seed was an Angrezi father who died when I was a child. He willed me little except the puzzle of the bull in the green field, his regimental crest. And because of that, the Colonel took me and trained me as his agent. My skin and my adoption aren't enough to make me an Angrezi, a stranger to the land I love. A man cannot be trapped by his birth, no matter how high or how low. He must forge his own path in life.'

'Even if it leads to his death?'

'It only leads to death. And to rebirth. In spite of your own self, Narain, you will not be born a cockroach in your next life. Brahma will make you an Angrezi for helping me.'

Narain fell off the bunk, laughing. He thrashed on the floor and howled. Kim too howled, both sounding like wolves, tears streaming down their faces, their stomachs aching.

'I shall be born the next Viceroy of India,' Narain managed finally. 'If Brahma is listening to me – I've no wish to be an ordinary Angrezi but the Viceroy. I shall have fifty-one guns firing salutes for me daily. I shall order all the women in the land to spend one night with me. It will be the law.' He fumbled at the latch of the suitcase and opened it. On top of the rocks were Kim's clothes – kurta, pi-jama, turban and chappals. Narain unwrapped the turban and drew out a bottle of arrack. He drank, and passed the bottle to Kim. 'And what will you become?'

'A sunyassi who will come to Viceroy Narain and be kicked for being a damned native.' He too drank and passed the bottle back to Narain.

As the bottle emptied they fell silent but still stayed

sober. The Nagpur Passenger was the slowest train. It came to a halt at every village and, for no particular reason, in between stations as well. There was a waxen moon and the land was full of shadows. Kim didn't know whether the journey was a futile one. Parvati might be dead by now, while they wallowed in the luxury of this train. He stilled his impatience, beat down his torment that even as he crawled towards her so slowly, she might be snatched from him by death. The wheels click-clacked her name and when they stopped, the silence swelled to choke him.

She dreamed of demons with bloody fangs and enormous tongues and eyes as red and large as the evening sun. They cavorted over her body, crushing and tearing at her. Blood dripped from their long, sharp talons; her blood, scooped like river water from her gaping entrails, and licked from their fingers. She thrashed and struggled, her mouth open with a scream which never left her throat. And when they receded and she believed death had claimed her, she would be haunted by many-headed serpents with flickering tongues, coiling endlessly over her arms, her legs, her throat, her head. They weren't as large as Siva's cobra, but worms with evil flat heads and silver eyes.

She had woken awash with sweat and exhausted from the nightmares every morning since Bahadhur sahib had left. Mohini knew she was trapped in a spell cast by Gitabhai. Each night her mind spun more evil images, monstrous in size, and she knew Gitabhai summoned them out of the darkness to kill her. If only she had cast a swift spell, one which would kill her immediately, Mohini would have been grateful. But Gitabhai wanted her to die slowly, from terror, from the exhaustion of sleepless nights.

Three times a day, Gitabhai and the women attended on Mohini. The servants would carry in silver platters of food, lovingly prepared by Gitabhai. Biriyani, kofta curry, keemas, chicken makhani, dhal, curd, lassi, bhadam kher, metais. Inexplicably, though she knew the spells were within the food, Mohini couldn't ignore her appetite. She ate ravenously; the blood drunk by monsters needed replacing.

'See how well I look after my daughter-in-law,' Gitab-hai would croon and pinch Mohini's cheeks painfully. 'My son cannot say that I do not care for her. Give her some more chicken, give her some more bhadam. She must look beautiful for when he returns from Calcutta.'

The servant hastily complied, but were baffled by Mohini's appearance. She did not grow fatter, but became gaunt. Her eyes had darkened and her hair dulled. They saw the bones of her ribs when they bathed her; she was so thin that she was vanishing before their eyes. Yet, if Bahadhur sahib asked, they would swear she ate like a rani. And like a rani dressed each day afresh in satins and silks, they would place her on the balcony and watch her stare listlessly out at the hills.

Mohini barely noticed the bright green jungle, still invigorated by the monsoon, which in summer would turn as grey and brittle as her mood. She barely noticed the colourful splash of peacocks and parrots, and the lithe brown chital and sambar coming to drink on the far shore, or the perfect blue sky in which an eagle circled endlessly above her head. Her mind remained as vacant as that sky; no thoughts crossed it. She was lost to her fate. She no longer remembered Kim, or the message she'd given the brothers who had once come to sing to her.

At the village of Sawai Madhapur, where the broad gauge crossed the narrow gauge line, Kim and Narain got off the train. They found themselves on the edge of the jungle, and far away glimpsed the Aravalli hills. They looked too distant for them to walk to, and Kim was impatient. Narain would have been content to wait for him in the village. Narain was uncertain about the jungle, believing he would be attacked and eaten by tigers or torn to pieces by bears. He fervently wished he was back in Bombay, among men no less savage, but who didn't frighten him. Resolutely, he followed Kim into the village. They found a camel owner who earned a meagre living by hiring out his beasts as pack animals to sahibs who came for shikar. He showed little interest in Kim and Narain. Kim, in grubby kurta and pi-jama, looked Pathan to him, and Pathans never gave away any money. Narain he dismissed immediately. Zakir Khan, who was considered the richest man in the village because of his astuteness, asked the exorbitant fee he always charged sahibs.

'Salah madhar chuth,' Kim said. 'I'm no sahib, and if you think you can cheat us I will take you into the jungle and beat you to within an inch of your miserable life. The wall eye you have on the left side of your head will go over to the right.'

Zakir Khan reconsidered. Both these men, especially the foul-mouthed one, looked desperate enough to fulfil their threat.

'Sahib, how was I to know you are such an influential man? I will give you a proper excellent price for my camels.'

They bargained and haggled. The camel owner hoped only to make a little more than he had from the last three men who'd passed through the village and rented his camels. Two of them had frightened him; they seemed to threaten not a beating, but death. The elder, who moved like a cat, had stared at him with black, dead eyes, and the younger one, who limped, bristled with danger. The third, who followed a little later, a strange man thin as a reed, and lost in his dreams, had somehow tricked him into agreeing to a few paltry rupees. It still puzzled Zakir Khan how that had come about.

Kim and Narain bought food from the railway stall-holder for the journey. When they returned to Zakir Khan's, he had the camels ready. One was a huge, sleek beast, arrogant as a prince; the other, small and scruffy, watched Kim and Narain with mean eyes and teeth as large as daggers. The arrogant one was Zakir's racing

493

camel. The camels, grumbling, knelt down and Kim and Narain mounted cautiously, Kim on the racer, Narain on the mean one which, he swore, had eyes in the back of its head. It was a two-day ride north into the jungle. Zakir Khan himself would lead them to the ancient fortress of Ranthambor.

There was no road, but a cart track that wound through the scrub grass and thorny bushes, some of which grew to the size of trees. They passed small herds of underfed cattle browsing on the new grass, followed by one or two small boys who stared at Kim and Narain in curiosity. They walked along beside the camels and wanted to know where the strangers had come from. Kim told them Lahore, a city of which they'd never heard. Zakir Khan proudly informed them it was far to the north from where centuries ago his ancestors had descended to the plains in search of plunder. By dusk they reached a small village of mud and thatch, encircled by a fence of thorn. Already the cattle and goats were inside the enclosure and the sar-panch, recognising Zakir, allowed them to spend the night within. Ranjit Singh, whose white stubble hid the scars of pock-marks, was disappointed that Kim did not carry a jezail. He had sent word to the Deputy Collector of the district that there was a tiger which had stolen two village goats, and if it wasn't killed it would snatch a man or a woman or a child next.

After the evening meal, sitting in the darkness of early night, they smoked a huqqa with Ranjit Singh and the other villagers.

'Do you know Bahadhur Ram Shanker?' Kim asked him.

'Yes. He's a very powerful man around here, a personal friend of the Maharajah of Jaipur whose hunting lodge is five kos away. Bahadhur sahib has his own lodge on the lake.'

Kim knew feudal loyalty was a powerful force in Rajputana. The peasants obeyed and served the Maharajah faithfully. If Bahadhur sahib was the Prince of

Jaipur's friend, they wouldn't betray him to these two strangers.

'Is he as kind a man as the Maharajah?'

Ranjit Singh squinted at Kim, drew on the huqqa and considered the question. He didn't like Bahadhur sahib at all, but as a friend of his Prince he was reluctant to speak against him. But Bahadhur sahib wasn't Rajput and his servants had severely beaten one of his own people. If he spoke ill of him, he wondered if Kim would tell the Prince.

'Are you his friend?'

'His enemy,' Kim said boldly, and then lied swiftly. 'He is married to my cousin, Parvati, and treats her badly. Narain and I are planning to take her back to our household.'

'Ah! Good. He is a very cruel man.'

'Is he there now?'

'No. He was there a few days ago, but I heard he had to go to Calcutta. It's strange that he should be spending so much time here without going hunting. He thinks himself a very good shikari, but I have known him to wound a tiger and then not hunt it down to kill it. Then it turns maneater and we have to send for the DC and ask him to kill it.'

'Who is at his lodge now?'

'I'm told his mother is living there. No one has ever seen her.'

'No one else?' Kim waited tensely for the sar-panch to draw on the huqqa.

'There is a young woman with her. One of the women who cleans the lodge and comes from the next village, says she is the wife of Bahadhur sahib. This woman could be your cousin. She is locked in her room for most of the day. Our woman hasn't seen her. All your cousin's needs are taken care of by Bahadhur sahib's mother and her personal servants who came with her from Delhi.'

'Is it easy to reach the island?'

'Before I answer, you must tell me: if you do take your cousin by force, will Bahadhur sahib complain to the

Maharajah? If he does, he will come and punish me and the village.'

'He will never know you have told me this. I swear it.'

The sar-panch believed Kim. In the darkness he sensed the young man's sincerity and strength of purpose.

'You can only reach the island by boat. In summer when the water is low, it is possible to walk on a stone path that lies below the water. The old Chuhan princes built it, from the banyan tree below the fortress to the island. You can't walk on it now, because the water is high.'

They left the village while it was still dark, and by the time the sun tipped over the horizon they had reached the Aravalli hills. Zakir Khan led them cautiously along narrow winding paths. The brush tugged at their clothes and scratched the camels, who sighed in irritation. Narain's beast tried to nip Kim's dangling foot more than once. The sides of the hills, where the jungle had been cleared, revealed pink gashes, raw and reddening as the sun fell on them. It was the stone the Jaipur princes used for their city palaces. Just where the path became steep, a stream ran through the gaping mouth of a large marble buffalo's head, set into a granite wall. The head was yellowed with age, moss-covered, but nothing could disguise its beauty. Kim wondered at the nature of men who'd spent years carving such an exquisite piece, only for water to flow through.

At midday, Zakir Khan called a halt. The ground was too steep for his camels. High above the dense jungle foliage they could just see the ruined walls of the fortress.

'There are two ways to get to the lake,' said Zakir Khan. 'One is around the hill, which will take another whole day. Or else you can climb by a small path which leads to the fort walls. You can enter by an underground stream and follow it. It will bring you out on the other side.'

'Will you wait for us here?'

'Not for ever. Until dawn.'

'Dawn, then.'

Kim and Narain followed the winding path. The light in the jungle was dim, making it easy to imagine wild beasts lurking. They sent peacocks scurrying in panic to fly into the tree tops and call their warning: 'mayur-mayur', and the langur high up above them sent its boom echoing across the jungle. They encountered no other wild animals, but when they passed they glimpsed the movements of chital returning from hiding, and a wild pig with its litter scrambling away. Kim stopped to cut himself a stick, using Narain's knife.

'What if we meet a tiger?' Narain whispered, for the jungle had grown ominously silent around them. It simmered with living things, but always at a distance, as though they were surrounded by an evil aura.

'You will throw your knife at it.'

'I'm not a circus performer. I'd miss and then it would leap on us and kill us both.'

'It is best not to think of such things, Narain,' Kim muttered, his whole being concentrated on reaching the lake. He couldn't consider dangers or obstacles until they arose. He let Narain, a step behind him, worry for them both.

They reached the foot of the cliff drenched in sweat. The stream ran through a low cavern and the cool water revived them as they waded down the tunnel. The stream's bed was smooth granite. It wasn't more than twenty feet long and quickly they found themselves in a roofless hamam. The walls were made of pink granite and the baths, through which the stream ran, were of the same yellowing marble as the buffalo head. The four interconnected baths, each half the depth of a standing man, were circular and large enough to accommodate half a dozen people.

'Those princes must have had a good time,' Kim said. 'They would bathe with all their women here every day. When you are Viceroy, you should revive the practice of mixed bathing.'

'No hot water,' Narain said, unimpressed.

Above their heads was open sky and the area around the baths was ankle-deep in dead, dry leaves. Steps led up into the fortress grounds and they climbed up to the ruined palace. They passed the durbar hall and the small temple and the fallen walls of the women's quarters to the far side of the battlements. The splendour was muted by the strange, sad silence. Men had laboured centuries ago to clear the jungle and build monuments for themselves, but nature had outlasted them, had waited patiently until the kingdom fell, and had then embraced the granite and marble and brick again. Kim foresaw that in a thousand years these walls and battlements would revert to boulders and sand. The cycle would be complete. The earth was permanent, not men. It would wait for the next cycle, and wait again for that to end too.

It was nearly dusk by the time they reached the far battlements and looked down. The jungle was full of shadows, but they could clearly see the hunting lodge in the middle of the lake, as stately as a becalmed ship, unruffled and serene. Its walls rose directly out of the water, and the windows were beyond reach. The entrance faced south and steps led down to a boat tied to the wall.

In the very middle of the island, surrounded by the lodge, Kim saw a tree. It had no leaves but its flowers were the most beautiful and strange he'd ever seen. They were pink and gold and shaped like goblets.

'I had a vision of a wondrous tree, and now I can see it there in the bagh.'

Narain peered out, polishing his spectacles, before returning them to his nose. He looked again, and then at Kim.

'What tree?'

'There.' Kim pointed. 'In the middle of the island.'

'I see nothing. You must have sunstroke. You Angrezis cannot take our Indian heat.'

'I swear I can see a tree.' And he told Narain of the vision he'd experienced in the temple.

'If you want to see a tree in that bagh, then your mind will present you with a tree. But I can see no tree. I only sense danger there.'

Suddenly Kim understood that its reality was meant only for his eyes.

'Do you see anyone inside, then?' he asked after a while. The tree was fading into the darkness now, as were the island and the jungle.

'No one. Maybe the sar-panch was lying. He is more afraid of Bahadhur sahib and the Maharajah than he is of you and me.'

'He was telling the truth.'

They were observed from deep within the temple by the black panther, who had been startled by their appearance. When they left the battlements it padded along the cobbled path to watch them descend the wide steps to the lake shore. Now that they were so close, Kim and Narain moved cautiously, trying not to make any sound, but they were not men of the jungle, and the jungle fell silent until they passed. They stopped beneath a banyan tree that covered half an acre of land, its branches spanning the distance between the cliff and the water. It was so dark they could barely see each other and the evening chill bit through their thin clothing. A lamp was lit in one of the rooms, and then in another.

'We'll wait for them to go to bed, and then cross by the path the sar-panch told us about. Can you swim?'

'Of course I can. In Bombay, I swam in the sea.'

'I can't,' Kim confessed. 'If I slip, grab me.'

There was a small pink pavilion at the edge of the lake beneath the tip of the banyan's branch and they slid into its shadows to watch the pale lamplights.

'How shall we get in, even if we get across?'

'There will be a way,' Kim said. 'I'll find even the smallest crevices to climb.'

Narain did not share his friend's confidence and would have complained about the madness of racing across the country to find a woman. Women always caused trouble, and he felt it surround him now. When they sat silent, the jungle returned to normal. They were deafened by crickets and cicadas, the rustle of animals moving through the undergrowth, the call of chital and sambar in the distant hills. As the moon rose, the hills beyond the hunting lodge were silhouetted against the night sky. They seemed to form the contours of a giant woman sleeping on her side. Her head faced north and her ankles south, and in between the hills curved to outline her shoulders, her waist, hips and thighs. They could see occasional movement in the lodge, a flutter of shadows, a lamp moved from one room to another. Kim wondered which was Parvati's room. Ranjit Singh had said she was locked up. No voices carried across the water, but the breeze wafted the smell of cooking to them and their mouths watered at the odours of pilao and chapatis and curry. They had no food left and their stomachs growled.

'Have you thought about where you will take her after getting her?'

'Rescuing her,' Kim said absently. 'No. I thought we'd go up to some mountains I know well. I'll find a village and we'll hide out there.'

'Which is exactly where Colonel sahib will send his men to look for you. He knows your mind, knows your hiding places. Lahore. The mountains.' Narain sighed and continued. 'I don't know why I am doing this. Listen. We will go to my family in the south. My village is near to Madurai in the Cumbun valley. Only my brother and his family and my wife are there now.'

'Your wife?' Kim whispered in surprise.

'How could I help it? I was married off when I was thirteen to my brother's wife's sister. I have never slept with her and now she hangs like a rock around my neck. That's why I stay in Bombay as an agent. If I go back, she will catch me and make my life miserable for having deserted her. But it's a beautiful valley. It will take the Colonel sahib a long time to find you there, for it's very remote. But I know, eventually, he will find you, Kim. He will never forgive either of us now. My brother's name is Kumar and he owns a coconut plantation and

500

some paddy fields. I'll take you there and leave you.'

'But you can't return to Bombay now.'

'Well, I certainly cannot live in a little village with a wife who will give me troubles. Women never forget things like disappearing husbands. I'll find another place. Madras, perhaps. But I'm told that's only a slightly bigger village than mine. What will you do with this Parvati?'

'Marry her.'

'Ahre bhai. She's already married to this scoundrel Bahadhur sahib.'

'What difference will that make?'

'Difference? Difference? Apart from Colonel sahib looking for us, we shall have Bahadhur sahib searching too. She must be a wondrous woman for you to love her so much, but she will be more trouble than a whole harem of unhappy women. Are you quite certain of this woman?'

'Who is sure of anything in this life?' Kim said. 'I'm only certain of what I remember of her, and even that may be false by now. But I do remember that she made me feel a great calm when I was in her company. We could be together in silence without feeling the loneliness that we all live in. And when she spoke, I enjoyed the sound of her voice. We could laugh with each other and at each other. And at night, lying beside her, I felt at peace. I slept as light as air and woke up wanting only to look on her again, to spend the hours with her. It is the most men can ask of another human, man or woman.'

'What if she no longer feels the same way for you?'

Narain felt rather than saw Kim shrug. 'The most I can do then is to free her from the captivity of her husband.'

'I've never felt like that for any woman. I fall in love too easily with their bodies. It's very distracting to one's true emotions, those bodies and faces they have.'

Across the water, they saw one lamp extinguished, then another. The moon lit the water, turning it silver;

the jungle beyond looked ghostly and dark. They waited a while longer, then Kim went down the steps and slowly entered the cold water. At first, near the bank, he felt only mud and weeds, but as he waded further in and the water reached his knees, he felt the stone path beneath his feet. He probed ahead with his stick and watched the ripples spread away, occasionally spying the splash of a fish. Some distance away a log floated in the water. Halfway across, the water had risen to his armpits and he found it difficult to keep his footing on the slippery stone. Narain was paddling gently behind and Kim wished that he had learned to swim. When the water covered his shoulders he began to worry. The cold felt like a metal band around his chest and legs. But imperceptibly it began to recede, and once he reached the wall of the lodge, it only lapped at his calves. They looked up. There were no holds for them to climb, and the windows were protected by strong jalis. They edged along the wall, went round the corner and continued to the other side. Kim saw a small door at the rear. It was set low down for the servants to throw out the rubbish and collect water. The door was locked, but the crossbeams gave him a foothold and he climbed to the wall and cautiously looked down. Below him was a small courtyard littered with firewood. In one corner was a small tank and beside it, a copper hamam. The courtyard led into the main building but the door appeared to be bolted.

He and Narain balanced on the wall and made their way to the sloping tiled roof. They crawled up on their bellies, and when they looked down the other side found themselves above the interior garden. Kim stared down in astonishment. At the far end was a fountain shaped like a lotus and nearer them a large marble bench. There were rose bushes growing up the walls, and bougain-villea smothered the roof. But there was no tree.

'Where is your tree, then?' Narain asked.

'I *saw* it,' Kim insisted, and wondered if there were another garden, wondered again at the power of his own imagination. 'It was here, I swear. It had pink and gold flowers shaped like goblets.' He remembered the lingering perfume of honey and incense. 'I can smell it.'

'I can only smell water. Where will she be?'

'Behind a locked door.'

They slid down the tiled roof, dangled from the edge and dropped a foot down onto the lawn. They remained in a crouch, tensely waiting for a challenge. None came. As Kim crossed the garden, he caught the glow of an object on the lawn. He scooped it up and held a pink and gold flower. He showed it to Narain in triumph and Narain wondered at the capacity of his friend to attract such strange magic. He only hoped it was watching over them now.

They tried all the doors leading out of the garden. None had locks, until they came to the last one by the marble bench. A heavy padlock hung on the hasp. The shutters too were bolted and they couldn't see in.

'What now? If I had my tools I could open that lock. My uncle taught me.'

'There must be another way.'

Using the trellis that held up the bougainvillea, they climbed back up to the roof directly over the room. They crawled to the peak and saw that it sloped directly down to a balcony overlooking the water. They suspected it would be protected, like the other windows, by a jali. They slid along sideways until the roof ended and saw a small open passageway that led towards the rear court-yard. Kim lowered himself down and found a door which, if it could be opened, would lead back to the locked room. The door was bolted but had no padlock. He motioned Narain to stand guard and slid the bolt back and stepped quickly into a dark bathroom.

He waited again for his eyes to adjust, and saw another door across the room. It was ajar.

In Mohini's bedroom, he saw shapes and colours swirling in the crowded air. Demons and serpents writhed above the divan and he heard the moans and whispers of the sleeping woman battling the horrific creatures that hovered above her. It made him feel ill to look at them and he struck out at them with his stick. When he saw the demons and serpents retreating he believed in his own power, and not that of the stone which hung in a pouch around his neck. Not until he felt its heat on his chest, felt its vibrations and heard its hum. The monsters retreated, but didn't vanish. They opened a path to the divan and Kim knelt down beside his Parvati. She was drenched in sweat and continued writhing to escape.

'Parvati . . . Parvati . . .' He shook her gently. She stirred but did not wake. He tried again and saw her eyes flicker as she struggled to escape the nightmare. When he kissed her, she came wide awake with a start and would have cried out in fright if he hadn't put his hand over her mouth.

'Parvati, it's me, Kim. I have come for you,' and he removed his hand.

'Kim.' She gazed at him and slowly the terror subsided. 'Kim.' She said his name in a voice filled with wonder. 'I never thought I would see you again. Is this only a dream, too?'

'No, my darling. I'm real. Come, we must leave at once.'

'It must be karma that you are always there when I need you, my Kim. I prayed for you but had lost all faith in a God who plays evil tricks on me.'

He helped her up and she leant against him. He felt her thinness and knew she wouldn't have the strength to climb over the roof. He picked her up and found her to be as light as a child. The demons crowded back into a corner, and when they left the room, rushed with howls and screams to Gitabhai who slept with her eyes and mouth wide open; they were the conduits for her malignant powers. Their din almost woke her as they pushed and jostled to stream down to the darkness through her eyes and mouth. She knew, however, what had happened; someone had woken Mohini from her spell. Gitabhai would have called out to Mahender and

Rajender in their quarters, except that she would have had to shut her mouth before screaming, which would have been fatal as she would have barred the way for the monsters to escape.

Narain's hair stood on end. He had heard the eerie howls and wanted to take to his heels. When Kim appeared carrying Parvati, he planted a kiss first on Parvati's cheek and then on Kim's, unable to contain his relief. It was too dark to see the woman Kim loved.

The passage led into the garden and they crossed quickly to the main door, which was made of wood and iron and intricately carved. It wasn't locked but it took all Narain's strength to pull back the bolt and swing it open.

Kim laid his Parvati tenderly in the boat and would have helped Narain pole them to the banyan tree, but she clung to him and wouldn't let go. Even though she felt his arms and touched his face, Mohini believed she was still asleep. If dreams of evil were real, why not good ones as well? She imagined she was afloat in the sky, drifting among the stars with Kim. She heard a man whisper, 'Will she live?' And Kim's sad reply: 'I don't know. Hurry.' Mohini wanted to tell him she was no longer afraid, and though she would like to live for him, she felt dreadfully tired.

They reached the shore and Kim picked up Parvati again. Narain hurried ahead, holding back the jungle for them until they reached the steps of the fortress.

'We must take her to a doctor,' Kim said as they climbed.

'We might find one in Sawai Madhapur.'

They were close to the massive rotting gate that led into the fortress when Narain looked back and saw two men emerge from the jungle and start the climb.

'Bahadhur sahib's servants,' Narain called in a low voice.

They were far below, hurrying through the shadows and the moonlight. Kim noticed one of the men begin to fall behind, obviously climbing with difficulty. He was limping and Kim felt a sudden chill. Now he knew who was pursuing him.

'No. Those are the two men I hunted in Simla and then found in Bombay. I broke the ankle of the one behind, and he shot me. How did they know we were here? Who told them?'

Narain shrugged and drew his knife. If they had been alone they could have outrun the two men, but with Parvati they were as handicapped as the man with the limp. The place where they stood had been built to be defended. The steps narrowed to pass through the gate and under the archway. Within the arch were recesses for soldiers to launch their attack on an enemy.

'They are dangerous men,' Kim said. 'I know they want me. Here, take Parvati and run quickly. Save her.'

The two men were already halfway up the steps. The one in front paused to wait for his companion. Kim saw the glitter of knives. Out of the corner of his eye, he caught a flit of movement far behind the two men just where the stairway passed under a battlement. It could have been another man or the moonlight catching the passage of some animal.

'What do you think Narain is? A coward? You are correct, but I will stay. You take her.'

Mohini heard their furious whispers over her head, and not understanding the dilemma, snuggled closer to Kim, thus helping Narain settle the argument. She heard the other man whisper: 'Go . . . go. There are only two of them,' and felt a slowness in Kim's tread as they went on.

But Kim couldn't go far. He hurried to the ruined durbar hall and gently laid Parvati down on the marble bench on which the Chuhan prince had centuries ago sat in judgment. The stone made her feel cold, and she stirred from the languor of comfort.

'I shall be back, Parvati. But now I must help Narain. I love you. Wait for me to return.' And then she realised she was alone again, slipping back into the shadows. Kim had been but a dream.

Kim ran back, clutching his stick, leaping over tumbled walls and shattered carvings. He sprinted through the archway and found Narain on the top step. Several steps below, the two men, their knives held out in front of them, were ascending in a crouch.

'I have always thought you crazy, Kim,' Narain whispered. 'But I am glad you came back. Those two goondas look mad with rage and murder.'

The two men hesitated, and then continued to advance. The air hummed as Kim twirled his stick. The older man said, 'Strike, Madan!' and the man who limped answered,

'In time. I want that one. He's the chuthia who crippled me. I have waited all these years to kill him for that.'

'Come, then,' Kim said. 'This time you won't escape me.'

Kim could only sense the quick dart of the older man to his left, and Narain's parry. Kim jabbed forward with the stick and Madan knocked it aside with his knife. Kim feinted towards his heart and Madan turned to avoid the blow, but not before he felt the end drive hard into his spleen. The pain was agonising and he retreated a step. Kim followed and struck him on the knee.

'I'll kill you,' Madan whispered.

'Reach me first. Who sent you?'

Madan lunged out, thinking he would slash Kim's legs, but Kim jumped back and drove the end of the stick into Madan's left shoulder, deadening a nerve. The arm dangled uselessly, and Madan retreated another step, desperately trying to shake it back to life.

'I can kill you with a touch of this stick. Who sent you here?'

Madan spat. He suddenly shifted his glance to behind Kim and grinned with malicious delight at what he saw. Kim heard the clatter of a knife on the steps and spun around. The older man's left arm was locked against Narain's throat and the right, holding a knife, soared up in the air and plunged down into Narain's side – once, twice. And before Kim could move, he tossed Narain aside and came at Kim.

He heard Narain's clear whisper rise into the night: 'Ram . . . Ram . . .'

Kim screamed in such rage and anguish that he startled the sleeping birds, causing them to rise out of the jungle in panic, filling the air with the frightened beat of wings. Kim spun and struck Madan on his right elbow, shattering the bone, then turned to meet the lunge of the older man. With no time to wound him or knock him unconscious, and blind with anger, Kim struck him at the exact spot which would cause instant death. The man's eyes widened in surprise. He had expected to die from the knife or a bullet, weapons he understood, but not from the agonising jab of a stick.

Kim spun around even before the man had fallen, but Madan had no stomach for further fighting. He was stumbling down the stairs, heading for the jungle where Kim couldn't follow him. Kim hesitated, then dropped his stick and ran to Narain. His glasses had fallen off and shone like two eyes on the steps; Kim tenderly replaced them on his nose. The wounds in his side were savage, but he was still breathing.

'Viceroy sahib, you must live to accompany us back to your village.'

Narain sighed: 'Ahre, even a nagging wife would be better than this pain.' He turned towards Kim, but couldn't open his eyes any more. He rested his face against Kim's arm as he died.

Halfway down the steps Madan knew he too was going to die. He accepted the reality of Isaac Newton's sword pointing at him. An ebony walking-stick was in his left hand and the sword kept circling and coming closer and closer. The swordsman was thin as a stork and looked frail, certainly incongruous in a suit and tie, grubby even in this dim light, but he held the sword firmly. Madan managed by sheer luck to dodge the first thrust and lunged at Newton in the hope he could bring him down. But Newton was too quick. He gashed

508

Madan's side. Madan saw no alternative but escape. He scrambled up the battlement, even as Newton slashed at his heels, just missing him, and fell down the other side into the darkness. He limped away, swearing, vowing to find Kim and kill him one day.

Kim cradled Narain and wept. He called up to Vamana to bring life back to his friend in exchange for his own, but his cries were met by silence. He couldn't change Narain's karma. His death had been ordained.

'BA. First-class loafer,' Isaac Newton said softly, coming to kneel beside Kim. He began to weep, looking down at his dead nephew. 'He would have preferred to die in one of his dens, rather than in this jungle.'

'Newton. What are you doing here?' Kim asked.

'Later. All later. Look down at the lake.'

Kim stood and squinted down over the battlements. Two men were floundering across, using the same submerged causeway he'd taken with Narain. They both held rifles high in the air. But Kim couldn't leave Narain yet. He carried him to the durbar hall and laid him next to Mohini on the marble bench. Mohini woke to the movement. The light was gradually changing as dawn approached, and for the first time she could see Kim clearly.

'You are real? But why are you crying?'

Kim told her. When she saw Narain, Mohini couldn't help crying too. Newton crouched by her side, placed a finger on the nada of her right wrist and felt her pulse.

'She is only weak and will live. You must take her to the temple and have her purified.'

'How did you arrive so suddenly?' Kim asked Newton again, now that the shock was wearing off.

'I followed those two men all the way from Bombay.'

'How did they know I would come here?'

'You would only escape from prison for one reason – your woman. One of Bahadhur sahib's servants – and I do not know which, but he is well paid – passed on information that your woman had been brought here.'

'Who sent them?'

Newton considered the question as deeply as he would have one of his puzzling inventions. He weighed his employment against his great affection for Kim. If he answered truthfully, and Kim accused the Colonel sahib, the Colonel sahib would guess that Isaac Newton had told Kim. He would be dismissed for disloyalty, or worse, jeopardise his own life. The Colonel sahib and his people were the real power in India. He was nothing but a humble native. And what good would it do Kim to know such things? The men were dead, a fact. Another fact, Kim was no longer the Colonel's Imperial Agent. Another fact, he had chosen the wrong side. Weighing these facts precisely, Newton finally answered.

'I cannot tell you that. And I do not want to know where you and this young woman are going. I should, as a government servant, report your whereabouts to the Colonel sahib, but I will not. And should he enquire, "Where is Kim?" I will truthfully answer that I don't know.'

But, in Isaac Newton's evasion, Kim knew who had sent those two men. The knowledge of such duplicity made him cold. His friend had died, and so had many others, all because an alien power wished to continue ruling his country. India was changing. Her long sleep was ending. How much longer could the Colonel and men like him continue to control India's destiny? Kim knew that one day their time would come, that they would cross the kala pani and never return. He had changed, as had so many Indians who no longer wanted to be ruled by the British. He had been used and manipulated by the man to whom he'd given all his love and loyalty. The reward was betrayal. He had thought himself different from the other agents, but in the eyes of his master he was only another pawn in the Great Game.

'I understand,' said Kim. 'What shall we do with Narain? I cannot leave him here to the jackals and vultures.'

'He is my nephew. Though I am not a Brahmin, I will

perform the pujas as prescribed by the Vedas, and recite the sastras. I will light his pyre with my own hand. You must go now, Kim. Hurry, before Bahadhur sahib's men come. Take her. Go far away.'

Kim knelt once more beside Narain, kissed his cheek, and prayed that his soul, when it returned in the eternal cycle of birth and re-birth, would enter the body of another brave man. He went to his Parvati and picked her up and strode out of the durbar hall.

'Where are we going?'

'Far away. To hide. It will be a long journey. Do you have the strength to go on?'

'Kim, you have given me the strength. I will live only as long as you live.'

Kim knew his own story had yet to end. He had chosen his side and would now have to play the Great Game against the Colonel, the man he had loved as a father. Kim also knew he would have to continue his wandering across India in search of those arrows which marked the turning points of his life; just as his dear Lama had searched for a mythical river, so he would search for arrows which did not exist, except in his vision. He looked up. It was going to be a clear, bright day. As they made their way down the steep path, far above, only a speck in the sky, he saw Jatayu circling and watching over them.

T. N. MURARI

TAJ

Shah Jahan, Sovereign of the World, the Scourge of
God, the Shadow of Allah, the Conqueror, fell in
love once only.

And when his one love, his Empress, died, he had a
vision of a monument to their love that would
endure for ever. Then, for twenty-two years, twenty
thousand men and women laboured to create his
vision. In marble, in gold and silver, they worked to
build the Taj Mahal, perfect image of their ruler's
passion and wonder of the world.

'An exotic, passionate novel, sensual and violent by
turn, always compelling'
Woman's Own

'A lush saga of India'
Daily Mirror

A Royal Mail service in association with the Book Marketing Council & The Booksellers Association.
Post-A-Book is a Post Office trademark.

T. N. MURARI

THE SHOOTER

He waited, alone.

He'd been a good cop; street-wise and dedicated.
Now, three years after his disgrace and prison, he
waited for Harry, his last friend on the police force.

Then, the news, told with a savage delight. Harry
wouldn't come calling. Harry was dead – shot down
that morning.

He knew then with a still-sure instinct that someone
from his past, a killer, was out for revenge. Knew
that he was friendless and facing a fight for survival
in the bitter Christmas snow of Manhattan.

'A real gripper'
The Scotsman

'Brilliantly traces the extraordinary nightmare that
skirts the shores of affluent Manhattan'
The Standard

NEW ENGLISH LIBRARY

MORE SAGAS FROM
HODDER AND STOUGHTON PAPERBACKS

T. N. MURARI

| | 05813 1 | The Shooter | £1.95 |
| | 05897 2 | Taj | £3.50 |

CHRISTIE DICKASON

| | 41219 4 | The Dragon Riders | £3.95 |

NOEL BARBER

	34709 0	A Farewell to France	£3.50
	41553 3	The Other Side of Paradise	£3.95
	28262 2	Tanamera	£3.50
	37772 0	A Woman of Cairo	£3.95

HILARY NORMAN

| | 41117 1 | In Love and Friendship | £3.50 |

*All these books are available at your local bookshop or
newsagent, or can be ordered direct from the publisher. Just
tick the titles you want and fill in the form below.*

Prices and availability subject to change without notice.

Hodder and Stoughton Paperbacks, P.O. Box 11, Falmouth,
Cornwall.

Please send cheque or postal order, and allow the following for
postage and packing:

U.K. – 55p for one book, plus 22p for the second book, and 14p for
each additional book ordered up to a £1.75 maximum.

B.F.P.O. and EIRE – 55p for the first book, plus 22p for the second
book, and 14p per copy for the next 7 books, 8p per book thereafter.

OTHER OVERSEAS CUSTOMERS – £1.00 for the first book, plus 25p
per copy for each additional book.

Name ....

Address ....

....